THE DAUGHTERS
OF
CANNAE

The Daughters of Cannae

Anthony Horne

JANUS PUBLISHING LTD
Cambridge, England

First published in Great Britain 2014
by Janus Publishing Company Ltd
The Studio
High Green
Great Shelford
Cambridge CB22 5EG

www.januspublishing.co.uk

Copyright © Anthony Horne 2014

British Library Cataloguing-in-Publication Data
A catalogue record for this book is available from the British Library

ISBN 978-1-85756-819-6

All rights reserved. No part of this publication may be reproduced, stored in a retrieval system or transmitted in any form or by any means, electric, mechanical, photocopying, recording or otherwise, without the prior permission of the publisher.

The right of Anthony Horne to be identified as the author of this work has been asserted by him in accordance with the Copyright, Designs and Patents Act 1988.

Cover Design: Janus Publishing
Cover Picture: W Knight

Printed and bound in the UK by PublishPoint
from KnowledgePoint Limited, Reading

Map of Italy

Key

1. River Ticinus
2. River Po
3. Placentia
4. River Trebia
5. Ariminum
6. Faesulae
7. River Arno
8. Arretium
9. Lake Trasimene
10. Spoletium
11. Veii
12. Tibur
13. Rome
14. Ostia
15. Antium
16. Tarracina
17. Capua
18. Beneventum
19. Cumae
20. Nola
21. River Aufidus
22. Cannae
23. Venosa
24. Paestum
25. Tarentum
26. Locri
27. Rhegium

Map of Rome

Key

1. Capitoline Hill
2. Sublician Bridge
3. Palatine Hill
4. Great Circus
5. Forum
6. Cattle market

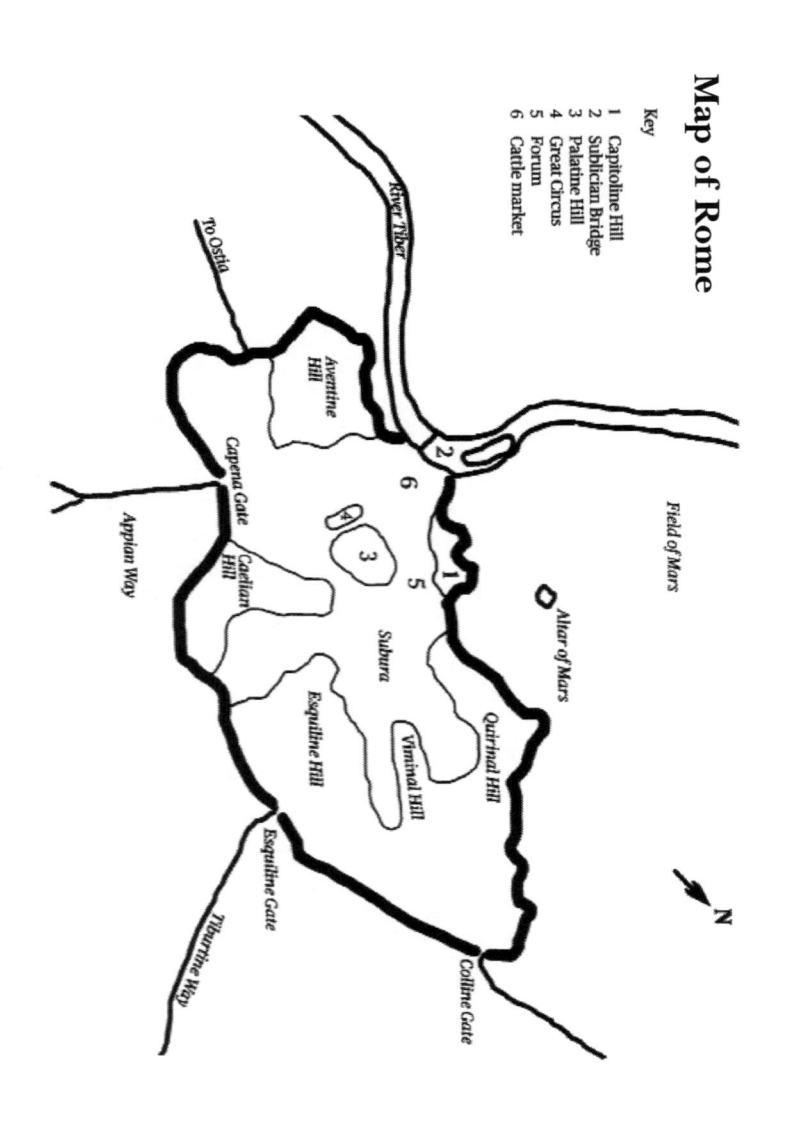

Around the Forum

Key

- ■ City wall
- ||||| A – The Hundred Steps
- ||||| B – The Gemonian Stairs

1. Temple of Juno Moneta
2. Senate House
3. Tullianum (prison)
4. Rostra
5. Temple of Concord
6. Temple of Jupiter
7. Temple of Saturn
8. Shops
9. Regia
10. Temple of Castor
11. Carmenta Gate
12. Temple of Vesta
13. Pool of Juturna
14. Temple of Hope
15. House of the Vestals
16. Sublician Bridge

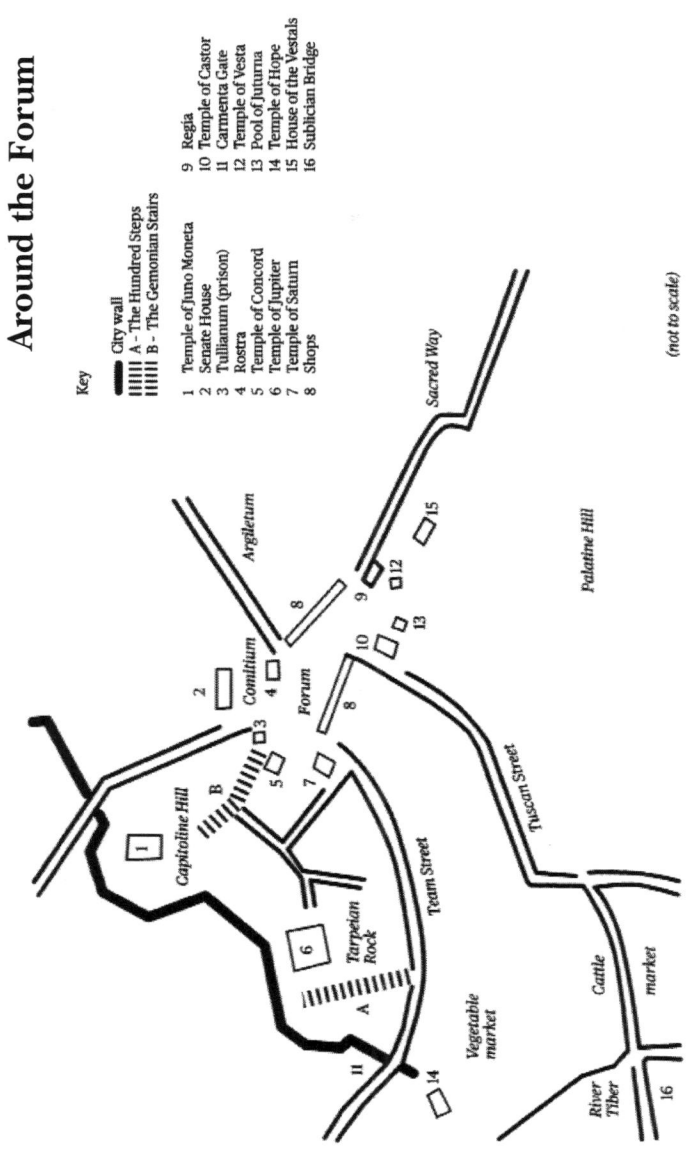

(not to scale)

Prologue

264–241 BC

Twenty-three years of war. Carthage lies exhausted, defeated, humiliated. Sicily is lost, together with all the other islands between it and mainland Italy. The fleet, Carthage's pride, lies near the Aegates Islands, west of Sicily, but it's at the bottom of the sea. Ironic this; the Romans won the action using ships copied from a Carthaginian design. Then there is the war indemnity. 3,200 talents of silver, payable to Rome by instalments over ten years. In every sinew of his body Hamilcar Barca burns for revenge. He meets the Suffetes, the chief magistrates of the Carthaginian senate.

'Let me go to Spain. Silver, copper, cereals, men, good horses. It's all there. We can build a new Sicily.' In his mind he sees a fresh base from which to attack Rome. The Carthaginian senate let him go. They're still ambitious. Carthage lives by trade. They know how to buy and sell. Spain can produce revenue and goods. No harm, then, to see what Hamilcar can do.

238 BC

The sun is setting on the Carthaginian camp near Cordoba. The jagged teeth of the high sierra, silhouetted against the deep red sky, bite into the western horizon. An altar, topped by the figure of the great god Baal, rises in the centre of the compound. In front of it has been placed a huge bronze bowl filled with burning oil and flames that seem to lick the image of the god. Hamilcar stands at the table on which his sword rests. In a broad circle around him are gathered his lieutenants. Their tanned faces gleam russet-coloured in the evening light. The last rays catch the iron armour. You can smell the sweated leather of their jerkins. A boy steps forward, nine-years old. He's well built for his age, lean and tall, but not thin. He advances easily towards Hamilcar, this man with a mane of shaggy hair to his shoulders, whose great hooked nose betrays Phoenician blood in a face that's beaten and chiselled by the desert winds of Africa, then dried to the colour of a palm date. The boy, with both hands, lifts the sword from the table and raises it above his head. The silence is broken by the rasp of forty swords drawn from their sheaths and raised aloft in imitation. Hamilcar fixes the boy with eyes that burn in the fiery light. It's time.

'I, Hannibal, son of Hamilcar, prince of the Barcid family, do swear by this sword and before the great god that I shall be the enemy of Rome for so long as I shall live, that I will avenge Carthage for the wrongs done to her and that I will do everything in my power to bring down the might of Rome and destroy its empire and its citizens for ever.'

218 BC

Spring is approaching. Hamilcar and his son-in-law, Hasdrubal, are dead. Hannibal, twenty-eight years old now, leads out his men from New Carthage[1]. This is the start of the long march to Italy, a thousand miles to the valley of the Po. His heavy Libyan infantry move steadily, their faces barely visible behind the cheekplates of their helmets. The Numidians dart about on their African horses, riding with one hand on the mane, the other holding a lance decorated with a pennon. They laugh madly and joust with

---

1. A city on the Mediterranean coast of Spain.

Prologue

one another. 'Not far to go on a horse!' they shout. Poor bloody infantry. The swarthy Spaniards, quick and nimble over rough country, press-ganged but loyal, carry lighter weapons. They can fight.

It's tough going through southern Gaul. Ambushes and false guides. A few desert. The Numidians ride them down, despatch them, no questions asked. Rome knows Hannibal is on his way. Its citizens are confident. Armies are manoeuvring in northern Italy. Before that, the Rhone's a barrier. We can stop him there. A large force of Gauls has assembled on the eastern bank. Under cover of darkness Hannibal orders his nephew, Hanno, to cross the river upstream. As Hannibal launches his rafts and canoes into the water, Hanno attacks the Gauls from the rear. It is enough; they turn and flee. Now for the elephants. Hannibal builds heavy rafts with tree trunks, laid criss-cross and lashed together. Stamp soil and twigs on top. Find the matriarch cows and lead them on. The bulls will follow. The horses swim across, attached to ropes behind the rafts. Not such a barrier after all, but a bigger one's to come.

The ground is rising steeply now. He needs guides to help him find the passes through the mountains. The Gallic tribes, Allobroges, are unpredictable, treacherous. The army traipses upwards; elephants feel the cold, packhorses stagger, sometimes trip. The muleteers goad them forward, always upwards. A sudden rumble from above. Heavy stones and rocks rain down; men and horses are knocked from the narrow path. They tumble to the valley floor, an avalanche of screaming men and flailing horses. Their climbing's done. Hannibal strips specially selected men of everything but weapons. Never mind the cold, the climbing will be warm work. They seize the heights left unoccupied at night; no more storms of rock by day.

The cold is bitter. Men die of frostbite. They're short of food and so are the horses, carrying heavy loads on emaciated bodies. Their hooves and fetlocks cut by the sharp screes, some die where they stand overnight, equine statues in the morning light, legs frozen to the ground. We're nearly at the watershed, he says. And then this, a vast rock that blocks the path. Nothing can get past. The general calls for timber. Somehow they drag up great logs and lodge them underneath the rock. With straw they set the wood alight and pour sour wine on the stone. It steams and sizzles; the colour of its surface turns to black and ochre, but it does not crack. More logs, more flames, more sour wine. The heat becomes intense and parts of the rock glow pink. A wind springs up; acting like bellows it fans the flames to help their work. The rock is becoming friable. Men seize picks and slam them savagely down into the cracks. Their feet are burning through their boots, but they cut through to form a path wide enough for horses and even the surviving elephants. Hannibal shows them the plains of Italy stretched out below.

It's a miserable winter's day in northern Italy, squally showers and sleet that burns your face. The sort of day so overcast that daylight never really manifests itself. Hannibal lies encamped not far from the River Trebia, a tributary of the Po. Sempronius[2] with his legions is stationed on the other side of the river. At first light the Carthaginian sends out his Numidians to ride up to the Roman camp where they taunt the Roman legionaries and hurl insults at them. Hannibal instructs his men in camp to eat a solid breakfast while they wait. Out come the legionaries, infuriated by the insolent Numidians. The freezing rain and sleet drive into their faces. They're hungry and cold. This is no way to start the day. The cavalry retreat, drawing the Romans on towards the river and the open ground beyond. That's where we'll fight, Sempronius says. Cheeky Spaniards and Gauls will cut and run. They're not in sunny Spain now.

---

2. Tiberius Sempronius Longus, consul in 218 BC.

Prologue

Into the water wade the legionaries, up to their waists in parts. Hands are so numb that they can hardly hold their javelins, but discipline is good. They advance to engage the enemy, clashing their spears against their shields. It's hand-to-hand stuff, silent butchery, for men make no small talk when they're killing. The groans of the dying are drowned not by screams but by the metallic clang of sword on armour. Hannibal's men, well breakfasted and dry, have their work cut out. Now he springs his trap. Out of a ditch where they have lain concealed overnight, his younger brother, Mago, leads his force of picked infantry to take the Romans in the rear. Some of the legionaries succeed in breaking through to Placentia, but many die trying to recross the icy waters of the Trebia, or on its banks where they're skewered as they seek to regain the safety of their camp. One–nil to Hannibal, or two if you count the earlier skirmish at the Ticinus. He's suffered casualties as well. Now he rides the sole surviving elephant. The cold has finished off the rest.

217 BC

We need a winner, desperately, cry the citizens of Rome. Their eyes fall on Flaminius.[3] He's got a good track record, admittedly against lesser opposition, the Insubrians, a Gallic tribe whom he defeated six years ago. They elect him consul again. It's not ten years since he last held the post, the normal period required, but needs must. He can't wait to get at Hannibal. No ritual sacrifice on the Alban Mount[4] for him, or New Year vows on the Capitol. He rides north immediately to take over the command.

---

3. Gaius Flaminius, a rather impetuous and demagogic plebeian who rose to become consul in 223 BC.
4. A mountain situated about twelve miles south-east of Rome on which the Latin Festivals were held and where newly elected consuls were supposed to sacrifice in the temple of Jupiter.

The Daughters of Cannae

Hannibal has crossed the Apennines. The swampy ground through which he leads his army takes its toll. Men and horses struggle through the quagmire. In the perpetual wet many of the horses lose their hooves. Men and beasts sink, never to be seen again. His own left eye becomes infected. He will lose the sight of it. No matter; it's nothing to the suffering of his men. At last they reach firm ground again, around Faesulae and the valley of the River Arno. Here the soldiers can plunder to their hearts' content. The area's rich in cattle, grain and wine. Hannibal encourages them. This hothead, Flaminius, must be provoked into attack. The latter's furious. The destruction is intolerable and what's more, it's very bad for Rome's reputation in the eyes of its allies and subject cities in Italy. Many Gauls from north of the Po have already joined the Punic army.[5] Who's to say more won't go over if this carries on? The Roman general tracks Hannibal as he moves southwards. At the first opportunity he must attack and put an end to this impudent invasion.

Hannibal keeps Flaminius in his wake, not too far behind, just enough, so that the Romans can see the burning farms and the cattle being led off. The Carthaginian follows the first principle of war; know your enemy. He is leading the consul into a trap and devastating defeat. The greatest crisis in the history of the Republic is about to unfold. Someone will have to take the blame. The gods must be appeased. Perhaps the punishment of a few might be sufficient to atone for the sins of many. The year of the scapegoat is at hand.

---

5. Punic is another word for Carthaginian.

Chapter One

c.263 BC

Lucius Opimius Veianus,[6] son of Gaius, a Roman knight, is being escorted to school by one of the family's slaves. He wears a tunic and the scarlet-bordered cloak of a young Roman citizen. Round his neck hang three small golden balls on a leather thong, given to him as a protective charm on the ninth day after his birth. He will wear them until he reaches manhood. In his hand he carries a small bag containing his stylus and wax tablets upon which to write.

The school is outside a butcher's shop in the street of the sandal makers, towards the bottom of the Esquiline Hill. A rough awning indicates its extent. Lucius takes his seat on a bench with six other boys. The master sits in a high-backed chair. Behind him the butcher is gutting rabbits and hanging them on hooks. The master lives in two rooms above the shop, part of a tenement. Occasionally a customer appears, to bargain with the butcher who chops more meat. A cart loaded with amphorae containing wine for the taverns and cookshops rumbles by. The horse pauses to unload a steaming pile and then moves on. The master

---

6. A Roman citizen normally had three names: the praenomen or first name given by his parents nine days after his birth, the gentilial or tribal name common to all members of the 'gens', in this case Opimius, and the cognomen which was originally an individual appellation but gradually became hereditary, in this case Veianus.

breaks off from dictation to curse the driver, who ignores him. People come and go from the tenement block. Children less fortunate than Lucius – he does not think so at this moment – are chucking a small leather ball about.

There's always something happening. It's hard enough to concentrate as it is, without all these distractions. Lucius watches a dog that he has not seen before. It's sniffing round the butcher's shop, no doubt hoping for some scrap. Every time it gets close enough the butcher curses and aims a kick. The dog can't resist the chance of food; it keeps coming back to have another go. Then, to Lucius's and his friends' delight, it cocks its leg and pees on the back of the master's chair. He hasn't seen it, boring man. The master looks up, sharp.

'What was I saying, Lucius?' He has no idea. The stick comes down hard. It hurts, but Lucius doesn't move his hand. A flash of irritation in the master's face. He can't get this boy to flinch. Up comes the stick again. The boy's face is expressionless and he thinks better of it.

The learning's tedious, by rote. Spelling, dictation, rudimentary mathematics. Lucius must recite a speech, declaim it to the other boys. It's difficult against the background of the butcher's cleaver. He writes his words ponderously. Progress is a little slow for he has no particular aptitude.

He tries to pay attention, usually, for he is by nature diligent and serious minded. Carefully he forms the letters with his stylus. Marcus, sitting next to him, has brought a white mouse in his satchel. He sets it free. It scuttles about under the bench and then makes off along a wheel rut down the street. Marcus doesn't care; his father's a senator. He's away to recapture it. The master shouts, then shrugs his shoulders. What's it to him? When the boy grows up he'll have plenty of scribes to do his writing for him.

With half an ear Lucius listens, with half a mouth he repeats spellings in chorus with the other boys and with

Chapter One

half an eye he's watching the shadow slide slowly down the tenement wall. Sometimes it seems to stop. It's dividing the rough stonework of the ground floor now. When the sun reaches into the narrow street itself, that's school done for the day. A holiday tomorrow; after that the grind resumes for another eight. He runs with two other boys out through the city wall and onto the Field of Mars.[7] They're training for selection to run for the Fabian wolf-boys against the Quintilians in the race round the Palatine Hill at the festival of the Lupercalia in a few months' time. His father has told Lucius that he cannot take part unless he's faster than all his friends. Every day he runs barefooted twice round the field. Nothing to eat for the rest of the day if he's not first back to the Carmenta Gate.

c.253 BC

Dawn over the Field of Mars. A wispy mist lingers just above the River Tiber, olive green in the dank morning air. In a few minutes the sun will burn the mist away and the rushes will begin to stir as waterfowl move out in search of food. Close under the city wall half a dozen tents are pitched, Gauls of the Cenomani tribe, north of the River Po, come to Rome to plead their cause to the Senate about incursions by their neighbours, the Boii. They wander out, wearing strange trousers, rekindle their fires and take fodder to their tethered horses. Already a couple of letter writers have taken up position nearby, hoping to catch some trade. They squat on the ground, pulling their cloaks tight against the early morning chill.

A few cattle meander slowly down towards the river, leaving behind a dead calf. A crow, keeping watch from the city wall, summons its mates with a mournful cry, before

---

7. A large expanse used for military gatherings and where young men took exercise.

flapping down to peck at the carcase. Moments later the birds rise, flailing the air like keening widows at the approach of two dogs who assume possession of the putrefying flesh. A group of priests, the Salii, dressed in tunics and robes of red and green, emerge from the Quirinal Gate. They carry spears and shields curiously indented on each side, like those of ancient Greeks, and embossed with the image of a woodpecker, sacred to Mars. It is the first day of his month, his special festival. They reach the god's altar, a stone edifice about ten feet high carved with reliefs of rustic scenes. One side depicts a farmer at the plough with his two oxen; the other shows figures reaping corn. The priests gather round and begin to sing their morning hymn, the words of which have come down from generation to generation. Their meaning is lost to history. Yet they sing with scrupulous care. The Chief Priest holds up his hand; somebody has sung one word incorrectly. They must start again to avoid offending the gods.

Meanwhile a steady trickle of citizens is emerging through the gate, coming to apply themselves to various forms of exercise. Wrestlers rub themselves with an ointment of oil and wax to make their skins more supple, then smear dust on top to prevent slipping from each other's grasp. Small boys gather round to watch, play bladder ball or roll hoops with a stick. Beyond, young men of the upper classes are engaged upon more martial arts. They throw javelins and fence with each other, using wooden swords. Lucius, aged eighteen now, assumed the manly toga some months ago and has dropped his first beard of fluffy hair, preserved in a silver casket. He rides out every day on the Spanish colt his father gave him. He must learn to steer with his heels and gallop holding a small round shield in one hand and a lance or sword in the other. At first he fell off several times and was covered in bruises and cuts.

'Catch the horse and get back on immediately!' How many times has his father shouted that? Again and again

Chapter One

Gaius puts his son through his paces. These skills must be mastered by a young man aspiring to serve in the cavalry. 'You have to ride that horse as if you were born on it.' His friends say that Gaius is so hard that the nails would bend if you tried to crucify him. 'Metellus[8] will only take you to Sicily if you're good enough. You must be the best, get yourself appointed to command a squadron. Come on, beat me to the bridge!' Gaius swings his horse round. She's a mare, nine-years old but still with a fair turn of foot, and Gaius knows how to get the best out of her. His father's cloak is streaming out behind him before Lucius can gather up his reins. He digs his heels hard into the colt's flanks.

'Go for it, boy, you can catch that old mare.' They're racing down a track. One day, before Lucius is dead, it will have turned into the Flaminian Way, running northwards to the Adriatic coast. Now it's rough, strewn with potholes and loose stones. Lucius is gaining on his father. His colt has a fine action, smooth and long striding. Soon, he thinks, I'll be upsides him. One more big effort. His head is down on the horse's neck, its sweat lathering his face. His father glances behind him, gives a little nod and kicks his mare sharply in the flank. Her head goes up. She veers violently to the right, but Gaius keeps control. Instinctively Lucius tries to follow. He jerks the rein. The colt can't respond. His foreleg catches a rut and he's down in a flurry of dirt and grass. Lucius is lucky. Nothing's broken but his ribs are agony.

His father laughs. 'I thought that might catch you out.' Lucius tries to speak, but turns away to spew up instead. Don't show it hurts. He forces out a smile.

---

8. Lucius Caecilius Metellus, consul in 251 and 247 BC. He became Pontifex Maximus (Chief Priest) from 243 to 237 BC and was said to have been blinded when rescuing sacred objects from the temple of Vesta during a fire, after which he was granted the privilege of riding to the Senate House in a chariot.

240 BC

The war in Sicily is over and Lucius has returned to Rome. He's done well, no disputing it. At Panormus, on the north coast of the island, the Carthaginian general Hasdrubal attacked the legions of Caecilius Metellus. The Roman skirmishers were running back like rabbits before the enemy's elephants coming on in a grey tidal wave, threatening to overwhelm them. Lucius, captain of a squadron attached to the first legion's second line, lay concealed with the rest of the cavalry in a wood. Orders were to wait until the Carthaginian infantry had reached the city walls and were engaging with the legions. At that point they were to charge the enemy in the rear.

'Make them feel your spear tips up their arses.' That's what Metellus said. Lucius and a few of his fellow captains saw the danger, took the initiative and charged the elephants, putting them to rout. Mahouts and elephants turned tail with javelins hanging like leeches from their flanks. It was the first occasion on which the Romans had withstood an elephant attack. Lucius had led the charge and received the personal congratulations of the consul afterwards, for showing the courage to disobey orders when the situation required new tactics.

At the long siege of Lilybaeum on Sicily's western coast where the Carthaginians had their main base, Lucius had again distinguished himself in the great fire. Himilco, the canny commander of the Punic garrison, had observed the Roman siege engines drying under months, indeed years, of wind and sun. The timbers had turned from brown to silver grey, tinder dry. One night his Greek mercenaries, encouraged by the promise of Punic gold in their pockets, row round from the seaward side and climb out onto the beach. The Romans wake and think the world's turned round. The sun is rising in the west! No, the glow is from the inferno that is their siege works. Fires fanned by the wind have turned the sky pink. Legionaries and cavalrymen

Chapter One

run from both camps, clamber across the protective earthworks joining them and try to rescue what they can. In among the chaos of flames, sparks and smoke Lucius saves the life of a centurion trapped under a siege hut which has fallen sideways when a tower collapsed on it. With the help of a trooper, Lucius pulls the man to safety. In the process an arrow stikes him on the arm. For ten days he lies unable to move. The inhalation of smoke makes it feel as though molten lead has been poured down his throat. The field surgeons despair of him. But Lucius is tough and gradually he recovers. Unguent of pine oil heals the wound in his arm and before long he's back in action. During the long years of the siege, Regulus, who commands, loses two of the tribunes from the six appointed by the People's Assembly for his first legion. Lucius is his choice for one of the replacements, a signal honour. Promotion in the field to military tribune happens rarely.

In Rome Lucius's status is further raised by the death of Gaius during the war in Sicily. Lucius is now head of the family, no longer in the power of his father or at his whim. He ought to feel a sense of relief. He's no longer the recipient of perpetual chidings to do better, indeed to be the best at everything he undertakes. Yet the spirit of his father lingers on. Lucius visits the family tomb to see the urn containing Gaius's ashes, placed on a shelf with those of other ancestors inside the small mausoleum beside the Appian Way. In the dank gloom of the building he stands still and silent. Despite himself a few tears trickle down his cheeks. Here was a Roman in the best tradition, a man of simple virtues, piety and duty, who brooked no compromise with anything or anybody. He has instilled in Lucius this same sense of duty. He reaches out to touch the cold piece of earthenware and vows to follow in the dead man's footsteps of service to the state before the interests of his family.

His mother, Marcia, has moved into a small house near the Esquiline Gate. Here she lives simply with her maids, weaving and tending her garden. Lucius must look to the family property. His father's death has caused him to become a landlord, owner of four tenement blocks on the slope overlooking the valley between the Esquiline and Viminal Hills. Two of these blocks are three storeys high and all contain one- or two-room apartments on the upper floors. The ground floors giving straight onto the street are mostly tenanted by small-shopkeepers. To save himself the trouble of collecting individual rents, Lucius's father let each block to one lessee at a fee covering the whole building. This head lessee lets out the individual rooms at the best rent he can obtain. So much the better for him if he can turn a profit, but he must also deal with repairs and perpetual complaints. The apartments are cold and draughty in the winter, prone to outbreaks of fire from the open braziers used by the occupants to keep warm. Hardly a day passes in the city when some jerry-built tenement does not tumble down because of fire or rickety floors giving way. The water carriers often deliberately slop their pails on the stairs to keep them damp.

Lucius decides the time has come to build himself a house. He has found a good plot looking out over the valley towards the Capitoline Hill and the temple of Jupiter. The solid walls are of limestone blocks interspaced with small pyramids of tufa packed together. No outside windows interrupt this barrier against the noises and smells of the surrounding tenements, but a stout door in the wall facing the street leads to a passageway giving access to the atrium.[9] On each side of the doorway he constructs one-room shops. One he rents to an ivory carver, all the rage since the war with Carthage, and the other to a candle maker, quiet occupations which will not disturb his household.

---

9. The central courtyard of a Roman house.

Chapter One

The atrium's roof is supported by thick beams of oak and has an opening in the centre to let in rainwater, collected in a shallow basin beneath. Round this covered courtyard are ranged small rooms, the doors and windows of which face inwards. Some will serve as storerooms while others will accommodate his family, he hopes. At the back of the atrium a pair of heavy doors made of ash and mounted on swivels guards the tablinum, the main reception room, and to the right of this one enters the triclinium, the formal dining room where Lucius will entertain his guests to dinner. On the other side of the tablinum he's had a smaller living room constructed where his family can eat informally. Its hearth will be the centre of the family's life. Set into the wall next to it are niches where clay statuettes of the household gods will reside.

Lucius walks out from the tablinum into a small peristyle[10] lined with a portico of smooth travertine columns supporting doric capitals. It is the area of his new home which gives Lucius the most pleasure, a place of privacy and quiet where the mind and the body can both rest. In the centre a raised basin is filled with water lilies and a small colony of frogs, which have been quick to take up occupation. From this central point radiate four gravel paths lined with low hedges of box. At each corner, stone plinths support bronze statues, like ones he remembers from the Greek colonies in Sicily. Here's a statue of wing-footed Perseus, copied from an original mural by Nicias of Athens. In his right hand he holds aloft the reflective shield. In his left he carries the sickle presented to him by Hermes to slice off the Medusa's head. The dripping head hangs from the sickle's hilt by its hair of serpents' tails. In the opposite corner, Andromeda, chained to a rock, holds out her arms to Perseus, begging to be rescued before the sea monster devours her. She is naked except for a bracelet on her wrist. Lucius was worried that his mother might not

---

10. A row of columns forming a cloister round a square open court.

approve, but years of weaving in poor light have dulled her eyes. She makes no comment except, 'Very nice,' when her chair is carried in so she can look around.

His carpenters are working on the pergola which will run across the back of the peristyle and support the roses he plans to grow there. In his mind's eye he sees lavender, violets, hyacinths and poppies to add colour to the beds between the paths. Beyond the peristyle he's set aside a small area for growing vegetables. He wants fresh peas, first-cut sprouts, crinkly lettuce and crisp radishes. His friend Brutus has ordered cartloads of good soil to be brought from his estate in Campania.

The builder has persuaded him into a little extravagance. The floors of the tablinum and the triclinium are to be laid with black-and-white mosaics. For the triclinium Lucius chooses a design of fishing boats. Round them in the sea swim a profusion of tuna, mullet, eels, octopuses and shellfish. He can hear the workmen tapping down the tiny tiles of marble and stone. The floor in the tablinum is already finished. He thought at first of having the enlarged face of a goddess, perhaps Minerva, tastefully framed in a chaplet of ivy, peering up at him.

'Better not,' said Brutus, 'goddesses don't like having their faces trodden on, any more than we do.' Instead he's gone for safety, a hunting scene with hounds in pursuit of stags running through the forest.

Lucius's slave, Naxus, arrives carrying the masks of the family ancestors, including that of his late father. Lucius supervises the hanging of them in a special room off the atrium. He cannot help himself from stroking the deep creases on his father's face. Gaius looks so old compared with how he remembers him. Naxus wants to wash the linen corselet that Lucius wore in Sicily. It's stained with dirt and blood, but Lucius refuses and orders him to hang it up as it is, next to his shield. 'I want my son to see them.'

* * *

Chapter One

Lucius is at the play. It's one of the new comedies based on a Greek model by an up-and-coming young man from Campania called Gnaeus Naevius.[11] Lucius pretends to laugh at the antics of Achilles, who's trying to get inside his tent to sulk but getting the arrow in his heel tangled up in the stays and pegs. All the while he is really watching a young lady called Naevia, the playwright's adopted daughter. She's definitely a looker and is someone to whom Lucius has been paying court for some time. Her father was at Lilybaeum, killed by a slingshot in the throat. Lucius remembers Junius Naevius as senior centurion of a maniple in the second line of his legion, a rugged man who liked to go fishing, occasionally tossing live sprats into his mouth and swallowing them whole. His brother is of a different hue, cultured and always scribbling something. Naevia lives with her adoptive father in a house set down in the valley below Lucius's new home. She is gay and cheerful, with a spark of wit. At the same time she exhibits the simple virtues of a Roman matron, keeping a well-ordered household for Naevius whose mind is not occupied by such trivia.

On the day of the betrothal the family and friends of each side gather at Naevius's house near the Viminal Hill. Despite her poor sight Marcia has baked some little wheat cakes sweetened with honey. She cannot rise from her chair and Naevia bends down to receive the gift, a mark of approval of her son's choice by the old lady. Lucius has brought a present too, a sandalwood box containing combs of horn and a mirror of burnished bronze. From the folds of his tunic he produces the ring, a circlet of gold set in iron. He forgets, of course, on which finger to place it. Naevia shows him the finger of her left hand from which a delicate nerve runs straight to the heart. All Roman women know that!

---

11. A Roman poet and playwright thought to have been born in Campania about 270 BC.

The Daughters of Cannae

In front of the families as witnesses the marriage contract is signed on wax tablets secured between two sheets of wood. Before he was conscripted to fight the Carthaginians, Naevia's father was a small farmer not far from Nola, almost in the shadow of Vesuvius, where the soil has been fertilised by the deposit of volcanic ash over centuries. There he owned land, which two stout white oxen took ten days to plough, rich soil producing good crops of turnips, cabbages, lentils and beans. He grew spelt and millet, regularly taking two crops a year off the same land. The barn housed a press to extract the juice from grapes and olives. Its floor of beaten earth was used to thresh the corn. Sunk into the yard beside the stone farmhouse lay rows of large casks for the fermentation of wine and nearby the trees in the orchard bore apples, pears and fat figs. Olive trees and vines mingled there, producing sufficient for the family with enough over to sell. This farm comes with Naevia as her dowry.

The marriage is fixed for the Calends of Quintilis, the first day of the fifth month.[12] The day before, Naevia looks out the rather battered straw dolls she played with as a girl on the farm. To mark the change in her status she places the dolls on the little shrine to the gods, which occupies a corner of her adoptive father's atrium. The figures of Janus and Vesta show no sign of gratitude. Later, in her bedroom, her maid helps to dress Naevia in a simple white tunic, woven according to the ancient method and secured at the waist by a double knot. 'Don't tie it too tightly or Lucius will never be able to undo it.' The slave girl giggles and Naevia tries to look severe. Next they do battle with her hair. Laboriously the girl combs and divides it into six locks

---

12. Originally the Roman year had only ten months and began on the Ides of March. It is said that King Numa added January and February. At some stage the beginning of the year was moved to the Calends of January, so that Quintilis became the seventh month, later named July after Julius Caesar. The Calends were the first day of each month, the Nones were the fifth or the seventh, and the Ides were the thirteenth or the fifteenth.

Chapter One

separated by a narrow band, then she joins them into a coil in the style worn by the Vestal Virgins. Naevia peers doubtfully at herself in the mirror given to her by Lucius. Perhaps it will look better in the morning. She tries to lie stock still all night, hoping not to spoil the girl's handiwork.

They're both up at first light to complete the preparations. Despite Naevia's efforts, the hairstyling seems to have taken a battering overnight and some rebuilding has to be done. Fortunately, it's going to be largely covered by an orange-coloured veil and topped off with a wreath of verbena and sweet marjoram. Eventually the maid assures her mistress that nothing is going to fall off at the wrong moment. Naevia steps gingerly into new sandals, dyed to match the veil. The ensemble is completed with an ample shawl, which she wraps around her shoulders.

In the garden of Naevius's house the families and guests are waiting. Somebody is playing a flute loudly, to drown the unpropitious squeals of a sucking pig who seems well aware of the part he is about to play in the celebrations. The deed is done. Two small boys appear. One carries a jug for libations and a wooden platter on which the pig's liver has been carefully arranged. He places it on the altar as an offering to the spirit of the family. The second boy swings a censer in one hand. In the other he carries a linen cloth into which the ritual cake of spelt has been folded. A respectful silence falls to enable the haruspex[13] to give his full attention to the job in hand, the interpretation of such signs as the gods shall choose to give. Old Julius, an uncle of Lucius, gives a little cough and hobbles forward on his stick. With it he pokes about among the bits of pig's liver for a suitable length of time. His qualifications as a haruspex are nil, but nobody minds at a private ceremony. The important point is

---

13. A haruspex was a man trained in the interpretation of the propitiousness or otherwise of some proposed action by inspecting the entrails of sacrificed animals.

to observe the formalities. Julius requests a knife which is hastily brought to him. He cuts open a bit of liver and has a good sniff at it. One of the boys stifles a giggle; it reminds him of a dog sniffing over its food before guzzling it. At last the old man pronounces the omens to be auspicious, which is fortunate because otherwise everybody would have to go home and come back on another day. Amid relieved applause Julius retires to a stone bench where he promptly falls asleep. His place is taken by Camilla, an old friend of Naevius's family. Her only husband died some years ago and she has not remarried. According to ancient tradition this makes her the ideal person to perform the marriage ceremony, despite the fact of her weekly assignation with Calvinus, a lecherous old member of the College of Pontiffs. Camilla takes the couple's right hands in hers and administers the nuptial vows with suitable solemnity. The last of these is pronounced by Naevia to confirm her status as the servient partner in this union. 'Wherever you are, Lucius, there I, Naevia, shall also be.' The ceremony is complete. Naevia has passed from the power of her adoptive father into the power of her new husband.

The rest of the day is spent in feasting, consuming the pig and sacrificing the ritual cake, the remains of which are eventually tossed to the dogs as nobody likes it much. Lucius chats with his two closest friends, Titus Junius Brutus and Gaius Laelius, both of whom fought alongside him in Sicily. Brutus comes from a very ancient family. An ancestor was one of the first consuls, with Marcus Horatius, to be appointed after the expulsion of the Etruscan kings. They dedicated the temple of Jupiter Capitolinus and signed a treaty with Carthage 250 years ago. That's how far the Brutus clan go back. They are staunch republicans, so much so that Lucius remembers Brutus once telling him that this same ancestor put his own son to death for involvement in an alleged conspiracy, because he feared for the safety of the Republic. Laelius is less intense, more

Chapter One

interested in good living and women than politics. He has a rugged handsomeness about him which endears him to the women, if not the men, who are jealous of his effortless success. 'Make a woman laugh and you're half way up her leg.' Lucius faintly disapproves, but Laelius amuses him and what's more he knows him to be a very brave horseman who singlehandedly saw off two elephants and their archers at Panormus. In outlook he is much closer to Brutus who has the same sense of duty ingrained in him. Yet he cannot help admiring Laelius. They take off their togas once the formalities are over and sit in the shade of an awning which Naevius has had rigged up for the occasion.

'So, Lucius, what are you going to do now?' Laelius twists the stem of his goblet while watching a couple of girls who are dancing to a tune that Naevia is playing on a set of pipes. Occasionally she pauses to sing about a Sicilian shepherdess bringing her flock down from the mountain for winter. Her voice floats above the chatter and at first Lucius does not reply. He cannot take his eyes off his new wife. She is sitting on a little stool and throws her head back, laughing and smiling at the applause. Lucius longs to put his arms around her.

'I've got my beautiful wife to occupy me,' he replies when the clapping dies away.

'My dear fellow, you can't spend the rest of your life in bed. The state has need of men like you.'

'It's flattering of you to say so, but I haven't really given it much thought. I've been rather busy since we came back from the war, what with my father's estate, building the house and getting married.'

'Your military service qualifies you to stand for one of the quaestorships.[14] I think your father would have liked

---

14. The quaestors were junior magistrates who either supervised the treasury at Rome, held administrative posts in Italy or assisted consuls or pro-magistrates abroad.

that.' It's the more serious-minded Brutus who speaks now. Lucius would not admit it to his two friends, but it is not strictly true that he has not given his future any thought. His success in the war and his new status as head of the family have ignited in him a tiny spark of ambition. His days at school, however hard he had tried, had not imbued him with great confidence. He was always conscious that many of the other boys were cleverer than he. It was rare that he ever received anything but muted praise from the master; more frequent were the tickings-off.

'A good effort, Lucius,' was the best he could hope for. Never 'Excellent!' or 'Good boy, go to the top of the class!' Well tried, that's how he'd sum up himself. And yet in Sicily there was no doubt that he had shone, surprising himself and earning the respect of his commanders. At night he lies in bed and sometimes dares to ask himself, 'Perhaps I'm more capable than I thought.'

Laelius takes a lamb pasty and chews it thoughtfully. 'You're right, Brutus. I can just see Lucius as a quaestor now. We're going to need a few sensible magistrates to counterbalance the idiots. Buggerlugs is proposing to stand, you know.' Buggerlugs is one Publius Umbrenus, so called for his large protruding ears. At Panormus, Laelius had suggested that earrings would look well on him when Umbrenus bragged of looting jewellery from a Carthaginian corpse. This had not gone down well, especially as, moments later, Umbrenus refused to take part in the cavalry charge, citing the general's orders to wait, and then found himself derided for showing no initiative. He is the rather arrogant son of a very rich plebeian rumoured to have made his money from dubious dealings in a Spanish silver mine.

'I heard Umbrenus was off to Saguntum to see if he could make even more money than his father. He keeps telling everybody that he's got a lot of friends there,' says Brutus.

'That was his plan, but things are changing in Spain,' replies Laelius, tucking into another pasty. 'Apparently the

Chapter One

Carthaginian influence is growing by the day and they're collaring all the silver to pay our war indemnity. In any case, I reckon his father's got ambitions for Buggerlugs.'

'Anybody else you know that's going to stand?' Lucius tries not to sound too interested.

'I should be very surprised if Catulus[15] doesn't put himself forward, by right of birth if nothing else. He'll be following in his father's footsteps, like shit comes after an ox.'

'Really, Brutus, you're much too kind about him,' says Laelius straightfacedly. 'That pointed snout of his always looks as if somebody has just held it over the main sewer. I'm surprised he can actually see anybody, he's so damned superior.' The conversation drifts into reminiscences about the war, but Lucius does not forget his friends' advice. It helps to dispel self-doubt.

Venus has risen in the western sky by the time preparations begin for the bridal procession to Lucius's house on the Esquiline. At the front the flute players mingle with the torch bearers, who lead the way. The boys carrying the torches wave their brands vigorously to induce strong flames. Weak flames portend a bridegroom with a feeble cock. 'Quite unnecessary,' Lucius assures his friends, who bring up the rear in a ragged column. They sing bawdy songs, some of which make ill-disguised references to the genitalia of both bride and groom. More demurely, Naevia walks accompanied by the two altar boys, one holding each hand. Their task is to ensure that the new bride does not stray on the way and arrive at the wrong house. Just in front of her skips Antonius, a little lad of seven years. He holds aloft the bridal torch of tightly bound hawthorn twigs. Naevia keeps pushing him gently forward as the sparks

---

15. Gaius Lutatius Catulus, who later became consul in 220 BC. His father, of the same name, won a naval battle off Lilybaeum on the west coast of Sicily in the First Punic War and had been consul in 242 BC.

threaten to ignite her veil. To the accompaniment of waving from the tenements and shouted good wishes of passers-by, the cortège winds its way up the narrow alleys of the hill.

The threshold of Lucius's house is spread with a white cloth and decorated with fresh sprigs of laurel. To mark her entry and status as a wife, Naevia smears the doorposts and lintel with oil from a small jar. Lucius looks round anxiously. He must find two men who are both strong and sober. The first part is easy but the second proves more difficult, as most of the guests are not known for their sobriety. It is essential that they do not stumble or, worse still, drop Naevia when they lift her over the threshold and into the house; that would be a terrible omen for the marriage. Licinianus, his cousin and a sheep farmer from Praeneste, rushes up and begs to be accorded the privilege. He is exceptionally strong but also exceptionally drunk and his bid falls by the wayside, literally. Lucius decides on Brutus, who never drinks too much, and Mucius,[16] a serious young man training to be a lawyer, who steps forward diffidently, almost overcome by the compliment. Together they lift Naevia, who is light and slimly built in any event, through the doorway and along the passage, and deposit her safely in the atrium. Naxus, dressed in a fresh tunic of brown linen, steps forward with a little bow.

'Welcome to the house of my master. I offer you the traditional gifts of fire and water.' He holds out a lighted lamp and a shallow dish of water. Naevia smiles and touches the lamp and the dish to signify her acceptance. Lydia, chief bridesmaid, bustles in carrying a distaff and spindle, ancient symbols of virtue and domestic diligence.

'Where do you want these?'

'Out of sight preferably.' Lydia frowns in disapproval, but Naevia only laughs. She's happy and has drunk a drop

---

16. This is Quintus Mucius Scaevola who became praetor in 216 BC and governor of Sardinia in 215 BC.

Chapter One

more wine than she's used to. Several guests have followed them into the atrium. Lydia shoos them all out. The final event of the day ought to be held in private.

Their friends predict that the marriage will be a happy one. Perhaps this a surprise, for in some ways it is a joining of opposites. The war has hardened Lucius. He is slowly becoming more like his father. Gaius Opimius was the embodiment of the old paterfamilias: stern, simple in his ways and always conscious of his duty. In a slightly diluted form Lucius has inherited the same qualities. Less unbending than his father, he is more able to relax, enjoy life's pleasures. He likes good wine, a visit to the play or the races in the circus beneath the Palatine Hill. He is strict with his slaves, as Gaius taught him to be, but does not punish them unnecessarily. You will not see any slave of Lucius Opimius with scars from beatings on his face or back. He does not even possess a whip. To him all men come the same, be they citizens, freemen or slaves. The experiences of war have taught him that being a patrician or a collector of street dung makes no difference in the thick of battle. Yet behind this relaxed air, almost amiability, there lurks a nagging sense of obligation. He needs to serve. It's in his blood, his breeding. Lucius does not speculate why he should feel this way. It is enough that he cannot escape from it. It was not so much his courage, though he is not short of it, but his status as a member of the equestrian order that made him fight bravely in Sicily. The wound in his arm is barely visible now. Few people, apart from Naevia, are even aware of the scar, which resembles the skin of a plucked chicken leg. Deep down Lucius is ashamed of it. He would feel more comfortable if the wound had been much worse; if he had lost the use of the arm altogether.

Lucius loves Naevia as a Roman of the upper classes should, fondly but from just above. Like his father, he views his wife as a beautiful woman who will serve him faithfully in her task of bringing up his children and in performing her duties as mistress of the household. The children will, of course, remain under his sole control at all times, as will Naevia. Fortunately for Lucius, Naevia, twenty-five years of age and older than usual for a bride, expects nothing else. She has been brought up in the knowledge that this will be her role in married life. Her new status is not very different from her previous one. A husband has many similarities to a father. She has only moved from the power of one man to that of another, having already kept house for her adoptive father for several years.

It would be a mistake, however, to think that Naevia is not happy. She is a naturally cheerful person who adapts easily and accepts life as it comes. She makes the best of whatever situation she finds herself in. She buys a good cook, Orrius, for fifty denarii.[17] It's a high price for a kitchen slave who has not worked in a private house previously. He will need some schooling before he can be let loose on Lucius's friends. Nevertheless he's young and free from disease, and Naevia knows he makes good pastry. He worked in a takeaway near her old home until his master died from a tumour that made his stomach swell as if he were pregnant. People joked that he had changed sex, but the poor fellow suffered terribly. He asked the knife sharpener next door to cut out the swelling. The sharpener practised a little crude surgery in the neighbourhood and was known to be a reliable lancer of boils and exciser of verrucas, but as he inserted his blade the baker gave out a terrible groan and died almost instantly. His widow let the shop to a tenant who didn't want Orrius.

Naevia has a natural grace in the way she carries herself. Her upper body is slim but her wide hips are a good sign in a Roman matron. They betoken the easy birth of children.

---

17. The denarius was a silver coin introduced in about 269 BC.

Chapter One

Her hair is long and of a pale chestnut colour. She usually sweeps it back from her face and ties it with a ribbon at the nape of her neck. She has an unblemished skin, a little darker than you might expect – the product of many hours under the sun working on her father's farm. She has inherited pale grey eyes from her mother, who died in childbirth. As she walks about the house, the passages and courtyards are filled with snatches of old songs that her wetnurse and surrogate mother, Phoebe, taught her as a girl in Nola. She is an accomplished player of the lyre and weaves her own clothes. Her hands and fingers also betray a rustic childhood. The sophisticated matrons of Rome would descibe them as sinewy. On the farm she spent many hours wielding a hoe or pulling buckets of water from a well to fill the oxen's trough. It's not long before the garden plot beyond the peristyle is sprouting Lucius's favourite vegetables and her own turnips, melons and pumpkins. From a corner comes the gentle murmuring of quails. They both like the eggs.

Lucius is not neglectful of a husband's duties. Indeed, why should he be with such a pretty wife? Although they have many friends, nothing delights him more than to sit in the peristyle on a warm summer evening, listening to the warbling of the doves in the eaves and watching the stars slowly brighten in the darkening sky. Naevia sits at his knee and plucks at her lyre, trying to recall some tune from her youth. A female slave, olive skinned and barefooted, moves silently from pillar to pillar. She carries a jug of oil to fill the little terracotta lamps hung from bronze brackets. With a taper she lights the lamps one by one, until the whole peristyle is bathed in a shadowy glow and tiny wisps of oily smoke climb upwards in the still air. Orrius appears, bearing a dish of grilled red mullet garnished with fresh lettuce. Lucius cuts a slice from the fish and hands it back to Orrius, the traditional portion to be tossed back into the fire as an offering to the gods.

Naevia gently stirs the crater[18] of wine brought by the girl, adding a little resin and plenty of water. They share a silver cup. The statues cast distorted shadows over the gravel paths. Slowly Perseus, holding up the Medusa's head, Theseus unwinding his spool of string and Sisyphus rolling the rock up the unending hill, dissolve and meld into the enveloping darkness. The lamps sputter and go out.

Naevia soon feels a stirring in her belly. She sends to Nola for her old nurse. Phoebe's reached her fiftieth year and her gait's a little laboured now, but she's a tough old bird who relishes the prospect of helping out. A few weeks later she's rattling up the Appian Way,[19] then making Naevia laugh with her description of the journey. She's had to remonstrate with Naxus for going much too fast, when she wanted to stop and look at everything. It's the first time she's been more than two miles from where she was born. Young Gaius, named after his grandfather, emerges safely into the world. A year later, coinciding with the feast of the Saturnalia, a little girl arrives. Officially she has no name, but like all daughters she will take the clan name of her father. She will be called Opimia.

---

18. A large flat dish used for this purpose.
19. The great highway first conceived in 312 BC by Appius Claudius after whom it was named. It ran southwards from Rome to Capua and eventually all the way to Brundisium, now Brindisi.

Chapter Two

237 BC

'Lucius Opimius Veianus, son of Gaius, knight and former military tribune, for quaestor. He is worthy of your vote.' These red- or black-painted signs are all over town: on the walls near the city gates, at crossroads where carters in from the countryside stop to display their wares, on the walls of supporters' houses, near the temple of Ceres at the foot of the Aventine Hill and in the big vegetable market by the river.

Lucius is campaigning with the help of his friends Laelius and Quintus Mucius, whose father is a senator. They're in the Subura, a long, narrow street in the valley between the Esquiline and Viminal Hills. It's the seediest part of town, lined with shops, takeaways and dingy taverns that provide cheap drink and a bed for the night, if you've nowhere else to go. You can have a woman as well to keep you company, provided you don't mind getting something you haven't paid for. The street's seething with humanity and quite a few forms of animal. Carts block the road, women shout at their urchins, who run about getting up to mischief of one kind or another; a scribe struggles along carrying his folding stool on his back; shopkeepers stand in doorways shouting for custom; and fumes from the cookshops hang in the fetid air. Washing, shapeless brown garments like giant bats, is strung across the street between the ramshackle tenements. From the smithies comes a cacophony of bangs and clangs as the metalworkers hammer out ironware on their anvils. Don't look up the side alleys, which usually end in middens piled high with excrement. Lying on top you might glimpse a little bundle, exposed. It could survive a couple of days, warmed by the heat generated from the ordure. Perhaps in the night a barren wretch will come creeping, listening for a whimper, and present her man with a surprise in the morning.

Lucius, with his friends beside him, progresses slowly. In front walk a few hired slaves, carrying placards and clearing the way. Behind come men who are budding clients, troopers from his squadron and other veterans of the war. They look to Lucius for favours, perhaps a loan or a quiet word in the right ear to secure a job. In return he can rely on them for political support. He's given them a few coins each, quarter asses,[20] which they toss into the crowd. The children fight like rats to grab them.

A man emerges from the throng and shouts, 'Hey, Lucius Opimius, what are you going to do about the hole in my ceiling? Your bloody tenants on the floor above piss through it every night.' The man's flat on the ground before he's finished speaking, held down by two of Lucius's retinue.

'That's why you stink all the time, Rosco,' somebody calls out. Lucky for Lucius; he's forgotten the man's name, if he ever knew it. He recognises him as the occupier of two rooms in one of the blocks on the ropemakers' street.

'All right, all right, let him up.' He's here to win votes, not to lose them by antagonising the locals. 'You know the terms of your tenancy, Rosco. Tullius on the ground floor is responsible for all repairs.'

---

20. An as was a copper coin of low value.

Chapter Two

There's some muttering among the bystanders. 'Typical bloody landlord, doesn't give a toss as long as he gets his money.' It could turn ugly very quickly. Rosco's strong and well built. Lucius has an idea that he works on the docks, lugging bags of grain off the barges. He can see a dagger tucked into his belt. He grins.

'You're a strong fellow, Rosco, anybody can see that. I bet you could piss upwards through the same hole with a bit of practice.' He gets a laugh and even Rosco looks less surly.

'He sticks it up most nights anyhow,' shouts a woman in a ragged dress streaked with tallow.

Another woman joins in. 'Well, you'd know!' General mayhem breaks out and Lucius moves off swiftly.

Down in the vegetable market Lucius has hired a stall for eight days. Orrius comes into his own. He sets up his charcoal brazier and a brick oven. Soon he's turning out pasties filled with spiced mutton and spinach, given away free. The customers can't miss the big sign hanging from the awning. 'Have a pasty on Lucius Opimius, your candidate for quaestor.' He strolls around, joshing with the other stallholders. To his surprise he's rather enjoying this electioneering.

A tiny man approaches. He just reaches Lucius's waist and it's made worse by the fact that he is hunchbacked, so that his tunic at the front comes down almost to his ankles, but behind it barely covers his bottom. His head is sunk into his shoulders and he turns his whole body to look round. Behind him he drags a small handcart. At first Lucius thinks he's selling furs. The man tugs at his toga and mumbles something. Lucius bends to listen.

'Sir, you see this bundle in my cart. It's all that's left of my dancing bear.' Lucius looks down. He can see now that it's the body of a small bear. One or two flies are crawling over it.

'So, what do you want me to do about it?'

'What I want is compensation.'

'Compensation, why? It's a dead bear, I'm sorry.'

'You don't understand, sir.' He lets go of the cart's handle. It drops to the ground and the body of the bear slides forward with a sloppy thud, revealing a large gash on its head. 'That's why I want compensation.' He jabs a stubby finger at the wound. 'I was in the Argiletum[21] yesterday, you know, where they're building those new shops for the butchers and the fishmongers. Lots of people and I had a good crowd watching my Salty. He's a wonderful dancer, well was. He could balance an apple on his snout and do a caper on his hind legs at the same time. Then he'd go round the crowd and collect money in his paw. You should have seen him; wonderful he was, really. Course he was completely tame. You could have curled him up with a baby.'

'Fascinating.' Lucius turns to look over to the stall. He's wondering whether Orrius will run out of sheep meat. He ought to send a slave for some more. He feels another tug on the rim of his toga. Beside him Mucius smiles and nods him back towards the dwarf.

'So, what happened?'

'What happened, sir? It was terrible. Just as Salty, that's his name, was finishing his act, there was this great crash from above. All this scaffolding came tumbling down and a big bloody brick lands smack on poor Salty's head. Stone dead and no mistake. I went to see the contractor straight away. He wasn't having anything to do with it. He sent me to the owner, some bloke called Vettius. I expect you know him. Apparently he owns the whole site. You know what, he told me to bugger off.' Lucius is conscious of a small splutter next to him, but he keeps a straight face himself. 'Course he's valuable, you know. Paid this bloke from Ostia a small fortune, I did, five hundred asses. It was about the time of the feast of the October horse, this three years

---

21. A street running off the Forum.

Chapter Two

gone. He was worth twenty times that after all the training I gave him.'

'I suppose you want some damages, but I'm afraid I'm not a lawyer. Perhaps you should go and see the Urban Praetor.'[22]

Mucius, who's training for the bar, assumes a learned expression. 'Did you say your bear was completely tame?'

'May Jupiter's bolt strike me, sir, if he wasn't as harmless as a lamb, though I say it myself.'

'I see. That might be a problem. I suspect your claim lies under the Aquilian Law which imposes liability for unlawfully killing slaves, farm animals, dogs and wild animals. I don't think there's any provision for tamed animals.'

'An interesting case for you, Quintus. You might make your reputation by establishing that a tame bear is still a wild animal within the meaning of the Act. Vettius is a rich fellow by all accounts. Double the penalty, isn't it, if a defendant denies liability and then loses?'

Mucius is a big man, well built. They make a curious pair, the tall aristocrat and his hunchback client dragging his cart behind him. They disappear together towards Team Street[23] and the praetor's tribunal in the Forum. Meanwhile Lucius wanders down in the direction of the cattle market, keeping an eye out for the kitchen boy he sent to fetch more meat for the stall. On the way he meets Pomptinus, once a client of his father. He greets Lucius, who has to slow his pace

---

22. The praetors were senior magistrates, second only to the consuls. Originally there was one praetor, the Praetor Urbanus, who supervised the administration of justice. In 242 BC the Praetor Peregrinus was added to deal with lawsuits involving foreigners. Their number was further increased to four by 227 BC when praetors were appointed to govern the newly acquired provinces of Sicily and Sardinia following the First Punic War. As the number of provinces increased during the later Republic, so the praetorships were added to, in order to provide governors who went out to a province after their year of office at Rome. Caesar raised the number of praetors to sixteen.
23. A street leading from the vegetable market into the Forum.

considerably to match the old chap's hobbling gait. He can't eat meat, he says, no teeth left, so he's bought a bit of eel and cabbage to stew for his supper. Lucius can tell without looking in the bag he carries. The wife can't get about now. He doesn't mind. It gets him out of the two rooms on the Aventine which they share with his son and his family. At the Sublician Bridge a gang of slaves is repairing the wooden piles. Some are standing up to their necks in the river, pulling on ropes to keep the timbers vertical, while men on the decking above heave squared lumps of stone up on pulleys and then let them drop to drive the beams into the river bed. The sun beats down on the bare backs of the slaves, stained with sweat and blood where the gangmaster's whip has found its mark. Lucius and Pomptinus exchange a few more words before the old man limps away, richer by a few coins that Lucius has slipped him. His father would have wanted it. He turns round to head back to the stall and all but bumps into Gythius, leader of a small guild of carpenters.

'Just the fellow I wanted. I've got some repairs need doing to the floors of one of my blocks on the Esquiline. Come and have a pasty and a cup of spiced wine.' The guild is worth a vote or two.

The morning of the election dawns bright and fine. Lucius rises early to be shaved by his body slave, Creto. It's an irritation, and sometimes a painful one at that. His father never submitted to the razor except to have his beard trimmed every other day. Lucius must endure the latest fashion. Gingerly Creto places the cloth around his master's neck, knowing full well how much Lucius dislikes this tedious chore. He dabs his master's face with warm water and draws the thin iron blade across the whetstone, hoping not to break it. Anxiously the slave scrapes away until the worst of the stubble is removed. For once Lucius emerges from the operation without the appearance of someone who has just taken part in a tavern brawl. It is not unknown for senators and even consuls to be seen dabbing

Chapter Two

at their faces in the Forum, trying to staunch a dribble of blood after the morning encounter with the razor.

In the atrium a few of his clients are already waiting to escort him to the Comitium, the place of assembly in front of the Senate House where voting will take place. Orrius is handing round freshly baked rolls filled with thin slices of chicken liver and asparagus. Naevia enters, leading little Gaius by the hand. He reaches up to touch his father. Naevia kisses Lucius on the cheek, then bends down to the boy dressed in a white tunic fringed with a red stripe. 'Wish your father good luck.' Lucius pats his son on the head. Then, almost as an afterthought, he picks him up in both arms to kiss him on each cheek. Gaius squirms; he's not used to such displays of affection by his father. And here's Phoebe cradling Opimia. She steps forward to let the child stretch out a chubby arm and stroke her father's face. Her hair is growing now, but so blonde that you can hardly see it. Lucius tickles her tiny foot, stoops to kiss her forehead, then turns to go.

The procession makes its way at a leisurely pace down the hill. Lucius knows how important it is to be seen with plenty of people round him. Roman citizens don't like a candidate for political office who stands or walks alone. He who stands or walks by himself may be seeking power only for himself. Such men want to be king and no true Roman will vote for that.

They enter the Forum via the Argiletum. To their right lies the Comitium. On the far side the Capitoline Hill rises, ascended by broad flights of steps leading to the temples of Juno Moneta and Jupiter. The temple of Jupiter itself is obscured by the slope of the hill and other buildings which hide all but its pediment and the finials on each side, statues of Juno[24] and Minerva.[25] Beyond, the skyline is

---

24. The patron goddess of womanhood.
25. The patron goddess of the arts and crafts.

The Daughters of Cannae

broken by the jagged outline of the Tarpeian Rock[26] where carrion crows are poking about in the crevices. Occasionally one flaps away, clutching in its beak a scrap of flesh, torn from the body of some criminal thrown over the precipice a few days before.

His retainers disperse into the throng while Lucius, accompanied only by Laelius and Mucius, walks to the platform on the southern side of the Comitium. This platform,[27] from which the magistrates and tribunes are accustomed to address the people, is decorated with gaily coloured beaks, trophies captured from the prows of enemy warships in a battle 100 years ago. Some of Lucius's fellow candidates are already there. He greets Catulus who responds with a thin smile but does not pause in his conversation with Lepidus, one of his patrician supporters. He hears Umbrenus before he sees him, talking loudly to nobody in particular about how he hopes to top the poll.

'If bribery's got anything to do with it,' mutters Laelius, 'he should win the votes of every tribe. He was chucking silver around in the circus yesterday as if the coins were just pebbles. Apparently he buys them up from Greek traders in return for ingots from his Spanish mine. A lot of toughs followed him into the Forum. I can see one or two hanging around the voting pens. Let's hope the stewards keep them under control.'

'I've warned our lads, but he's probably bought the stewards as well. Keep your eyes skinned for any buggering about once the voting starts. Umbrenus has never liked me

---

26. The Tarpeian Rock was a precipitous outcrop near the south-western corner of the Capitoline Hill over which convicted criminals were thrown to their death. According to legend it was named after Tarpeia, the daughter of a Roman commander. She is said to have betrayed Rome by letting some besieging Sabines, who were trying to recover their womenfolk, into the Capitoline citadel.
27. The platform was known as the Rostra, from the Latin for the beaks of ships.

Chapter Two

since Panormus. It's lucky we're not all competing for just one job.'

The Comitium is a relatively small area capable of accommodating only a few thousand citizens at one time. It is paved with black marble, distinguishing it from the rest of the Forum, which is covered only by earth, beaten down solid over the years. You can't miss the tall gnomon of the sundial brought back by Valerius Messalla from Sicily during the war against Carthage. Because of its relocation the sundial no longer shows the hour correctly, but it's near enough and the citizens enjoy the novelty. Nearby stands a large tomb flanked by two stone lions on plinths. The sides of this tomb are carved with a strange inscription in a language nobody can translate. Some say that the tomb is as old as Rome itself and that it contains the body of Romulus. This must be nonsense. Every Roman child knows that he was carried straight up to heaven to join the gods when he died. The sacred fig tree, which grows close by, marks the spot where Romulus and his brother were found in their wicker basket, caught up by the flood waters of the Tiber and then rescued by the she-wolf. Others say the fig tree was on the Palatine Hill near the grotto they call the Lupercal. In either case, a bronze statue depicts the twins being suckled by the wolf. Don't desecrate the tree or the statue, unless you want to be trussed up in a sack with a monkey, a cockerel and a dog, then thrown into the river.

Today the Comitium has been sectioned off with ropes and hurdles. Representatives of the thirty-five tribes of citizens assemble in their allotted pens. The poorer men wear only a grubby loincloth and a tattered tunic. Others, from the richer tribes, sport light cloaks over their tunics and broad-brimmed hats to guard against the sun. A few conservative types have put on the toga, considering it to be an occasion when formal dress should be worn. Naturally all the candidates and their supporters on the platform are wearing theirs. Some voters are lingering in the shade of the awnings draped from the shop fronts down near the temple of Saturn. The sun has reached its zenith, high in the sky between the speakers' and the ambassadors' platforms. The doors of the Senate House swing open to reveal a trumpeter, who marches forward. Not everybody has noticed him. The mighty blast of his trumpet soon alters that and the crowd falls silent. Here's the consul's herald. He walks forward solemnly to announce that the sixth hour has ended and the seventh has begun. It is midday.[28]

The crowd remains hushed. All eyes are trained on the entrance to the Senate House. In stately procession the lictors[29] emerge, swathed in their togas and carrying the fasces on their shoulders. In two files of six they walk to the steps leading down to the Comitium and pause, then each file takes two paces sideways to leave a space between them, like parade-ground soldiers. Nothing but the cawing of a crow breaks the silence. Even those citizens who were eating have stopped. They stand open mouthed, expectant like the rest. A tall figure appears in the doorway, the whiteness of his toga contrasting starkly with the dark interior. He stands there for a few moments as if to check that all is ready, then steps forward into the bright sunlight. Once again the trumpet's notes ring out across the Forum. Lucius Cornelius Lentulus Caudinus,[30] Consul of Rome,

---

28. The Roman day and night were each divided into twelve hours. The first hour of the day began at sunrise and the last hour ended at sunset. Similarly the first hour of the night began at sunset and the last hour ended at dawn. Consequently the hours were not of fixed duration. As the day hours were longer so the night hours were shorter, and conversely, according to the time of year. The hours would only be equal at the spring and summer equinoxes.
29. The lictors were executive officials in attendance on a magistrate. The consul on duty was entitled to twelve lictors, who preceded him, clearing the way and calling upon citizens to salute him. They carried bundles of rods (fasces) from which protruded an axe-head symbolising the magistrate's power, except inside the city's boundaries where the axe-head was removed.
30. Consul in 237 BC and Pontifex Maximus (Chief Priest) from 237 until his death in 213 BC.

Chapter Two

advances to pass between the two files of his lictors and stops at the head of the steps. This man exudes an air of absolute authority. To look at him you would not believe that his power lasts only for a year. The Cornelii, patricians and one of the city's most ancient and distinguished clans, have produced many consuls. He knows he will not be the last. The self-assurance is bred into him over centuries of service and influence in the affairs of the Republic. He is not noticeably arrogant, but few would care to interrupt when he speaks, and he would not expect it. Even before his election to the consulship his fellow senators would give way if he indicated that he wished to speak in a debate. You can almost feel the effortless superiority. His tall figure and lean face betray his aristocratic breeding, as his sharp grey eyes survey the scene. His short hair is tightly curled in rings of pale bronze that nearly match the smooth tan of his face, not wrinkled by long days of toil in the sun, unlike many of his less fortunate fellow citizens. He raises his right arm, a gesture that is at once a greeting to the people and a sign demanding silence, unnecessary for there is not a whisper from the mob beneath him.

He retires a couple of paces to stand at the head of his lictors and an augur[31] mounts the steps. He wears a long white gown trimmed with fur and a hood over his head. The crowd watches him quartering the sky with a curved wand, seeking to observe the flight of birds. The mysteries of this arcane ritual are known only to the augurs. Cynics say that they preserve their status in this way. Fortunately birds are not in short supply. Many are perched on buildings around the Forum or are hopping about on the ground, pecking at the titbits left by citizens given to eating

---

31. An augur acquainted men with the wishes of the gods by interpreting the flight of birds, the appetite of the sacred chickens and other fortuitous events. If the omens observed by the augur were not propitious the business in hand would not proceed.

while they wait to vote. A pair of ravens appears in the sky above the Comitium. They flap lazily down to settle in the Grove of Vesta underneath the Palatine. On the basis of this slender evidence the augur pronounces that the omens are propitious. The elections may proceed.

Caudinus advances to speak. 'Jupiter, best and greatest, grant that this day the citizens of Rome may elect as quaestors the best candidates, who will well and faithfully execute their duties.' Preceded by his lictors, he descends the steps of the Senate House and walks to the speakers' platform. You might catch a glimpse of purple as he raises his right arm once more to give the traditional instruction. 'Citizens, disperse to cast your votes.'

The motley throng gradually resolves itself into some semblance of order. Representatives of each tribe take their places in the pens assigned to them. Lots are drawn to decide the order in which the tribes will vote. As each citizen shuffles forward in the queue, he takes a pebble. Lines of baskets bearing the names of individual candidates stand ready to be filled. Lucius watches carefully. It's the narrow gangways down which the voters must pass that are critical. It's hard to see. There are so many people milling about, pushing forward, stopping to talk, so that a crowd builds up behind. Laelius is whispering to him.

'That's one of Umbrenus's men. Look, there.' Laelius points to a tall, thick-set ox of a fellow with hair cut very short. He's standing close to the entrance to a gangway with a couple of other men who seem to know him. 'He runs a tavern down on the docks and a brothel at the back. I think he knew Umbrenus in Sicily and now they import elephant tusks from a merchant based in Carthage. Somebody told me he's got a shed full of the stuff which he sells at a massive profit. I might have a chat with him.'

'Got anything on you?'

'I wouldn't come without.'

Chapter Two

Laelius slips away. Moments later Lucius spots him among the crowd, pushing gently through the bystanders near a gangway. Umbrenus's man has positioned himself nicely where he can have the last word before a voter reaches the baskets. Laelius is right behind him now, admiring the spiked iron bracelets on each wrist and the thick fingers covered in rings. He could touch the sweaty brown tunic and the roll of fat hanging over the leather thong which passes for a belt. This lump's never tasted the legionary's biscuit, more likely too many sows' bellies.

'Who you voting for today, mate?' An old man with a dead chicken hanging from his belt looks up. 'Better make it Publius Umbrenus if you want to keep that for your supper.'

Laelius sticks a dagger's point into each side of the man's ribs. The man stiffens but he doesn't move. Whoever is behind him knows his business. Laelius is in his ear.

'Listen, fatso, you won't get to supper if you play that game. Now bugger off, before I cut your giblets out. Move!' He gives him a sharp kick up the arse by way of further encouragement and, with the dagger points still pressed into the man's flanks, guides him over to the stewards. 'The consul has seen this turd interfering with voters. Keep him under close arrest until sundown or Caudinus will want explanations from you.' Laelius is gone before anybody can ask questions.

Voting has scarcely finished before the herald proclaims the sunset hour. To nobody's surprise Umbrenus has topped the poll. He is carried on the shoulders of his supporters to the foot of the Capitoline steps, where he announces that he will sacrifice an ox to Jupiter the following day, to celebrate his election. Lucius has been successful too. He's pleased and perhaps a little surprised. His friends clap him on the back and clients offer their respectful congratulations. He has stepped onto the first rung of the political ladder. His confidence and ambition have received another boost.

Orrius prepares a special meal of quails' eggs and mushrooms. Lucius and Naevia drink Falernian wine and break open walnuts brought up from the farm in Campania.

'What happens now?'

'That depends on how the Senate allocate the various posts. They say it's done by lot, but I'm sure the senators fix the draw. I might be appointed as aide to one of the consuls. I wouldn't mind that. There's work to be done in Picenum, settling colonies, or I suppose I could be assigned to one of the criminal courts; not very likely without legal experience. Then there's the treasury.'

Naevia leans her head against her husband's knee. 'I hope you get a job at the treasury. Then you'd stay in Rome.'

'I'd serve wherever they sent me.'

In the event, Lucius is lucky in the draw. He receives one of the posts at the treasury. On business days he makes his way to the temple of Saturn at the foot of the Capitol. There he presides with his colleague Manlius on the quaestors' tribunal. Fresh to the office, they rely upon the clerks to guide them through the daily routine of paying out money for minor public works, checking the expenses of those on official business and receiving money or securities for debts owed to the treasury. Lucius applies himself dutifully to these mundane tasks. It takes time before he can spot the corrupt contractors who submit inflated claims for materials not used, or diverted to some other project, like the invoice for basalt slabs said to have been required for repairs to the Appian Way, some of which turned up as cornerstones on the gangmaster's new house near the Esquiline Gate. On another day Lucius orders the claim for the death of a slave to be checked. The contractor states that he was a strong young man who drowned in the Tiber helping to float off a barge that had run aground while unloading at the port. He wants compensation of one

Chapter Two

hundred and fifty denarii, a lot even for a skilled slave. In any event the river is low at this time of year; no reason why a strong man should drown. What's more, Lucius suspects that the clerk and the contractor have an arrangement by which the former gets a percentage of every successful claim. He sends for the corpse. No sign of drowning, but several stab wounds on the body of a rather aged slave with three fingers missing from the right hand, not even any use as a urine collector or a water carrier. He hands the contractor over to the people's Aediles[32] for prosecution and has the clerk flogged on the steps of the temple as a warning to the rest.

---

32. The two plebeian aediles were junior magistrates concerned with temples and markets, the corn supply, keeping the streets clear and in repair, and with matters of hygiene, water supply and the organisation of certain games.

Chapter Three

231 BC

Opimia can just make out the dark red and ochre walls of her little room off the peristyle. The faint grey light of dawn filters through the linen cloth which serves as a curtain. Somewhere outside in the street the iron rims of a cart squeak and the bolts of the shutters on the candlemaker's shop rattle as he opens up. There's a chill in the air. She wraps herself in a woollen shawl woven by Phoebe and gropes with her feet in the semi-darkness, searching for her rabbit-skin slippers. The smell of tallow from a candle lingers in the room.

In a corner set aside for cooking Orrius is lighting the first fire of the day. Opimia watches him strike a piece of iron against a lump of quartz. Sparks fly onto a thin strip of dried fungus which curls and punctures with the heat. Gently he places bits of straw on the fungus and Opimia leans forward to blow. In a few moments there's a wisp of smoke followed by a burst of flame as the straw ignites. Orrius smiles and the little girl gives a cry of delight. She skips away, pausing in the atrium to scoop a handful of water from the basin.

Her father's room lies at the end of a short passage in which Creto sleeps at night. When Opimia enters, Lucius is already sitting in his tunic on the edge of the bed. She goes to the simple wooden table, the only other piece of

Chapter Three

furniture in the room, and takes from it a goblet of water which she hands to her father. He throws it back in a single gulp and taps her fondly on the arm as she passes him the heavy leather sandals from the rush mat at the foot of the bed. She rests against his knee while he leans forward to tie the thongs. Creto appears, carrying a black jug decorated with red figures of two men wrestling. Lucius sighs. It is a business day and he must submit to the razor before going down to the Forum. Opimia chatters gaily while the sharpened iron performs its crude work. She thinks she can see a nest in the eaves where the doves settle for the night and Gaius has found some frogspawn in the peristyle basin. Lucius dabs his face gingerly until Creto returns, this time bearing a toga fresh from the fullers. He stands up straight as Creto drapes the garment first over his left shoulder, then round his back, under the right arm and once more round, before placing the last fold over his master's left arm. Lucius takes a step, adjusts a fold and gives a nod to signify his satisfaction. Opimia is already holding the shoulder clasp, which she hands to Creto. It is of bronze, shaped like a shield into which a cornelian has been set, taken from the cloak of a Gaul killed in battle many years ago by Lucius's father. Creto secures it with a silver pin. By the end of the second hour Lucius is ready for his day's work. Since his quaestorship he has been a member of a ten-man commission engaged upon the establishment of colonies in Campania for veterans of the war with Carthage. He is regarded as a coming man whom the censors[33] may soon consider for elevation to the Senate.

---

33. The two censors, elected for five years but normally expected to complete their tasks within eighteen months and thereafter resign, were senior magistrates commissioned to take a census of the citizens and their property. They also drew up the list of senators and knights and were responsible for the letting of contracts to collect taxes and for major public works. The censors were often men of distinction towards the end of their political career.

A few clients await him in the atrium. One moves forward, assuming a more than usually deferential air. He has a cousin with a wife and child, threatened with eviction from a tenement on the Aventine for arrears of rent. The man has been sick, unable to work as an attendant at one of the public lavatories. Could Lucius see his way? Lucius nods and tells the man to send his cousin the next day. He'll never get his money back, but it would be useful to know where he can have a free crap every now and then.

Soon after Lucius leaves it's time for young Gaius to go to school. He drags his feet and looks a little sulky. Naevia scolds him. He has lost his stylus yet again. Eventually Rullus finds it on the edge of the basin in the peristyle, where Gaius has been using it to spear the frogspawn. Gaius complains that it is too hot to wear his cloak, but Naevia insists. At last the pair set off. Rullus carries the bag where Gaius has hidden a small frog. Opimia has seen him do this and nearly says something, but a look from her brother is enough. She settles down in a corner with her dolls made of linen stuffed with wool and horsehair. She arranges them on a stone bench in front of her, pretending to be their master and reprimanding them, just as Gaius has told her happens at his school. Sometimes the mornings drag and she longs for her brother to return.

On fine days Naevia has her hair combed outside. They sit side by side on a bench and Opimia learns to tell what hour it is by the position of the sun in relation to the roof of the house. Then Naevia shows the little girl how to add and subtract, using pebbles from the paths. With a wax tablet Opimia forms her letters and learns to read and write. One day, her mother says, she will have to do the household accounts for her husband.

Phoebe's getting on now, but she can still remember many of the songs they sang back in the old days on the farm at Nola. Opimia is quick to learn and wants to please. Like her mother she has a good singing voice. It is not long

Chapter Three

before she can play a small set of pipes made for her by Orrius from an ash tree in the garden.

Orrius is fond of the little girl and she can often be found helping him to tend the vegetables in the kitchen garden. He has made her a small mattock. Carefully she steps between the rows of lettuces and turnips, carving channels for Orrius to fill with water. He cuts bunches of violets, irises, narcissi and lilies. Opimia buries her nose in them as she carries the flowers into the house. Her mother arranges them carefully in large marble bowls on the tables in the atrium and the tablinum, to impress visitors. Lucius says this is most important. At the end of each week they fill a trug with sprigs of laurel. Opimia runs to find Naxus and together they go to the room off the atrium where the masks of the family ancestors hang. Naxus takes down the old laurel and drapes the fresh sprigs round the waxen faces. Opimia gazes up at them, trying to remember who is who. Outside again, she finds Orrius picking parsley, which he sprinkles into a bowl to decorate a mixture of eggs, olives and sour goats' cheese. Opimia is allowed a spoonful before it's set aside for the evening meal, together with the flat bread which she can smell baking in the little brick oven.

When the sun's rays start to warm the basin in the atrium Naevia takes her seat at table with her daughter and Phoebe. They eat some of the fresh bread, spread with a relish of garlic, cheese, oil and vinegar ground in a mortar by Orrius. They drink barley water. Orrius slips Opimia a chicken wing to chew and brings a plate of almonds and figs fresh from the market. Gaius is back from school. Alas, the frog did not survive the journey in the bag and the children bury it surreptitiously beneath the ash tree. Soon they're running up and down the paths with hoops, scattering the doves who are pecking at the breadcrumbs. Gaius splashes Opimia with water from the basin and threatens to make her eat frogspawn. To defend herself, she seizes the tamarisk broom used by the slaves to sweep the paths. Naevia emerges to say that there will no supper unless this stops immediately. The children know that this is no idle threat and settle down to play micatio. Simultaneously they both raise the fingers of one hand, changing each time the number of fingers raised, and shout out the combined total. The winner is the one who guesses the correct number of fingers raised. Gaius often cheats by raising his fingers fractionally later than his sister, but she likes him to win and does not mind. Orrius sometimes plays with her in the morning and she always wins then. Father has told them that you only really trust people if you can play micatio with them in the dark.

One morning, on the eighth day when Gaius has no school, Orrius is instructed by Lucius that on his way to the meat market by the river he is to deliver a message to the head tenant of one of Lucius's tenement blocks. Gaius is to be allowed to go with Orrius and, after much persuasion and a few tears, for she is not yet six years old, Naevia agrees that Opimia may go as well. Phoebe, of course, disapproves strongly. Apart from anything else, she won't eat cattle meat. Like many of her generation she considers that cows and oxen should only be slaughtered when sacrificing to the gods. Otherwise they should be preserved for work in the fields. She insists that Opimia wear a shawl over her head. 'The streets are dirty and you never know what might be thrown out of those upstairs windows. And mind you don't let go of Orrius's hand, even though he's a slave.'

They set off down the hill with Gaius walking ahead, pretending he knows where to go, and Opimia keeping a tight hold on Orrius. At first she is a little disconcerted. The other children are mostly dressed in tattered tunics and many have nothing on their feet. She sees them staring at her tiny leather boots and shawl. They fall silent from their play and step aside. Gaius walks confidently in his cloak, seemingly unaware of those around him. But Opimia looks about her. The street is very narrow so that the sky is only a

Chapter Three

thin strip hemmed in by grubby-looking tenements, some with wooden balconies which overhang and almost touch each other. The walls are covered with graffiti and signs. On the side of one house she sees a niche in which has been placed an erect phallus as tall as her and painted a gaudy pink. A man approaches and strokes it with his hand, muttering a few words as he does so. Curious, Opimia drags her feet but Orrius's grasp is insistent and she has to crane her neck to watch. Nobody else takes any notice.

At the next corner, where Gaius has to wait, she whispers to him, 'Did you see that pink thing on the wall and that man talking to it?'

'Oh, they're just good-luck symbols. You see them all over the place. Look, there's a small one outside that shop. People think they'll have a good day if they say a prayer to one in the morning.' Gaius assumes a knowledgeable air and strides ahead again.

Soon they turn another corner and come face to face with a large block of tenements. At the entrance a man is squatting on his haunches. He seems to know Orrius and raises the vine stick in his right hand by way of recognition. His left arm is tucked inside his tunic and Opimia wonders why he never removes it. When he stands he uses the stick to support himself. On his feet he wears a pair of very battered old boots held on by strips of leather wrapped round the soles.

'I have a message from Lucius Opimius for Salvius.' The man waves his stick in the general direction of the entrance to the block. There's no door, just a gloomy gap in the wall. To Opimia it looks like a cave leading to the underworld. Inside it feels chilly after the warmth of the sun. At first she can make out nothing in the darkness, but as her eyes grow accustomed she notices a stout wooden door and beside it, stone steps leading to the two upper storeys. On the floor in a far corner lies a heap of rags and close to the bottom of the steps stands an enormous cask, mounted on a block of tufa. The whole area is filled with a sickly sweet smell, so powerful that Opimia covers her nose with the end of her shawl. Orrius raps on the door and Opimia jumps when the bundle on the floor suddenly turns over and farts. The door is opened by a woman in a long tunic reaching to the ground, secured at the waist by a thin piece of cord. The tunic is colourless, but clean and neat. She has combed her hair and tied it in a bun from which protrudes a hairpin of polished bone. Behind her, in a basket made of rushes lined with straw and lying on the floor, Opimia can see a baby who seems to be awake but makes no sound. Light comes from a small window in front of which stands an unlit brazier. The middle of the room is taken up by a table with nothing on it but a couple of empty wooden platters and a jug. There is a bed in the corner covered in a coarse woollen blanket and next to it two heavy wooden chairs, pushed back against the wall to make more space.

The woman knows that Orrius has come from Opimius and that he is only a slave. She does not ask him in. Salvius, she says, is at work in his woodyard down by the docks, where he fashions timber for use in the barges plying between the port and Ostia. She will take a message. Orrius has dealt with the woman before. For all her defiant look, he knows that his master's instructions will be passed on. Salvius is lucky to be head tenant of the block, even if he has to let out the remaining rooms on the ground floor to make ends meet.

Opimia hears footsteps behind her and turns to see a man shuffling into the entrance. He carries several jars in a net and sets them down next to the stairway. Carefully he places one of his jars beneath the stopper at the foot of the large cask that she saw earlier. Dark yellow fluid gushes out. The man repeats the process until each of his jars is full and replaced in the net. Without looking up he hoists the net over his shoulder and puts it on a handcart waiting outside, before continuing on his way.

Chapter Three

Outside Gaius has been talking to the old man with the stick. As they walk on down the hill he tells Opimia that he is a veteran who served in the first line of a legion in Sicily. His left hand was crushed between the ship and the pier as they were tying up on their return to Italy after the war. He also suffered a wound to his leg.

'He showed me his hand. It looked like a piece of flat bread. You couldn't see where his fingers had been. It was all red and yellow, just like your face.' He runs on ahead again before Opimia can retaliate.

'Your father gave him the job of doorman,' Orrius tells her. 'He couldn't return to his farm at Tusculum. He wouldn't be able to handle a plough or animals. Now all he can do is try to keep unwanted people out of that block and the one next door. He can't really do that, but he fought alongside your father in Sicily. That's what he told me.' Opimia feels sorry for him and cannot help herself from trying to imagine the crushed hand. She squeezes Orrius's to make sure it feels right and he looks down with a smile.

The Forum is milling with people, many of them men dressed formally in togas like her father. Most are on foot, but some ride in litters or chairs carried by burly slaves who seem to think that they can push anybody about because of the importance of their passenger. Orrius points out the temple of Saturn where Lucius used to work. Then they pass a row of shops before turning right into Tuscan Street.

Gaius shouts out excitedly. 'That's the temple of Castor. I know because our master at school told us that it had a pool next to it.' Opimia gazes up at the columns of the temple towering above her. She remembers the story told by her mother. Hundreds of years ago the Romans had fought a great battle at Lake Regillus against the Latins. During the fighting two horsemen on chargers had appeared on the Roman side. They were the Dioscuri, the sons of Jupiter, called Castor and Pollux. Later, glistening with the sweat of battle, they had been seen in the Forum, watering their horses at the pool sacred to the nymph Juturna and thereby announcing the victory. Thereafter they vanished. Her little face breaks into a deep smile. It all seems so real now. She wants to run to the pool and dip her hands in it, but Orrius thinks that only the Vestal Virgins may touch the water.

As they walk on down Tuscan Street the noise from the cattle market grows louder and louder. Oxen, cows, sheep, goats, pigs and horses are herded into wooden enclosures with only narrow walkways between them. The mixture of braying, mooing, bleating and squealing is deafening. The sickly smell of blood fills the atmosphere and everywhere frightened animals toss their heads and crash against each other in their agitation. Butchers cleave great chunks of meat from carcasses to be hauled away on carts. The traders seem oblivious to the noise and smell, but Opimia is thankful again for her shawl, which she wraps tightly round her ears and nose. What are these men doing with their hands? It looks as though they're playing micatio, but something's not quite right. She tugs at Orrius's tunic and he bends to listen.

'Why do they wave their hands about like that? I can't see anyone shouting numbers.'

'It's their way of counting. You see that man selling those two goats. He's holding out his right hand with his thumb and all his fingers extended except the little one which he's tucked into his palm. That means one hundred and on his left hand he's tucked his thumb behind his palm, but all his fingers are extended. That means twenty. So the price of the goats is one hundred and twenty asses.'

Opimia nods but she's still a bit mystified. The sellers move their hands so quickly. It's impossible to keep up, even with Orrius explaining.

Things grow a little quieter as they reach the part where the poultry and the rabbits are displayed. Chickens hang upside down in pairs from hooks where they've been since

Chapter Three

early morning. The occasional weak flap of a wing indicates that life persists. After close examination to make sure they are not diseased, Orrius selects a pair which he puts into his bag. He'll wring their necks just before he plucks them. They walk on past row upon row of rabbits in wooden cages. Opimia wants to stop and tickle their twitching noses pressed up against the bars, but Gaius has disappeared again and Orrius is anxious to catch him up. They find him by a man with pots spread out on the stall in front of him. He's holding up the lid of one and Gaius is peering inside. By stretching up on tiptoe Opimia can just see over the rim, only to find herself looking straight into two tiny black eyes and a twitching nose. It's a fat mouse and gives her such a jump that she nearly falls over with surprise. When she is persuaded to look inside the pot again she can make out several mice moving about. The stallholder shows them the tiny spiral staircases moulded on the inside of the pots, up which the mice run for exercise. Gaius, of course, wants to take one home. Orrius shakes his head. These mice are expensive delicacies to be roasted in honey for the table and his mistress would not approve of such an outlay, unless they were entertaining very important guests. Opimia says that she would never eat one anyway and turns away her face.

On the way home Orrius buys each of them a roast chestnut and helps Opimia to open hers. She feels more confident now and no longer holds his hand as they make their way back towards the Forum. At the side of the street a rough platform has been set up. On it stands a motley group of men and women dressed only in dirty loincloths. When they get closer, Opimia can see that they are all shackled at the ankles and that one or two have the lower part of their legs whitened with chalk. Orrius says that this is to show that they are newly imported. One woman has a child about Opimia's own age standing next to her. She too is chained but completely naked. Most have wooden plaques hung from their necks with short descriptions: 'Strong and can read and write a bit', or 'Caught stealing a chicken/good cook'. They all stand motionless with downcast eyes and seem more like statues than real people.

A man, Caepio, scrambles up onto the platform and approaches one of the women, really a girl. He lifts up the plaque and feels her breasts before fondling her buttocks. The girl betrays no sign that she is even aware of his presence. He pushes up her chin and sticks his hand inside her mouth. Finally he turns her round and satisfies himself that there are no marks or scars on her back. Meanwhile the slave dealer, Petrinus, is talking all the time, pointing out the girl's good features: fresh from Greece, slim and comely with a fine, unmottled skin. The customer has heard it all before. He jumps down and continues his appraisal from below. The question is whether his master will like her. She's young, perhaps sixteen years old, her teeth are firm and her breath doesn't smell too bad. Not like the last one whose teeth were all rotten, as he found out too late when he presented her to his master and received a sound beating for his pains. The dealer is standing next to the girl, ignoring the customer who has shown interest and addressing the little knot of people who have gathered in front of his stand. He strokes her hair and demonstrates the firmness of her breasts. He wants them on his side when it comes to the bargaining.

'Not often you get goods of this quality,' he cries. 'I'd have her meself if I could afford it.'

'I bet you've had her already,' shouts one of the onlookers. Petrinus glares, probably because it's true. He's keeping his eye on Caepio, who has not wandered off but is standing at the back. He knows that Caepio works for Marcus Cethegus, the senator, who is partial to Greek girls and has the purse to pay well for them.

'Straight off a boat from Corinth when I bought her.' Petrinus is pushing his luck a bit. The girl does speak Greek

Chapter Three

and he did buy her near the Marine gate at Pompeii from a sea captain who had just docked. 'Must be worth two thousand asses of anybody's money.' One or two bystanders catch their breath. It's a high price for an untrained slave. A man, probably in business with Petrinus, tells everybody that the girl's good value at that. He's seen similar ones go for much more on the last trading day in the Forum. Caepio snorts with laughter and turns as if to leave.

Petrinus shouts after him, 'I'll take fifteen hundred and no warranties as to quality or provenance.' Caepio shakes his head and continues walking. 'Twelve hundred and fifty and you've stolen her.' Caepio pauses, then half turns.

'I've got a budget of one thousand, take it or leave it.'

'You'll ruin an honest man, Caepio.' This is not entirely true as Petrinus got the girl for five hundred. The sea captain needed to raise money quickly when a lighter carrying part of his cargo into the port capsized. Petrinus takes a key from the bunch hanging on his belt and unlocks the girl's shackles. She almost stumbles as he pushes her towards the steps leading down from the platform. Her eyes remain firmly fixed to the ground as Caepio steps forward to take possession. With a leather thong he ties her wrists behind her back while he holds the other end like a leash. None of the slaves still on the platform looks up, but the naked child shuffles closer to her mother. Who knows? She may be next.

Orrius knows the Greek girl may be lucky. Better to live in the comfortable house of a senator than doing backbreaking work on a farm under the whip of a gang foreman. That way lies painful and distorted bones from carrying loads that are too heavy, sleeping on dank straw and eating rotting food. He is grateful that he lives in a household where the slaves are treated almost as members of the family.

They are back in the Forum and there seems to be a rumpus going on at one of the shops that line the side opposite the Comitium. A small crowd has gathered to harangue the shopkeeper who, apparently, has been giving short measures on sales of wine and oil. The aedile arrives, resplendent in his shining white toga. As he passes, Opimia catches the hint of sulphur and ammonia, familiar in her father's room at home when he dons a toga fresh from the fullers. His assistants push the angry customers aside to make way for the magisrate, who towers over the cringing shopkeeper. He blabbers something about his jugs being from the country where they don't bother with these things. The aedile is unimpressed and orders his men to test the jugs against their standard measuring ones. Sure enough, the shopkeeper's jugs are short by about a fifth and the shout goes up that he's been diddling for weeks at another site behind the sheep market. The aedile knows how to make himself popular. Within minutes the disgruntled customers are helping themselves to the contents of the amphorae stacked behind the counter, filling their own containers with free wine and oil. Meanwhile the shopkeeper has to watch his jugs being smashed and the day's takings seized.

By the time they've climbed the hill and reached home again Opimia is quite tired. It has been a long morning full of new experiences. She sits down on her favourite stone bench in the peristyle. For once she does not miss Gaius, who now goes every afternoon with his father to exercise on the Field of Mars. Like his father before him, Lucius is teaching his son to ride and to handle the javelin and the sword. With half-closed eyes Opimia watches Naxus on the roof, scraping up the droppings of the doves, which Orrius wants for the vegetable patch. Soon the warmth of the sun does its work and she is fast asleep.

Lucius has become a very busy man. His tunic now bears the purple stripe to show he is a senator. On business days he rises at first light and rarely returns before the end of

Chapter Three

the eleventh hour. Opimia treasures her early-morning chat with him, for otherwise she sees little of her father. When summer comes, however, Naevia likes to escape from the heat and smells of the city. She and Opimia pile into the family gig and rattle out through the Esquiline Gate towards the hills at Tibur. Phoebe follows at a more leisurely pace in a cart driven by Naxus with clothing and a few other requisites for the stay. The villa sits at the head of a valley in the foothills, on a gentle slope facing westwards. It is a modest building with simple accommodation and sparse furnishing. To one side lies an old olive grove where the silver-grey leaves and the twisted trunks shimmer in the summer heat. A little way above rises a belt of small oak trees which emerge from tangled undergrowth inhabited by rabbits, deer and wild pigs. Towards the top of the hills the trees give way to short grass and craggy outcrops of rock over which kites circle and hawks hover, their wings etched sharply against sky the colour of pale lead.

Opimia's excitement grows as her mother shakes up the reins and they begin to climb the bumpy white track to the villa. She runs into her room and disturbs a tiny lizard, which scuttles across the ceiling. The shutters on the little opening in the wall are closed to keep out the worst of the heat. She remembers the mornings, when the sun rises over the hills and a beam of intense light shines through the crack between the shutters, so that a long narrow shaft like a brilliant wand appears on the wall next to her bed.

On some mornings, soon after dawn when wisps of pale mist still cling to the sides of the hills and the dew sparkles in the damp grass, Naevia sends Opimia with a small bucket, not too heavy for her to carry, down the slope to a tiny farm on the floor of the valley. There the farmer draws milk from one of his two cows and fills Opimia's bucket. She sets off back up the slope but, as often as not, she pauses to dip her finger in the warm liquid. Sometimes she cannot resist the temptation to lift the bucket to her lips.

With her free hand she tries to wipe her face clean, but her mother always knows and gently chides her.

In the afternoons they go for walks, gathering mushrooms that spring up in the warm weather after rain. Opimia likes to make for a stream which trickles down over the rocks of a gulley carved between the trees. In the winter it would be a raging torrent, but now the flow is slow and gentle. Opimia loves to dangle her feet in the cool water and scoop up handfuls to her mouth. It tastes so much better than the stale water in the atrium at home. Then Naevia opens the basket which Phoebe has prepared. Inside they usually find wheat cakes flavoured with honey, and perhaps almonds or figs picked from two trees behind the house. Afterwards Opimia runs into the woods to find a couple of ivy tendrils into which they plait flowers and grasses to make garlands. Naevia helps Opimia to finish hers before placing it in her hair. She kneels down to allow Opimia to put the larger one on her own head. Laughing, they help each other to their feet, clasp hands and perform a little jig on the soft moss.

On the way back down to the villa they gather kindling for the fire. Opimia tries hard to carry as much as her mother. On one occasion she trips and falls, crushing her garland. Naevia hands over her own which eventually slips down round the child's neck. It reminds Naevia of an animal decorated for sacrifice being led to the altar. Occasionally they spot the farmer walking in front of his pigs, blowing his horn to make them follow him down from the trees where they feed on acorns during the day.

In front of the villa is a small area of flat ground, no more than beaten earth, which becomes hard and cracked during the summer. Here Opimia likes to sit with her straw dolls on a bench set against the warm stone walls of the house. Over to the west, as far as the eye can see, the land stretches away in a plain leading towards Rome. The departing sun leaves a sky of the palest magenta shot with

Chapter Three

shards of brilliant orange, while the shadows creep like thieves up the valley slopes to where she sits, still bathed in the last dusty rays. One by one a million cicadas fall silent. The thrushes and the woodlarks in the trees cease their chatter, the evening breeze dies and the white ox belonging to the farmer below fades to an indistinct grey, then disappears. The rabbits have long since scuttled back into the woodland, having spent the day grazing or basking on the grassy hillside.

Gazing upwards Opimia tries to count the stars beginning to appear in a sea of tarnished bronze mottled with a few white sails. A motionless silence heralds the approach of night. The little girl is startled from her reverie by Naxus, who comes round the corner. He's been out trapping partridges and has caught six. A few minutes later she detects the sweet smell of wood smoke flavoured with sprigs of rosemary which he has thrown onto the fire.

One evening, when the shadows have almost reached the terrace, Opimia glimpses the dark shape of an animal loping across the slope below. At first she thinks it is a dog. It stops and looks round, crouching low to the ground. Three more grey shapes appear, bumbling along in a confusion of legs and tails, barely discernible in the fast-fading light. Instinctively, for she has never seen one before, Opimia realises that it is a she-wolf with her cubs. She calls out to her mother to come and look, but it's too late; the wolf has led her litter into the trees.

Naevia brings an oil lamp and sits down beside the little girl. The air is so still that the tiny flame does not even flicker. She begins to recount the ancient story of the birth of Rome. Opimia listens attentively to her mother explaining how Rhea Silvia, the first Vestal, was forced to sleep with the god Mars and then gave birth to twin boys. This made her uncle, Amulius, frightened that the boys might one day usurp his throne at Alba Longa, a city close to where Rome now stands. He was a cruel man who ordered Rhea Silvia to be imprisoned and had the two boys placed in a basket and thrown into the river. But the boys did not drown as Amulius intended. Instead the waters of the Tiber saved them and washed the basket aground under the sacred fig tree which still stands in the Forum. It was here that the she-wolf found the boys and suckled them until a shepherd called Faustulus discovered them. He took the twins home to his wife who nursed them.

In time the boys, whose names were Romulus and Remus, grew strong enough to look after themselves. They were ambitious young men and they decided to found their own city away from Alba Longa which had become too crowded. Unfortunately, however, both of them had inherited the quarrelsome nature of their ancestors and though they could agree on the site of the new city, they could not agree on its name. Each insisted on calling it after himself. They therefore consulted the gods who declared that the issue should be resolved by observing the flight of birds. And so it came about that Romulus went to stand on the Palatine Hill where he saw twelve vultures fly overhead. His brother climbed onto the Aventine Hill and claimed that he saw six vultures before Romulus had seen his birds. Each claimed victory; Remus because he saw his birds first and Romulus because he had seen twice as many. A great quarrel ensued and the young men fought to the death. Remus was killed and Romulus named the new city after himself.

By the time that Naevia has finished telling the story it has grown dark and the air has lost some of its warmth. She opens her shawl and wraps it round Opimia as well. For a few minutes they sit on in the tiny oasis of light provided by the oil lamp at their feet. Moths begin to flutter round it.

'It's very rare to see a she-wolf with her cubs, isn't it?'

'Oh, yes. I once saw a wolf when I was about your age on the farm at Nola, but it was by itself. Wolves had to be kept away from the farm animals. I've never seen one since.'

Chapter Three

Naevia pauses and then puts her arm round the little girl, drawing the shawl closer. 'What you saw tonight was very special. Perhaps it was an omen.'

'What's an omen?'

'An omen is a sign given to mortals by the gods. I once heard of a cow that gave birth to a calf with two heads. That was a kind of omen to the farmer.'

'How horrible!'

'Not all omens are like that. Some omens are good, when the gods are pleased with us. That's why we take the auspices on important occasions, to make sure the gods approve. Sometimes if they're really cross, they shake whole towns or cities and knock the buildings down.'

'Do you think my omen is a good one? I hope I haven't done anything to displease the gods.'

'I'm sure it is. I think it is a sign that you're important to them.' Naevia turns and kisses the little girl on the head before picking up the lamp and leading her indoors. Soon Phoebe comes fussing in and settles Opimia for bed. First she has to hear all about the she-wolf and her cubs and that it is an omen. Phoebe tells her not to mind about that and blows out the candle. In the pitch dark Opimia can see nothing, but in her mind's eye she watches the wolf over and over again. She longs to see it once more and makes up her mind to wait every evening at sunset.

Though the days are still hot, the evenings are turning cooler. Opimia borrows her mother's shawl as she sits on the bench, hoping to catch another glimpse of the wolf and her cubs. The scent of lilies is strong in the air, almost intoxicating to her sharp senses, alert to any sound or movement. Far below the farmer has just lit his fire and the smoke drifts across the valley, hanging in the trees. Her imagination wanders over the landscape. She's dancing to the music of her own pipes up by the stream, wild rosebuds in her hair. Now she's lying in the grass under the olive trees, looking through half-closed eyes at the tracery of leaves painted on the sky. Dryads, the wispy spirits of the woods, clothed in puffs of diaphanous white, pause in their crazy dances through the contorted boughs to smile down at her with their cunning, twisted faces. She opens her mouth to speak but they evaporate in the softly undulating air. She's standing at the top of the hill, opening her arms to the wind and almost toppling over when she tries to lean against it. The she-wolf does not come but she does not mind.

In the morning they make ready to return to the city. Opimia always feels sad to leave the villa but she helps her mother and Phoebe to pack up and load the cart. As the gig trundles down the track she turns her head for a last view of the valley. The farmer looks up from repairing his plough and waves goodbye.

Back in the house in Rome she carries the last garlands that she and her mother made to the family hearth and places them in the niche where the lares[35] keep their vigil.

---

35. Household gods.

Chapter Four

227 BC

It is the Ides of May, sacred to Jupiter, Best and Greatest. Opimia is a few months into her ninth year. In Rome it is hot, but above all it is dry. There has been no rain for weeks and the corn is not growing in the fields. Everywhere the soil is parched. In the Field of Mars you cannot stick a spear into the ground. The Tiber runs only sluggishly, with boats and barges aground on the muddy banks. Fish lie flat and white on the surface. The current is too slow to carry away the city's effluent and the Cloaca Maxima[36] is blocked with rubbish and human excrement. Slaves have been sent in through the mouth in the riverbank to clear it. Even the Aqua Appia,[37] which brings water into the city from outside the walls, to flow underground to a basin in the cattle market, has a queue of slaves and citzens waiting patiently with their buckets. A miasma hangs in the valleys and round the hills on which the city stands. The air is putrid and the stink of excrement is everywhere. In the streets people cover their faces with a cloth to avoid the worst of the smell. Fortunately last year's vintage was plentiful; there is no shortage of wine to drink, but very little water to dilute

---

36. The main drain which ran through the city and discharged into the Tiber near the Sublician Bridge.
37. The city's first aqueduct, built by Appius Claudius in 312 BC.

it. Men unused to the strength of their tipple stagger in the street or lie semi-comatose in any shady spot they can find.

The Senate meets to discuss this unsatisfactory situation. They consult with the Chief Priest who consults with his fellow members of the College of Pontiffs. After due deliberation they advise that the old ceremony of *aquaelicium* must be revived. This rite, they say, is the only solution to a long drought, which is the consequence of having displeased Jupiter, the god of the sky. In a small temple dedicated to Mars down by the Capena Gate[38] there is a stone, ignored for many years. It is the rain stone and it must be brought to the temple of Jupiter on the Capitol.

With her father and brother, Opimia stands beside the Sacred Way.[39] They are not alone. A throng of citizens lines the way, many of them clutching jugs or water skins, which occasionally they hold up to the sky and then turn upside down to show that they are empty. Somewhere in the distance they can hear a rumbling and soon, over the rise at the southern end of the Palatine Hill, a cart appears hauled by four slaves bent almost double as they heave on the ropes. The stone rests in the cart, which continually creaks and jolts over the basalt slabs. Immediately behind walk the three senior priests of Jupiter, Mars and Quirinus followed by the minor priests assigned to other gods. They wear woollen cloaks clasped at the throat and leather caps topped by a spike of olive wood.

Outside the house of the Vestal Virgins, beneath the slope of the Palatine, the little procession comes to a halt and for a few moments nothing happens. Eventually the door of the house is opened by an unseen hand and Claudia, the Senior Vestal, appears. She pauses to survey the scene, as if to approve it, before advancing with slow,

---

38. A gate in the wall on the south side of the city leading to the Appian Way.
39. The Via Sacra (the Sacred Way) was the most important street in Rome and ran through the Forum.

Chapter Four

steady paces. She is tall for a woman, a member of the patrician Claudian family, who are well known for their haughtiness. Her body is thin and angular, like her face over which the skin seems tightly stretched, producing a permanently severe expression. Her forehead is high with a thin nose and a jutting chin beneath. She certainly has none of the good looks for which many of her family are famous. It would be unfair to describe Claudia's bearing as arrogant, yet there is no mistaking the air of authority she exudes. The crowd lining the way parts to let her through. She gives no sign that she has even noticed them. A moment later the five other priestesses follow her. All are dressed in similar fashion. Their long gowns almost reach the ground and their heads are bound with chaplets of red and white bands which hang down over their shoulders. The headdresses are topped with the white cloth to be worn for sacrifice. The crowd watches respectfully as the priestesses take their place at the head of the procession and the priests incline their heads in recognition. Opimia is curious. She has never seen a Vestal before, but knows that they play a very important part in the city's life. One catches her eye. She looks young, more of a girl than a woman. She came out of the Vestals' house last and is walking by herself, behind the others who are in a line of four following the Senior Vestal. The girl looks a little frail and exposed. She seems to be carrying something which Opimia cannot identify. She feels rather sorry for her.

When all are in position Claudia raises her hand to signal that she is ready. The slaves bend once more to their work and the cart rumbles ponderously forward, but only for a few yards. Outside the Regia, old King Numa's palace, it grinds to a halt again. This ancient building is now the office of the Pontifex Maximus, who emerges accompanied by his attendants to take his place in front of the Vestals. He carries the traditional symbols of his office, an iron knife and a libation saucer. The Pontifex is none other than

Caudinus, who presided when Lucius was elected to the quaestorship eight years ago. The chestnut hair is tinged with iron now and there is the hint of a stoop in his gait. A few wrinkles line the once smooth face. Still, he remains slim and fit, walking everywhere and disdaining the use of a chair or a litter.

Lucius, in the company of other senators and knights, follows the procession along the Sacred Way into the Forum. Everybody is moving slowly and Opimia has no difficulty in keeping up. She is a little awestruck by the appearance of the priests. Their silent faces look neither left nor right, but are fixed on the stone in the cart. She feels a nudge in her ribs from Gaius who is pointing at something. At first she cannot see for the crowd, but then she spots it, a great white ox. She has never seen such a large animal. His flanks glisten in the sunlight for he has been scrubbed clean and his coat combed to a beautiful sheen. Round his horns coloured fillets have been bound and a garland of flowers hangs from his neck. A man leads him by a halter and another gently wafts a palm frond over his broad back so that flies do not disturb his calm demeanour. It is important that this noble animal, selected for his fine proportions, should come quietly and willingly to the altar. Only this will satisfy the gods. The soft brown eyes turn occasionally to the crowd and the great head nods as if to say, 'Yes, you were right to choose me.' Behind him a slave walks with a bucket and sponge to wash down his rear quarters if he should defecate on the way, but he shows no sign of nerves. Opimia breaks away and walks beside him for a short distance before her father calls her back.

In the Forum the procession swings left into Team Street. At the base of the steps leading up the Capitoline Hill to the temple of Jupiter the two consuls are waiting. The slaves must unload the rain stone from the cart and carry it on the final stage of its journey. Meanwhile the consuls have mounted the steps and turn to face the crowd.

Chapter Four

To Opimia they seem a long way up, like statuettes silhouetted against the sky. She thinks she can see a wisp of smoke floating up behind them. Then everybody is moving again. Eight slaves have hoisted the stone onto a wooden frame and are moving steadily towards the top of the stairway. Each step presents a barrier to Opimia's short legs, but she is determined and refuses the helping hand proffered by her father. At length they reach the top where there is a little jostling as people seek a good view of the proceedings. Gaius and Opimia squirm their way to the front where a few other children are also standing. Most of them have never mounted the Capitol before and they look about them wide-eyed. In front of the temple is a flat paved area around which the people are ranged. A large stone altar stands at the foot of a flight of steps leading to the portico of the temple itself. The temple's walls are of tufa supporting a pitched roof of tiles. Opimia gazes up at the pediment surmounted by a statue of Jupiter, who rides in a chariot drawn by four prancing horses. In his right hand the god is carrying a spear and in his left a wreath of oak leaves. The pillars of the portico are painted bright red and behind them Opimia glimpses the double doors of bronze leading to the triple cella[40] inside, one each for the shrines of Jupiter, Juno and Minerva.

The rain stone has been set down by the slaves before the altar. Beside it a brazier of charcoal smoulders in the sunshine. The men leading the ox come forward to take up a position on the other side of the altar. A third man appears whom Opimia has not seen before and she cannot restrain a slight shudder. For a moment she wants to turn round and wriggle her way back through the throng of people to where she cannot see. Yet something stops her. She has asked to come with Gaius who will mock her if she backs away now. This new man is swarthy and naked to the

---

40. The inner chamber of a temple housing the cult image of a god.

waist. Resting on his shoulder as if it were a mere toy is the biggest axe that Opimia has ever seen. Occasionally, when he moves, the sharpened blade catches the sunlight. He wears a loose skirt with a purple hem and a thick belt into which a large knife has been stuffed. Nobody takes any notice of him, but Opimia cannot take her eyes away. The ox shakes his head, causing the ribbons on his horns to flutter as the boy gently wafts the palm frond. Opimia knows that the sacrifice to the gods is necessary. Her father and everyone else say so, otherwise the rain will not come. She feels a strong urge to ask Jupiter whether some lesser animal would not be adequate, anything rather than this sturdy creature standing so bravely in the sun. She fights to suppress the tears that well up inside her. Gaius and the others must not see that she is upset.

Now the consuls have mounted the steps of the temple and the murmuring of the people increases in anticipation. To one side of the altar the priests are standing, while on the other the Vestals are seated on folding stools of wood and leather. Nearest to the altar sits Claudia, bolt upright and seemingly oblivious of those around her. A herald emerges from the shadows of the portico to proclaim silence. From the group of priests Caudinus steps forward and stands by the brazier. Opimia notices that he has gathered up part of his gown and draped it over his head in the form of a hood. He holds out his hands and she wonders if he is about to pray to Jupiter, but instead two acolytes appear dressed in short white tunics. One carries a box and the other a small silver flagon and a goblet. From the box the Pontifex takes a handful of incense and tosses it onto the brazier where it flares up, emitting a small cloud of yellow smoke which hangs like a shroud in the still air. He adds a few drops of wine from the flagon before handing it back to the boy. Now his arms are raised again in supplication to the god. He intones a long prayer repenting on behalf of the citizens their fault or neglect in the respect

Chapter Four

due to Jupiter, Best and Greatest. He asks the god to accept the people's sacrifice as an atonement for their wrongs, which have upset the equilibrium between the Romans and the gods. Finally he pleads for rain to save the city from further suffering. A third attendant steps forward with a jug and the Pontifex walks over to the rain stone to pour the symbolic water on it. Opimia looks up to the sky expecting at any moment to feel drops on her face, but there are no clouds, only unending blue. Privately she hopes that it will not rain until they are home.

Looking down again she is surprised to see the young Vestal she had noticed earlier rise from her stool. She is carrying a small leather pouch. The girl walks forward a few paces until she is opposite Claudia, then turns to face her. Claudia nods, almost peremptorily, and the girl, with trembling hands, so it seems to Opimia, opens the pouch and offers the contents to Claudia. The latter rises stiffly from her stool and takes the purificatory cake cupped in both hands. Together she and the Pontifex approach the ox, who stands quite still; only his tail swishes gently to and fro. First the Pontifex pours a little wine on the great white head and then Claudia follows with the cake which she crumbles along his back. Opimia gives a little gasp; the priest has the iron knife in his hand and with an arcing movement of his arm he draws it across the ox's throat. She expects to see a stream of blood, but there is nothing, for it is merely a symbolic gesture. Opimia cannot help feeling a surge of relief. Perhaps they will not kill the ox after all and she turns to say something to Gaius. At that moment the axe of the slaughterman comes crashing down with practised accuracy on the unsuspecting neck. For an instant the ox seems to stand unmoved before his flanks heave and collapse, his hooves thrashing the empty air in a flurry of white and spurting red. The slaughterman is quick and skilful with his knife. In no time he and his assistants have extracted the sacred parts: the liver, heart, gall and lungs. Each piece is first laid on the altar for inspection by the haruspex to ensure there is no abnormality, for nothing that is not perfect must be offered to the gods. The Pontifex moves forward again to supervise the transfer of these gory pieces to the brazier where at first they sizzle and then burn in the formal sacrifice to Jupiter. Meanwhile the priests advance one by one to pour water on the rain stone while the people murmur their own final supplication to the god. Now surely it will rain.

As they walk home Opimia searches the sky again for signs of the downpour which must come soon. On the southern horizon a few white puffy clouds linger in a windless heaven, otherwise all is as before. She is puzzled. Surely the great god Jupiter will not ignore such a sacrifice.

'Why isn't it raining, Father? I wish they hadn't killed the ox if it's not going to work.'

'It will work, you'll see. Jupiter will keep his part of the bargain. Provided we citizens of Rome observe the proper rituals and make due sacrifice to the gods they will aways rescue us in the end.'

But it does not rain that day and for seven more days and nights the sky remains obstinately clear. Opimia gives up putting a bowl outside her door when she goes to bed, hoping that it will be full in the morning. Then on the eighth day something wakes her. For some time she listens, wondering what it can be. Suddenly she realises and runs outside. Water is pouring into the pool in the atrium. She turns her face and hands upwards, delighting in the sensation of the sweet drops spattering her skin. She opens her mouth wide and sticks out her tongue. After a few moments of this she gathers some water in a bowl and runs happily to her father's room to present it to him.

Rome has acquired two new provinces, Sicily and Sardinia with Corsica, following their conquest in the war against the Carthaginians. She needs governors for this expansion

Chapter Four

of her territories and so two more praetorships have been created. Encouraged again by his friends, Lucius has decided to stand for one of the offices and is holding a series of dinners to canvass support in the run-up to the elections. Tonight is particularly important, for no fewer than three ex-consuls are to attend.

Naevia is busy with her servants preparing the formal dining room. They decorate the walls with swags of deep-red roses to offset the ochre-coloured stucco. Bowls filled with irises, lilies, violets and narcissi stand on tables of marble with curved legs of bronze. Fresh ivy, acanthus, laurel and oleander are draped round the columns lining the room. The scent is a little overpowering, but Naevia knows that it will help to cover up the smell from the oil lamps. Opimia helps her mother to carry the sprigs of evergreen and the long trails of ivy. Occasionally she is allowed to snip with the heavy iron scissors and hand up cuttings to the slave girl perched on the ladder, while Naevia directs. Other slaves hurry to and fro, sweeping and polishing the mosaic floor with fine sand, arranging amphorae of wine and bringing plates and bowls. The bolsters and coverlets for the couches are brought out of store to be brushed and checked, even though this was done when they were put away on the last occasion.

Naevia has hired two assistant cooks for the evening. Orrius, surrounded by baking utensils, pans, spits and pestles, assigns their various tasks. Meanwhile he is preparing a large platter of peahens' eggs, goose liver, truffles and mushrooms garnished with slices of lamprey, eel, crab, lizard fish and sardines. This will be followed by millet cakes sweetened with honey. His assistants are stuffing pies with wild pig, hare, venison and wood pigeon from the Laurentine Forest outside the city. In wooden bowls they pile black and green olives, juicy figs from the garden and apples and pears from the farm at Nola. Well out of sight behind the peristyle Naxus slits the throat of a goat, eviscerates it and begins to roast it on a spit. A slave boy gathers up the innards in a bucket, then runs to throw them into the street where dogs will make short work of them. Nearby, Creto slices lettuces, radishes, turnips, lentils, pumpkins and beans.

Amid all this bustle Lucius announces to his children that they are to demonstrate their speaking and singing skills to his guests. Gaius must recite a poem. It is not quite so bad as it seems, for he already knows it pretty well and has performed it in front of his fellow pupils at school. As the sun touches the apex of the roof around the peristyle Gaius can be seen pacing up and down the gravel paths between the box, pausing occasionally to consult the wax tablets on which the words are scratched. Sometimes he raises his arm in a declamatory gesture, imagining himself to be his father addressing the Senate. Opimia has retreated to her room where there is less noise, to practise a song that she learnt from her mother a year ago. Phoebe stands in for Naevia on the lyre. The little girl works hard. She wants to be perfect for her father.

Meanwhile Lucius wears a worried frown. He has a problem. Who is to occupy the couch of honour with him? He does not wish to offend any of his important guests; indeed he cannot afford to if his progress up the political ladder is to continue. Should it be Metellus, a member of one of Rome's most distinguished families and his old commander at Panormus? He has been consul twice and Pontifex Maximus when he was blinded, rescuing sacred artefacts from the temple of Vesta during a fire several years ago. But then there is Fabius, consul only last year and once before that. He has held the censorship as well. And what about Caudinus, the present Pontifex and the man who presided at Lucius's election for the quaestorship? He ponders hard and long. Finally he selects Metellus. After all he is the oldest and being blind, he deserves special consideration.

Chapter Four

The light is beginning to fade. Soon the slave girl will be making her way around all the lamps with a taper. The doves have ceased their cooing and the shadows are starting their evening journey across the peristyle. The paths and the paving are swept for the final time. Orrius and his temporary assistants are busy cooking. Pale blue smoke curls up over the roof tiles from the charcoal braziers and a faint aroma of roasting meat pervades the air. Naxus is still turning his spit. Naevia checks the couches once again and counts the knives, spoons and toothpicks. She straightens coverlets and plumps cushions which are already straight and plumped. The wine-mixing bowls are in position on a side table, but has Creto remembered the resin? Anxiously she scans the roses in case any have wilted. She stretches up to adjust a spray of acanthus. A boy hurries in carrying a large bowl of saffron mixed with sawdust, for sprinkling on the mosaic between courses. Naevia chides him for not remembering it earlier. She takes a last look round before instructing the slave girl to stand at the entrance to the room and let nobody else in until the guests start to arrive.

The comings and goings of the day subside. Everything that can be done has been done and the house lies silent and expectant. At any moment the first guests will appear. Opimia is curious and hides behind a pillar in the atrium. Soon she hears the clatter of wheels outside in the street and a few moments later Metellus is led in by his body slave who guides him to a seat in the atrium. Creto comes forward with a bowl of water and a sponge. The old general says nothing but raises one foot for Creto to remove the sandal. Carefully Creto washes that foot, then the other. He does not replace the sandals, which he will clean with those of the other guests while they dine. Lucius knows Metellus has arrived but does not enter the atrium until the foot washing is complete. That would be undignified. Now he greets his guest and helps him from his cloak. Metellus mutters gruff thanks and extends his arm for Lucius to conduct him to the dining room. Opimia slips away to her room where Phoebe is waiting to help her dress. She puts on a long pale-green tunic reaching to her ankles, secured at the waist by a slim cord dyed expensively in purple. Phoebe arranges a chaplet of young oak leaves and jasmine in her hair, which she combs out to hang loosely in a wave of yellow gold.

In the dining room the men recline on three couches arranged in a U round a square table of black marble. Bolsters separate each guest from his neighbour. On the central couch, in the place of honour next to his host, Metellus leans on an elbow and picks at a selection of fish meat. He's nearly bald. His face is disfigured by a livid patch of skin, which runs from his cheek down one side of his neck and onto his left shoulder where he was burnt in the fire. His eyes are cloudy but they move as he follows the conversation round the room. From time to time he passes a hand across his face as if he were trying to wipe the blindness away. He has grown a little stout in his old age and occupies more than his proper share of the couch. Lucius takes good care to give him plenty of space. At his feet, behind the couch, his body slave stands ready with his personal napkin, which Metellus summons frequently with a snap of the fingers.

Quintus Fabius has not reached fifty and yet to look at him you might think he was older than Metellus. The face is heavily lined and the impression of age is reinforced by the wart on his upper lip for which he has acquired the nickname 'Verrucosus'[41]. On his plate he has only a few slices of lizard fish spiced with garum.[42] These he cuts up into small portions but then lays aside his knife and ignores the food. They say that he only eats the bare minimum to maintain his strength and the bones in his hands show

---

41. 'Warty'.
42. A sauce made from fermented fish and salt, much favoured by the Romans.

Chapter Four

through like the webbed feet of a large bird. Yet he is a man of great stamina, with muscular legs and arms. But the most striking thing about Fabius is the gravity of his manner. Not many people have seen him laugh. The best you get is the flicker of a smile. His speech is slow, almost laborious; so much so that when he was young his classmates used to mimic him, like a chorus, when he had to declaim in front of them.

This slowness of speech, however, is deceiving. Quintus Fabius is no fool. He never says anything without first having thought out his argument. Woe betide anybody who contradicts him. Fabius will regard the other with disfavour for a few moments, then slowly and with painstaking thoroughness dismantle his reasoning. His watchword is caution. He listens while others speak, but when he rises in the Senate he is heard in respectful silence. He takes occasional sips from his goblet in which the wine is so diluted with water that you can hardly taste it. Creto bends before each guest and offers the silver platter on which to place his offering to the gods. With a small pointed spoon Fabius pushes onto it all but one piece of his fish. He is a pious man, a stickler for observing the correct rituals when sacrificing, a patrician of the old school with a strong sense of duty. Lucius often thinks that his father would have got on well with him.

On the couch opposite, Gaius Laelius and Quintus Mucius present a lighter mood. They are discussing a wild boar hunt the previous day in the hills near Praeneste. Apparently there has been an incident involving Gaius's son, also called Gaius,[43] and young Publius Scipio. Without telling anybody the two lads wandered off into a thicket where Publius was gored by a pig that trapped him with its tusks against a tree. Fortunately Gaius senior heard the

---

43. This is Gaius Laelius the younger, a lifelong friend of the great Publius Cornelius Scipio Africanus who defeated Hannibal at Zama in 202 BC, when Laelius commanded the Italian cavalry.

boys' cries and arrived in time to despatch the boar before any serious injury was done. Both lads have been soundly beaten for their ill-disciplined behaviour and forbidden to go to the Field of Mars until the feast of the Ambarvalia.[44] Laelius pretended to be furious with his son, but secretly is pleased that the boys showed a bit of initiative and did not simply follow the others.

Next to them Caudinus, the third consul present, is devoting all his attention to a plate of asparagus and walnuts. The Pontifex rose at first light and went by carriage to the Alban Mount. On the summit he sacrificed to Jupiter, to whom the hill is sacred. On the slopes below, hundreds of slaves were hacking at the flanks of the old volcano, hewing out slabs of hardened tufa which will be used to line the streets of the city. The climb has given him an appetite.

The slaves are going round with finger bowls while the next course is carried in. Lucius, anxious not to let the conversation flag, turns to his old commander, Metellus.

'So how do you see the situation in Spain, sir?'

'I don't like it at all, young man.' To Metellus, Lucius is still the junior cavalry captain of twenty-odd years ago. 'That Hamilcar Barca fella is dangerous. I'm sure he's intent on revenge, you know.'

Fabius looks up from his empty plate and says quietly, 'I don't think he's much of a threat now. He died a couple of years ago, if you remember.'

'Yes, of course!' harumphs Metellus, brushing his hand across his eyes. 'But you know who I mean. That other fella with a similar name, I can never remember it.'

'I think you're referring to Hasdrubal, his son-in-law.'

'That's right, equally dangerous man.' Metellus holds out his goblet to be refilled and Lucius hastily beckons up

---

44. A religious ceremony involving the purification of the fields for the welfare of the crops. It normally took place towards the end of May, depending on the state of the crops.

Chapter Four

Creto. 'If you ask me, we ought to attack in Spain before those Punic buggers get too powerful again.'

'I don't think Hasdrubal is as aggressive as his father-in-law,' opines Caudinus, chewing thoughtfully on a nut.

'All those Barcids are aggressive. It's in their blood,' mutters Metellus.

'That may be, but the Saguntines[45] say that where Hamilcar proceeded by conquest Hasdrubal works through negotiation and bribery. He's formed a network of alliances with the tribes in the south.' Caudinus is about to continue but Metellus interrupt him testily.

'Exactly! Our influence there is nil. You mark my words, we shall pay for our complacency one day.' Caudinus again makes as if to speak but sees Fabius raise his hand and falls silent.

'There may be something in what you say, Metellus, but I don't believe the Carthaginians are ready to attack us yet. Besides, we have our hands full dealing with these tiresome Celts in the north of Italy. We must secure our frontier there first. If we are not careful we shall have Gauls on the Capitol again.'[46]

Metellus grunts and his goblet slides on the table as he feels to put it down. 'You make a point, Fabius, but Punic leaders are devious. Before we know what's happening they'll have their fingers into Massilia[47] and we shall have lost a useful ally. They're already doing a good trade in copper and horses for Massilian pottery and wine. Surely we could send a couple of legions to northern Spain to steady their ambitions?'

---

45. Saguntum was a town on the Mediterranean coast of Spain having a treaty with Rome. It was the attack and capture of Saguntum by Hannibal, the son of Hamilcar, in 219 BC that provoked the Second Punic War.
46. This is a reference to the siege of the Capitol by Gauls in 390 BC, when tradition has it that a nocturnal scaling party was foiled by the cackling of the sacred geese from the temple of Juno.
47. Marseilles.

The Daughters of Cannae

'It would take more than a couple of legions to control that vast area. In any event we can't afford the men. Our best policy is to try to control the spread of Punic influence north of the River Ebro while we deal with the threat on our doorstep. Spain must wait.' Others in the room nod in agreement but Metellus shakes his head irritably.

'It's always the same with you, Fabius. Where's your spirit of attack?'

'There's a time to attack and a time to wait. Spain is a long way away. The Celts are pounding at the gates.' Fabius's slow and solemn delivery has an air of finality about it.[48]

His remarks are followed by an awkward silence. Lucius looks anxiously at his old general. The last thing he wants is for a quarrel to develop. It will hardly help his candidature for the praetorship, especially now the voting is only a few weeks away. Naevia is standing close to the door, supervising the mixing of more wine in a large crater. He catches her eye, gives a little nod and she disappears to fetch the children.

It's the turn of Gaius first. He's nearly eleven years old now and more confident than his father at that age. Like his sister he has fair straight hair cut in a fringe across his forehead. His white tunic is freshly laundered and he sports a small sheathed dagger in his belt. The three golden balls hanging at his neck have been polished for the occasion and gleam in the light of the lamps. Lucius cannot restrain a sense of pride as the boy steps into the room. He is well built, but not heavy, and Lucius detects bravery in the grey eyes, which gaze calmly around at the men reclining in front of him. At the boy's entrance all eyes are trained on him. They are curious to see how Lucius's son has turned out and Lucius is well aware that part of him is on trial too.

---

48. The following year, 226 BC, Rome concluded a treaty with Hasdrubal under which the Carthaginians agreed not to cross the Ebro.

Chapter Four

Gaius begins to recite his poem, with suitable declamatory gestures of the arms in the manner the master at school has taught him. He relates the legend of the time when Rome was being besieged by the Etruscans under the command of Lars Porsenna. A young Roman aristocrat called Gaius Mucius resolves to infiltrate the Etruscan camp and assassinate Porsenna, even though it will inevitably result in his own death. At the mention of Gaius Mucius there is a slightly amused stir among the guests and Quintus Mucius, smiling, puts down the honeyed fig that he was about to pop into his mouth. Young Gaius, however, is well into his work and does not even notice. Mucius has reached the enemy's camp where he seeks out the Etruscan king. Unfortunately he thrusts his dagger into the wrong man. Hauled before Lars Porsenna, he is threatened with being burnt alive unless he tells all he knows of the Roman plans. Mucius is defiant. To show he is not frightened of the flames he places his right hand in the altar fire beside him and leaves it there. The king admires his bravery and pardons him. Mucius's hand is so badly burnt that he can no longer use it. He becomes left-handed and is given the name 'Scaevola', which means just that.

By the time that Gaius has finished his father is smiling broadly. The boy has recited the poem confidently and well, just as Lucius knew he would. His old friend Quintus Mucius Scaevola jumps up from his couch and claps an arm round the shoulder of Gaius, who looks a little bewildered.

'Well done, lad! Your taste in poetry is excellent!' laughs Quintus. 'You will make a fine speaker in the Forum and the Senate one day.' He reaches into his tunic and presses something into the boy's palm. When Gaius looks down he sees a shining coin of silver. On one side it bears a picture of the goddess of victory riding a chariot drawn by four horses and on the other the two-faced god, Janus.[49]

'I think you might have given him the coin with your left hand,' says Fabius with mock severity, although you can never be quite sure in his case.

The Daughters of Cannae

'Oh, we Scaevolae can still use our right hands, but only for torture and other special occasions, like this.' Mucius grins and the others clap their hands as Gaius walks backwards from the room, still a little uncertain what it's all about. Outside, his mother explains that Mucius traces his ancestry all the way back to the hero of his poem, which is why he was asked to recite it. She bends to give him a kiss before taking Opimia's hand and leading her gently into the room. In her other hand the little girl carries a single white flower.

Naevia seats herself at a stool and begins to pluck her lyre, slowly and with long pauses, so that the notes seem to linger wistfully in the air before fading away into the shadows. She looks up, smiles and nods to Opimia who lifts her head and begins to sing. Her voice is pure and lilting, like the lyre. One by one the men stop eating or picking at their teeth, to fix their eyes upon this girl. Caudinus raises a lump of venison to his mouth and then returns it to his plate, as if forgetting why he picked it up. Metellus drops his napkin and it lies bright red on the saffron dust. If you were an optimist you might even detect the trace of a smile on Fabius's solemn features. Laelius is listening too. At the same time he observes the undulations of Naevia's dress and feels a little envious of his friend.

Narcissus, the son of a nymph called Leiriope, is a very beautiful boy and he knows it. His meandering path through life is strewn with swooning lovers of both sexes who want to lie with him. Narcissus, however, is heartless and rejects them all. Nobody is good enough for him. One day he is strolling in the woods trying to net stags when another nymph, Echo, who has already been seduced by that old goat Pan, catches sight of him. Echo is entranced and immediately falls for Narcissus. She starts to follow

---

49. A quadrigatus, so called because of the depiction of the four-horse chariot. This coin preceded the denarius.

Chapter Four

him, flitting behind the trees. She longs to call out to Narcissus, but she can never speak first. Soon he realises that he has wandered away from his companions and feeling lost, he shouts, 'Where are you?'

'Here,' cries Echo. Narcissus looks round, a bit mystified for he can't see anybody.

'Come to me.'

'Come to me.'

'Please join with me,' Narcissus calls again.

'Please join with me,' comes the reply. Echo can resist no longer. She runs out from her hiding place and tries to embrace Narcissus, but he shakes her off roughly and flees into a thicket.

'I shall die before anyone can lie with me!'

'Lie with me,' repeats Echo. The poor nymph is so heartbroken that she pines away to nothing. No body, only her voice survives. Much later the vain Narcissus is travelling through Thespia where he comes upon a pool of the purest clear water. He stoops to drink from it and glimpses his own face. It is enough. So enraptured is he by his own beauty that he cannot endure the thought of possessing such looks and yet not be able to lie with the possessor. He seizes a dagger and crying, 'Alas! Alas!' plunges it into his own heart. Echo, who has never left him, repeats his last words. The blood spills onto the grass beside the pool and from it a white flower edged with crimson springs up.

As the last notes die away Opimia raises the flower to her lips and kisses it. For a moment there is silence. Then all at once these hardened men clap their hands and shower praises on the diminutive figure before them. Opimia smiles happily; she knows she has pleased her father.

Chapter Five

Three days have passed since the dinner party at Lucius's house. Close under the Palatine Hill in the house of the Vestals the slaves move silently about their tasks, heads bent and eyes averted. By not seeing, they hope not to be seen and thus not disturb the priestesses whose attention is focused on one room. Despite the heat the doors and shutters remain closed, for the pollution of imminent death must be contained. The priestesses have walled themselves off, both physically and mentally, from the clamour of the city. It is as if the gods had thrown a dark mantle over the Vestals' house from which they cannot emerge until the crisis is past. In the cooking area a female slave is preparing an evening meal of polenta which will probably never be eaten. The priestesses are too preoccupied to take much notice of their food. Only in the temple next to the house is there a semblance of normality. Here the junior Vestal, Floronia, keeps watch over the fire. She gazes absent-mindedly into the bronze casket of smouldering wood and charcoal. Her hands hold a scroll on which are scratched the words of a hymn that she has been given to learn, but it is difficult to concentrate.

Inside the house itself the other priestesses are gathered outside the chamber of the Chief Vestal, apart from Camilla who sits by Claudia's bed. For ten days now, unknown to the citizens of Rome, Claudia has lain unable to move, sometimes awake, sometimes unconscious. Her face has

Chapter Five

sagged on one side and her skin feels cold to the touch. Occasionally Camilla reaches tentatively forward with a goblet of water and tries to make Claudia take a few sips. At first she was able to swallow, but even this seems beyond her now. It can only be a matter of time. Camilla waits patiently for the final moments, when she will bend close to Claudia's mouth to catch the last breath of her departing soul. She has none of Claudia's angular severity or haughtiness. Indeed Camilla is much shorter of stature and a little on the plump side. Her eyes do not dart like those of the Chief Vestal. She surveys the world with a kindly look that seeks only the good in everybody. The skin of her face is soft and downy. Her appearance is always one of unhurried calm. In her twenty-five years as a Vestal she has hardly uttered a cross word or even reproached her fellow priestesses for any neglect or error in their rituals. If she has a fault, it is a tendency to believe that others conduct themselves as well as she.

Tuccia enters the room and almost in a whisper offers to relieve Camilla, who has been at Claudia's bedside for several hours already. Camilla shakes her head, gesturing towards the prostrate figure, whose breath is now coming irregularly in little gasps. Claudia's eyes are wide open, staring vacantly. For a moment it seems that she is trying to speak, yet no words come, only a slow gurgle from her throat. The gasping stops suddenly and Camilla bends forward to listen. The struggle for life is over. Tuccia turns to beckon Postumia and Livia into the room. Camilla, still seated, in a clear, calm voice, begins a prayer to Vesta for Claudia's safe journey to the underworld. Postumia stands erect, unblinking, but tears well up in the eyes of the other two. Camilla leans forward to close the dead woman's eyes. She takes the scrawny hand and presses it for a moment, as if to say farewell. Tuccia and Livia each take a hand, while Postumia nods a little uncomfortably in Claudia's direction.

The second hour of the night has begun. The priestesses remove Claudia's clothing, wash her body with warm water and annoint it with pine oil. With deft hands from years of practice Camilla dresses the long streaky hair in the six coils and arranges the chaplet and headbands.[50] In death the tautness of the skin seems to have relaxed a little, but she takes care to drape a fold of the headdress over the lopsided mouth.

'There, I think that is all we can do for the night. Livia dear, would you be kind enough to relieve Floronia in the temple and ask her to come? She must be wondering.'

The junior Vestal comes red eyed and looking a little frightened. Floronia is thirteen years old and has been a Vestal for just over three years. She has never seen a dead body before. At the sight of Claudia she gulps and her hand flies to her mouth. Gently Camilla leads her forward to the bed. Apart from introductions when she first became a priestess, Floronia has spoken only occasionally to Claudia, who left her tuition to the others. It had not occurred to the little girl that this remote and rather austere figure could die. She stares unbelievingly at the frail and vulnerable body with its unfamiliar smell. Camilla motions to her to touch the hand stretched out on the bed. At first Floronia shrinks back from the bird-like claw, but Camilla smiles and nods reassuringly. With an effort she touches it, then wills herself to hold it firmly. She feels the comforting warm hand of the older woman on her arm and turns away.

'Well done,' murmurs Camilla. 'Now you must get some rest. We shall all be busy in the morning.' She turns to the others. 'I shall stay with Claudia. Can I leave it to you, please, to cover the night watches?'

A small clay oil lamp burns on the table in Floronia's room. By its flickering light she loosens the coils of her hair and lays her bands and shawl carefully aside for the morning. The emotion of the last few days has tired her, but

---

50. Vestals wore their hair in a particular style consisting of six coils or braids held together by bands. Brides also dressed their hair in this way.

Chapter Five

sleep does not come. Instead Claudia's gaunt face hovers in the darkness above her head. Why does she look so odd? Floronia turns aside and buries her head in the rough bolster. She tries to repeat the lines of the hymn she is supposed to be learning. Postumia has told her to be word perfect for the festival of the Consualia.[51] At last tiredness overtakes her. This slip of a girl with the pretty oval face and light blue eyes falls asleep.

Hours later she wakes with a start. The oil lamp has long since sputtered out. From somewhere in the darkness a noise comes. She lies quite still, wondering if it was a dream. No, there it is again! Somebody is calling out Claudia's name. Has Libitina, the goddess of funerals, stalking the house swathed in her black robes, come to carry the corpse away to the underworld? Floronia shivers and draws her blanket up over her face. If only the morning would come. Once more she tries to sleep. It's no good. Fear has made her alert.

'Claudia! Claudia!' The voice is familiar, but how strange. Floronia slips off the bed and feels her way towards the door from where she can see out. The pillars round the atrium stand like grey sentinels in the semi-darkness. In the centre the basin reflects the moonlight as if it were a dish of tarnished silver. From somewhere behind one of the pillars, near the door to Claudia's room, Floronia detects the glow of a lamp and beside it, half hidden by the pillar, a seated figure. The marble is cold under her bare feet as she walks forward, past the sleeping statues of earlier Vestals on their pedestals. She gives a little cough, anxious not to disturb whoever it is in the chair. But Camilla has heard the footsteps.

'Is that you, Floronia? I thought I heard your door open. Can't you sleep?'

---

51. A harvest festival at which the Quirinal priest, accompanied by the Vestals, made an offering at an underground altar in the Circus Maximus (the Great Circus), specially uncovered for the occasion.

'I heard you calling out Claudia's name. I just wondered if anything was wrong.'

'No, no, my dear, there's nothing wrong. When somebody dies, we call out their name for a little while afterwards. It's only to make sure they're dead. If there's no reply, we know for certain. That's all.'

'Oh. How many more times will you call out?'

'Perhaps once more before first light. Now I think you ought to get back to sleep. Tomorrow will be a long day. When you fetch the water from the sacred pool, I want you to go round by the end shop in the Forum. Do you know the one I mean, the one nearest the temple of Castor?' Floronia nods. 'The man there, I think his name is Servilius, specialises in producing death masks. Ask him to come here at the beginning of the fourth hour. By that time Claudia's death will be public knowledge.' She stretches out and pats Floronia on the arm. 'Now off you go and don't lie awake.'

Floronia does not mind her early-morning trips to fetch water from the pool of Juturna. In the past few months she has become conscious of her developing figure. Men and women draw back as she approaches. Floronia tries to look steadily ahead. Nothing must detract from the dignity of her status. Men pause from their tasks to watch her go by. She drifts off to sleep, looking forward to her visit to the Forum.

Soon after dawn two slaves carry Claudia's body to a couch near the entrance of the house. They place it with the feet towards the door. Camilla adjusts the robe again and sends for oak leaves and rose petals to scatter round the corpse. She places a sprig of rosemary in the dead woman's hands. Despite lack of sleep she is alert, in a new robe and with her hair freshly coiled.

'I have sent a message to the Pontifex that I shall call to see him at the beginning of the second hour. Until then I think we must be careful that no word of Claudia's death gets out.' She pauses and the other priestesses murmur their agreement.

Chapter Five

'I have asked Leto to go into the wood and cut pine and cypress branches to hang by the door when we expose the body.' Livia speaks softly. Of all the Vestals, she was perhaps the closest to Claudia and is most affected by the death. She has a simple purity which Claudia, despite her haughty manners, had grown to respect.

'I will ride out to the Esquiline Gate and sort out the best firm of undertakers. We don't want any mishaps on an occasion like this. It's not every day that the Chief Vestal dies.' Postumia's tone is brisk and matter of fact. She speaks as if she were organising a banquet, not a funeral. There is silence for a moment.

'Yes, of course. I'm sure Caudinus would agree,' Camilla nods.

The sun is rising in a clear blue sky when the door to the house of the Vestals opens briefly and Camilla emerges, accompanied by a lictor who escorts her the short distance to the official residence of the Chief Priest. Not long afterwards a herald appears to announce the death of the Chief Vestal and notices are pinned up on the Rostra in the Forum. The door opens once more and Claudia is brought forward to lie in state, surrounded by pine and cypress branches.

Two days later it is still dark when the undertakers leave their encampment in the woods beyond the city walls and tramp through the Esquiline Gate, making their way down to the Forum. On their shoulders they carry the bier, now empty, but soon to be occupied by Claudia's shrouded body. Crowds are beginning to line the Sacred Way to watch the procession. In the atrium the Vestals wait in awkward silence. Postumia taps her foot, complaining at the delay in forming the procession. Though she tries to disguise it, the others know that the real cause of her irritation is the appointment by Caudinus of Camilla as Chief Vestal to succeed Claudia. This should come as no surprise, since Camilla is the oldest and most long serving of them. At last Camilla leads them outside to take their places at the head of the mourners. Livia, who is already upset enough, trips on the threshold and receives a sharp rebuke from Postumia for making herself look foolish in public. Livia whispers an apology as Camilla takes her arm.

By the time all the dignitaries have assembled it is daylight. Many in the crowd carry burning torches, a relic of the past when funerals took place at night. The silence is broken by the flute players and trumpeters whose solemn notes roll out over the city. Camilla takes her place at the head of the procession with Postumia, Livia and Tuccia in a row behind her. Floronia walks just behind them, watching the other two taking care not to get ahead of Postumia. She feels the eyes of other mourners a few paces back from her. Can they see that her bands are too tight this morning and that her head aches from lack of sleep? She concentrates on Livia immediately in front and tries to copy her steady walk. She cannot see the mimic who imitates Claudia's peculiar upright posture with chin thrust defiantly forward, or the members of the Claudian family who follow in a group, some sporting masks portraying distinguished ancestors.

The cortège reaches the Comitium. On the Rostra a row of folding chairs has been set out, resembling the curule chairs of the senior magistrates, inlaid with ivory and elaborately carved. Camilla leads the priestesses up the steps to take their seats beside the two consuls and the Claudian family. Floronia is uncomfortably aware of the sea of faces beneath her. The paleness of the women contrasts with the men, weather-beaten and tanned to the colour of old leather by years of work in the sun. Their grubby tunics are stained with sweat and dirt. The smell of unwashed bodies hangs in the air. The brightly painted beaks of the ships' prows, yellow, red and green with big black eyes like giant crows waiting to peck at carrion, jut out over the melee of upturned faces. Her eye is caught by the tight ginger curls of a well-built man standing a few paces back from the platform. He is taller than the average, with a

Chapter Five

broad chest clothed in a tunic cut away at the shoulders to reveal powerful arms. Her gaze rests on him until suddenly she realises that he is staring back at her. Did he smile? Floronia can't be sure in the fleeting moment of contact before she averted her eyes. Without realising it she shrinks back in her chair, which feels too large in any case. Postumia, two seats along, hisses at her to sit up straight. A solitary tear runs down her cheek but she dare not wipe it away. Instead she sets herself to watch as the last of the procession moves slowly into the Comitium. The crowd parts to let the undertakers through. A few paces before the Rostra they halt and raise the bier into an upright position, so that the shrouded figure appears to be standing. No part of Claudia is visible, for the Chief Priest must not look upon death. Why is she made to stand? Is this is a pretence that she is still alive and must listen to her own eulogy before the flames consume her? A terrible thought strikes Floronia. Perhaps Claudia is not really dead. After all, Camilla was calling out to her. She stares at the shrouded figure, trying to detect some sign of movement. Has Claudia committed some crime for which she is now, in death, to be arraigned and tried before the people? If only she could ask. Perhaps Livia next to her knows the truth. She half turns to her neighbour, but Livia seems wrapped in her own thoughts, staring blankly in front of her, her hands clenched together. Best to keep still and not imagine things.

The dissonant notes of the flutes and trumpets die apologetically on the dusty air, leaving only the low murmur of the citizenry. Somewhere to her left a chair scrapes back and Floronia turns to watch Caudinus get to his feet, helped up by the consul sitting next to him. He fumbles in the folds of his toga, searching for something. Finally he produces a scroll, which he holds up close to his face and then lets drop to his side, having reminded himself of his notes. He begins to speak of Claudia's ancestry, though, truth to tell, it is of little interest to his audience. They know nothing of Appius

Claudius the Blind, the builder of the Appian Way and the first aqueduct to serve the city. How can they know, when most of them can neither read nor write? It is enough that their carts have smooth basalt to travel on and that water flows to the fountain near the market. A man sitting on the Rostra raises the great man's mask in the air. This provokes a diffident cheer from a few citizens, probably clients of the Claudian family who recognise their cue. Caudinus's delivery is slow and mechanical, with frequent pauses to consult his notes. The crowd listen patiently, knowing their place. It is not wise to chatter when a patrician is speaking. You never know when he might be able to help with a loan or perhaps a word in someone's ear to secure a job. One of his clients may be standing next to you. He rambles on, raising a slight titter when he mentions Claudia's father, another Appius Claudius, for some reason known as 'Blockhead'. He, Caudinus informs his audience, was the man who sailed his fleet by night across the strait between Italy and Sicily and later raised the siege of Messana by defeating Hiero of Syracuse and the Carthaginians.[52] A veteran shouts out that he was there and receives an enthusiastic cheer.

Fortunately Caudinus neglects to mention Claudia's cousin, Publius Claudius the Beautiful, who lost ninety-three warships at Drepana in Sicily when he allowed his fleet to become trapped between the coast and the Carthaginian galleys. The poor fellow died in ignominy. His son, however, who lacks his father's arrogance, is making his way up the political ladder and has come to pay his last respects by walking in the procession, not riding in a chariot as some have done.

---

52. The citizens of Messana, a town on the Sicilian side of the strait dividing Italy from Sicily, were originally from Campania in Italy. They appealed to Rome for help when they were threatened by the Carthaginians. Appius Claudius commanded the expedition sent to assist them. The subsequent engagements against the Syracusans and the Carthaginians marked the outbreak of the First Punic War in 264 BC.

Chapter Five

The sun beats down relentlessly. Floronia tries to listen in case one of the older Vestals questions her later about what Caudinus said. She too has never heard of Claudia's various ancestors. Her mind dwells on the distorted face behind the shroud. Can poor Claudia hear what is being said? It's very hot and her headdress affords little protection for her neck, which feels as though a piece of burning wood has been laid against it. All the men have their heads covered for the funeral. The women must go bare-headed, though some, Floronia notices with envy, have drawn close to their menfolk and pulled a fold of their husband's cloak or toga over them. She fidgets in her seat, trying to find a position where the sun is not shining directly on her neck. Gently Livia lays a restraining hand on her arm and whispers that it's nearly over.

With the air of a man who has just completed a disagreeable task, Caudinus thrusts his notes back inside his toga. Floronia is disappointed. She had hoped to learn something about the austere woman whose house she shared for three years. Instead she has been obliged to listen to a recitation of the achievements of her ancestors. It seems a strange way to say goodbye.

It's a relief to come down from the Rostra and be back in the relative anonymity of the procession. The pyre, erected on open ground between the Capitoline and Viminal Hills, comes into view. It is large and within the city walls, a privilege only accorded to members of patrician families who have achieved high office.

Nearby a group of senators has assembled. The whiteness of their togas and the purple stripes catch the sun. Floronia looks towards them, hoping that her father may be among them. She knows in her heart that he will not be there. Marcus Floronius has hardly stirred from his house these past two years, since a fever left him permanently short of breath and unable to walk more than a few paces. On rare occasions, when she has a little time off from her duties and training, Floronia takes her carriage to the house on the Caelian Hill where her parents live.[53] There, as often as not, she finds her father dozing on a day couch laid out for him in the peristyle, with her mother sitting quietly next to him. At first she used to chatter gaily about her new life in the Vestals' house, but it never seemed to arouse any great response in either parent. Often Marcus dropped off to sleep soon after she arrived and her mother was tired or preoccupied with worry about him. Long silences took the place of conversation, so that recently her visits have become less frequent. Sometimes there might be a letter from her brother, Publius, with his legion in north Italy. However, he is no great correspondent and his letters read more like military reports, which mean little to either Floronia or her mother.

She is conscious of a vague longing to restore the link with her family. Her parents always say how pleased they are to see her, and yet some unseen barrier has installed itself between them. She dreads the leave-taking at the end of her visits. It is not because she does not want to go. She has grown used to that. It's the indifference that she senses. Her father, if he is awake, only grunts when she stoops to kiss him. He offers no physical response, no touching with his hand, no words of affection. Her mother smiles bleakly. There's no warmth in that smile. She might be saying goodbye to an unwelcome guest, rather than her daughter. She could accompany Floronia to her carriage, but usually summons a slave to see to it. Once, when Floronia asked her mother why she seemed so distant, the response had been vague, a little embarrassed, something about no longer being a member of the family.

The days are too full and busy to feel lonely. Floronia reserves her weeping for her bed at night, where nobody can see or criticise her. It's here in the silence and the

---

53. Vestals had the privilege of riding in a two-wheeled carriage.

Chapter Five

darkness that the isolation grips her like a vice. The other Vestals are much older than she, and though they are friendly enough, apart from Postumia, Floronia knows it is out of kindness rather than any real interest in her.

The head undertaker removes the death mask from the bier and hands it to Camilla, who passes the wax image carefully to Livia. It will hang in the atrium with the masks of previous chief Vestals. Everybody waits while the awkward task of hoisting the bier on top of the pyre is performed. At last it is in position and Camilla and Appius Claudius approach together. Each takes a flaming brand and thrusts it into the wood. They step back quickly as the flames leap hungrily through the dry timber, drawing an audible gasp from the citizens. Some take a pace or two forward to toss trinkets or flowers into the flames. Others begin to wail a funeral dirge and later smear their faces with the warm ash. Floronia watches pieces of Claudia's shroud float up in the vortex of shimmering air above the pyre. She almost cries out when the body moves, but it is only the timbers collapsing as the fire consumes them. With the other priestesses she goes as near as the heat will allow and tosses a handful of myrrh towards the flames. Hers scatters in the air, then settles on the ground in front of her. She steps back, feeling a little foolish, but nobody has noticed. Camilla stands apart, gazing fixedly at the fire, while the other three huddle in a group. Floronia is unsure what to do. It seems presumptuous to join Camilla and the backs of the others preclude her joining them. She watches by herself, waiting for it all to end. She can feel beads of sweat trickling down her neck and her feet ache.

The crowd is beginning to disperse. It would be nice to go with them. Some are swallowing handfuls of water from a nearby fountain or throwing the water over themselves. Floronia longs to join them but she cannot move. There's nothing much left now except a pile of smouldering wood. The pale blue smoke gives off the gentle scent of myrtle as

The Daughters of Cannae

it drifts across the beaten earth. Floronia looks intently into the blackened pile. She cannot help herself from searching. A bone sticks up obscenely, a wisp of smoke trailing out of its charred end. She wonders what it is; an arm, a leg perhaps? She feels no emotion. The strangeness of these last few days has drained her. The undertakers are throwing dark red wine on the embers to douse them. Some of it trickles out from the sodden ash and wood, which hisses and steams in the harsh light. Claudia's blood is flowing back into the underworld.

An eerie quietness descends upon the scene. Where there were crowds and movement there is now just emptiness, an atmosphere of loss and desolation. The undertakers move in to gather ashes and bits of bone for presentation to the family. Camilla is beckoning the others to her, but they seem not to have noticed. She walks over to the group where Postumia is talking. They fall silent at Camilla's approach and Floronia, though she cannot hear, senses that whatever was being said was not for Camilla's ears. They arrange themselves in a line with Floronia on the end, facing the smouldering pile of ash. Together they recite the last words to the departed:

'Farewell, farewell, farewell. We shall all follow you as nature shall direct. May the earth sit lightly upon you.'

Camilla turns away to begin the walk back to the Vestals' house. The sun's rim is nearly resting on the long flat ridge of the Janiculum,[54] bathing the Senate House and the temples of the Forum in the soft radiance of early evening. Floronia feels the accumulated heat in the basalt slabs beneath her feet. All around her the air wobbles in the warmth thrown off by the walls of pale red brick and stone. The shadows cast by them are an oasis and the gaps between them a desert to be crossed. Her gown clings to her body and, looking down, she sees that smuts from the

---

54. A hill on the far side of the Tiber.

Chapter Five

fire have soiled it. The act of trying to brush them off with sweaty palms makes matters worse.

In the Forum a man emerges from one of the stalls, followed by a young woman with a small child at her side. Floronia recognises him as the man to whom she was sent to order Claudia's mask. He stops outside his own shop. The woman laughs at something he has said while the child tugs at her arm. They stand close to each other and a moment later he stoops to kiss her. She touches his arm before allowing herself to be pulled away. The woman's long tunic is of a dull dark brown, frayed at the sleeve ends and spattered with dirt around the hem. She carries herself lightly, while the boy skips along beside her in bare feet as they walk off down towards the river. Floronia's footsteps falter to watch until the pair disappear from view. She has to hurry to catch up before the others reach the house and the round temple next to it, now in the shade of the hill up the slope of which the grove of pine and oak trees climbs. The house looks cool and inviting, a refuge from the heat. In her little room she throws off her sandals and revels in the chill running up her legs from the marble floor. She soaks her arms in a basin of the water brought that morning from the pool. Soon enough she will be in the temple, watching over the fire until the sun sets. For now it is comforting to be unobserved. She wonders whether the woman in the brown tunic has reached home and if the man who makes the masks is her secret lover.

Chapter Six

227 BC

In the Senate the debate grinds forward. Catulus, patrician and silken voiced, complains that the city's woes are all the product of the policy of Gaius Flaminius five years previously, when the Senones were driven out of Picenum[55] and the area was colonised by Rome. Of course, he does not say in direct terms that Flaminius is a demagogue whose only interest is self-promotion by ingratiating himself with the people through grants of land, but everybody knows that is what he means. Catulus sniffs the air as if he has detected some bad odour caused by even mentioning the name of this upstart tribune who, to his mind, carried through the popular assembly a measure that was properly the business of the Senate.

'Now, after so many years of peace with the Gauls, they are restless again. We hear that the Insubres and the Boii[56] have come together in an alliance and are in contact with other tribes who live across the Alps by the banks of the Rhone. Why? I will tell you why. These people are fearful that Rome is going to expel them from their territories and eventually exterminate them. They have seen what happened to the Senones and our greatly mistaken policy there.' Murmurs of

---

55. An area of central Italy east of Umbria and bordering on the Adriatic.
56. Tribes of northern Italy.

Chapter Six

assent rumble from the mouths of conservative elements who have grouped themselves round Catulus. 'It is shameful that, with this growing threat from the Gallic tribes, we have to watch the Carthaginians gorge themselves in Spain.' The snout, as Lucius privately refers to him, drones on. At last he sits down to one or two polite shouts of support and a pat on the back from old Lepidus, during whose consulship Flaminius pushed through his land bill.

This business day is drawing to a close.[57] High above, the latticework of the windows shreds the setting sun into bars of white gold which lance downward through the speckled air. Looking across the chamber to where Fabius sits in his customary seat, Lucius notices that the wart on his lip is grotesquely enlarged by the angle of the shadow on it. The knot of people who have been lingering at the great double doors listening to the speeches begins to disperse. Lucius's thoughts turn to dinner with his old friend Brutus, who sits with hooded eyes a few feet away. His dining room will be cool in the young night, fanned with palm fronds in the hands of soft-skinned slaves. Lucius wonders idly who else will be of the company as Flaccus, the consul who presides over the debate, rises to his feet. May it please the gods, he will wind up now, thinks Lucius. The fetid air, staled by worn arguments, hangs heavily on Rome's governing elite. A few senators, the more aged ones, are actually asleep and an occasional snort rings out over grey and thinning pates. Some time ago Metellus's stick clattered on the marble pavement and still lies where it fell. Lucius leans forward from his seat behind, thinking to pick it up and be ready to help the old man to his feet when the House adjourns. But Publius Umbrenus, 'Buggerlugs', as Laelius likes to call him, beats him to it. With a sly smile at Lucius he nudges

---

57. Generally speaking the Roman year was divided into two kinds of day, those on which civil and judicial business might be transacted and those on which such business was suspended in order not to offend the gods.

the old general to consciousness and puts the stick into his hand. His trouble is rewarded by an irritated grunt.

Umbrenus is running a bit to flab these days. The sweat trickles down his cheeks and arms, like the fat of a sucking pig on a spit. He's spent most of the afternoon trying to catch the consul's eye, hoping to be asked to speak. As a new man[58] his chances are negligible and in any case Lucius suspects that he will only whine about the loss of the family's silver mine, which has been seized by the Carthaginians.

Flaccus puts the motion that envoys should be sent to the Veneti and the Cenomani,[59] with a view to shoring up Rome's alliance with these peoples in the event of an attack by the Boii and their allies. Nobody can disagree with this and the House rises in a collective air of relief.

Outside, Lucius lingers on the pavement above the Comitium, chatting to Laelius and Mucius about his campaign for the praetorship. It's not long now until the elections in Quintilis. His timely contribution to the cost of refurbishing the wood merchants' hall on the banks of the Tiber has gone down well with the leaders of the city tribes, but other candidates have not been slow to advance their cause. New bronze doors gleam at the entrance to the temple of Saturn, accompanied by a notice in large red letters proclaiming that they have been paid for by C.Terrentius Varro. The friends agree to meet again on the morrow to discuss tactics, after which Lucius sets off on the walk back to the Esquiline. He declines the offer of a ride in a litter, preferring the company of a few clients who escort him through the crowd milling in the Forum.

A press of people surrounds the consul and his lictors have difficulty in clearing a path for him. A deputation of Greeks has arrived from the island of Rhodes. They wear long tunics hitched up in folds over their girdles. Most sport broad-

---

58. A man who is the first of his family to reach the Senate.
59. Gallic tribes north of the River Po.

Chapter Six

brimmed hats and some are draped in short cloaks dyed with Phoenician purple or deep indigo. Their interpreters importune the lictors, seeking an immediate audience with Flaccus. An earthquake[60] has devastated their city, bringing down many public buildings and a giant statue of the sun god Helios which towered beside the entrance to the harbour. All that remains are two enormous feet implanted on a rock above shards of shattered bronze and rubble. The Greeks cannot rebuild the statue. An oracle has advised against it. But large areas of the city need to be cleared and restored. They have come to Rome for help. They beseech, implore and generally wave their arms about in supplication. One throws himself upon his knees and wails like a widow at a funeral. Flaccus eyes them stonily and orders his lictors to push them aside. It is not the Roman way to submit to such emotional behaviour. He will consider their appeal on the next business day. Perhaps a temporary exemption from customs dues might be appropriate. The Rhodians retire to the platform at the side of the Forum reserved for foreign deputations. Here they continue their lamentations. A wag in the crowd shouts out, asking them to show what the statue looked like. A number of them clamber up on each other and stand unsteadily until the human edifice collapses in a heap, much to the delight of the spectators.

Lucius turns away past the new shops and into the Argiletum.[61] As the ground begins to rise a litter draws level with him and he hears a peremptory order to stop. The curtains draw back to reveal the face of Caudinus who is apparently looking for him.

'Good afternoon to you, Opimius. I was hoping to catch a word with you after the debate in the House, but I missed

---

60. This earthquake occurred in 227 or 226 BC and brought down the statue known as the Colossus of Rhodes.
61. A street leading out of the Forum. It later became lined with banks and bookshops.

you in that terrible scrum of Greeks making such a scene. Anybody would think they were the only people who suffered from earthquakes. It's probably a punishment of the gods for loose living. They looked a bit dissolute.'

'The envoys say that large parts of the city and harbour have been destroyed.'

'Indeed, indeed,' replies Caudinus dismissively. 'But I have not stopped to talk about that. Another matter has been engaging me these past few days which I should like a moment to discuss with you. I have no time now. I am on my way to dine with Lepidus. Perhaps I might call upon you tomorrow around the fourth hour?'

Lucius is a little startled. Why should the Chief Priest trouble himself to call upon him?

'Oh!' Then, 'Yes, of course, but I would be most happy to come to the Regia.'

'No, no. On this occasion I should prefer to talk at your house.' Caudinus nods, smiles drily to indicate that the conversation is over and orders his bearers to proceed. Lucius continues up the hill, puzzling over this strange interview. What can a powerful man such as the Pontifex want from him? It must be something to do with his candidacy for the praetorship. Does Caudinus want him to stand aside in favour of someone else?

Lucius is still thinking uncomfortably about this when he arrives at Brutus's house high up on the slopes of the Janiculum, away from the smells and corruption of the city centre, as his host likes to put it. Tonight Brutus is entertaining his guests on the roof, which affords a view stretching over the whole city. His slaves have carried up couches upon which the guests recline in the cooler evening air. Slowly a thin mist is rising from the river. Like a tide sidling in from the sea it gradually swallows up the houses in the valleys below, before breaking in a splashless foam on the hills, until only a few apartment blocks rise like stubby fingers above it. The temple of Jupiter on the

Chapter Six

Capitoline rides like a roofed boat at anchor on a milky lagoon studded with islands of treetops.

Brutus orders a brazier to be brought up to warm his guests, who have called for their togas. Round the oval table the couches radiate outwards. Oil lamps on low stands underlight the diners' faces, which resemble the masks carried at funerals, detached from their heads and bodies by the engulfing darkness behind. Slaves move noiselessly among them, dispensing from shallow craters wine of high quality but well watered, and asparagus fresh from Brutus's estates in Campania with slices of juicy capon wrapped in lettuce leaves. The conversation is quiet, gentle and courteous. Lucius listens with half an ear. He is still distracted by the curious interview with Caudinus. He had been considering arranging for a gathering of the men in his squadron in Sicily, at any rate those who still live in the city. Many of the veterans have returned to their farms after the war, but others, particularly those with disabling wounds, have lingered and never returned to the countryside. They would be useful for drumming up votes in his election campaign. Perhaps it is all a waste of effort. A vague feeling of irritation disturbs his evening.

On the other side of the city, in the district of the Aventine Hill, where many of the plebeians make their home, a gathering of a different kind is taking place. The stone-and-tufa walls of the house of Publius Umbrenus stand out against the rough wooden tenements that surround it. Tonight he has invited several guests, ostensibly to dinner. The real reason, however, for his invitation is to show off his latest acquisition which, he says, comes from an ivory merchant in Leptis Magna[62] who bought it in Corinth some years previously. The guests are a mixture. Many, like Umbrenus himself, have done well for themselves in trade as a result of the expansion of the city's

---

62. A city on the north coast of Africa in modern Libya.

interests beyond the confines of Italy. Others are young men, some from patrician families or at any rate of senatorial rank, who in due course will don the purple stripe and occupy positions of power in the Republic, future praetors or even consuls. They are men who may one day be useful to Umbrenus in the furtherance of his career. Meanwhile these scions of some of Rome's most noble families are not averse to a little free wine and food, even if it means keeping strange company.

Such a one is Marcus Furius who has only lately adopted the manly toga.[63] His father, Publius Furius, will become a consul in four years' time. The young man has come with a few aristocratic friends to gather in the atrium, where lavish food and strong unwatered wine are being served. Marcus and his companions take full advantage of the largesse. Umbrenus watches with satisfaction. It may be costing him now, but he is confident that one day he will reap the benefits.

He has an eye for the dramatic. As dusk falls he ushers his guests into the spacious peristyle. A gauzy mist from the Tiber lingers in the smoky haze of the cressets set at intervals round the colonnade. In the wavy yellow light patched by the shadows of unlit corners the guests wait expectantly. Umbrenus advances towards a cloth-draped figure set up in the centre. He raises a chubby hand decorated with the gold ring of a Roman knight. Conversation stutters into silence. He jerks at the cloth which unfortunately catches on some invisible obstruction, so that the theatrical gesture of revelation loses its panache while Umbrenus fiddles to release it. After a short struggle he tears the cloth free and announces in words carefully rehearsed, 'Behold the goddess Aphrodite rising from the Aegean sea near Cythera!'

---

63. The assumption of the *toga virilis* (manly toga) marked the passage from boyhood to manhood.

Chapter Six

Despite Umbrenus's clumsiness the effect on his guests is indeed striking. For there, set in a fountain of phosphorescent amber, rises the lifesize Greek goddess, carved in sheer white marble shining with a smooth luminescence of its own. Umbrenus has not miscalculated. His audience murmur appreciatively at the lissom curves of this naked young woman riding effortlessly on the gentle waves. Tresses of hair trail languidly over one breast. Nothing more conceals her femininity. Her fingertips almost touch in a shy greeting beneath a smile which beckons the onlooker to the pleasures of her cult.

Young Marcus has drunk plenty of the wine, which is a lot stronger than the heavily diluted mixture to which he is accustomed. The sausage pasties are not to his taste. Dumbfounded, he gazes at the statue and, as he does, the sap in him begins to stir. He has no experience of sex and the sight of this inanimate but very female body fascinates him. One or two of his friends, brought up in households with several female slaves, make lewd remarks but are otherwise unexcited. It is not so with Marcus. His austere patrician father is not cruel or even unkind but, unlike Opimius, his slaves have always been kept at a distance. As a small boy it was made clear to Marcus that slaves were untouchable except when it was necessary to punish them. Watching with undue care some slave girl going about her work in the house is as close as he has ever been. The prospect of the lash, or worse, has kept him in check. Pausing several times to disguise his interest, he begins to sidle round the voluptuous figure. He is curious to see the back. Is it flat, as if carved on a slab? To his relief the body is whole in all its shapeliness. He pretends to avert his eyes in case anybody is watching. Perhaps he could touch her thighs when nobody is looking. But Umbrenus is strict.

'No hands!' he shouts more than once when guests stretch forward to stroke the polished flesh. Above well-fed cheeks little black eyes sparkle with satisfaction. A self-deprecating smile accepts congratulations, tributes to his good taste and another step up the social ladder.

Soon the smoky tallow and the cool mist combine as an excuse for the guests to drift back inside where they can continue to sample more of their host's generous hospitality. Marcus must follow after a last furtive glance. A slave appears at his side, carrying a jug of rich dark wine. It seems churlish to refuse and Marcus holds out his goblet till it overflows. Men and women lean for support against pillars or recline untidily on couches. Some are silent, flushed and bleary from too much to drink, occasionally muttering slurred inanities to their neighbour. Most of Marcus's friends are still upright, talking loudly. Titus Aemilius has torn the arm of his tunic, which hangs quaintly off his shoulder, and Sulpicius is covered in wine stains.

Marcus surveys the scene a little uncertainly. His eye is caught by a woman propped on one elbow against a long bolster. Beside her sits a man who is evidently wealthy, to judge from the thick gold bracelets on each wrist and his belt of intertwined snakes in heavy silver. The woman extends a slender leg along his thigh to reveal a delicate sandal mounted with pearls. She smiles and dabs a kiss onto his sweaty arm, which rests indiscreetly on her knee. Her face, powdered with chalk or perhaps white lead, reminds Marcus momentarily of the glistening marble outside. There is no further resemblance. Deep red lips, stained from the lees of wine, slash this face like a wound, while antimony accentuates the eyebrows and bruises the sockets below. A pale arm manacled by a jewelled bangle sneaks out to stroke the man's attentive hand. Marcus stares, mesmerised by such behaviour. He cannot imagine what his mother would make of it. This is a world of which he had no inkling, a world in which he does not feel at ease. He turns away in search of Aemilius and the rest. Suddenly the room seems to be full of people he does not know. His friends have disappeared. He takes another swig of wine.

Chapter Six

He feels a little isolated. Perhaps the others have gone back outside. No harm in going to take a look.

Nobody pays any attention, even when he stumbles at the doorway. There she is; alone, magnificent and pure woman, swathed in the dank vaporous air. Marcus walks slowly round, his feet crunching on the gravel. The peristyle is deserted. He has the lady to himself and her smiling eyes transfix him. Surely it would do no harm to touch her, despite what Umbrenus said. That could be a secret between the goddess and himself. Marcus giggles at the thought. He takes another gulp of wine and puts his goblet on the ground. A couple of steps and he is almost within touching distance. Only the plumes of water on which the goddess rides keep her just out of reach. He leans forward, stretching out his arms to clutch at her hips. He loses balance and his body strikes the statue with all his weight. Slowly, but ineluctably, Aphrodite falls backwards. Marcus struggles frantically to recover. It's too late. With Marcus's arms locked round her waist the pair crash to the ground. He pulls his arms free, rolls away and scrambles to his feet. One of his teeth is loose from impact against a marble breast and his right arm aches, but otherwise he is unhurt. The goddess has not fared so well. Her head lies separated from her shoulders, one forearm has broken off at the elbow and two watery plumes have lost their tips.

Marcus stands terrified. What a moment before was irresistibly attractive has now become an object of horror. He looks round. Nobody seems to be about. He can hear the sounds of revelry coming from inside the house as, half running, half walking, he creeps past the atrium. He fumbles clumsily with the bolts on the door. The dozing slave wakes and mumbles something. Marcus does not wait to talk but yanks open the door and almost falls into the street.

Outside it is very dark indeed, for there are no lights and the moon, if one has risen, sails above the mist. Despite the coolness of the air Marcus is sweating and his head is fuddled.

The Daughters of Cannae

Swaying slightly, he forces himself to stand still. He is consumed by an urgent desire to put distance between himself and the house. He rests a clammy hand against the wall. The river must be to his left. Before that he should reach the city wall running beside it. If he can find the wall, he should be able to follow it back towards the family home on the far slope of the Capitoline. At first he cannot even make out his hands held in front of him as he shuffles uncertainly forward. Gradually his eyes grow a little more accustomed to the blackness. He can just distinguish the outline of the tenements lining the narrow alley from the paler streak of mist above. Occasionally he trips over some unseen object or bumps into a wall. His sandals, he knows, are caked with the filth of the street which he cannot see to avoid. The groping forward is slow and painful. His arm is hurting and his toes sting from continually stubbing them. He begins to feel giddy and props himself against an unseen doorpost. Suddenly his stomach turns upside down and a stream of purple liquid erupts from his mouth. For a moment Marcus wants to die there and then. His limp body slides down to rest on the beaten earth, which feels damp and cold.

The chill air pulls him to his feet. He's feeling very weak and unsteady. The nausea has filled his eyes with tears which he tries to wipe away with the sleeve of his tunic. Dimly he becomes conscious of a gentle slapping sound. It must be a sail on one of the boats moored in the river disturbed by a momentary breeze, or perhaps water plopping against a hull. For a second the mist parts and Marcus glimpses the city wall, solid black behind a ragged line of rooftops. The listless Tiber makes no sound but Marcus thinks he can smell the river. Almost immediately the mist closes in again. If only he can keep going, he must eventually reach the road leading to the Sublician Bridge. Somewhere ahead an ox bellows from his pen in the cattle market. The sound carries eerily through the fog. Soon Marcus finds himself passing empty stalls and hutches. He

Chapter Six

bumps into a gate and rests against it, trying to focus. A few sheep, suddenly conscious of his presence, jostle each other to get away from this intruder. From the far corner of their enclosure they eye Marcus balefully. He tries to count them, but gives up, confused. His head throbs and his mouth tastes foul.

The damp and cold are beginning to eat into him. Somewhere he has mislaid his cloak. Why did the door slave not give it to him when he left? He cannot remember. If only this mist would clear. Put a foot forward, past the first one. That's what he must do. Here's another stall with the remains of some turnips on it. Two rats scuttle down the wooden legs and disappear. He must have reached the vegetable market close to the temple of Hope. It can't be far now to the Carmenta Gate and Team Street running beneath the Capitoline. Marcus stoops to pick out a stone or something sharp which has lodged in his sandal, loses balance and pitches forward. His head strikes the ground and for some moments he lies dazed. His head swims when he tries to stand and he has to grab the side of another stall to steady himself. The fall reminds him of his earlier one and the terrible events of the evening. How is he going to face his father? He, the son of a patrician, has run away from the house of a plebeian, unable to accept responsibility for his drunken behaviour.

The shame and fear well up in Marcus's fuddled mind. Blinded almost by mist, darkness and fright, he blunders on, not sure now whether to go home or somewhere else. His foot strikes a paving stone, the bottom of some steps. Instinctively he begins to climb, hoping to emerge from this suffocating mist. On all fours, placing one hand on the step two above, he hauls himself painfully upwards. The dank blanket that envelops him shows no sign of thinning. Angrily he tries to swish it away with a swing of his arm and topples sideways to lie gasping on the loose stones beside the steps. Surely he can't be far from home now. One more effort and he'll soon be rattling the door to wake the slave behind it.

Something is not quite right about these steps. They're too wide and steep. Marcus sits down to try to think. He must be sitting on the Hundred Steps leading up to the Capitol. The Gemonian Steps, where he wants to be, are further over, by the Comitium. He just needs to climb a little higher and then turn to his right. That should do the trick. If only he could see. The damp stone has soaked through to his bottom, so that his tunic clings stickily when he stands. 'Ten more steps, that should be enough,' he mutters to himself. He counts out loud, 'One, two, three ... ten and one for luck.' He turns aside, relieved to escape from this wretched climb. His knees feel wobbly and almost give way, but he gropes forward on the rough, sloping ground. The mist seems thicker than ever, wrapping poor Marcus in its confusing and disorientating cloak. His foot slides on a wet piece of scree and then hangs momentarily in the empty air. His left hand searches desperately for a hold, encountering only a piece of cruelly smooth granite. Nothing can save him now and he tumbles headlong, thrown from one jagged outcrop to the next, until his ragged body lies still.

In the morning Lucius decides to receive the Pontifex in the shade of the colonnade. He orders sherbet and his best wine to be made ready, though he habitually takes only water for himself until the lamps are lit. From the tone of the conversation the previous day Lucius surmises that whatever is to be said is confidential. Naevia and the rest of the household are instructed to retire elsewhere.

The slaves have set out two chairs of bronze with strong leather seats and backs, and placed a small table between them. Caudinus gives a little grunt as he settles himself. He loosens the thongs of one sandal which he eases gently off his foot. Lucius observes that the toe is swollen but Caudinus makes no apology or comment. He looks round

Chapter Six

with the air of a man who is used to the superior things in life and allows himself a few casual remarks about the pleasant flowers and statuary.

'You've made yourself a decent enough spot here, Opimius.' The tone is not quite condescending, but establishes the terms upon which the conversation is to take place. Lucius offers the wine or the sherbet. His guest looks down, surprised, and Lucius senses that he would not expect to receive refreshment straight from the hand of his host, only from a slave. Caudinus hesitates, as if he does not wish to incur the obligation of hospitality, then agrees to take a small cup of sherbet. He leaves it untouched on the table while Lucius pours himself some water to occupy the moment.

'I enjoyed our little dinner here the other night.' A pause. 'Most enjoyable.'

'It was a pleasure to have your company. I hope the food was to your taste.'

'Oh indeed! Your wife, Naevia, isn't it, seems to have some competent cooks.' Caudinus adjusts himself in his chair and clears his throat. 'You know, of course, that we have just lost our Chief Vestal. Wonderful woman, Claudia. Knew exactly how to behave at all times. Set such a good example to the people.'

'I thought your eulogy was most fitting, if I may say so.'

'Ah! Quite. One must observe the rituals. The people insist on it, you know. I'm afraid I'm no orator, but one does one's best.' Lucius feels that further words of praise are called for, but can think of nothing and remains silent. Another cough from Caudinus. 'Anyway, that brings me to the reason for my calling upon you this morning. I wonder whether you might consider offering your daughter to fill the vacancy in the Vestal order.'

'My daughter! You mean Opimia?' Lucius is so surprised that he struggles to get out the words.

'Of course, this will come as something of a shock to you, especially as you are not of patrician stock.[64] Despite

The Daughters of Cannae

this, it seems to me that your family and she have the necessary qualifications. I believe I'm right in saying that there have been no slaves among your ancestors and that Opimia has been in your power since birth and remains so.'

Lucius turns his head to nod at Caudinus who continues, without looking at his host.

'It's normal to recruit between the ages of six and ten years. I took the liberty of inquiring and I understand that your daughter was nine at the feast of Saturnalia. You are probably not aware of this, but a Vestal must have no impediment of speech or bodily imperfection. Bad pronunciation or a misspoken word in a prayer is offensive to the gods. I saw for myself that your daughter is perfectly formed and indeed has a most beautiful voice. I believe that she has all the qualities that would make her acceptable to the gods and to the Senate.' He hesitates and this time gives Lucius a sly glance. 'I'm sure I don't have to ask you if she is a virgin.'

Lucius's mind is racing. 'Oh, of course.' He takes a long pull at the water in his cup.

'You will understand,' continues Caudinus in an almost confidential tone, 'that I consider your daughter to have that essential element of purity required in a Vestal.'

'Is there not a procedure for the election of a Vestal? I thought a list of acceptable candidates had to be presented, followed by a vote in the Senate to select one of them.'

'Technically that is correct. But if a man of good family offers his daughter and all the qualities for a Vestal are fulfilled and the Senate approves, then such a girl may be accepted into the priesthood without further formality.'

'I see.' Lucius tries to think of something more to say. The whole idea is confusing and yet very flattering. His

---

64. The patricians were the aristocratic class of ancient Rome. In the early years of the Republic most of the magistracies and other offices of state were occupied by patricians. Gradually the plebeian class, the ordinary people, obtained the right to stand for these positions.

Chapter Six

little girl, Opimia, could suddenly become a member of the only female priesthood in Rome. One day she might even become Chief Vestal, the most important woman in the city.

'You're standing for the praetorship, are you not?' Almost abstractedly Lucius agrees. 'To offer your daughter as a Vestal will certainly do your chances no harm. Assuming that I can obtain approval in the Senate, which should present no difficulties, your status in the city will be greatly enhanced.' Caudinus picks up the cup of sherbet and takes a small sip. 'I'm sure you appreciate that.'

'It's a great honour that you should consider my daughter suitable.' Lucius stumbles over the words and then mentally kicks himself for being so servile. 'Perhaps you would allow me a couple of days to think it over.'

'Naturally. Opimia seems to me to be an exceptional child, worthy of elevation.' For the first time Caudinus refers to Opimia by name. 'But you must have time to reflect.' His tone suggests that he does not think such reflection necessary. 'It would represent a big advance for your family.'

Caudinus replaces his foot in the sandal. 'Now, perhaps you would be so kind as to summon a slave to relace this sandal and then fetch my litter. I have business to attend to in the Regia.' Opimius claps his hands for Naxus, who appears hurriedly from behind a pillar. Caudinus extends his foot and then, limping slightly, walks towards the door with Opimius a step or two behind. Without turning round the Pontifex climbs into his litter and settles himself on the cushions.

'My compliments to the lady Naevia. Proceed!'

Lucius watches the slaves carry their master at a brisk walking pace down the hill before returning to his chair. His mind clears. The confusion of a few moments ago evaporates. This is a great step up for both him and Opimia. For the sake of both of them it would be madness to refuse. Besides, it is a notable service to the state to release one's daughter to become a Vestal. Her future in society is guaranteed. Admittedly she will not be able to marry for thirty years, but there's no harm in that, and she will enjoy great privileges by way of compensation. Lucius feels a sense of pride. Before the herald in the Forum has announced the noonday hour Lucius tells Naevia about the conversation with Caudinus and of his decision.

Chapter Seven

It is the first hour of the same day on which Caudinus will call at Lucius's house. Rome awakens to a sunless dawn. Above the city the mist has risen a little to skirt the hills, leaving a threadbare blanket streaked with grey from the smoke of early-morning fires. From a house on the north side of the Capitoline Hill a young slave, Milo, emerges. He is on his way down to a chandler's on the river to fetch some rope needed to secure scaffolding for repairs to his master's house. His tunic is dun coloured with short sleeves beneath a jerkin of rough untreated leather. At his waist he wears a broad belt and on his feet a pair of heavy sandals secured with thongs strapped round his calves. As he descends the steps leading towards the Forum he can see the line of shops gradually coming to life. Men are unbolting shutters and erecting awnings against the sun, as yet invisible, but which in a few hours will make the basalt slabs of the Sacred Way too hot for bare feet. A steady rumble does not herald the approach of a summer thunderstorm. It is the noise of carts, some pushed by hand, others pulled by mules or oxen, creaking along narrow alleys from outside the city's walls towards the vegetable market. Milo can just hear the shouts of the stevedores in the distance, starting their day's work of unloading small boats and barges that have come up the river from Ostia. A few slaves, bent on errands like himself, hurry about their morning tasks. Two, brandishing long poles tipped with cloths, are engaged in polishing the heavy bronze doors of the Senate House.

Milo crosses the Forum and makes his way along Team Street. He tucks his jerkin inside his belt for a little extra warmth. Above him the ground rises steeply to the Capitol. Soon he reaches the base of the Tarpeian Rock where a small knot of people has gathered round something Milo cannot see. Taking no notice he hastens on towards the vegetable market and the river. He is almost past the Rock when someone shouts.

'Hey, Milo. Is that you? Come over here. You ought to see this.' Milo recognises the voice of a slave of Julius Sabinus, owner of the property next door to his master's. He pauses, wondering whether to ignore the summons. The contractor wants the rope and he will be in trouble if he is late back with it. The man shouts again. He seems concerned and is beckoning insistently. Reluctantly Milo steps aside and walks over to the group standing close to the bottom of the Rock. At his approach the group separate a little and Milo can see the prostrate body which has attracted their attention. The man, whom he now recognises as Sabinus's steward, points to the figure lying on the ground.

'Isn't this the son of your master, Publius Furius? He's in a bad way. We ought to get him back home. He needs a doctor. Not that he'll be able to do much for him in that state.'

Milo looks down. Marcus is lying where he fell during the night. Blotches of congealed blood mingle with wine stains, so that his tattered tunic resembles the rags used by field surgeons to bind the wounds of legionaries. His whole body is covered in bruises, some of them almost black and others a sickly yellow. One leg is stretched out at a contorted angle. Even to Milo's untrained eye it is obviously broken. A piece of white bone protrudes from the shin. The other leg is a mass of red raw flesh where the skin has been sloughed off. The right arm appears relatively unharmed but the left has a mangled and dislocated look about it.

Chapter Seven

'Well? It is young Marcus Furius, isn't it?'

Milo is young. He has never seen a man in such a state. His body recoils from the sight and yet he cannot take his eyes away. He nods slowly, afraid to speak lest his voice should break.

'He's still alive. Just. I knelt down and could feel his breath when I spat on my hand. Don't know how much longer he'll last. He needs moving anyway or the crows'll have his eyes.' The other bystanders, all slaves, start to shuffle away, not wishing to get involved. Marcus's head moves, his mouth twists and a faint moan emerges from swollen lips.

'You'd better get back to your master's house and fetch help quick,' the older man tells Milo. 'I'll wait here and guard what's left of him. Here, give me that jerkin. The poor bugger might as well die warm.' Still wordless Milo removes the jerkin and the steward bends to tuck it round Marcus's chest.

Publius Furius, senator and member of an ancient patrician family, has risen at first light as is his invariable habit. Dressed only in a loin cloth and heedless of the early-morning chill he walks from his chamber to the peristyle, an area devoid of ornament apart from a pool in the centre. There he performs his routine of exercises: bending, stretching, skipping with a rope and finally lifting lead weights laid on his back. He works up a good sweat before climbing onto a cold marble slab where he lies to be scraped with a strigil, then massaged and rubbed down with palm oil. The slave is hard at work on his master's body. After the rigorous exercises and the tedious scraping, Furius, though he would not admit it, derives a sensuous pleasure from the slapping and pummelling of his body, the rubbing and smoothing of his muscles. He is not pleased by the interruption that Milo's appearance brings.

Panting and rather frightened by his master's glare, Milo relates what has happened. Slowly Furius sits up and swings his legs off the marble slab. He betrays no emotion apart from the grim line into which his mouth sets when he is not speaking.

'Otto,' he turns to the body slave who still holds a phial of oil, 'send four men with the litter. Milo, go with them and guide them to the spot and then carry on to fetch the rope. The builder must make a start.'

Lollia Sabina, Publius's wife, is summoned by her husband and informed of what has happened. She wears a pale green tunic reaching to her ankles. Her hair is swept back from her forehead and tied with a ribbon at the nape. She is slim and flat chested. Like her husband she lives frugally, eating sparingly and drinking only the most diluted wine. Her days are spent weaving and attending to the smooth running of her husband's household. Excursions are rare and then only to attend religious festivals, or perhaps once or twice a year to watch the races in the Great Circus. She speaks so quietly to her maids that sometimes they do not hear and Publius becomes angry that instructions have not been carried out. There is no pomp and little sparkle, but this lack of colour disguises a strong and resolute character.

The news of the attack on Marcus, for both she and Publius assume that he has been robbed and beaten up by thieves, Lollia receives calmly. A doctor must be sent for. She knows the best man to bind the wounds and prescribe the healing ointments. Philistion helped the midwife to deliver Marcus into the world and he again must save the boy from exiting it too early. Lollia despatches a runner to fetch him.

By the end of the second hour of the day Marcus lies on a couch in the atrium of his father's house. Carefully Lollia washes his wounds in warm clear water fetched from a spring rising near the citadel. She cuts away the blood-soaked tunic and lays a woollen blanket on his chest. The boy is breathing slowly, but his eyes remain closed and he

Chapter Seven

makes no response to his mother's soothing words. His mouth gapes to reveal broken teeth and beneath the matted hair a gash runs from one ear across the top of his head to the opposite shoulder. Gently Lollia lifts her son's head and holds a silver cup to the thickened lips. She trickles the water into his mouth. It seeps out down his chin. She strokes his face as she wipes it away. Her husband, grim and silent, turns aside to face the other way.

Philistion, the surgeon, is a Greek from Locri in the deep south of Italy. It is not his real name, but one that he has adopted from a famous doctor who lived over a hundred years before Philistion was born. A little borrowed goodwill does no harm, especially when one is trying to build a practice. As a young man he studied the work of Hippocrates and all the treatises collected under his name. Soon he decided that Locri was not big enough to contain his ambition. He made his way to Rome and there he settled in a ground-floor tenement with a courtyard attached, on the Aventine Hill and not far from the Great Circus. He reasoned that there would be plenty of work tending the injuries of the charioteers.

Round the walls of his little house are arranged in racks the tools of his trade: scalpels, bone hooks, forceps, saws and arrow extractors. In one corner a cauldron sits, for Philistion is meticulous about boiling his instruments before and after each procedure. In the yard he grows herbs: garlic for the heart, fennel to calm the nerves and oregano for its antiseptic properties, cardamom seeds for their healing aroma and sesame seeds from which he extracts soothing oil.

Lollia has sent the litter in pursuit of her runner. Philistion scrambles into it, leaving his assistant to walk alongside. Reaching the steep flight of steps leading up to the house the doctor is obliged to dismount to complete the remainder of the journey on foot, followed by the panting assistant who carries a stout leather bag filled with instruments and sundry medicaments. Philistion has grown a trifle portly with prosperity. His practice is widespread throughout the city and he counts many of the leading families of Rome among his patients. By the time he is shown into the atrium he too is breathing heavily and dark patches have appeared under his armpits, across his back and over a distended belly. He sinks into a chair while Lollia waves a slave forward to wash his hands and feet from a silver basin. She has a soft spot for the doctor and is patient with him.

'Now, my lady, perhaps I may look at your poor son.' He heaves himself out of the chair and walks over to where Marcus lies unconscious. Gently he pulls back the woollen blanket to reveal a naked torso, washed and pale. Some of the wounds are suppurating and Lollia bends forward to wipe the gore away but Philistion raises his hand to restrain her. He calls for his bag and removes from it a bunch of fresh oak leaves. He soaks the leaves in pine oil and delicately applies them to each wound until they are all covered. He observes the dislocation of the arm. His chubby fingers seem clumsy, yet they move swiftly up and down the inert body, like Pan playing his pipes, probing, feeling, manipulating. 'That must wait until he is a little stronger and can withstand the shock,' he mutters to himself and turns to consider the broken leg. His fingers close round the fracture and with a sudden squeeze the splintered bone is forced back beneath the flesh. Lollia stifles a cry but there is no reaction on the face of Marcus. Philistion and his assistant deftly apply a pair of splints secured with twine.

'I shall need some of your finest wine, please, in a shallow dish.' Lollia nods to a slave and meanwhile Philistion produces from his bag some sheep's wool, the leaves of a lemon plant and some oregano. The leaves he crushes, using a mortar and pestle fashioned out of granite.

'These have antiseptic properties, my lady, and will combine with the cleansing qualities of the wine to guard

Chapter Seven

the wounds against infection.' He stirs the crushed leaves into the wine with a vine stick. Once the infusion is to his satisfaction he soaks the wool in the mixture and applies it to each wound in turn, having first removed the oak leaves. This process takes some time for there are many cuts on Marcus's body. At length Philistion is satisfied. Finally he takes a needle made of bone and, dipping it frequently in the wine, he sutures the worst of the wounds with a fine thread. The young man does not stir. His breathing is hardly discernible. The battered body has taken on an air of peacefulness. Philistion stands back to contemplate his work. He wears no look of satisfaction, well aware as he is that Marcus is still deeply unconscious and has injuries that he cannot see.

For the first time since the doctor's arrival the senator speaks.

'Will he live then?'

Philistion does not look the senator in the face. 'I, I cannot say, sir. I have seen worse after a chariot race, but his injuries are very bad. I have done everything I can for the time being.' Publius Furius grunts but makes no reply. The assistant is gathering up Philistion's instruments in an awkward silence, which is broken by the sound of loud knocking followed by raised voices from the front of the house. A moment later a harrassed-looking slave enters the atrium, stuttering an apology for his unbidden appearance.

'Sir, a man calling himself Publius Umbrenus is at the door. He's got another man with him whose name was not given to me. They're demanding to speak to you.'

'What do you mean, demanding?' Furius glares at the slave who stands looking at the ground. 'Today has started badly enough without such importunities. Kindly inform Umbrenus and his friend that I am engaged and cannot see them now.' He waves the slave away. The latter scurries off but a moment later returns, bent almost double at the prospect of his master's wrath.

'Sir, they refuse to leave without seeing you.'

This really is too much. Furius turns on his heel and strides out. At the door he finds Umbrenus in the company of a man whom he recognises as a lawyer called Statilius. He does not invite them to enter.

'This is an unfortunate time to call, Umbrenus.' Innate discipline controls his voice, but an unmistakeable acerbity betrays his irritation. 'I have a son lying gravely injured from an attack by thieves and I really cannot receive you now.'

'I shall not detain you more than a moment,' replies Umbrenus evenly. 'You may not be aware that last night your son destroyed a valuable statue belonging to me, for which I require compensation.'

The lawyer steps forward and gently tugs at Umbrenus's toga. A whispered exchange takes place. Umbrenus turns back to Furius who is now both cross and confused.

'I am, of course, sorry to hear that your son has suffered a mishap. You say that he is seriously hurt?'

'He is unconscious. The surgeon is with him at this moment. What is this allegation about a statue? My son is not in the habit of destroying such objects.'

Statilius steps forward. 'My client has incontrovertible evidence that your son, Marcus Furius, was at his house last night and there destroyed a marble statue of the goddess Aphrodite. The particulars are contained here.' He holds out a small scroll which Furius takes without looking at its contents. 'I fear that the matter has become urgent because of your son's condition. On behalf of my client, therefore, I must insist that you appear before the City Praetor this day at the sixth hour. You will be aware that if you do not attend personally or by your representative, force can, if necessary, be used to secure your presence.'

In the Forum a small crowd has gathered in front of the praetor's tribunal. Gaius Atilius sits in a curule chair on a platform shaded from the sun by an awning supported on

Chapter Seven

four poles. Beside him stands a clerk who holds wax tablets and a stylus with which to take a note of the proceedings. On the other side an African boy waits, whisk in hand, ready to swat away any flies. On a table supported by a tripod of gilded bronze legs a basin filled with water, a drinking cup and a jug of wine have been placed. The praetorian lictors in togas and bearing their bundles of rods are ranged below on each side of the tribunal.

News of the action by one senator against another has spread quickly among the gossips of the Forum. A murmur of expectation ripples through the crowd as the parties make their way to court. Umbrenus, surrounded by a group of supporters, arrives first. It is noticeable that he does not wear a formal toga, but has chosen instead a dark-coloured tunic and a short cloak of faded blue beneath a wide-brimmed hat. Experienced court watchers mutter that this is a deliberate tactic. He has suffered a serious loss to his patrimony and does not want to look cheerful about it. With a heavy sigh he removes his hat and lays it on the bench reserved for the plaintiff.

From the other direction Publius Furius approaches. The spectators part respectfully to let him through. Beside him walks Quintus Mucius, Opimius's friend, who has been retained for the defence. At first Furius refused to acknowledge the summons and said he had no intention of attending court at the behest of Umbrenus. Lollia and Mucius had to persuade him that the humiliation of being dragged forcibly before the praetor would be an even worse affront to the family's dignity. Mucius carries the scroll that his opponent handed to Furius earlier in the morning. Furius looks straight ahead, his face expressionless. One or two of his old family clients approach as he passes and offer words of sympathy. He nods politely but does not reply.

When all have taken their seats the clerk steps forward. 'Who appears in this action?'

Statilius rises to his feet to introduce himself and to indicate that Mucius appears for the defence. For the first time Atilius looks up.

'I understand there may be some urgency in this matter, Statilius.' The praetor wears the expression of one who is continually put about.

'Sir, my client and I are very conscious of the pressure on your time.' Atilius gives a peremptory nod. 'I hope the reason for putting you to such inconvenience will shortly become apparent.'

'Very well, very well. Open the matter to me.'

'Sir, my client, Publius Umbrenus, who sits beside me …'

'Yes, yes, I think we all know the plaintiff.'

'Indeed so, sir. As I was saying, my client brings these proceedings under section three of the Aquilian Law.'

'That section deals, does it not, with damage to inanimate objects?' Atilius is not a trained lawyer but he likes to show off his knowledge.

'I'm grateful for your help, sir. That is, of course, correct.' Umbrenus beckons to a slave who steps forward with a cloth. He mops his brow and wipes his hands, a gesture which he contrives to make resemble that of a man who has suffered a great loss. Statilius continues by outlining the events of the previous evening.

'You say, Statilius, that it is the defendant's son who is alleged to have caused the damage?'

'Indeed, sir. However, we rely upon the old law of the Twelve Tables which prescribes that a man shall be liable for damage caused by a slave or a son in his power at the time.'

Atilius nods and turns to Mucius, who rises to his feet. 'Without making any assumptions about the cause of any damage, is it conceded that Marcus Furius was and remains in the power of your client?'

'That point can be conceded, sir, but we make no other admissions.'

Chapter Seven

'Very well. Perhaps you would continue, Statilius.'

'You will, I'm sure, appreciate that our haste to appear before you this morning, sir, is necessitated by the condition of the defendant's son.'

Atilius cannot restrain a smirk at the chance to display his knowledge again. 'I take it that you are referring to the rule that a noxal action lapses if the perpetrator of the damage dies before joinder of issue.'

Statilius inclines his head a fraction. 'Once again, sir, you are ahead of me. The Aquilian Law allows this type of action in relation to damage to property, but the old rule of lapse remains.'

'I presume, Mucius, that your client would not wish to exercise his option of surrendering his son to the plaintiff instead of paying compensation.'

'My client would never contemplate that, sir.'

'Very well. Let me see the statement of claim, please, Statilius.'

'Unfortunately there has been no time to agree the wording with my friend, but I have prepared a draft which I hope may be considered and agreed now.' Statilius produces three scrolls, one of which is handed up to the praetor and one to Mucius, while he retains the third for himself. Atilius scrutinises his document for a few moments and looks up at Mucius.

'Do you want to make any comments?'

'I repeat, sir, that none of the allegations is accepted as true and the plaintiff should be put to the proof on all points.'

Atilius turns to dictate to his clerk who makes a note with his stylus and then hands the tablet to his master. The praetor peruses it, scratches something out and mutters a few words to the clerk who makes an alteration before giving back the tablet.

'Very well, gentlemen. My direction to the judge will be as follows: If the plaintiff, Publius Umbrenus, shall prove that property belonging to him, namely a marble statue of the goddess Aphrodite, shall have had a value at any time in the last thirty days of five hundred denarii and that the said statue has been destroyed by one Marcus Furius, in the power of the defendant at the time of such destruction, then let the defendant be condemned to pay to the plaintiff the said sum of five hundred denarii or such lesser sum as the judge shall find to be the value of the said statue.'

Statilius is on his feet again. 'There remains, sir, the question of security for the appearance of the defendant at the trial.' Furius, who until this moment, appears almost to have ignored the proceedings, turns in his seat to glare at his opponent's advocate. The colour rises in his face at the suggestion that he might flee the city to escape the trial.

Mucius rises hastily to his feet, sensing the affront to his client's dignity. 'Sir, my client comes from a patrician family who count many consuls and praetors among their ancestors, not to mention generals who have ridden along the Sacred Way clad in the garments of Jupiter.[65] My client is also, of course, a man of considerable substance and in all the circumstances I submit that it is an unwarranted slight to require him to provide security.'

Atilius appears to reflect. He is rather enjoying the momentary power that he has over Furius, who has never asked him to dine at his house. 'The matter is a serious one and the possible damages a considerable sum.' He pauses to eye the effect on Furius, whose face is a pleasurable mixture of anxiety and fury. 'However, I propose to make

---

65. This is a reference to the celebration of a triumph granted by the Senate to a victorious general. The general would ride in a chariot through the streets of the city to the Sacred Way followed by his soldiers displaying their spoils and prisoners to the cheers of the citizens. He was clad in a purple tunic and toga embroidered with gold. In his hand he held an ivory sceptre mounted with an eagle and on his head he wore a laurel wreath. As the personification of Jupiter his face was painted red. At the foot of the Capitol he dismounted and climbed the steps to give thanks before sacrificing to the gods.

Chapter Seven

no order for security in this case. The circumstances are embarrassing enough for the defendant, without adding to them.' He turns to Statilius. 'To preserve the legality of the action I make a formal order that there is joinder of issue. I shall notify you shortly of the judge whom I have appointed to hear the case.'

With a curt nod to the parties Atilius rises to his feet, steps down from the tribunal and, escorted by his lictors, sweeps out of the Forum.

The next few days witness no noticeable change in the condition of young Marcus. His mother hardly leaves his side. Occasionally she places a hand on his face or arm and strokes it gently. Softly she speaks his name and once she thinks she sees his eyelids flutter as if he were about to wake. Philistion calls every day to bathe the wounds and apply ointment. He recommends that the boy should be kept uncovered as far as possible to aid the healing process. Only at night does Lollia Sabina place a light blanket over her son and have screens drawn around the couch to keep away the draughts.

On the fourth night Lollia sits as usual by an earthenware oil lamp whose flame, unwavering in the stillness, projects her silhouette onto the linen screen beside her. Sometimes her head drops onto her chest, only to jerk upwards again as she struggles to control the drowsines. The boy seems peaceful tonight and his breathing is regular, though faint. Lollia rests her hand in his and keeps hold of it. Perhaps the life in her will seep through this physical connection and bring her son back to consciousness. Her maid, Tullia, brings in barley water with some bread and fish, which she sets down beside the lamp. Lollia makes no move to eat or drink. The maid, who has served her mistress for many years and normally sleeps at the foot of her bed, speaks in a whisper.

'You ought to have something, my lady. You have hardly eaten these past three days.' But Lollia shakes her head, which never strays from looking at her son. 'At least have a little to drink.' Tullia picks up the cup, places it in Lollia's free hand and with her own presses her mistress's arm. She sips reluctantly. 'Would you let me sit with him? You could get some sleep.' Lollia shakes her head again.

'I cannot leave him. Go now and come again in the morning. Perhaps I shall eat a little soon, or perhaps my son will wake and want something. Where is my husband?'

'He has had cakes of cheese and wheat flour baked at the hearth and offered to the household gods. He is still sitting there, listening to Cethego, who is reading to him.'

Lollia hopes that Publius will come to sit with her. He has left the house only once since his son was carried home, and that was to answer the summons before the praetor. He sits alone, silent and morose. To him this situation is unacceptable, one that must be dealt with by shutting it away. If his son survives, he must leave the city and never return. Publius will not go to sit with his wife. For him Marcus Furius no longer exists.

The watches of the night slip by. Lollia's hand never leaves her son's. The flame of the little lamp burns bravely, comfortingly, in the surrounding silence. Marcus's breath is slow, almost imperceptible. Lollia's body bends forward and then back, as subconsciously she moves in time with the rise and fall of the boy's chest, willing him to stay alive. No sound comes from the rest of the house, apart from the occasional scuttle of mice in search of the remains of food. They feast upon the wheat cakes left in front of the hearth and pitter-patter away into the crevices.

Soon after dawn Tullia rises stiffly from her crude mattress of cloth stuffed with reeds and gropes her way into the atrium. She pulls aside the screen. Her mistress is fast asleep, her head lolled over to one side. The hand that held her son's has slipped and rests inertly in her lap. The boy lies still; too still. The lamp no longer burns and Lollia's vigil is over.

* * *

Chapter Seven

Glabrio, a rather aged senator with only a tuft of hair behind each ear, presides at the trial. Some say he is a little deaf, but the truth is he hears only what he wants to listen to. An advocate labouring his points will get short shrift from Glabrio, who will shut his eyes and give every appearance of being asleep. He is not averse to a bit of sarcasm if he considers the occasion requires it. Once a nervous young barrister instructed by the plaintiff in a case concerning the theft of a swarm of bees, having finished his speech to sum up his client's case, was asked for which party he was appearing. Nevertheless, Glabrio is not incompetent and is sharp enough on points of law, particularly if his interest is engaged. Beneath him on a table are displayed the remains of the statue. The decapitated body lies beside two pieces of broken wave. The head of the goddess sits incongruously next to the severed arm, like the fragments of a skeleton left by tomb robbers.

Statilius is taking a slave of Publius Umbrenus through his evidence. 'Did you see the son of the defendant on the evening in question at the house of your master?'

'I did, sir.'

'How do you know that he was the son of the defendant?'

'I heard him announced when he arrived. He came in the company of Titus Aemilius who I recognised from previous visits.'

'What was Marcus Furius wearing when he arrived?'

'A red cloak.'

Statilius reaches behind him and holds up a red cloak of fine sheep's wool. 'Is this the cloak?'

The slave does not answer immediately when it is passed to him for examination. He has been well coached. He hesitates. 'I cannot say for certain, but it is very like the one that was left behind at my master's house that night.' Umbrenus is staring hard at him. 'In fact I feel sure it is the cloak that Marcus Furius was wearing.'

Glabrio looks up. 'Did you actually see the man whom you understood to be Marcus Furius wearing a red cloak?'

'Oh yes, sir. He had it on when he arrived.'

'I'm grateful for the clarification, sir,' Statilius purrs and turns back to his witness. 'And did you see Marcus Furius later that evening?'

'Yes, sir.'

'Where was that?'

'I heard a noise and went to see what it was about. I went into the peristyle and saw Marcus Furius running towards the door.'

'Did you see anything else?'

'I saw the statue. It was lying on the ground in pieces, sir.'

'Did you say anything to Marcus Furius?'

'No, sir. He'd disappeared by that time. It all happened very quickly.'

A few more questions and Statilius sits down. Quintus Mucius rises to cross-examine. He manages to establish that it was dark and misty in the peristyle, and that it was only a fleeting look that the slave had of the fleeing figure, but he fails to shake the slave on the issue of identity. He remains adamant that the person in the peristyle was the same person as arrived wearing a red cloak.

The door slave is of no assistance either. He says only that a man rushed past him. He says that he was not wearing a cloak, but cannot describe him. He is careful to deny that he was half asleep at the time.

Next Statilius calls a sculptor called Circon, a man from the old colony of Poseidonia founded by Greeks from Sybaris who named the settlement after their god of the sea. The Romans have renamed it Paestum and built a Forum over the old agora. There, temples built by the Poseidonians still stand and among them are works by Circon, including marble statues. He has travelled to Rome up the Appian Way, making the journey in a cart pulled by two mules. Circon is old and a straggly beard hangs down

Chapter Seven

almost to his waist beneath a head that is completely bald. His long fingers, gnarled and arthritic from the years spent with mallet and chisel, seem more like the claws of a large bird than those of an artist. The tanned face, etched with deep creases, resembles the shell of a walnut. Unsteadily he gets to his feet, supporting himself with a nobbly stick of ash which he tucks under his armpit like a crutch.

Glabrio, who can be considerate as well as impatient, eyes him sympathetically. His joints too are not what they were. 'Perhaps your witness could resume his seat, Statilius. I have no objection to his not standing to give his evidence.' Circon remains upright, apparently unaware of the judge's remark and Statilius has to persuade him to sit down.

The old Greek's voice is high pitched but surprisingly clear and firm, although Statilius frequently has to repeat his questions. He asks about the value of the statue before it was damaged. Circon agrees that five hundred denarii is a reasonable price to pay; indeed his opinion is that the statue may perhaps be worth more. The carving displays great artistic skill. Though he cannot say who the sculptor was, he confirms that the marble is of the highest quality and originates from the quarries on Mount Pentelicus near Athens.

Mucius has some questions for the defence. 'You have created many statues in your time, Circon?'

'My hands will no longer allow me to carve, but I think my work is quite well known, even here in Rome.'

'Indeed, I have had the pleasure of admiring some of it myself.' Mucius smiles encouragingly. 'But I suppose from time to time your works have been damaged, perhaps pieces chipped off or even a broken limb?'

'That does happen. Occasionally I have been called upon to repair not only my own work but that of other sculptors also. I remember some years ago a figure of Lucretia was brought into my workshop. The arm holding the dagger with which she was about to stab herself after the rape by Sextus Tarquinius had broken off. I fixed it back into position and you could hardly tell where the break had been.'

'I can well believe it, judging by the quality of your own work.' Mucius, too, knows the value of flattering a witness. 'So a statue may be repaired and be as good as it was before the damage?'

'It depends on the extent of the damage and the skill of the repairer.'

'Of course. But the diminution in value might be minimal if a man of your talents carries out the repairs?'

'Yes.'

'Suppose,' continues Mucius, warming to the witness, 'that you were asked to repair this statue. That could be done, could it not?'

Circon surveys the fragments on the table. 'It would take some time. Without further examination I cannot vouch for the result.'

'But it could be done.'

'It could.'

'Can you estimate what that would cost?'

'As you know, sir, I can no longer work. But I would put the cost at one hundred denarii. Perhaps more. I don't think you would get it done for less.'

Statilius senses the drift of his opponent's argument and rises to his feet to re-examine his witness. 'Circon, you would agree, I suppose, that there is a world of difference between a house and a statue. One is merely a structure made by workmen, while the other is a work of art made by a craftsman.'

'Oh indeed, sir.'

'So, if I have a house and my neighbour accidentally knocks down part of the wall of my house, or perhaps an earthquake causes it to collapse, then I can have it rebuilt. The stones, bricks and rubble infill are reassembled. My house is as good as new, perhaps even better. That's true, is it not?'

Chapter Seven

Circon nods. 'But it is different with a work of art. A statue, for example, made of one solid piece of marble, is indivisible. It possesses its own integrity. Once a part of it is damaged, though it may be repairable, the original work of the artist is lost. It is unlike a wall, which any man may rebuild. It is the work of an individual artist, a unique craftsman whose work cannot be replaced. The integrity of the object has been destroyed.'

Glabrio lifts his chin from the palm in which it has been cupped. 'Your point, Statilius, is that this statue has been destroyed, not merely damaged. Suppose that only a finger of the statue had been broken. Surely you would not argue that the statue had been destroyed in that case?'

'I respectfully agree, sir. Where the damage is only very minor it would be a distortion of language to say that the statue had been destroyed. That is not the case here. The most important part, namely the head of the goddess, has been severed from the torso and an arm has been broken off at the elbow. A solid piece of brilliantly carved marble has been shattered into three pieces, to say nothing of the damage to the base.'

Glabrio considers for a moment and turns back to Circon. 'Perhaps you would care to explain how the repairs would be executed.'

'It would be very difficult. First you would have to bore holes into the neck and head. Then you would insert an iron bar to hold the two pieces together. Sometimes I have used resin from a pine tree as an additional adhesive. The arm would require great care. The break is at the elbow and the iron rod would need to be shaped accordingly. There is a severe risk that the marble would crack or, more likely, splinter. Even if the joins were a perfect fit, which is very hard to achieve, you would still see a thin line which is impossible to disguise. The statue would no longer be one piece, which is the sculptor's art, but at least three pieces visibly joined together.'

'What do you say to that, Mucius?'

'I accept, sir, that the damage in this case is serious, that it would be expensive to put right and would result in a considerable diminution in value of the statue. Nevertheless, the witness has said that the repairs could be made. The terms of reference formulated by the praetor, and agreed on behalf of the plaintiff, require the plaintiff to prove that the statue has been destroyed. If it has merely been damaged, as we contend, then the plaintiff has overclaimed and thereby deprived the defence of the option of arguing that the damages should be confined to the cost of repairs, rather than the full value of the statue. This is a case of overclaim and the plaintiff's case should therefore be dismissed.'

Statilius again. 'I hear my friend's argument, but I submit it is fallacious. The actual marble may only have been damaged, but the work of art has been destroyed.'

Glabrio takes a few moments to ponder, gazing down at the assorted pieces laid out before him on the table. 'I must say that my initial view is that the damage is too serious to contend that repairs, however skilfully carried out, can restore the original work of the sculptor. If you wish, Mucius, you may address further argument to me in your closing speech.'

Mucius looks across to his client who stares blankly in front of him. Publius Furius has only one concern, that this public humiliation should end. He will pay whatever is found to be owed to Umbrenus. For a man of his substance this presents no difficulty. He can then dismiss the affair from his mind and his son from his memory. Mucius, though he is careful not to show it, feels a trifle dispirited. His client appears to take no interest in the proceedings and the trial is not going as he had wanted. Any real doubt about the identity of the perpetrator of the damage has disappeared with the production of the red cloak. Mucius has an uncomfortable feeling that he should have

Chapter Seven

anticipated this, which does nothing for his confidence. Now it appears that the judge is going to reject the main plank of his defence, the issue of overclaim on which he had rested his hopes.

Statilius is on his feet again. He is not arrogant, but Mucius detects an air of satisfaction. His case is proceeding nicely. Glancing down at his notes, Statilius calls forward his client to give evidence. Umbrenus is resplendent in senatorial toga. His face is freshly shaved and the tight curls on his head have been lightly oiled to make them glisten. As he steps forward the sun catches the gold chain round his neck. Gone is the doleful expression that he assumed before the praetor. He looks over to his lawyer, smiles and inclines his head a fraction to indicate that he is ready. There is a stir of interest in the idlers who habitually hang around the courts.

Statilius takes his client through the routine particulars. Umbrenus gives his answers loudly and clearly. 'Now I want to come to the crux of the matter. Perhaps you would tell the judge how you came to purchase the statue.' Glabrio motions to his scribe to be ready to take a note of the evidence.

Before speaking, Umbrenus gives just a hint of a bow in the direction of Glabrio. 'Sir, you may possibly be aware that I have business interests in the city.'

'Not strictly permissible for a senator, but that is not a matter which concerns us today,' Glabrio interjects. 'Carry on.'

Umbrenus is momentarily disconcerted, then recovers his composure. He has become accustomed to remarks of this kind from impoverished patricians and rather relishes their jealousy. He looks over to Statilius who nods encouragingly.

'Since the end of the war against the Carthaginians I have been importing ivory from Africa. I have a contact who is a merchant from the city of Leptis Magna, a man called Trebellius. One day, I believe it was about the time of the feast of Ambarvalia, I was down at this man's warehouse by the Tiber inspecting some ivory that I wanted to buy. My eye was caught by a beautiful statue standing in a corner. I asked if it was for sale. At first Trebellius said that it wasn't. He said it came from Corinth and he intended to put it in his own house. I eventually persuaded him to sell and we did a deal at five hundred denarii.'

'Did you pay for the statue there and then?'

'No. We agreed that I would collect the statue the following day and that I would pay for it at the same time.'

There is a disturbance among the spectators as somebody pushes his way forward. Glabrio looks up, irritated. A man dressed in a long-sleeved tunic decorated with swirls of a russet-coloured material has elbowed his way to the front. He sports a short black beard. A large green jewel sparkles on one hand and on his head sits a cone-shaped felt hat which flops in a comical fashion over one ear. He carries a leather bag. His chest heaves as he tries to catch his breath. It is evident that he has been in a hurry to reach the court.

'Would somebody kindly get rid of this man?' Glabrio addresses his remark to nobody in particular, but a burly slave advances from somewhere behind him. The intruder is not deterred and, having recovered his breath sufficiently to speak, glares at Umbrenus before turning to face the judge.

'I am Trebellius, the man who sold the statue. It is not true that Umbrenus paid me in denarii. He paid in bars of silver, or so he said they were.'

Statilius is quickly on his feet. 'Sir, it appears that this gentleman wants to give evidence that my client was about to give. Perhaps he might be allowed to continue.' Glabrio nods, but waves away the slave who already has a hold of the sleeve of Trebellius's tunic.

Umbrenus smiles and gives a tiny shrug of the shoulders. 'Sir, the agreement was that I would pay either in denarii or, if I wished, in silver bars to the value of five hundred denarii. I chose to pay in ingots as it suited me to do so and I had deliberately stipulated for this.'

Chapter Seven

'Yes, and here is one of the bars.' Trebellius steps forward again and tips open his bag onto the table in front of Glabrio. Out falls a bar of metal, landing on the table with a heavy thud. For a moment there is silence as everybody surveys it. Then Trebellius continues.

'I took this bar to the temple of Juno Moneta this morning, expecting to change it for fifty denarii. The moneyers there said it had to be tested first. Do you know what they found? This bar,' Trebellius picks it up and holds it aloft before tossing it back on the table, 'is adulterated with lead!'

Up springs Statilius again. 'Sir, we have no idea whether this allegation is true. It is not even established that the bar this man has produced is one which my client used to pay for the statue.'

'I think I can satisfy you about that.' Trebellius picks up the bar again and turns it over. 'There! What's that?' He jabs with a stubby finger at a stamp in one corner. 'I'll tell you what it is, sir, it is the seal of Publius Umbrenus. All the other bars bear the same seal.'

Glabrio holds up his hand. It is time to resume control of matters. 'This clearly calls for further investigation and evidence. I presume from what has been said that your client paid for the statue with ten bars, each purporting to contain silver to the value of fifty denarii. Kindly take instructions, Statilius.'

'Sir, my client has already informed me that that was the position.'

'Very well. I take it that you still have the remaining nine bars in your possession, Trebellius.'

'I do, sir. It was only this very morning that I took this one to exchange for coin.'

Glabrio turns to Mucius. 'No doubt this man will want all the bars to be tested for purity. I suggest you arrange for the assayer to attend before me. I shall adjourn for three days.'

* * *

The Daughters of Cannae

When the court reassembles following the adjournment it is noticeable that on the judge's table lie a number of scrolls. Mucius rises.

'I am grateful for the adjournment, sir. It has enabled us to carry out tests on all the bars in question. You see them laid out on the table before you. My friend has acknowledged that each bar bears the seal of his client. With your permission I will now call the assayer to give his evidence.'

Labeo is a small man of dwarf-like appearance who has worked at the mint housed next door to the the temple of Juno Moneta for fifteen years. From his belt hangs a heavy iron key with which he fiddles throughout his questioning. His job, he says, is to test metal for purity, especially silver, before it is pressed and turned into coin.

'And you have assayed each of the bars lying on the table before you?'

Labeo peers at the bars and appears to count them before answering. 'Yes, that's right.'

'How was that done and with what result?'

'I cut a different section from each bar, sir, melted it down and found that in every bar a quantity of lead had been mixed with the silver.'

'Can you tell us the proportion of lead and silver in each bar?'

'All the samples contained approximately one part of lead and nine parts of silver.' As Labeo says this he looks nervously round the court and clutches the key at his belt. He is well aware that many people are staring at him and he is not used to such attention.

'Do you consider that the whole of each bar was contaminated in the same way?'

Labeo looks down at his feet, almost as if he were frightened to answer the question. 'Well, sir,' he pauses again to gather himself, 'if you want my opinion, all the lead and all the silver have been melted down together and then divided into ten identical bars.'

Chapter Seven

Umbrenus rises from his bench and tries to say something but Statilius hastily restrains him. A murmur goes round the spectators and Trebellius is seen to be nodding vigorously. Glabrio glares at the bystanders, who fall silent. He turns to Labeo, who has pulled a grubby cloth from beneath his tunic and is wiping his face with it.

'Assuming that what you say is correct, what value would you place on the silver in the ten bars?'

Labeo twists the cloth in his hands, then, remembering where he is, he stuffs it into his sleeve. 'It's difficult to be precise, sir. You would lose a little of the silver in the process of separating it from the lead. Perhaps four-hundred and thirty denarii.'

Glabrio looks over to Mucius who has sat down. 'Any further questions?' Mucius indicates that he has finished. 'Statilius?'

Statilius gets slowly to his feet and gazes for a few moments at poor Labeo, who has the appearance of a slave about to be whipped by his master for stealing.

'Supposing that what you say is true, can one tell simply by looking that the bars are not pure silver?'

'Well, sir, now that I know they are contaminated I can see that they do not gleam quite in the way they should.'

'But if you did not know that?'

'I can't be sure that I would have known, sir.'

Labeo is released from giving further evidence and trips over a bench in his haste to get away. The bystanders titter at his discomfiture, but let him pass through for fear of incurring Glabrio's biting tongue. Trebellius is requested to give formal evidence of the completion of the sale. He confirms that Umbrenus came with slaves and a cart to his warehouse the following day to fetch the statue. At the same time he handed over the ten ingots in payment of the price.

It is time for Statilius to make his closing speech on behalf of his client. He is tall and has a distinguished air, like his father who also had a successful practice. A high forehead and a strong nose protruding between piercing grey eyes betray considerable intelligence. Not for nothing is he known as the 'eagle of the bar' and the presents he receives from clients for representing them are more expensive than those of any other barrister. He speaks confidently and with a natural fluency. If he has any notes he does not consult them, but keeps his eyes firmly fixed upon the judge to gauge the effect of his words. Glabrio nods when he deals with the question of identity, cutting him short on the point. On the issue of destruction versus damage, the judge again advises Statilius that he need not labour the argument.

'I come now to the matter of the adulteration of the silver bars. My client was, of course, completely unaware that the ingots were in any way corrupted.' Behind him Umbrenus is nodding, turning to the crowd behind him as he does so. 'My client handed over the ingots in good faith, believing them to be in accordance with his stipulation for payment in silver bars instead of coin.'

'I don't think your client's state of mind as to the purity or otherwise of the ingots is material.' Glabrio has taken up one of the scrolls lying beside him on the table. While Statilius continues to speak he screws up his eyes and traces the writing on it with his finger.

'I am grateful for your comment, sir.' Statilius pauses as Glabrio's finger continues its laborious journey.

'Go on, go on. I'm listening.'

For once Statilius loses his customary poise. He is trying to guess what the judge is reading about.

'Er, as I was saying, sir, my client is most anxious that his good faith in this matter be not impugned. Indeed, since the discovery of the contamination of the ingots he has paid to Trebellius another one hundred denarii in respect of the balance of the price and something extra for his trouble.'

Statilius concludes by taking the judge through the directions of the praetor. His client has established his case

Chapter Seven

on all points and Statilius formally requests that the defendant be condemned to pay the full amount claimed.

Glabrio does not look up when Statilius finishes his speech. Instead he continues to read. At length he pushes the first scroll aside and reaches for another one. Carefully he unfurls it, smoothes it out and places a round lump of bronze at each side to prevent it from rolling up. Apparently oblivious of litigants and their representatives alike, Glabrio crouches over the text until his nose seems almost to touch it. Once again his finger, by stops and starts, moves jerkily from side to side. At one point he stabs down with his finger and gives a little grunt of satisfaction, as if he has found the passage he was looking for. Finally he cups one hand under his chin, looks up and says to Mucius, who has been standing patiently for some time, 'Yes, Mucius, tell me what you have to say.'

'Sir, at the risk of being accused of failing my client by not pursuing all the arguments that can be raised in his defence, in particular the issues of identity and overclaim, I propose not to address you at all on those matters as I sense that I should be knocking at a door which would not open.'

Glabrio nods. 'You would not have persuaded me on either point.'

'However, there is another matter which does arise from the evidence. It is not a question of fact, but of law.'

Glabrio brightens and sits back in his chair. 'Oh, I like a little law, Mucius, it relieves the tedium.'

'Sir, in this case we have a contract for the sale of goods, namely the statue of the Greek goddess Aphrodite for which the purchase price was five hundred denarii, to be satisfied either by payment in coin or by silver ingots to the same value. We are told that the bargain was struck at the warehouse of Trebellius by the river. The contract was a simple one to which no conditions were attached. The parties agreed to meet the following day, when the statue would be delivered to the plaintiff and he would hand over the price. There is no suggestion that payment of the price was to be postponed or paid by instalments. Indeed, the plaintiff clearly intended to pay the whole purchase price on taking delivery of the statue, as he handed over the ten ingots at that time.

'What is the legal effect of the agreement made at the warehouse when Umbrenus first saw the statue? Here we come to a curiosity in our system of law. At the moment of that agreement to buy and sell, the risk of the statue being damaged in some way, provided it was not caused by negligence or wrongdoing on the part of Trebellius, passed from him to Umbrenus. So, if there had been a fire at the warehouse that night through no fault of Trebellius, the loss of the statue would have been Umbrenus's. That is a strange thing, for until the statue had been delivered to Umbrenus the following day, it remained the property of Trebellius. Our ancient lawgivers decided that ownership of goods did not pass to the buyer at the moment a sale and purchase were agreed, and yet the risk of the property being damaged or destroyed did so pass.

'But there was, and remains, another way which our law provides as a protection against the buyer who fails to produce the price. The ownership of the goods passes to the buyer not just by delivery of the items, but also by payment of the price. Both conditions must be satisfied. Unless the parties have agreed to defer payment, ownership will not pass to the buyer simply by the act of delivery to him. It is clear in this case, as I have already indicated, that payment of the price was to be simultaneous with delivery of the statue. If the plaintiff had arrived at the warehouse with say, four hundred denarii, rather than the full purchase price, the ownership of the statue would not have passed to Umbrenus unless Trebellius had agreed to defer payment of the balance. Clearly, he made no such agreement. How could he? He thought he was being paid in full. It follows, therefore, that the plaintiff in this case, because he had not paid the

Chapter Seven

purchase price, but only part of it, did not become the owner of the statue when he took it from the warehouse. He has never had ownership of the statue and since he does not own it, he cannot claim compensation for its destruction.'

Glabrio looks up. 'Nevertheless, the statue was at his risk as you assert in your argument. Can the plaintiff, therefore, not claim compensation for its loss? Apart from that, he has now, presumably with the agreement of Trebellius, paid the outstanding balance and thereby perfected his title to the statue.'

'Sir, I accept that the plaintiff may now be the owner of the statue. However I submit that this does not validate his claim. The terms of the direction given by the praetor, to which this court is bound to adhere strictly, provide that the plaintiff must prove ownership of the statue. That can only relate to ownership at the moment of damage. He acquired the property in the statue only after the damage had been done. The plaintiff has failed to prove the claim in the terms of the praetor's direction and it must therefore fail.'

Glabrio permits himself a small smile of satisfaction. 'It will not come as a surprise to you that I, too, have been studying the law prescribed by the Twelve Tables and the opinions of our jurists on this subject.' He taps the scrolls in front of him. 'You need not trouble me with further argument, Mucius.'

Statilius hastens to his feet and tries to speak, but Glabrio waves him down. 'I can deal with this case quite shortly. I find as a fact that the son of the defendant was responsible for the damage to the statue. I also find that the damage was such as effectively to destroy the statue as a work of art. However, this claim must fail on the ground that the plaintiff was not the owner of the statue at the moment of its destruction. I therefore hold that the defendant is not liable to pay any sum to the plaintiff.'

Glabrio sweeps up the scrolls in front of him and thrusts them at his clerk. He inclines his head briefly to Statilius and Mucius before rising stiffly from his chair and hobbling from the court.

Statilius is gracious in defeat, smiling and saying quietly to Mucius that the judge was correct in law. Publius Furius stands silently to one side. The victory is meaningless to him. It is a mere technicality. The judge has found that his son destroyed the statue of a plebeian and fled the scene. Nothing can remove the stain on his family's honour. For his part, Umbrenus looks stunned as he watches a number of Mucius's friends, among them Lucius Opimius, recently elected a praetor for the following year, gather round to offer their congratulations. They all seem so pleased that the upstart plebeian with all his money has been given one in the eye. It is not something Umbrenus will forget.

Chapter Eight

One hot morning, twelve years almost to the day since Lucius and Naevia were married, Opimia sits with one of her straw dolls at the base of a pillar in the peristyle. The stone feels warm and comfortable on her back. She looks around at the familiar features of her life up until this day, a place where she splashed in the fountain with her brother, though she sees less of him now that he spends so much time either at school or exercising on the Field of Mars. This place where her mother taught her old songs from Campania and showed her how to weave, where Phoebe dresses her hair with a comb of carved and polished ivory, where she has helped Orrius tend the garden and pick fresh flowers, where every morning after she has greeted her father the doves flutter round as she scatters corn for them. This is a happy place. And yet the thought of her imminent departure from it does not trouble the little girl. She waits calmly. After all, she will not be cut off completely from the family and it's what her father wants. He says it is a great honour that cannot be refused. She will be able to visit them and when she is older they will meet from time to time in the course of her duties. She will miss them all, especially Phoebe, and Orrius who, these past few days, has picked violets each morning to put in her hair.

The gravel is stirred by the house snake who emerges sinuously from a crack in the wall. He slides sideways, leaving a dry wake behind him in the disturbed pebbles. The sun beckons him from the cool shade where Opimia sits. His mottled skin glistens in the sharp light and yellow eyes stare unblinkingly out of a sleek black head. The long winding body basks, still as a curved stick in the welcoming heat. Does he know that he is a revered member of the household, the symbol of its genius? No evil must befall him, for if it should, then it is certain that misfortune will strike the master of the family. Though she knows he does not see her, Opimia smiles benevolently at this creature, motionless and silent, seemingly indifferent, like the image of a god, all-seeing and yet seeing nothing. Perhaps he's only like me, she thinks, warming himself in the sun and taking everything as it comes.

Naevia comes to sit beside her. She takes her daughter's hand and begins to stroke it. The snake, disturbed by the woman's approach, slithers away towards the garden where Orrius is scratching with a hoe. Opimia senses the anxiety in her mother's inquiring fingers.

'Don't worry, Mother. I'm going to be all right, you know. I shall not be far away and we shall see each other often. It pleases Father that I am becoming a Vestal and so it pleases me.'

This reversal of roles engendered by such self-possession does not entirely surprise Naevia. This child has an awareness of her destiny and an inner calm, a maturity beyond her years. Naevia remembers the incident of the she-wolf and the feeling she had then of an omen. She turns to smile, puts an arm around Opimia's shoulder and kisses her on the cheek.

'How funny that you should comfort me.'

That afternoon, in the sultry heat, when citizens and street dogs alike creep away into any shady corner and the city dozes until roused from its collective trance by the cool of evening, the Chief Priest, never neglectful of his duties, arrives at the house on the Esquiline. He finds Opimia

Chapter Eight

seated on her father's lap in the pose required by tradition. Naevia stands at their side, staring into nothingness, as if unwilling to acknowledge her own presence. Phoebe's hand rests lightly on the shoulder of her mistress. On the other side of the courtyard, respectful and wordless, the household slaves have arranged themselves in a line. Caudinus eyes them, as if they were displayed for possible purchase, and then turns away. Naxus watches his master in case of any command. Next to him Orrius has his head bowed and his fists clenched together.

Solemnly Lucius takes his daughter's hand and offers it to Caudinus in whose grasp it is completely enveloped. In flat tones Caudinus pronounces the formula: 'I, Lucius Cornelius Lentulus Caudinus, Chief Priest, take you thus, Opimia, as a Vestal priestess, who will perform the rites which it is proper that a Vestal priestess perform on behalf of the Roman people, on the same terms as she who was a Vestal on the best terms.'[66]

So saying, Caudinus lifts Opimia from her father's lap and leads her through the peristyle into the atrium and thence to the door of the house. Camilla awaits her in a carriage which will bear them away to the house in the Forum. It is all over in a matter of moments.

Lucius does not utter a word. His hand rests limply in his lap. He stares down at it, this last vestige of contact. The slaves shuffle away to resume their tasks, except Orrius who stands still, oblivious of their departure. His fists clench and open repeatedly. At last he turns, his head slumped on his chest, and walks towards the garden, bumping into the archway as he does so. Naevia cannot restrain a sob and buries her face in the old nurse's neck. Phoebe gently takes her hand and guides her inside. Lucius sits on, alone. Nobody comes to speak to him. He has given his daughter

---

[66]. The meaning of this terminology is uncertain. The reference to a previous Vestal is presumably to Rhea Silvia, the first Vestal.

away to Rome. He knows his father would have done the same. Duty requires it.

The two-wheeled carriage carrying Camilla and her young passenger travels briskly along the narrow alleyways and streets, unimpeded by the normal press of people and carts. The citizens of Rome are quick to recognise the approach of a Vestal and move smartly to one side. Opimia takes it all in her stride, apparently unperturbed by the transition taking place. Camilla observes the child's self-possession with approval. When the carriage draws up in front of the Vestals' house the muleteer assists Camilla to alight, but Opimia jumps down unaided and looks about her. She is surprised to see that on either side of the entrance the wall is lined with small shops facing the Sacred Way. A few bystanders pause to watch respectfully as the Chief Vestal enters the house. Inside, the only priestess in evidence is Livia who comes forward, smiling, to introduce herself. At Camilla's invitation she takes Opimia by the hand and shows her to a small chamber off the atrium.

'This is the room normally occupied by the junior Vestal. Floronia, whom you will meet soon, has moved out. She's a little older than you, but I hope you will be friends.'

Opimia takes in the tiny room. There is not much to look at. A small table supports an earthenware basin and ewer. In one corner stands a wooden cupboard whose open door reveals a pile of woollen blankets. Next to it is a wooden chair, not particularly comfortable by the look of it. Most of the rest of the room is occupied by the bed, at the foot of which sits a chest with an oil lamp on top. The fittings are completed by a rush mat running from the door to the side of the bed. There is no window and the only natural light comes through the doorway from the atrium.

As Opimia's eyes grow accustomed to the dimness she perceives that on the bed various garments have been laid out, together with something that looks like a wig. Livia follows her gaze.

Chapter Eight

'These are the clothes that all priestesses of Vesta wear. We have to dress you in them now. They should fit. They have been made specially for you.' Opimia eyes the gown a little doubtfully. It looks heavy, with long sleeves and elaborate folds compared with her own simple tunic. Livia helps her into it.

'Don't worry. It may feel odd at first, but in a few days you won't notice it at all. Now we have to put on your special hair.' Livia picks up the wig-like object and carefully places it on Opimia's head. It consists of six braids of hair wound in circlets on top of each other and Livia secures it with coloured ribbons of white, green and red. The hair does not exactly match Opimia's own. Livia tucks away any loose strands beneath the braids so as to make them invisible. She stands back, then reaches forward again to make a minor adjustment to the ribbons.

'There; it suits you very well. The ribbons are not too tight, are they? You'll learn quickly how to tie them yourself and in a few days you won't even notice you're wearing them. Would you like to see?' Livia picks up a mirror of polished bronze lying on the cupboard. Opimia walks over to the door and holds it up. The headdress makes her appear taller. The effect is not unpleasing.

'As you get older and your hair grows longer, you will be able to replace some of the braids with your own hair. Two of my braids are my own. Never forget to put on your headdress each morning. You must never be seen without it.'

'Why do we have to wear it?'

'Nobody really knows. They say we are the successors to the daughters of King Numa. Brides always dress their hair in the same way. They are virgins, as we have to be. Perhaps that is the reason.'

'But we are not allowed to marry.'

'After thirty years of service a Vestal can retire if she wishes and marry. Until then she must remain a virgin, a bride of the Roman state, and dress her hair accordingly.'

Livia stoops to gather up Opimia's old tunic, which she tucks under her arm, watched a trifle wistfully by Opimia who realises she will never wear it again. 'Come, I want you to meet Floronia. I'm sure she'll help you get used to our way of living here.'

They walk across the atrium where a female slave is sweeping the floor, while another is at work arranging acanthus leaves mixed with blood-red poppies in large urns set on pedestals. At the north end of the house they reach a wide double door of oak through which they step outside. The weather has changed and a gentle drizzle greets them as they walk the few steps to the temple. This small circular building is topped by a tiled roof from which protrudes a chimney covered with a coping tile. A colonnade of fluted doric pillars surrounds the drum of the temple to which a heavy iron door gives access. The whole building stands upon a plinth divided into four shallow steps.

Through the open door Opimia glimpses the sacred fire. It is not as she had expected. In her mind she had pictured a single flame fed by oil from a lamp. What she sees is a large casket of bronze raised from the floor on a tripod. Beneath sits a tray to catch the ash. The fire itself consists of a glowing mixture of wood and charcoal producing a thin ribbon of blue smoke which climbs languorously through the warmed air to the chimney above.

Opimia is so preoccupied by the fire that for a moment she does not notice the figure sitting on a bench pushed back against the wall. When she does, she sees a young priestess gazing at her steadily. Opimia immediately recognises the slim girl who took part at the ceremony of the aquaelicium on the Capitol.

'Now, I hope you two will make friends,' says Livia briskly. 'Opimia, this is Floronia who is guarding the fire today. The junior Vestals do most of the watching during the day, but we older ones also do our bit.'

Chapter Eight

Before either can say anything, Opimia becomes aware of another priestess who has followed them to the temple. Postumia eyes the newcomer up and down.

'I hope you're going to keep your gown a bit cleaner than that. You've only just put it on, haven't you?'

Opimia looks down. The rain has splashed specks of dirt onto the hem which, to make matters worse, has trailed on the ground, being fractionally too long.

'Oh, we can soon put that right,' Livia intervenes.

'Mind you do.' Postumia ignores the older woman and addresses herself directly to Opimia. 'It is important that a Vestal be immaculate in her conduct and her appearance at all times. Don't forget it.' She turns on her heel and walks out. A momentary silence follows before Livia, her voice a mixture of embarrassment and irritation, smiles at Opimia who is still looking down uncomfortably at the offending hem.

'Well, I'll leave you two to get to know each other.'

When Livia has gone, Floronia lets out a short laugh. 'Typical Postumia, she always knows how to make herself unpleasant. Come and sit over here.' She smiles and beckons to Opimia whose eyes have filled with tears. 'Don't worry, she's always like that. She's testing you, just like she did with me. I try to keep out of her way, but it's difficult when there are only six of us. She'll probably set you a prayer to learn later and expect you to be word perfect before the light fails.'

Opimia nods and blows her nose. 'Thank you. She does seem a bit different from Livia.'

'Yes, she's nice. She'll mother you a bit until you get used to things here.'

'Is it true we have to spend all our time watching the fire?'

'Somebody has to be here all the time to make sure it doesn't go out. I'm in here for part of every day and sometimes I take one of the early night watches.'

'Why is it so important not to let the fire go out?'

'Oh, you'll be taught all about that. This fire is the essence of what it is to be Roman. That's what they'll tell you. It's the hearth of the Roman state, like the hearth we have in our houses. So long as this fire burns, the City of Rome will flourish and our power will increase. If the fire goes out, then Rome is put in danger.'

'But what happens if it does go out? It might do, mightn't it?'

'It's never happened since I've been a Vestal, except at the beginning of the new year. We let it go out then and light a fresh one. It has to be a completely new fire which we kindle ourselves. We cannot take an ember from somewhere else. That would be impure.'

'Oh. Is the flame of the fire really the spirit of the hearth goddess, Vesta, then?'

'I suppose so.' Floronia gets up and with a pair of tongs she takes a lump of charcoal from a box beside her and places it on the casket. 'Anyway, it's the first thing you learn here, the importance of the fire; that and virginity.' Floronia gives a sly giggle.

Next morning before first light when Floronia, armed with an oil lamp lit for her by a slave, enters Opimia's room, she finds her already sitting on the bed, dressed in her gown and sandals.

'I'm glad you've come. It's impossible to see in here. How are we supposed to put on this headdress in the dark?'

'You're not, silly.' Floronia puts her own lamp down on the cupboard. 'I forgot to tell you. Orestilla is supposed to come every morning at dawn and place a fresh lamp in your room. Make sure you tell her to include you from now on. Now, where are your braids? Try to put them on by yourself. You've got to learn.'

Opimia has nimble fingers and with minimal help she soon has the headdress adjusted.

'Well done. You're a quick learner. What a shame, though. You've got such nice hair.'

Chapter Eight

Opimia has noticed that Floronia has left a few curls of her own pale blonde hair protruding at the nape of her neck. 'Your hair is beautiful too.'

Floronia grins mischievously. 'I always leave a bit hanging out, just to annoy Postumia. Come on. You've got to perform your first task as a Vestal.'

She leads her new friend out into the pale grey light of the first hour. The air has a nip in it and Opimia is glad of the heavy gown which she hitches up above her ankles. To her left the slope of the Palatine Hill climbs to a long low ridge, like the belly of some slumbering sow waiting to be roused by the first sunbeams. The umbrella pines, charcoal against a streaked and starless sky, form a complex fretwork of boughs, branches and spines which remind Opimia of the olive grove outside the villa at Tibur. She brushes aside a pang of nostalgia and concentrates on keeping her gown dry. Animals are snuffling in the undergrowth somewhere above, perhaps a flock of goats pastured there the night before being taken to market. Coming up the Sacred Way a cart filled with stone drawn by two mules grumbles over the paving. The smack of a whip crackles through the dark, followed by the clunk of iron against iron. Behind the cart shuffles a line of shadowy figures, manacled and attached to each other by a short chain. The staccato of chisels striking granite and the occasional spark betray the destination of the cart, a building under construction in the Forum.

In the temple Tuccia is arranging logs round the brazier to dry, so that they will burn with a clear flame. Carefully she rinses her hands using water from a jug, which she pours over one hand and then the other, allowing the water to flow into a basin out of which it runs straight into a drain.

Floronia reaches up to a wooden rack from which a row of bronze pots hangs. She selects one and hands it to Opimia. 'Feel the weight of that. Do you think you can manage two, or just one? They will be full when we come back and you can't put them down. Do you see how the bottoms are shaped? They're designed to fall over and spill their contents if you put them on the ground. Mean, isn't it?'

'That's enough of that. I think perhaps just one would be enough to begin with.' Tuccia eyes Opimia's diminutive figure. 'We'll give you two to carry when you're a little bigger and stronger. Are you nine years old yet?'

'I shall be ten at the Saturnalia.'[67]

'Very well. Floronia, take Opimia with you and make sure you teach her the correct procedure. You know how important it is. When you return, get your breakfeast and then come and relieve me at the beginning of the second hour.'

The two young priestesses emerge, carrying three water vessels between them.

'Why must we fetch the water from the pool of Juturna?'

'You're always asking questions, you are. Juturna is the goddess of eternally flowing streams and we are supposed only to use running water. The pool is fed by a spring which keeps it fresh and clean. It's the purest water in the city. Come on. Walk a few paces behind me, trying to make your steps as even as possible. Do not look to right or left, even if somebody speaks to you. Carry the pot in front of you with one hand on each side.' Floronia demonstrates. 'Watch me at all times, but do not speak unless I say something to you.'

They set off along a narrow earthen path worn by generations and from which the roots of trees protrude to trip the unwary. It winds through a copse of olive trees, the Grove of Vesta, to emerge close to the pool beside the temple, which Opimia remembers from her walk with Orrius and her brother to the market. Floronia kneels on the smooth blocks of tufa surrounding the pool.

---

67. A festival celebrated near the winter solstice. Saturn watched over the fertility of the soil. The atmosphere was similar to that of a modern carnival and normal restraint was abandoned. Slaves took the place of their masters for the day.

Chapter Eight

'Don't scoop up the water. Lower the pot into the pool until the rim is level with the surface and then let the water overflow evenly into it. Try not to get anything other than clear water into the pot. If you go back with water that isn't clear you'll probably be told to take it back and try again.'

On the way back to the temple a small child approaches them and says something to Floronia who ignores her. Opimia feels a little sorry for the infant who receives a scolding from her mother for daring to speak to a Vestal. By the time they reach the temple her arms are aching and she is glad to deposit her burden into a basin.

The water fetching done, the two girls have a little time before they must relieve Tuccia at the fire. Floronia hesitates, sizing up Opimia first, before making up her mind.

'Come on, I want to show you something.' She leads the way up the slope of the hill through the trees and along a path no wider than a rabbit run, glancing occasionally behind her to make sure they are not being watched. On each side myrtle bushes grow thickly, mingling with saplings of oak and pine to form an almost impenetrable undergrowth from the foliage of which droplets of morning mist hang like gemstones. Suddenly Floronia veers off and disappears behind some tangled bushes. Gingerly Opimia follows, stooping into a green tunnel formed by the arching branches of two fir trees standing like gateposts beside each other to form a low entrance. They emerge into a small glade enclosed by a natural wall of bushes and trees through which nothing can be seen of the outside world. Spongy moss and grass give way under the girls' feet and their gowns swish against the leggy stalks of dead flowers whose search for the sun is long past. In the centre of this enclave rises a large lump of granite the top of which is smooth and gently concave, so that a person may sit comfortably on it. This morning a pool of water has collected in the dip.

'Do you like it?' Floronia extends her arm in a proprietorial gesture. 'This is my secret place, where I come when Postumia or one of the others is after me for doing something wrong. If it's warm and sunny I sit on the stone and swing my legs in the air. Sometimes I even take off my headdress if it gets too hot.' She glances at Opimia, testing her reaction.

'It's all a bit damp at the moment,' replies Opimia cautiously, conscious of the marks her gown has gathered on their journey up the hill.

'Oh, don't worry again about that.' Floronia divines her thoughts. 'We'll change our dresses as soon as we get back. I get mine washed every day.' She laughs and walks over to the stone to give it a pat. The first rays of the sun are slanting down through the trees to create beams of light which play upon the granite in bars of chiaroscuro. 'He's my friend. He never goes away.'

'Does anybody else know you come here?'

'No, you're the first person I've shown it to. I think the others would stop me if they knew, but I will share it with you, if you like. There's been nobody until you arrived.' Floronia looks up and Opimia catches the appeal in her eyes.

'I like it here. Shall we be friends then, like Livia said?'

'Yes! For ever and ever.' Floronia hugs Opimia and kisses her on the cheek. 'We'd better get back before we're missed.'

Holding hands where the path is wide enough, they descend the hill and enter the house via a side door near the slaves' quarters. Here Floronia instructs a girl to bring fresh gowns to their rooms.

The weeks turn into months. Opimia becomes accustomed to the routine of life as a Vestal. She is not considered old enough to guard the sacred fire through the watches of the night, but every day she must sit by it for at least four hours, usually with Floronia. The girls have got to know each other well, telling stories of their childhood before they became

Chapter Eight

priestesses. Together they attend the festivals in which the Vestals are required to participate, but only to observe and learn the rituals.

'Ten years learning, ten years performing the sacred rites and ten years teaching the novices,' Livia tells Opimia. They are sitting at the fire where Livia is weaving a woollen shawl against the winter nights when duty means the bench in the temple rather than her bed.

'Why is it so important that we learn the form of words for prayers to Vesta and the other gods so perfectly?'

Livia sets down the shawl and rests her eyes on the girl beside her. 'To understand that, my dear, you have to understand the relationship between us Romans and our gods. You see, we mortals need the presence of the gods to whom we look for guidance and assistance. But in return for that help the gods require us to offer something back.'

'Like when a farmer sacrifices a pig, a sheep and a bull?'

'Yes, dear. He does that to propitiate the gods, who in turn, he hopes, will keep his crops free from disease and produce a good harvest.'

'Is it a kind of bargain, then?'

'Well yes, I suppose it can be thought of in that way. We believe that the success of the Republic is dependent on our keeping on good terms with the gods. To do that we must carry out our sacrifices and perform all our rituals meticulously. Otherwise the gods will be offended and punish us.'

'So that's why we have to learn everything so perfectly?'

'Anything that is offered to the gods must be unblemished. That's why, when we sacrifice an animal, only the best are chosen. Nothing less is good enough for the gods; for example, a fine ox which is washed and garlanded before it dies.'

'Postumia told me that a Vestal must conduct herself immaculately at all times.'

'She is right about that. Vestals are chosen as young girls, because then we are pure and without physical blemish. That makes us suitable to serve as priestesses of the goddess. So long as we remain chaste and perform our religious duties with strict accuracy it is said that Rome will remain safe and prosperous. But if we fail in some way, then Rome is put in peril. On us depends the continued existence of the city.'

'What happens if we Romans do something wrong in the eyes of the gods?'

'They will be angry with us. They will say that we have not kept to our part of the contract, so why should they keep to theirs?'

'How will we know when the gods are angry?'

'That can happen in a lot of ways. Perhaps the crops will fail, or an earthquake strikes, or the citizens are struck down by a disease. Then we must propitiate the gods with a sacrifice and make sure that it is performed exactly as it should be. That's what you are learning about now. We do not love our gods or pray to them to make us good. Our theology lies in the knowledge of religious rites and their due performance. The gods reward precise ritual, not good behaviour.'

Opimia is silent, digesting what Livia has said. 'I didn't realise that our conduct was as important as all that.'

'That's the reason behind all your training.' Livia picks up the shawl and resumes her weaving. She smiles at the frown on Opimia's face. 'Don't worry. I felt like that at your age. You'll have your ups and downs, but you'll come through them, just as we all do. We have great privileges you know, as well as our duties. Now, give the casket a poke and riddle down a few of those ashes. Put on a couple more bits of wood and some of that charcoal. Never, never forget the fire.'

In the crackling early-morning light of the Ides of February Floronia and Opimia carry large rush baskets filled with the sacred bread of first wheat flour and boiled salt, which the

Chapter Eight

senior Vestals have made the day before over the temple fire. Ahead of them on the frosty path skirting the slope of the Palatine walk Camilla and the other priestesses, silhouetted against the rising sun. Camilla has urged the girls to tread carefully for fear of spilling their baskets, and to take their time. This does not deter Postumia from turning round occasionally and beckoning them to catch up.

All around, young women, some with children and others without, are making their way in the same direction, towards the southern end of the hill. A few sport green or blue ribbons tied into their hair or round a wrist. The atmosphere is cheerful, broken at intervals by the sound of a trumpet shattering the crystalline air. Where the path turns up towards the top of the hill a small crowd has gathered round a stall set up on a cart, with a brazier next to it. Above the smouldering embers a spit holding two fat capons revolves fitfully. The boy charged with turning the spit is scarcely tall enough and has to jump up to nudge the handle on when it reaches its apogee. His father, perhaps, shouts to attract custom, at the same time deftly slicing strips from the capons or distributing hot sausage.

Camilla begins to ascend the slope at the crest of which the Priest of Mars and his acolytes await her. Beside them, chattering and swinging their arms to keep warm, stand two groups of boys, clad only in flimsy tunics and barefooted. Floronia and Opimia follow the others up the hill, struggling not to slip. Once Opimia trips on a tree root and nearly drops her basket, but Floronia is quick to help her to her feet. Fortunately the older priestesses have their backs turned and do not witness this undignified incident. Reaching the top they find themselves outside a dark recess in the side of the hill. Legend has it that this is the Lupercal, so called because it is where the she-wolf nursed Romulus and Remus after rescuing them from the waters of the Tiber. Scattered about on the slopes below, groups of women wait expectantly.

The Daughters of Cannae

From inside the cave emerges a large brown dog tethered to a leash on which it bites in a vain effort to escape. In the sudden light it bares its teeth to emit a long-drawn-out howl, audible even to the watchmen on the Capena Gate. An acolyte seizes the back of the hound's neck and draws his iron blade swiftly across the animal's throat. It rolls over onto its back, legs flailing the air in the throes of death.

'Why do they kill a dog?' Opimia whispers. She has grown accustomed to the sacrifice of animals and can watch dispassionately.

'I think it's supposed to represent the she-wolf, but I don't see why,' replies Floronia doubtfully.

The silence brought on by the slaughter of the dog is broken by the sound of anxious bleating. Six goats are led forward, each hobbled by one foreleg to the next one. In their agitation to break free they dart this way and that, kicking their hind legs in the air and butting one another. The smell of the dog's blood only serves to increase the terror that infects them. Once again the acolyte's blade performs its lethal work. Swiftly he skins two of the animals and, laying their pelts aside, he cuts the remaining hides into thin strips. His butchery complete, the acolyte hands the dripping blade to the Priest of Mars, who beckons forward the respective leaders of the Fabian and Quintilian boys, dressed in their blue and green colours.

Floronia nudges Opimia and nods towards one of the boys. He is exceptionally handsome, with curly blond hair and the chiselled lips of a woman rather than a boy. 'Good looking, isn't he? I know him, he's called Marcus Claudius.[68]

---

68. This is Marcus Claudius Marcellus who became consul in 196 BC. His father, of the same name, was consul four times and was a leading general in the Second Punic War. The fine on the aedile, Capitolinus, was used by the father to commission some silver libation bowls which he dedicated to the gods.

Chapter Eight

He used to come to our house with his father. There was a scandal about him last year. One of the aediles seduced him. He got fined by the Senate.'

Opimia is not to be outdone. 'My father led the Fabians one year. The skin is still hanging in the atrium at home.'

Floronia, somewhat miffed by this upstaging, sniffs. 'I expect it smells terrible.'

With the flat of his blade the priest smears the forehead of each boy and then, taking a hank of sheep's wool dipped in milk, he wipes away the blood. He nods and the boys, recognising their cue, laugh out loud and run to pick up the two goat skins, which they place round their necks, securing them by the forelegs. The other wolf-boys seize the strips and the race round the hill begins. Shouting and laughing madly they hurtle down the slope, flailing about them with the strips of hide. Young women, anxious to conceive, line the route of the race and stretch out their arms, imploring a wolf-boy to strike them with his strip as he rushes past. In their horns and tails the two leaders resemble the rustic god, Faunus, while their followers race after them to celebrate the approach of spring.

Soon the fastest of the runners have completed the circuit of the hill. Breathless they return to the Lupercal where Floronia and Opimia hold out the baskets for each contestant to take one of the cakes of sacred bread. Marcus Claudius recognises Floronia, despite the headdress. He pauses for a moment. Smiling, she presses another cake into his hand and earns herself a severe rebuke from Postumia.

Lizards bask in the heat of the seventh hour. The girls, too, sunbathe on the stone in their secret glade. Only the humming of bees disturbs the tranquillity of the afternoon. Today marks the end of the Vestalia when the Roman matrons process barefooted to the temple to make homely offerings to the priestesses, who reciprocate with the sacred cake. Floronia and Opimia have swept and cleansed the temple before carrying the sweepings to the Tiber and throwing them into the river.

Floronia has taken off her headdress and tossed it onto the grass. Her white legs, which she has exposed by hitching up her gown, lie across the warm granite surface. She stretches back luxuriously, shielding her eyes from the sun with the sleeve of her gown. Opimia sits upright, her braids still firmly in position and her sandals only just visible beneath the hem of her gown.

'It would be nice to be normal, wouldn't it?'

'What do you mean by that?' Opimia replies, picking up a violet and twirling it round in her fingers.

'Well, like all those matrons who came to the temple for our festival.'

'What, getting married, having children and all that sort of thing?'

'Yes. I mean we're not normal, are we? No other girl in Rome is like us. We're on the edge of things. We don't even have a family to belong to any more. I don't think my parents regard me as a daughter now. Livia says that legally we are quite separate from them. We aren't subject to the power of our fathers, like other unmarried girls.'

'Yes, but we can still see them when we want to. I quite often see my father, especially now he's a praetor.'

'You're lucky. I'm not sure my father knows who I am any more and Mother doesn't seem interested.' Floronia covers her mouth with one hand. Opimia, sensing her friend's upset, leans back to put an arm around her waist and lays her head on Floronia's shoulder. They stay together in this position for some time, until Floronia turns her head to kiss Opimia on the cheek and then sits up.

'I shouldn't complain, should I? Your father's going to Sardinia soon as governor, isn't he?'

'Yes, he'll be off once the elections are over next month. My mother is going with him.' Opimia is kicking the heels of her sandals against the rock. 'I went back to the house a

Chapter Eight

few days ago. A lot of the slaves were depressed. They said the place wasn't the same without me, and now their master and mistress are leaving as well. Orrius, he was my best friend, found the house snake dead under the almond tree.' She pauses, still kicking at the base of the stone. 'Even Phoebe, that's my mother's old maid, has gone blind and says she wants to go back to her old home in Campania.'

The pair sit in silence, each immersed in her own thoughts.

'It's not so bad since you came,' says Floronia eventually. 'I don't feel so alone any more. Sometimes I wanted to kill myself.'

Opimia gives her friend a squeeze. 'Well, at least we've got each other. I suppose we're lucky in some ways. We have good food and live in a fine house with lots of slaves. Not everybody can sit in the best seats at the games or ride through the city in a carriage. Just think, one day you may be Senior Vestal, the most powerful woman in Rome.'

Floronia considers this. 'Yes, and I shall be nearly forty. Who will want to marry me then, after I retire?'

'Marriage isn't everything. You might have been given to a man you hated or died in childbirth, if you weren't a priestess of Vesta.'

'Perhaps you're right,' replies Floronia doubtfully, 'but I might not have minded the chance.'

225 BC

The heat of the summer solstice is subsiding into a roseate dusk. In the Grove of Vesta the thrushes are taking to their perches and the ravens, which habitually linger near the shops during the day in search of titbits, have flapped away to the roof ridges of the Senate House and the temples in the Forum where they align themselves like so many black sentinels. No breeze disturbs the air and the flames of the lamps in the atrium of the Vestals rise so still and straight that they resemble stalagmites of shining amber.

At a table next to the pool Camilla presides over a meal of fish and eggs, but nobody has much appetite and the slaves clear away platters almost untouched. Even the proximity of the pool does nothing to relieve the accumulated heat of the day radiating from the walls. The priestesses sip water and pick at nuts and dates from bowls of sandalwood which the slaves place before each of them.

Camilla moves restlessly in her chair. Her habitual serenity is discomfited by the stifling atmosphere and she longs for the isolation of her room where she can remove her gown and headdress. She rises from her seat.

'I'm afraid, ladies, that I must retire early. This weather is too much for me these days.' She looks round the table. 'You girls are watching the fire tonight, I think. I hope you won't be too uncomfortable. Good night to you all.' Her maid approaches bearing a lamp and together they move slowly away to her room.

'Well, I shall go now too.' Postumia likewise pushes back her chair and calls for a napkin to wipe her hands. She tosses it back to the slave girl who just manages to catch it. 'Are you coming, Livia?'

Livia puts down the goblet, which she has been turning slowly in her hands, a little trick to disguise the twitch she has developed in her fingers since the death of Claudia.

'Oh, I think I'll stay here until Tuccia comes and these two take over the fire. I shan't be able to sleep in this heat in any case.' She smiles weakly. 'Good night, Postumia.' A sharp ear might have detected an element of relief in her voice.

Tuccia appears, sweating and fanning her face with a handkerchief so that the lamps flutter momentarily before resuming their inertia.

'I don't envy you two girls in there tonight. It's unbearably hot even with the door wide open. I've let the fire die down a bit to try to reduce the heat. Mind you keep an eye on it. Don't let it get too low.'

Chapter Eight

'I'm sure they'll be careful,' says Livia reassuringly. 'Why don't you two take a bowl of dates or walnuts in with you? I expect you'll be hungry by the morning.'

'Oh, we shall be all right, shan't we, Opimia? We always seem to have something to talk about. Are you going to relieve us at first light?'

'It's really Postumia's turn, but I've said I would do it for her. She wants to meet her bailiff to discuss some property.'

'That woman is always fussing about her property,' mutters Tuccia.

'Well, I suppose she has a lot of it, mostly tenement blocks on the Aventine, I think.'[69]

A soft night greets Floronia and Opimia as they walk to the temple. Only the glow from the fire penetrates the wall of darkness and silence that envelops them. The moon and stars are concealed by thin cloud, so that their feet are guided to the temple steps not by their eyes but by endless repetition. In the doorway they find a chair where Tuccia has been sitting to catch some cooler air. Inside, the fire has sunk low in the casket but the heat from the grey charcoal still takes their breath away.

'Let's sit outside like Tuccia until the night gets a bit cooler,' suggests Floronia. There is no other chair in the temple, so together they carry out the bench and set it down between two of the columns. Both girls unstrap their sandals and rest their feet on the step to cool. The lamps they have lit inside the temple cast a shaft of yellow smoky light through the open doors, framing their two figures.

For some time they talk of this and that. Opimia has received a letter from her father in Sardinia. He speaks of his journeys through the island, adjudicating on disputes, and the discomfort of travelling by carriage on rough tracks. His soldiers have discovered a pocket of Carthaginians, sailors hiding on the island ever since the

---

69. The Aventine Hill, an area south of the Palatine largely inhabited by plebeians.

end of the war. Lucius has set them to work to build him a pleasure boat in which to circumnavigate his province.

Floronia has been to visit her parents. Her father is now permanently confined to a couch, which the slaves carry from room to room, depending on the time of day. His speech comes in short gasped phrases, which take such an effort that his days are passed in long morose silences from which his wife can no longer rouse him.

The conversation falters as both girls become more drowsy. At last the air grows a little cooler and, slipping on their sandals, they carry the bench back inside. Opimia refills one or two of the lamps which have burnt low while Floronia tosses a log into the casket. A cloud of ash flies up and hovers before slowly subsiding onto the stone floor. They settle themselves on the bench, pushed back against the wall as far from the fire as possible. Somewhere up in the woods on the Palatine an owl hoots. It evokes no answering call.

Opimia watches a tiny plume of smoke curl upwards towards the roof. Its sinuous progress into the shadowy recesses above is mesmeric. She pictures its escape through the chimney, at the start of a never-ending journey to the stars. She is riding on the wisps, floating on a scented sea. She feels Floronia's head resting gently on her shoulder. Her rhythmic breath ushers the meandering wisps higher and higher into the peaceful darkness. Soon both girls are asleep.

From time to time the smouldering fire lets out a crack or shoots a spark into the gloom, dead on arrival in the hearth. The log thrown in by Floronia drops down, to settle in the thick bed of ash that has collected in the bottom of the casket. There its glow is slowly stifled. No nocturnal breeze revives the dying ember, starved of air. The trickle of smoke evaporates into invisibility. The fire of Vesta has gone out.

Floronia awakes, roused by the urgent tugging of Opimia's arm. A chill has invaded the temple. The same thought seizes them. Floronia jumps up to grab the poker

Chapter Eight

with which she frantically riddles the ashes at the bottom of the casket. No spark or comforting glow is generated.

'Quick! In the cupboard, there are some bellows.'

Opimia, in her agitation, stumbles in the semi-darkness. Floronia hisses at her to hurry. She jabs the iron tube between the bars and slaps the leather lungs together. Clouds of ash fly everywhere, sending both girls into a fit of coughing. The casket feels warm to the touch, but of fire there is no sign.

Horrified, the pair stand facing each other. Opimia begins to weep, partly through fright and partly with pain from her foot where she has stubbed her toes. Their gowns are speckled with ash and Floronia's face is streaked with grey. Outside a pearly sky announces the approach of dawn.

'Don't just stand there crying!' Fear sharpens Floronia's words. 'We can relight the fire. Nobody will ever know if we're quick.'

'How?' gulps Opimia.

'Use an oil lamp to light a piece of kindling and build it up from there.'

'But that's against our vows. The fire has to be rekindled from a fresh flame, otherwise it's not pure.'

'There's no time for that.' Floronia snatches a lamp from one of the brackets on the wall. The meagre flame offers little heat. She rummages among the bits of wood laid by the casket to dry out and selects a piece of kindling. 'You blow with the bellows when I say,' she orders Opimia who kneels down beside her.

At the sound of footsteps entering the temple their heads turn guiltily to face the newcomer. Livia needs no telling. She grabs the lamp from Floronia's hand.

'How dare you defile the fire in that way!' Her hands shake as she replaces the lamp in the bracket. She speaks quietly but anger fuels her words. Gone is the gentleness which Opimia has grown used to. 'Stand up, the pair of you. You have betrayed the sacred trust placed in you. Do you realise the seriousness of this?' She does not wait for an answer. 'Not only have you placed the city in danger, you have defied your vows by trying to relight the flame in a way which you know is forbidden. The Chief Priest will have to be informed. What shame this will bring on all of us! Wait there.' With a glare at the two girls as if to fix them to the spot, Livia hurries from the temple, but on the steps she pauses and looks back. 'That floor is a mess. Make sure it's swept before Camilla comes.' Then, in a softer tone, almost as if she regrets her earlier outburst, she shakes her head sadly. 'I'm afraid there's nothing I can do for you now.'

Without speaking the two girls hasten to do as they have been told. When the sweeping is done they stand side by side, neither looking at the other. Opimia tries to put a comforting arm around Floronia's waist, but she moves over towards the door. For a moment Opimia thinks that she is going to run away. Instead Floronia leans morosely against it, her arms folded across her chest, staring into the distance. Suddenly she steps back to stand next to Opimia again. Camilla is advancing rapidly, with Livia a few steps behind, hurrying to keep up.

The Senior Vestal stares for a moment at the lifeless casket. She picks up the poker and begins to stir the ashes distractedly, as if she cannot believe what she is doing, then drops it with a rattle on the floor.

'I suppose you both fell asleep.' Her voice is calm, but resigned. There is no anger in it, unlike Livia's first reaction. 'You must know what a serious matter this is. I have no alternative but to report it to the Chief Priest. He will decide your punishment. It is not a matter for me. Go to your rooms and wait until you are summoned.' Camilla steps aside and motions to the girls to leave. As they do so, Livia whispers to them to make sure they change their gowns before they appear in the Regia.

'This is my fault of course. I should never have allowed them to guard the fire overnight. Postumia was right. They

Chapter Eight

are too young and immature. Claudia would not have made such a mistake.'

'I don't think you should blame yourself like that.' Livia lays a gentle hand on the other's arm. 'They had watched the fire together on several previous occasions. It was the heat last night. Tuccia said she had let the fire burn down low because of it.'

Camilla shakes her head. 'Would you fetch Tuccia and clean out the casket? Then light a new fire when the sun is hot enough. I shall have to escort Floronia and Opimia to the Regia. I fear for them.'

On a bench by the door to the house the two young priestesses sit together in fearful silence. They are clad in fresh gowns, their headdresses neatly secured with new ribbons. Outside, the hustle and bustle of the city proceeds in ignorance of these troubled girls. A squadron of cavalry clatters up the Sacred Way, ordered to escort the censors to the Field of Mars where a lustration[70] of the people is to be held. Meanwhile the Chief Priest has sent a message that all the priestesses of Vesta are to attend upon him at the Regia when he returns from his business at the lustration.

From the Forum a slave makes his way towards the house of the Vestals. Attached to his wrist by a cord, to ensure that he does not lose it and that it is not stolen, hangs a leather pouch. He speaks to the keeper of the door and, after a few words, hands to him a small package taken from the pouch. The slave waits outside, for he may not enter the house. Inside, the door-keeper hands the packet to Floronia without speaking and averts his eyes. She senses what it contains, but with steady fingers she unties the

---

70. A ceremony in which the citizens assembled on the Field of Mars, drawn up in their tribes in military formation. The censors led a pig, a sheep and a bull round the crowd before sacrificing them to the gods. This rite closed the purification (*lustrum*) of the people. The term 'lustrum' came to apply to the five-year period during which the classification of the citizens by the censors remained in force.

bands, which hold two pieces of wood together. A short message is incised on the wax inside. Her father has died of a seizure during the night. Floronia snaps the leaves of wood shut and hands them back to the door slave.

'Tell him there is no reply. I was nothing to him in any case.'

Opimia tries to comfort her, but Floronia roughly removes the consoling arm. She sits motionless for some time, staring at the floor.

'I suppose I loved him once and I suppose he loved me too. He was my father. Then, when I came here, it was as if I had dropped out of his life. That's when he died for me really. Not now.' Her fists clasp the rim of the bench. Opimia weeps for her friend, but Floronia sheds no tears.

'Well, I love you and we shall always stay together. Nothing is going to separate us.' Opimia takes Floronia's hand and holds it tightly. The two girls sit close together, waiting.

In the Forum the consul's herald proclaims the moment of midday. Still nobody summons the priestesses. Heedlessly, slaves pass to and fro on their daily tasks, frightened to look. News that the sacred fire has been allowed to die has spread like a ripple through the slaves and clerks of the house. None has experienced such an event before and they fear the consequences. Who knows what revenge the gods may exact for this default? Meanwhile, nobody wishes to have contact with the perpetrators. When Opimia asks a slave girl to bring some food and water she backs away hastily, pretending not to have heard. In this limbo the girls have lost their priestly status, so that even the slaves do not obey them.

The torpor of late afternoon is broken by the clatter of a carriage on the Sacred Way. Caudinus has returned from the ceremonies on the Field of Mars. He strides into the Regia and orders preparations to be made. A messenger is despatched to the house of the Vestals where Camilla receives instructions that all are to attend before the Chief Priest.

Chapter Eight

Tuccia emerges from her chamber and, head down, comes to stand by the door. She is followed by Livia and Postumia, neither of whom speaks to, or even glances at, the two girls. Finally Camilla appears. Her pale face contrasts with the red rims about her eyes. She addresses the figures huddled together on the bench, the first words spoken to them since they left the temple.

'The Chief Priest has announced that he is ready. You will walk immediately behind us.'

A lictor appears and Camilla signals to him to proceed. In single file the Vestals walk the short distance to the Regia. Guards, helmeted but with swords sheathed, open the gates into a courtyard paved with tufa, where two large bay trees grow. The sound of their dead leaves crunching underfoot accompanies the doleful procession to a wooden portico on the steps of which two acolytes wait. They push open double doors and step aside, lowering their heads in recognition of the Senior Vestal. Camilla makes no acknowledgement.

Inside the chamber Camilla and Postumia walk to one side of a dais while Livia and Tuccia stand opposite them. Camilla motions to Floronia and Opimia to remain where they are, facing the dais on which stands a large wooden chair. This central chamber is lit by two windows in the rear wall through which can be seen a garden dotted with cypress trees and an ancient bronze statue of King Numa clasping a sceptre. To one side of the chamber lies the shrine of Mars, where the shields of the Salic priests and the sacred lances are stored.[71] On the other, a narrow door gives access to another shrine, that of Ops Consiva, the goddess of plenty, which only the Chief Priest and the Vestals may enter. Opimia and Floronia, however, see none of these things. They stand with heads bowed, still and

---

71. The Salii were a priestly college founded, according to legend, by King Numa. They performed war dances in honour of Mars. The lances kept in the shrine were said to shake at the outbreak of war.

The Daughters of Cannae

silent. The older Vestals, too, wait in solemn silence, their faces uniformly expressionless, eyes staring blankly and hands inert at their sides. Above, the empty chair poses an unspoken threat.

The shuffle of sandals intrudes upon this motionless and wordless congregation. From the inner recesses the lean figure of Caudinus emerges. He pauses at the foot of the dais, nods to each pair of Vestals on either side and then takes his seat in the chair. With his right hand he drapes part of his gown over his head in the manner of a priest about to sacrifice. In his left hand he clasps a flat iron knife, the symbol of his office. He surveys the two girls in front of him coldly.

'So, Chief Vestal, let me have your report.' He speaks in the same flat tone with which he addressed the citizens from the Rostra at the funeral of Claudia.

Camilla takes half a step forward and briefly recounts the events of the previous night. She speaks hesitantly, as if the words escape unwillingly from her lips. Once or twice Caudinus asks her to speak up and a trace of irritation crosses that bland face. Camilla finishes her report by apologising, seeking to lay the blame upon herself, reiterating the ages of the girls and their comparative inexperience.

'You say that the matter was not reported immediately, but that the Vestal Livia found the offenders trying to relight the fire with an oil lamp. That seems to me to compound the crime.'

Camilla stands silent, her head bent forward and hands clasped together in an attitude of supplication.

'I take it you agree?' Caudinus's words cut through the air.

'I can only plead their inexperience, sir.'

'For which, of course, you are responsible. In any event that act is directly contrary to their vows. The fire must never be relit except by the sun and fresh soft wood ground until it smoulders. They knew that the flame must be pure and sacred, unadulterated?'

Chapter Eight

'They were taught this from the beginning. Every Vestal knows that the purity of the flame is vital to the safety of the city.'

Caudinus turns the flat knife over and over in his hand. The Vestals stand like statues, terrified to interrupt his thoughts by even the slightest movement. At last, directing his gaze at some point behind and above Floronia and Opimia and seemingly oblivious of his audience, he begins to speak.

'Our peace with the gods depends upon the conduct of our priests and priestesses and the strict observance of ritual. This is never so important as in the case of the Vestals, upon whom is placed the responsibility for the safety and wellbeing of the city, their foremost duty being the maintenance of the sacred fire in the temple of the goddess. That duty was neglected last night in the most shameful way and it may well be that the gods will see fit to punish the citizens of Rome for this grievous default.' Caudinus pauses, searching for words. For the first time since he entered the Regia he looks straight at Floronia and Opimia. 'I know your fathers well. Indeed I was instrumental in the induction of both of you into the Vestal order. It is therefore especially painful to me that you stand here today in such a state of dishonour. The Chief Vestal has spoken of your youth and inexperience, but this cannot absolve you from the ignominy which you have brought upon your priesthood and the danger to which you have exposed the city. It is my duty to sentence you to five lashes each, which I hope will be accepted by the gods as sufficient atonement for your crime.'

Opimia gasps but then clenches her teeth. Floronia looks up and stares stonily in front of her. Her mind retreats from her body, to float somewhere above her head. The only way she can escape the pain of the previous night and day is to inhabit a space from which all feeling is severed. She no longer senses Opimia beside her. Her Vestal gown and headdress are mentally divested. She is naked and alone, divorced from her family, from the priesthood and from Rome. She is nobody: neither of the class of Roman matrons nor of her virgins.

Caudinus taps his knife on the armrest of his chair. The two acolytes who admitted the Vestals to the Regia reappear. They carry with them an upright triangular frame of wood which they set up in front of the dais. Attached to the uprights on each side of the frame cords hang, roughly at shoulder height.

'Proceed!' Caudinus raps out the word. 'The younger priestess first.'

The two acolytes advance upon Opimia. She offers no resistance as they seize her arms and march her to the frame. Here they pause, awaiting further instructions. Caudinus is not slow with these.

'Pull down the gown to her waist and attach her wrists to the frame.'

Camilla's hands fly up to cover her eyes. Next to her Postumia nods. Tuccia takes a step back at the horror of a priestess being so defiled and Livia turns away her face.

'I require you to remain exactly where you are and to observe the punishment, which is partly yours as well.' Caudinus's voice rings out starkly like a military order. He steps down from the dais and takes from one of the acolytes a bunch of withies secured by an iron hoop to which is attached a wooden handle.

Opimia's slight figure, pale and with the vertebrae of her backbone protruding, rests against the crossbar of the frame on which her arms are stretched out as in a crucifixion. Her wrists are tied so tightly to the bars that her fingers begin to grow numb. She bites the crosspiece to stifle the sobs provoked by the shame of her body's exposure. Her feet hang above the floor.

Caudinus steps forward and with both hands he brings the withies smashing down on Opimia's bare back. Four more times he repeats the strike, each blow leaving fresh

Chapter Eight

stripes of raw pink on the white flesh. Each time Opimia convulses, but she makes no sound. Cuts litter her back where the sharp twigs have penetrated the skin and rivulets of blood trickle down to soak into the gown forced onto her buttocks.

'Release her.' Caudinus turns away and the two acolytes untie the cords. Half senseless, Opimia slides down the frame and crumples on the floor. Livia hurries forward, raises her to her feet and gently replaces the gown. With Livia and Tuccia supporting her, Opimia is told to stand and watch while the same punishment is administered to Floronia. Before the acolytes can reach her she rips off the bodice of her gown, revealing the firm breasts of a young woman. She stands defiantly for a moment until her arms are seized and she is tied to the frame.

Once again the lashes rain down upon the naked torso of a Vestal Virgin. It seems that Caudinus strikes even harder, incensed by Floronia's own baring of her body. She does not stir under the blows and when it is over she walks unaided from the frame. Camilla attempts to help her with her gown but Floronia brushes her aside. Red stains seep through as she eases the gown over the torn flesh.

Caudinus strides from the chamber without a word, followed by his acolytes, leaving the Vestals alone in the Regia. Outside, the afternoon sun is still bright and Camilla is concerned.

'We cannot have these two exposed to the sight of the people in this condition.' A firmer tone has returned to her voice. 'Tuccia, I'd be grateful if you would fetch two large shawls from the house and send for a closed litter for Opimia. She is in no fit state to walk.'

'I can walk. If Floronia can do it, so can I. In any case, he did not beat our legs. I want to walk with her.' Opimia moves towards Floronia who recoils at Opimia's approach and insists on walking by herself.

The Daughters of Cannae

That night Livia washes and bathes Opimia's cuts. A little unguent of pine oil should serve to stave off any infection. While Livia tends her back, Opimia tells her of the death of Floronia's father.

'She is a troubled child. I'm glad she has a friend in you, even though her behaviour is distant at times. I noticed how she backed way from you this evening.'

'Oh, I shan't take offence at that. She feels that the world is against her at the moment and even though I'm a friend, I'm still part of that world. She needs our support but she resents it at the same time.'

Livia smiles. 'For such a young girl, you have a very understanding mind.' She rubs in a little more oil and then draws a muslin sheet across Opimia's back. 'There, you will have to sleep on your stomach tonight and perhaps for a few more.'

'Thank you. I'm sure I shall soon be better.' Livia moves quietly about the little room, laying out a clean gown and bands for the morning. Opimia turns her head and holds out her hand to the older woman. 'I'm glad we were beaten. We deserved it for putting Rome in danger.'

'Best to forget it now. I'm sure that the gods will forgive you. Good night.'

In the temple Camilla is bent over the fire. With the wrist of her left hand she holds the palm of her right hand over a burning ember. The skin singes and turns an ugly brown. Still she holds it there, weeping with the pain. Some of the skin has burnt away before Tuccia arrives to take over the night watch. She finds Camilla slumped on the bench by the wall, clutching her hand in the folds of her gown. With difficulty she prises the hand free.

'You've done this deliberately, haven't you, with the flame from a lamp?'

Camilla shakes her head slowly, but then nods. 'No, over the fire. I had to do it. I had to punish myself. Those girls

Chapter Eight

can't take all the blame. I must accept responsbility as well, if the gods are to be appeased. It's our duty, isn't it?'

Tuccia stoops to kiss Camilla on her forehead before hastening into the house to fetch bandages and more pine oil.

Chapter Nine

217 BC

It is early summer, a time when the weather in the city is at its most benign. Yet the mood of the citizens is one of anxiety. It hangs like a pall over people and buildings alike. The last few months have witnessed a series of strange events, evil omens perhaps. In the cattle market an ox escaped from a pen, mounted two flights of steps to the second floor of an apartment block and, being frightened by the screams and shouts of the tenants, threw itself from a window. In the vegetable market the temple of Hope has been struck by lightning and cracks have appeared in two of its columns. It is said that in Cisalpine Gaul[72] a wolf pulled the sword from the sheath of a sentry and ran off with it.

These disturbing events, however, do not occupy the minds of Romans so much as the arrival of Hannibal and his army in northern Italy. He has won a battle at the River Trebia, a tributary of the Po, and has begun his advance southwards through Etruria. If the Alps and Publius Scipio[73] cannot stop this man, who can? Hopes are pinned on the new consuls, Gaius Flaminius and Gnaeus Servilius, who have gone north with their armies.

---

72. That part of Gaul between the River Po and the Alps.
73. Scipio the elder, father of Scipio Africanus, the eventual victor over Hannibal at Zama in 202 BC.

Chapter Nine

There have been changes in the house of the Vestals. Camilla retired three years ago and now lives in a small house on the Capitoline Hill, with only two freedwomen and a female slave to care for her. Her right hand is so deformed that she can no loner use it. The fingers have grown into the palm where it was burnt, so that the hand is permanently shaped like a fist. She wears a glove to disguise it. Postumia has assumed the office of Chief Vestal and, having achieved her ill-disguised ambition, makes herself less unpleasant. Livia has grown rather scatterbrained with advancing years, but enjoys looking after the new Vestal, Licinia, who is just eleven. Tuccia never changes, though she has put on weight and lost the looks that once nearly got her into trouble.

In the temple Opimia is waiting by the fire. Little Licinia sits with her, too young to be left in charge. Opimia cannot help feeling a trifle irritated. Floronia was supposed to relieve her at the end of the fourth hour and it is already well past that. This has become a regular occurrence since Floronia was appointed Vestal in charge of the shrine of Ops Consiva, the goddess of plenty, in the Regia. Hardly a day passes without Floronia spending at least two hours over in the Regia and Opimia sometimes wonders what can detain her for so long. She once asked Floronia about it, but had her head snapped off and does not dare to pry further. Despite Opimia's efforts to preserve their friendship they have grown a little apart in the last year or two.

At last Floronia arrives with mumbled apologies. She does not look Opimia in the face and speaks roughly to Licinia. Discomfited, Opimia hurries to her carriage. Soon afterwards she enters her father's house on the slopes of the Esquiline. These visits are becoming more and more frequent. Although her mother and she pretend otherwise, both know that Lucius is dying. It is the old wound in his arm, the Punic arrow at Lilybaeum all those years ago. Somehow it has become infected again and the bad blood, so Philistion says, is spreading through the rest of his body. Some months ago a sore appeared on one of his cheeks. It refuses to heal and it too is spreading slowly, so that it reaches now below the jawbone. The flesh has become necrotic and Opimia cannot help noticing a smell when she enters her father's room. She forces herself to stoop to kiss him on the other cheek and talks as cheerfully as she can. Yet these are sombre times. It is hard to look happy when your father is dying before your very eyes and your oldest friend seems to have abandoned you. Naevia is stoical. Only in the privacy of her own room does she weep for her husband's suffering. Philistion attends every day to apply oil of sesame, intended to soothe the wounds and relieve the pain. His optimistic words do not deceive. The expression on his face tells all to Lucius's wife and daughter.

Opimia goes into the peristyle to hide her tears. Through the arch at the far end she glimpses the bent fgure of Orrius in the kitchen garden. She tiptoes forward across the gravel. She need not worry, for he has grown very deaf. She watches him scratching at the rich black Campanian soil as he hoes his radishes and lettuces. There is a regularity and dignity about his movements. His mind is far removed from the troubles that afflict the city. He appears perfectly at peace with his environment and Opimia envies his serenity. It seems a shame to interrupt her old friend, yet she cannot leave without speaking to him. Stepping forward, she taps him lightly on the shoulder. Unhurriedly he turns and the familiar smile spreads like a gentle ripple across his face. Without speaking he rests his hoe against the almond tree, arrayed in pink-and-white blossom, and pulls a heavy iron knife from his belt. From the pergola he carefully selects six of the dark red roses which he ties together with the tendril of a vine. Already bent with age and the constant tending of his vegetables he bows still further to present the bouquet to Opimia. She kisses the thinning hair on his head and pats his hand to thank him.

Chapter Nine

On her way back to the Forum her carriage is surrounded by people all hurrying in the same direction. Many of the women are weeping and holding their arms upwards to the sky in gestures of supplication. Nobody takes notice of her carriage or attempts to make way for it. Her driver stops to make inquiries. The only firm news is that some disaster has occurred. Reaching the Comitium she finds a throng of people gathered outside the Senate House. They are shouting for a magistrate to give them firm information. At length the City Praetor, Marcus Pomponius, emerges from the Senate House to make his way to the Rostra. Despite his lictors, who try to clear a path, several of the women clutch at his toga before he can reach the platform. Somewhere a military horn sounds and the crowd falls silent, all eyes fixed upon Pomponius. His news is short and bad. A single cavalryman has reached the city to report that a great battle has taken place near Lake Trasimene, followed by an earthquake in the same area. The consul Flaminius is dead and most of his army destroyed. The mothers, wives and daughters of men in the consul's legions set up a wailing lamentation. They beat their breasts and tear at their hair and clothing, all fearful that they have lost a husband, son or father.

Opimia is also worried by the news. Her brother, Gaius, has been serving with the legions in the north. Is he with the army of Flaminius or with the other army of Servilius? She is not sure. Her mind is flooded with troubles as she enters the Vestals' house, ignoring a slave who raises a sponge to wash her feet and then lowers it again. She must be alone. She gulps for air on the hillside and hurries up the narrow path. The fronds and brambles in the green tunnel threaten to entangle her as she pushes her way forward anxiously. Somewhere in front the bushes rustle, probably an animal disturbed by her approach. The glade opens up and she stumbles over to the comfort of the stone surrounded by flattened grass which, in her unhappy state, she does not notice. The events of the day have so fatigued her that for several moments she leans motionless against it, recovering her breath. The tears flow freely until at length they have their own calming effect and she can begin to think clearly again. It is inevitable that her father will die. She must accept that, like any other child. And Gaius? Perhaps he has survived the battle, if he was there. But Rome. What of Rome, so assailed by evil portents and disasters? Something must be wrong. Has Hannibal been sent to destroy the city because its citizens have offended the gods in some way? It seems so to Opimia.

During the days which follow the announcement by Pomponius the streets of the city are strangely deserted. Even the cattle and vegetable markets lack the usual shouts of the traders and the bellowings of the beasts. The buildings of the Forum and the shops lining the square assume an air of desolation. The women of Rome, matrons and virgins alike, together with men too old and boys too young, are congregated on the Field of Mars. They light fires and pitch tents to avoid going home at night. A mixture of hope and fear infects them. From time to time a lone figure, or perhaps two or three together, appear in the distance, limping back towards the city from the north. They carry no weapons; some are wounded and all have tattered clothing. One man tells how he survived by wading into the lake and ducking beneath the floating corpse of a fellow legionary whenever the Punic cavalry came splashing about on their horses to finish off survivors. A matron sees somebody whom she thinks is her son. She rushes forward to clasp him to her bosom and then with a shriek thrusts him away, beating him on the chest with her fists when she realises her mistake. He has no strength to resist. One or two have hidden in the reeds at the edge of the water and then escaped by night. In a few days the trickle of survivors dries up. One by one the tents are struck and the fires go out. The citizens return within the walls, mourning their menfolk and fearful for the future.

Chapter Nine

The days pass painfully for Opimia. One morning she receives a message that Creto, her father's old body slave, is at the door. She prepares herself for bad news but is greeted by a beaming face. Gaius has returned home, having survived the battle at Lake Trasimene. Midsummer is a quiet time for the Vestals. There are few state religious festivals which require their presence. Opimia hurries to the house on the Esquiline where she finds her brother in company with another survivor, Publius Lentulus. Her father, overjoyed, has risen from his bed and the three of them are sitting in the peristyle under the shade of an awning. The cook has produced sow's paunch garnished with asparagus and mushrooms picked by Orrius from the garden. The two young men are tucking in voraciously.

Gaius talks about their escape. 'We were riding with the leading maniples,[74] right up in the van of the column. It was a bit misty, especially down towards the lake. You couldn't see a lot. Suddenly there was this great hubbub from behind. Men seemed to be running everywhere and we could hear shouts up above, in the hills to our left. Javelins and darts started to rain down on us and we realised we had been ambushed.' Gaius pauses to help himself to some more meat, held out for him by Naevia who is smiling for the first time in many days.

'Then the ground shook under our feet. That was almost more frightening than the attack. My horse reared and nearly threw me.' Lentulus speaks quietly. He is a tall man, square jawed beneath a head covered in tight chestnut curls. His eyes are of the same colour. The clean tunic, lent to him by Gaius after they had bathed and been shaved by Creto, reveals muscular arms and large hands, one of which bears a fresh scar on the back where a Punic dart struck him a glancing blow.

---

[74]. At this time a legion consisted of about 4,200 men divided into ten equal units known as maniples.

'We realised we had been trapped in the defile between the hills and the lake,' says Gaius, continuing. 'There was only one thing to do; try to fight our way out, which meant climbing the slope in front of us. At first we made good progress. The men scrambled upwards, keeping their shields above their heads to ward off the darts coming out of the mist. Then we hit the Libyans posted on top of the ridge, waiting for us. Some of the men turned to run back down the slope, but Lentulus here shouted at them to hold their ground.'

'You played your part in rallying the men as well. I saw you seize one of the standards from a bearer and hold it up, asking the men if they were going to allow it to be captured,' Lentulus interrupts. 'Your son was very brave. You would have been proud of him,' he continues, turning to Lucius whose disfigured face contorts into a smile. 'If it had not been for Gaius, I believe the legionaries would have fled back down the hill and been swallowed up in the general carnage by the lake.'

'Lentulus is kind but exaggerates. Anyway, the men steadied and drew their swords. It was grim work, hacking our way through. Even though they had the advantage of being above us, the Libyans eventually pulled back. Desperation gave us the edge in the end. Our weapons were superior and we kept our discipline.'

'I think a lot of them were still tired and ill from the march through the swamps in Etruria. We captured a few who looked as though they had scurvy. When we finally reached the level ground most of them just turned and fled. We were too exhausted to go after them.' Lentulus takes a couple of fat figs from the bowl in front of him.

'So what happened to those of you who fought your way out of the trap?' asks Lucius. 'Very few made it back to Rome.'

'We couldn't stay on the ridge in case Hannibal's men came after us, so we just started marching again. Somehow the men kept going all day, but it was slow progress. The

Chapter Nine

legionaries were shattered and many of them were carrying wounds. That night we pitched a camp and posted sentries. In the morning all seemed quiet when we set out. Suddenly the Carthaginian cavalry rode up and surrounded our men. I think they must have got ahead of us during the night and waited for us to strike camp. Lentulus and I had gone back to see if we were being pursued, so they missed us. We rode away with three other men from an allied cavalry squadron and reached Spoletium. At first the guards wouldn't open the gates. They thought we were scouts from Hannibal's army. They let us in eventually and we rested there for a couple of days. The citizens were very frightened and asked us to ride to Rome requesting help. They gave us fresh horses for the journey through the Sabine mountains.'

'We heard that Hannibal did knock at the gates of Spoletium and demand the surrender of the town, but the citizens refused. It seems he turned away eastward towards the coastal plain, looking for grazing for his pack animals and to allow his men time to recover.'

'I think you're right, sir,' replies Lentulus. 'I don't believe Hannibal will attack Rome, at least for the time being. He's recruited some Gallic tribesmen since he crossed the Alps but he's still lost a lot of his original troops and they need time to recuperate.'

Lentulus and Gaius continue to talk after Lucius retires to his room to rest. The need now is to find an experienced general to oppose Hannibal. Both men are anxious to return to the legions, but under the command of somebody who will not be led by the nose like Flaminius. Lentulus, in particular, is ashamed that they rode away instead of returning to face the Punic cavalry. Gaius points out that it would have been a futile gesture, certain death or capture for no purpose. At least they have lived to fight again.

Opimia sits listening to their conversation. Lentulus turns frequently to her, asking about the atmosphere in the city and who she thinks may be the next consuls.

The Daughters of Cannae

A class war is stirring between the people and the patricians, something that often occurs when the city is in trouble. The tribunes rouse the people in the Comitium with speeches accusing the patricians of producing incompetent leaders while the countryside is ravaged by some African interloper commanding nothing but a ragged band of ruffians. The senators themselves appear divided between the conservatives led by Fabius and the populists who curry favour with the plebeians.

Opimia finds herself enjoying the conversation. The views of real soldiers are interesting and, truth to tell, the fresh company is stimulating after the stifling atmosphere recently in the Vestals' house and the antipathy shown towards her by Floronia these days. She has no close friends now. Without realising it, she has become rather lonely. Her brother and Lentulus recount rough tales of life serving in the legions. Wine loosens their tongues and occasionally they apologise for their language. Opimia laughs at their jokes. She will be twenty-one years old in a few months. It's such a change from the cloistered life of a Vestal. She has not felt so relaxed for a long time.

Lentulus senses but cannot see the blonde hair beneath the headdress. When Opimia laughs she has an engaging way of throwing back her head a little, so that her breasts rise tantalisingly. He cannot help observing this. Her face reminds him of his mother, long since dead, with the pale blue eyes and a tiny dimple on her chin. He feels an urge to touch her, at least to stroke the delicate hands resting demurely in her lap. Surely a Vestal should not look as beautiful as this? She stands to pass a plate of honeyed almonds. The sweet smell of her body close to his is almost overpowering. It is all he can do to restrain himself from leaning forward to kiss her hand. She is a Vestal, he tells himself. She is sacrosanct, untouchable.

Opimia is not unaware of the effect that she is having on the young man next to her. She had intended to return to

Chapter Nine

the house under the Palatine some hours ago. On the other hand there is no need to go. No duties await her until the sun has set and the night watches begin. It is pleasant to sit here in the shade, in her old family home and in the company of amusing men. She feels Lentulus's gaze resting upon her. Why not stay a little longer?

The evening shadows are creeping across the peristyle when he rises to take his leave. He has no real home to go to, for both his parents died some years ago. He resides with an aged aunt, Livilla, in a large house by the Quirinal Gate. Naevia emerges from sitting with Lucius. Lentulus bows to kiss her hand. Opimia wishes that he would do the same to her, even though her status precludes any such gesture. Instead he turns, smiles and holds out both arms in a barely perceptible shrug.

'I had heard so much about you from Gaius, but I had no idea what a pleasure it would be to meet you. I hope it will be the first of many times.' He smiles again, turns to clasp Gaius firmly round the shoulders and strides away, his light cloak trailing behind him.

Naevia, who has a woman's sense for these things, sits down by her daughter. 'You certainly made an impression there, dear. Do be careful; you can't encourage him.'

Opimia suppresses a mild feeling of irritation provoked by her mother's remark. 'Oh, don't worry, Mother. I know my position and I'm sure he understands.'

That night, by the fire in the temple, she practises on the lyre her mother has given her to help while away the hours. She remembers the story of Arion, from the Greek island of Lesbos, who played so beautifully. His patron, the tyrant of Corinth, a man called Periander, was persuaded to allow Arion to visit Taenarus in Sicily to compete in a music festival. There he won all the prizes of gold and many gifts were bestowed on him. But on the voyage back to Corinth the sailors on his boat became jealous. 'You are too rich,' said their captain. 'You must die.' Arion pleaded for his life and offered to hand over all his winnings. The captain, however, refused, saying that Arion would renege on his promise as soon as they reached Corinth. Thereupon, Arion asked if he might sing one last song and, when he had finished, he leapt into the sea. Swimming beside the ship was a school of dolphins who had been enchanted by Arion's voice and the sweet notes of his lyre. Carrying him on their backs, the dolphins reached Corinth some days before the boat and deposited Arion safely on the shore. Periander, who knew that his favourite had already returned, asked the ship's captain for news of the young man and, on being told that Arion had been delayed at Taenarus by the hospitality of its citizens, had the whole crew executed on the spot.

In the morning Opimia retires to her room to rest after the night's vigil. Sleep comes quickly. She is riding on the back of a dolphin with her arms clasped around Lentulus. They plunge into the warm waves, then soar momentarily above them. He laughs aloud at the spray and the plumes of water that engulf them. The moon rises, but still the dolphin surges forward in a never-ending rhythm. Droplets of salt from the sea glisten phosphorescently on Lentulus's body, so that he resembles some jewelled god. She surrenders herself to the exhilaration of the journey.

The return of Gaius has produced a temporary improvement in the condition of Lucius. Each morning he takes a shambling walk in the peristyle, supported by Naevia on one side and by Creto on the other. Unfortunately the improvement is short-lived and in a matter of days he is once again too weak to rise from his bed. Opimia comes to visit every day. Gaius is usually there and often Lentulus as well. They are both at somewhat of a loose end. Soon fresh legions will have to be recruited for the defence of the city. Meanwhile there is little to do. They spend many hours at the house where Opimia often joins them. As she rides through the streets towards her old

Chapter Nine

home she cannot help herself from hoping that Lentulus will be there. When he is not, she tries to banish the tinge of disappointment. She chides herself that she ought only to think of her sinking father.

One day she arrives to find that they have been joined by another, younger man. He seems little more than a youth whose first cutting of the beard has yet to take place.[75] Yet this casually dressed fellow, with hair down to his shoulders and a languid air about him, exudes an aura of authority. When he speaks he appears often to imply that his remarks emanate from advice that he has received from the gods. He slouches in his chair, so that one might suppose him to be disposed to idleness and pleasure, but these are merely the physical attributes of youth. The mind is sharp and percipient.

'Who is that boy with Gaius and Lentulus?' asks Opimia as she and her mother leave Lucius sleeping in his room.

'Oh, that's young Publius Scipio, the son of last year's consul. He's a bit of a hero apparently.'

'What has he done?'

'His father was badly wounded in a skirmish with Hannibal's troops soon after they reached Italy, near a river called the Ticinus, or some such. The consul was surrounded by enemy cavalry and it looked as if he would be killed. Young Publius, there, saw the danger and shouted to his squadron to ride to the rescue. When they hesitated to follow him he rode into the enemy by himself. His men were ashamed of themselves and went after him. Somehow Publius extricated his father who offered him the civic crown,[76] but the boy refused, saying that he had only done his filial duty.

---

75. The occasion of a religious ceremony in ancient Rome. Aristocrats might preserve the shavings in a casket. The emperor Nero had the hairs of his first shaving sacrificed in a golden casket offered to Capitoline Jupiter.
76. The *'corona civica'*, Rome's highest award for valour, given for saving the life of a fellow citizen in battle.

The Daughters of Cannae

When Opimia joins them, the discussion is about strategy. Scipio believes that his father was right. Caution must be the watchword. Do not give Hannibal the chance of easy victories against inexperienced troops commanded by naïve generals. Let our raw recruits learn the arts of war before they offer battle. We have an inexhaustible supply of men and arms. Hannibal roams in alien territory, with no ready source from which to recruit. Africa is a long way off and Spain will be isolated when Scipio's father and uncle begin their campaigns beyond the Ebro.

Opimia watches. Occasionally her eyes meet Lentulus's. He has turned his chair to face hers. He speaks of his anxiety to return to the field. 'The African has taken himself off towards the Adriatic coast. He has given us a breathing space. We must use it wisely, as Scipio says, to recruit and train new legions. When the time comes, I hope to be appointed a junior military tribune. Gaius wants the same. I think we stand a good chance. There aren't so many candidates now,' he adds ruefully. 'Meanwhile, it's very pleasant to be in Rome, see old friends and meet new ones. I shall miss these afternoons spent here.' He pauses and looks away for a moment, sensing that perhaps he has said too much. Opimia examines her hands, trying to show no reaction, despite the implication of his words. A little too quickly he changes the subject. 'Let's hope that your father will soon take a turn for the better.'

'I'm afraid there's no hope of that. Philistion says his condition is incurable. All we can do is make his last days as comfortable as possible.'

'He has been a brave man. He did not run away to save his life at Lilybaeum. I still feel ashamed that we rode off and left those men to be captured.'

Opimia leans forward in her chair. 'Gaius says that you fought brilliantly in the ambush and that without your leadership the legionaries would never have reached the ridge. That's something to be proud of, not ashamed. It is

Chapter Nine

no cowardice to escape to fight again.' Involuntarily she pats his arm.

The praetors keep the Senate in session from sunrise to sunset over the course of several days. The fathers of the state debate what is to be done for the safety of the Republic, who should be the new leader and what fresh forces are to be levied. Quintus Fabius rises to speak.

'Fellow senators, we have listened to many criticisms of our generals in the conduct of the campaign since Hannibal invaded our country. From the reports we have received, it is clear that on the River Trebia Sempronius allowed himself to be provoked into battle and then tricked into an ambush. Flaminius was guilty of gross negligence in failing to reconnoitre the dispositions of the enemy at Lake Trasimene. Our generals have made shocking mistakes.

'But, gentlemen,' Fabius pauses to gaze sternly round the tiered circles of wooden benches, 'I suggest that much greater failings have taken place here in Rome. You look mystified. I am not surprised, for it is not only the common people but this House as well, who have neglected our duties to the gods. Consider what happened when the wretched Flaminius was elected consul. What did he do, but hurry from the city without even taking the auspices, believing that we would contrive to find them unfavourable and delay his departure? Has a consul ever before embarked upon his year of office without mounting the Capitol to give solemn vows to Jupiter? Which consul, gentlemen, has not first proclaimed the Latin festival and climbed the Alban Mount for the annual sacrifice? Flaminius neglected all these sacred rites, which, from our earliest days, have been performed for the satisfaction of the gods. Instead he slunk away, unaccompanied by lictors and not bothering to don his general's cloak, like some common criminal. Are you aware, members of the Senate, many of you former consuls yourselves, that this man assumed his robe of office in a wayside inn outside Ariminum?

The Daughters of Cannae

'You will justly point out that the miserable fellow was summoned back to the city to perform all these neglected offices. He refused and in any event it was too late. The gods had been sorely abused. Even before Flaminius set out on his ill-fated pursuit of the African, they gave us a sign of their displeasure. When the consul mounted his horse it reared up immediately, so that he was thrown from it. Worse still, one of the legionary standards could not be pulled from the ground when they struck camp.

'Gentlemen, the gods have been grossly offended by these failures to observe the traditional rituals. Until we offer adequate sacrifices by way of propitiation, the affairs of Rome will go badly, perhaps even so far as the destruction of the Republic.'

Fabius sits down. His audience are silent for some moments. This is not what they had been expecting: a tirade against the generals, a bid for the leadership perhaps, but not all this about the neglect of the gods.

A man pipes up from the crowd of citizens gathered at the doors of the Senate House, where they have been listening to the debate. 'I respectfully agree, Quintus Fabius. A laxity has developed in our observation of religious rites. The gods will not forgive us if no action is taken to rectify matters.' His words provoke a general murmur of support from the other onlookers.

Gaius Catulus, never slow to incense the common people, but a recent consul with a right to speak early in any debate, is called by Pomponius. He surveys the House from above his beaky nose.

'We have listened with interest,' he manages to convey that he knew it all along, 'to what the noble Fabius has said and many of us have been aware of these failings.' He sniffs and, turning towards the doorway, adds, 'This House was always bitterly opposed to the election of Flaminius as consul. Now we are reaping the rewards of the people's folly.' A howl goes up from the mob, some of whom

Chapter Nine

threaten to invade the Senate House and are only restrained by the spears of the guards stretched hastily across the entrance. Catulus is pulled down by his neighbour and Pomponius shouts for order as everybody begins to talk at once.

'Gentlemen,' cries the praetor, 'we are not here to debate the merits of Flaminius's election, but to consider what is to be done to save the state. Perhaps, Quintus Fabius, you would care to advise on the course of action you recommend to propitiate the gods.'

'Willingly, gentlemen. I propose that the Board of Ten be instructed to consult the Sibylline Books[77] and that whatever advice is found there should be followed to the letter.'

Pomponius puts the motion to the House, which passes it unanimously. By sunset the people, gathered in the Comitium and in the absence of a consul to appoint a dictator, have elected Fabius acting dictator by acclamation. In addition they approve Marcus Minucius Rufus to be his Master of Horse.[78]

The act of electing a dictator invigorates the citizens. They are roused from the torpor induced by the prospect of inevitable defeat and death. Fabius gives instructions for the defences of the city to be strengthened. The old wall, neglected for many years when there was no prospect of assault, crawls with masons. Pulleys haul fresh blocks of granite into position to repair the battlements. The city rings to the sound of armourers beating out the blades of swords

---

77. According to Roman legend the Sibylline Books were purchased by the last king of Rome, Tarquinius, from the sibyl at Cumae, not far from Naples. A sibyl was a prophetess. The Books were stored in a vault beneath the temple of Jupiter on the Capitol. The Board of Ten, normally ex-consuls or ex-praetors, were appointed to look after them and to keep their contents secret. The Books were consulted at times of crisis. The oracles themselves, written in Greek hexameters, were not communicated to the people, only the religious observances necessary to avert calamities and to appease the gods.
78. A dictator's second in command.

The Daughters of Cannae

and spearheads. From the Naevian Gate riders gallop their horses on their way to summon assistance under treaties with the towns of Latium: Ardea, Antium, Circeii, Tarracina and Veii. A posse of horsemen clatter through the Colline Gate en route to Umbria: to brave Spoletium with a request for cavalry, then north to Arretium and Ariminum. The guards stand back as another troop hurry through the Capena Gate, heading down the Appian Way for Capua and Beneventum. Others will penetrate deep into the south of the country, to Tarentum in Apulia, even as far as Locri and Rhegium in Bruttium. Rome needs cavalry, money and weapons. The allies will not fail them. Fabius inspires the city with a sense of purpose once more.

Gaius and Lentulus spend their days on the Field of Mars. As they had hoped, both have been appointed junior military tribunes. They and their colleagues are entrusted with the task of enrolling two new legions which Minucius has been authorised to raise. The order has gone out for all citizens of military age to assemble in their tribes. Lots are drawn to determine which tribe shall be selected first for the levy. Thereafter men are prodded forward in groups and the tribunes on their dais take it in turns to choose men for their respective legions. Standing by are others with tubs of paint to daub each man's arm in black or red to denote his legion. At last the process of selection is complete and the order is issued for those chosen to return in ten days, when the class of each fighting man will be determined and weapons will be distributed.

The Board of Ten consult the Sibylline Books with the assistance of two Greek interpreters. After much deliberation as to the meaning of the oracles, they announce that among the propitiatory rites, a public feast in honour of the gods must be held. The goddess Vesta is one of the twelve gods chosen to be honoured. She will share a couch with Vulcan.

Postumia rules that fresh sacred cakes are to be baked over the temple fire, even though it is not one of the three

Chapter Nine

occasions in the year assigned to the performance of this rite. She summons Livia and Tuccia to assist. Meanwhile Opimia and Floronia are instructed to go into the store room where the earthenware pot is kept that contains impure salt, baked hard over the fire at the previous Vestalia. They break open the gypsum seal, cut the salt into blocks and carry water from the pool of Juturna to make the sacred brine. It is the first time for many months that they have been together more than a few moments. Floronia looks relaxed and chats happily as they break down the salt before stirring it into the water. Afterwards Opimia suggests that they might climb up to the glade on the hill and spend some time together there, but Floronia recoils.

'I never go there now,' she says emphatically. 'I'm too busy at the Regia. In any case I think the place is inhabited by evil spirits. I should keep away if I were you.'

Opimia is puzzled. She feels sure that she has seen Floronia go in that direction not so long ago. Perhaps she is mistaken. It's something that relations with Floronia have been partially restored. Best not to take it any further.

The day arrives for the strewing of the couches decreed by the Board of Ten. Preceded by her lictor, Postumia steps out from the house of the Vestals. In her hands she clasps a statuette which the Chief Priest has authorised her to take from the inner sanctum of the temple, a place which nobody but a Senior Vestal may enter. This small object is the palladium, which fell from heaven and was brought from Troy to Italy by Aeneas.[79] It is the most sacred relic in the city, a symbol of the safety of Rome. No citizen has seen

---

79. In mythology Aeneas was the son of Venus. At the end of the war with the Greeks he fled the ruins of Troy and made his way to Carthage where he met the queen of that city, Dido. They became lovers until Aeneas, compelled by the gods to abandon Dido and travel on to Italy to become the founder of the Roman people, abandoned her on the shores of Africa. Thereupon Dido killed herself, but before doing so she uttered a curse that foretold the turbulent relationship between Rome and Carthage.

it before, and those who realise what it is gasp as Postumia passes by, holding it up in front of her. Tuccia and Livia follow, bearing the rush baskets filled with the sacred cakes. Behind them walk Floronia and Opimia, each carrying a silver jug of brine. Little Licinia clasps a small oil lamp to represent the Vestal fire.

A gentle breeze flutters the priestesses' headbands in their procession down to the Comitium, where the crowd is held back to provide an open space close to the grave of Romulus. Here six couches have been set up, each covered with a broad white cloth festooned with branches of laurel and sprigs of oak. Sprays of roses burst from vases of yellow marble placed between the couches. Apples, figs, dates, grapes and nuts are piled in profusion in bowls near the image of each god. Truffles, capons and sucking pigs, garnished with every kind of vegetable, overflow the platters. Pastries, bread and honey cakes tumble from baskets. The winged thunderbolt of Jupiter commands a pedestal by the couch that he shares with Juno. A silver helmet crested with purpled egret feathers signifies the couch where Mars rests in the company of Venus. His priest, none other than Publius Umbrenus, a bulky figure in his heavy woollen cloak and leather skull cap, reverentially leans a pair of Salian shields against the couch. Sheaves of corn are dedicated to Mercury and Ceres, a nod to the farmers of the plebeian class. There is no want of drink. Amphorae are propped everywhere among earthenware jugs and goblets of silver. It is a sumptuous feast for the gods, intended to placate their anger and to arouse pity for the citizens of Rome in their plight.

The three senior priests of Jupiter, Mars and Quirinus speak in turn, intoning prayers of supplication, requesting their particular divinity to accept the gifts of food and wine. Umbrenus, recently returned from the pro-praetorship of Sicily and all the better off for his term of office in that province, finishes his devotions by scattering silver coins,

Chapter Nine

some of which roll towards the people, who rush to gather them up. Caudinus, as Chief Priest, completes the ceremony with an address to the pantheon of gods, craving forgiveness for the recent wrongs committed by the citizens, in particular an offering to Mars made earlier in the war which was incorrectly performed and which the Board of Ten have decreed must be performed again. Umbrenus nods vigorously. It is no fault of his, he signifies. The wrongly worded rite occurred before his assumption of the priesthood. Caudinus, bald but for a few wisps of hair about his ears and bent almost double on his stick, calls for his litter and is borne away. The people surge forward to admire the feast while the ravens circle above, biding their time.

In the house on the Esquiline Hill, Lucius lies on a day bed in the tablinum. His breath comes stertorously. Occasionally he lapses into sleep, then wakes to ask for water. Opimia sits at one side of the bed while Gaius carefully lifts his father's head to help him drink. In one of his periods of wakefulness Lucius asks Naevia to bring her lyre. He wants her to play and sing the old songs from Campania which Phoebe taught her. She draws up a stool. Her gentle fingers caress the strings, persuading from them notes that linger like sunbeams in the still air. Lucius remembers the days when they were newly married. He sees again his fresh young bride, her gaiety about the house, the cheerful ripple of her laughter, the soft eyes and welcoming smile. He cannot smile. His face is too damaged by disease, but he can still hear. Opimia feels the slight pressure of his hand in hers. She bends to kiss him on the forehead, this man whom she has known so little and yet loves so much. Like his father before him, his overriding purpose in life has been to perform his duty to Rome. He has fought in her cause, trained his son to do the same and given his daughter to care for her safety. Opimia silently vows to emulate him.

It is the eleventh hour of the night when the suffering of Lucius Opimius Veianus comes to an end. The warbling of the doves in the eaves betrays the dawning of another day. The slaves come to stand silently in line, then shuffle away, some hiding their tears. Opimia fetches warm water to bathe her father's body. Gaius hurries away to see to the funeral arrangements that day, for on the morrow the new legions must march to Tibur where they are ordered to report.

Creto enters quietly to say that Lentulus is at the door. Opimia comes forward to greet him. He bends his head and his hand brushes the sleeve of her gown.

'I'm so sorry. I had come to take leave of your father. We march from Rome tomorrow. You know how much I respected him and I wanted to say goodbye. Please forgive me for being so importunate. It was not intentional.'

'There is nothing to forgive. You could not know. It has been a long illness. I am glad his suffering is over. My mother is resting but I'm sure she would want me to thank you for coming.'

They stand awkwardly for a moment, alone together, neither knowing how to continue.

'We shall pass by the Esquiline Gate tomorrow onto the Tiburtine Way at about the noonday hour. I expect a lot of people will come to see us off.' He hesitates and looks up. 'Do the Vestals normally appear on such occasions?'

'I have never known it.' Opimia tries to think but the emotion of the moment overwhelms her. No words will come. She turns her head away.

Impulsively Lentulus steps forward. Her grief and the desire to comfort lend courage. He kisses her damp cheek twice. She does not recoil.

'Goodbye then.' He turns hastily, embarrassed by his forwardness, and strides from the room. Opimia listens to his footsteps down the passage. She hears the muffled sound of conversation with the slave and then a bang as the heavy door slams shut, a terrible sound of finality.

The rest of the day passes in a blur. Everything must be done in haste before Gaius leaves. The family masks in the

Chapter Nine

atrium are brought down from the wall. The little procession sets off through the streets, with the body of her father on a carriage. Out through the Capena Gate and onto the Appian Way they walk, to the accompaniment of flutes. Mimers and mimics prance before the carriage, holding up masks of famous ancestors. At the family mausoleum the funeral pyre is lit and the spirit of Lucius rises up into a blue sky.

In the morning a sea of movement washes over the Field of Mars. Men and horses seem at first to be a tangled mob which will never resolve itself. Here and there armour glimmers in the sunlight. The eagles of the legionary standards hover above the confusion. Veteran centurions seconded from the army of Servilius, which Fabius has taken over, lay about them with their vine sticks. Gradually, orderly ranks and files of soldiers emerge, marshalled according to their fighting class. The circular horns of war blast out across the field and the column begins to snake round the outside of the city wall up to the Esquiline Gate, from where the pale blue hills of Tibur can be seen rising in the distance. In the van of each legion march the skirmishers, armed with slings, javelins and light shields. The wolf skins on their helmets increase their stature and give them a more fearsome appearance, for these are the poorest class of citizen, undernourished and therefore undersized. Behind them comes the steady tramp of the spearmen, their long shields and two throwing spears strapped to their backs. A short sword, pointed and sharpened on both sides, slaps each man's thigh as he swings along. A small breastplate covers the heart and their bronze helmets sport plumes of black or purple feathers which nod menacingly in the sun.

The men in the prime of life, the principals, form the third line of battle in front of which marches the legionary standard bearer clad in a leather corselet. From his head and down his back hangs a whole wolf skin. His breastplate and greaves are of polished brass. The oak staff which he carries aloft bears a silver eagle with its wings spread, a laurel wreath from which coloured ribbons flutter and a plaque inscribed with the letters S.P.Q.R.[80]

The fourth line of older men brings up the rear. These are the reserves, thrown into battle as a last resort. Their arms are similar to those of the other legionaries, apart from their spears, which are designed for thrusting, not for throwing. Leading each maniple strides its first centurion, while his deputy supervises the rear.

Old men, women and children trail along beside the column, shouting out to their loved ones. Others congregate outside the wall at the city gate. Some cheer, some weep. Most are looking out for a father, son or brother somewhere in the ranks of marching men. It's difficult to see through the dust churned up by the tramping of boots and the hooves of the horses. The augurs are waiting at the Esquiline Gate, where the giant serpent of nearly ten thousand men comes to a halt and the trumpets fall silent. Minucius dismounts to greet the Chief Augur, Lucius Junius Pullus, a man of nearly eighty summers who fought in the previous war against the Carthaginians. He advances unsteadily, bent over and using his wand as a walking stick. Like a priest about to sacrifice, he drapes part of his gown over his head before motioning to Minucius to retire a few paces. With a shaky hand his wand describes in the dust a rectangle inside which he steps. From here he will observe the flight of the birds to determine if the omens for the army are propitious. First, however, the sacred chickens must be fed. The cackling birds are released from their cages and an acolyte steps forward to give Junius a small bag of corn. He unties the cord and scatters the food over the ground. A murmur of relief tinged with approval goes up among the watching

---

80. *Senatus Populusque Romanus*: The Senate and The People of Rome.

Chapter Nine

tribunes and other officers who have similarly dismounted to observe the proceedings. The hens are eating enthusiastically. The campaign will be successful. Minucius claps his hand on his thigh and turns to remount his horse.

'Not so hasty, General. You would not wish to repeat the mistakes of Flaminius, I'm sure.' The old man places a restraining hand on the other's arm and looks up at the sky. Stepping back inside his square he begins to quarter it with his wand. The heavens are devoid of movement; no birds appear. Minucius is becoming restless, anxious to be on his way, but Junius will not let him go. At last some geese come from the direction of the city, flapping ponderously overhead and calling mournfully. They fly on towards the hills of Tibur. Reluctantly Junius concedes that it is sufficient sign that the army can proceed. With a triumphant shout Minucius springs back on his horse and waves the column forward.

On a hillock set back from the road and just above the second milestone a small carriage waits. Opimia remains in her seat, watching the columns slowly pass by. She knows that Lentulus will be riding with the second legion. The first legion, to which Gaius is assigned, has already gone on its way and she could not distinguish him from the other horsemen. Now the skirmishers of the second legion are coming into view. Without realising it Opimia leans forward in her seat. She can make out the silver eagle riding above the dust. Will Lentulus be on the far side of the column or on hers? Her heart is thumping and she stands up in the carriage, striving to catch sight of him. It's no use. In their armour and their helmets all the tribunes look the same. She sits back sadly, ready to order her driver to circle round the city wall and re-enter by the Viminalian Gate. There is no prospect of going through the Esquiline for many hours. Her eye is caught by a man on horseback. He seems to be gesticulating at the infantry, perhaps urging them to march more quickly. No, he is waving,

waving to her and smiling. Opimia raises her arm slightly to indicate that she has seen him. Lentulus cannot break away, but he turns repeatedly to look back over his shoulder. Opimia gazes after him until she can no longer distinguish his raised arm. Soon enough he is merely a speck which disappears into the dusty haze. She looks up, attracted by the sound of a flock of geese flying back towards the city from the direction of Tibur.

Descending from her carriage she hurries straight to her room. She feels the need to be alone. The past two days have drained her emotionally and physically. She lies on her bed and tries to calm herself. Really the death of her father has come as a relief. She must shut out the image of suppurating flesh and the anguish on her mother's face. It's over now. She will remember the too few happy days with him, when she saw him smile at something she had done which pleased him. She can only hope to fulfil her duty to the city as he did. Her mind drifts ineluctably in another direction, to the army marching away to fight unknown battles. She pictures Lentulus turning reluctantly back, to face forward on his horse. She wonders how he is feeling. She tries to stifle the realisation of her own loss. It is not right that a Vestal should harbour such feelings for a man. She turns over on the little bed to face the wall. A couple of tears escape and trickle down her cheek. Perhaps even at this moment they are approaching the hills not far from where her mother and she used to spend the summer. She is climbing the hill, with him holding her hand to help. On the craggy outcrop at the top they lean against the wind and laugh. Her eyes close and Opimia sleeps. On her lips rests the trace of a smile.

When she wakes she slips on her shoes and emerges into the atrium. Apart from a slave sweeping the pavement with birch twigs, nobody is about. From somewhere outside comes the scent of roses carried on the warm evening air. Opimia wanders out into the dusk and begins to climb the

Chapter Nine

hill to the glade above. The path has a well-trodden look though she has not used it for many weeks and she knows that Floronia has stopped going. At the entrance to the green tunnel she stoops and starts to make her way along it. A sound causes her to pause. She assumes it to be an animal, but it does not move away. She cannot define it. It is as if someone were running a race. The lush summer foliage conceals the view. Gently she pushes aside a branch so that she can see into the glade. At first she can make no sense of it. The rock has changed shape. It seems to throb as though it were alive. Then Opimia knows. She knows what she is looking at. Floronia is sprawled across the rock. Over her lies a man who is thrusting himself between her thighs. In horrified fascination Opimia watches until the fear of discovery grips her. Carefully she lets the branch slide slowly from her hand and retreats back down the tunnel. Reaching the path she begins to run. At the bottom of the hill she forces herself to walk sedately into the house and thence to her room. Once inside she throws herself on the bed, weeping and shaking uncontrollably.

Chapter Ten

217–216 BC

The burden of her discovery gnaws at Opimia. It will not leave her alone. Each morning when she wakes, the vision of Floronia on the rock intrudes like an unwelcome guest. She tries to distract herself by careful attention to her duties, but the routine of minding the fire, evening hymns and prayers for the safety of the state has lost its savour and turned into monotony. She is dragged down by her knowledge. It defiles her. She tries to avoid contact with Floronia, impossible in such a small community. When they meet she struggles to look her former friend in the eye. The prospect that Floronia may discover her secret through some slip of the tongue terrifies her. Strangely, Floronia seems friendlier than in the past. The tension and veiled animosity have gone, to be replaced by a more relaxed and cheerful attitude. Opimia tries to reciprocate, but the strain tells on her. She longs to be alone, escaping to her room whenever duties permit. Yet the bed offers neither solace nor sleep, only a ceiling which stares down remorselessly. It occurs to her that the other Vestals may already be aware of Floronia's unchastity. Is she the last to know? She watches for some sign that Floronia is being shielded from discovery. No sidelong glances, exchanges of looks or remarks betray suspicion or knowledge held by the others. Opimia becomes convinced that she alone knows.

Chapter Ten

Perhaps she should report what she has seen. She cannot bring herself to do it. In any case, who would believe it? She does not know the identity of the man. Faced with such an accusation Floronia would inevitably deny it, perhaps even try to reverse the position, knowing of Opimia's friendship with Lentulus. And what of her relationship with him? Is it proper for a Vestal to be kissed by a man, to long for his presence, to cry at night wondering whether he is safe and to pray for his return? Is her fault not as great as that of Floronia? Does unchaste behaviour lie only in physical acts or are her thoughts and longings not just as blameworthy, a dereliction of her sacred vows? Her silence is tacit condonation of an adultery committed against Rome, which is thereby put in danger. Her father would have put his duty to Rome before all else and reported what he had seen, even though it involved the betrayal of a friend. And yet she cannot do it. The betrayal of Floronia will not release her from her own sense of guilt. The very act of reasoning and arguing with herself signifies a breach of the trust placed in her to protect the city by the purity of her conduct.

The lonely days of summer begin at last to shorten. Opimia welcomes the longer hours of darkness when her isolation and despair are not so visible. Naevia receives a brief letter from Gaius indicating that he is safe and well. It contains no mention of Lentulus and Opimia dare not ask her mother to make inquiries in her reply. A month or two pass until one morning, at about the setting of the Pleiades and the rites of the October horse,[81] Naevia sends a message that a courier has called at the house leaving a letter addressed to Opimia. It is two days before she can

---

81. On 15 October each year two chariots raced on the Field of Mars. The right-hand horse of the winning pair was thereupon sacrificed by the Priest of Mars and some of its blood was taken by the Vestals to be burned. The resultant ashes were preserved as a purificatory substance for use by the priestesses at other festivals.

escape from her duties, two days of agonising over whether she should even open the letter or destroy it unopened. When at last her carriage pulls up outside the house on the Esquiline, Opimia does not attempt to disguise from herself the feeling of relief on finding that her mother is not at home. She has left the letter in Opimia's old room. It consists of a tube of wood sealed at each end with the stamp of the second legion. Her hand rests on the seal. It would be a matter of a moment to toss the whole thing into the brazier, but there can be no harm in opening the letter. Her fingers seem to anticipate her wish and prise off the seal. She draws out a roll of papyrus and carefully unfolds it on the table, placing a jug on one side to hold it down and a trembling hand on the other. She reads:

> To my dearest Opimia,
>
> I hope you will forgive my writing to you. I make my excuse for doing so the wish to assure you that your dear brother is fit and well. Though I do not see a great deal of him we do occasionally meet. He is a natural soldier and leader of men who relishes life on campaign. Like many of us, he is anxious to take on the Africans in a fair fight and rid our country of this plague. Quintus Fabius, however, is determined to bide his time. He believes in a slow war of attrition. Down here Hannibal cannot draw on the Gallic tribes for reserves of men, whereas we can look to our citizens and allies from all over Italy. Meanwhile we harry the enemy's foragers and rearguard whenever opportunities present themselves. This provides our new levies with experience and depletes the enemy's numbers.
>
> The campaign is not without its difficulties, however. Minucius and many of his tribunes are hot for battle. They openly criticise Fabius, saying that he stands idly by while Hannibal lays waste to the countryside, burning, looting and seizing our crops

Chapter Ten

and cattle to feed his army. He has been careful to leave untouched Fabius's estates in Campania, a fact which has caused great resentment. Some are even suggesting that Fabius has struck a bargain with Hannibal, that he is a traitor to the state and will eventually surrender to him. I am convinced this is not true and that Fabius's strategy is the right one. Hanibal is too clever a general for us to risk an open battle just yet.

I am writing to you from Falernum, near a river called the Volturnus which runs through the plain of Campania. Perhaps your mother remembers it. We are licking our wounds after another trick by Hannibal. The area is full of rich crops and they make excellent wine here. Hannibal has been ravaging the farmsteads while we stick to the high ground, tracking his movements. Fabius was convinced that he would retire back into Samnium to find a secure place in which to camp for the winter, taking his booty with him. We posted a strong force in the only pass through the hills which Hannibal could use and pitched our main camp on another hill opposite, called Eribianus. Our plan was to ambush the Carthaginians as they made their way through the pass. But during the night Hannibal created a diversion by setting fire to faggots attached to the horns of several thousand cattle which he caused to be driven up the hill towards a ridge above the pass. Our men thought the enemy were escaping by another route and set off in the direction of the lights. Meanwhile Hannibal escaped with the main body of his army through the abandoned pass. Fabius refused to leave camp, fearing another ruse by Hannibal. He was right. In the morning we saw that the enemy had got clean away. Minucius and his colleagues were furious, accusing Fabius of negligence and cowardice. There was a stand-up row in front of

The Daughters of Cannae

many of the tribunes, with Minucius shouting at the dictator. Fabius is stubborn and unwavering in his views. He just glowered at Minucius and then turned on his heel and went into his tent. I support Fabius, but there is a growing feeling among the officers that if we continue with this passive strategy our allies in Italy will begin to desert and go over to Hannibal to protect themselves from destruction.

I am sorry to have burdened you with military affairs. That was not my intention when I started this letter, but rather to let you know that I think often of you and our happy times at your parents' house. It was truly kind and brave of you to watch us leave on the road to Tibur. I hope you saw me wave and that it will not be too long before we meet again. Fabius has announced his intention of returning to Rome shortly to perform certain religious duties. I am to command his escort. It may be, therefore, that this letter, which a despatch rider to the Senate has agreed to deliver, will not long precede me.

I send you my warmest regards which please also convey to your mother. You are always in my thoughts.

Publius Lentulus

Opimia sinks to her knees, releasing the scroll which curls up against the jug. Her hands rest in her lap and tears trickle from her eyes. An intense feeling of relief wells up in her breast. Lentulus is safe and it seems he will soon be back in Rome. For all she knows, he may already have arrived. She picks up the letter again and rereads it, before rolling it tightly to fit back into the wooden tube. She ponders whether to burn it. It is not the sort of letter a Vestal should receive. Certainly it would be dangerous to take it back to the Vestals' house. Looking round, she sees her old chest at the bottom of the bed. She removes from it a woollen blanket into which she folds the tube before

Chapter Ten

replacing it beneath the others in the chest. Naevia has still not returned by the time her driver is slapping the reins of the two mules who draw her carriage back to the Forum.

As they rattle down the slope towards the Sacred Way a squadron of horsemen clatter past in the opposite direction, followed by a carriage in which Opimia recognises the austere figure of Fabius. She turns quickly in her seat but the escort has already disappeared from view, veering round towards the Capitoline Hill where she knows that Fabius has a house. The knowledge that Lentulus is again so close raises in Opimia both fear and excitement. While he is away from Rome their relationship poses no real danger. His presence is a threat which she tries not to acknowledge, yet it lingers in the back of her mind. Her love, she can hardly bring herself to think the word, is in conflict with everything she is supposed to represent. It is with a newly troubled mind that she enters the Vestals' house to resume the duties which the spirit of her father commands her to perform.

The following day Opimia is carrying bread to the table set up in the atrium, when the door slave approaches her with a note written on wax secured between two slivers of sandalwood. Suspecting what it may be, she excuses herself from the other priestesses and retires to her room. Lentulus is engaged on military matters for the next three days, but hopes that she may be able to come to the house by the Quirinal Gate in the afternoon of the Ides. Pocketing the message in the folds of her gown she returns to the table and takes her place. Her face betrays the tension which receipt of the note has aroused. Livia smiles kindly at her.

'You look a little pale, dear. Not bad news, I hope.'

Opimia forces herself to assume a cheerful expression. 'Oh no, indeed the contrary. It was simply a note from my mother to say that she has heard from my brother, Gaius, saying that he is fit and well.' She takes up a piece of bread, anything to engage her hands which she is certain will shake otherwise. How readily she lies now and, by way of compensation for this untruth, she adds, 'He's serving in the first legion, you know.'

Postumia looks up quizzically from the end of the table. 'Of course we do.' All resume their eating in silence. Opimia senses nobody believes her, that in that moment she has taken an irrevocable step. She glances round, almost defiantly; nobody meets her gaze. Floronia sits demurely opposite, carefully slicing an apple. The urge to shout out what she has seen is almost irrepressible. Instead she finishes her food as hastily as decency allows and begs to be excused. From the sanctuary of her room she hears the sound of the others talking, discussing her, no doubt. She takes out the message and opens it again. The words stare back at her. She holds the tablet over the flame of an oil lamp until the wax has become viscous. Then, with her finger she smoothes the letters until they are obliterated. There shall be no reply. The act of lying has troubled her too much. She will not go. This sensation of being drawn inexorably towards a rock against which her frail body will crash and break must end. This perpetual shadow over her existence must be lifted. If only she can resist, fulfil her duty as a priestess, as her father would wish and as Rome needs. Her happiness can be regained by sacrificing it first on the altar of duty. Over the next few days Opimia repeats this sentiment to herself while she goes about her tasks. She takes particular pains over the most trivial of matters, striving to escape and to put any thought of Lentulus out of her mind. The nights are most difficult, whether she is lying on her bed unable to sleep, or sitting by the fire through the seemingly interminable hours of darkness, until the comfort of another dawn arrives and she can immerse herself in activity.

The Ides of November bring flurries of sleet and dead leaves chased into corners by a bitter wind. Citizens do not linger to chat in the Forum or the street markets, but raise the hoods of their cloaks and hurry on. The fumes from

Chapter Ten

hundreds of braziers hover momentarily like gauzy veils in the narrow alleys of the city, before being swept away on the icy draughts. Fabius is to leave Rome on the following day and Lentulus will certainly accompany him. All morning the battle rages in Opimia's mind. The resolution of the previous days has been weakened by the realisation that this may be the last time she will see him. Sooner or later the issue between Rome and Hannibal will be tried once and for all. A battle cannot be postponed for very much longer. The people and the allies will not stand for it. Suppose that Lentulus were killed. She could never forgive herself that she had not said goodbye. The rota of duties has left her without commitments in the afternoon. She did not contrive it. It has fallen out that way. It would be wrong not to go.

The house near the Quirinal Gate fronts onto a narrow street running beside the city wall, beneath which carts are drawn up displaying the wares their drivers have brought in from the countryside. Rabbits and game of all kinds dangle from hooks, interspersed with vegetables among which the citizens pick, searching for the best. Dogs run about, scavenging for anything dropped on the ground and receiving the occasional kick for their troubles. The progress of Opimia's carriage is slowed. Her driver shouts for the way to be cleared and people stand back when they recognise the headdress of a Vestal. A man convicted of the theft of some firewood claims the right to be pardoned for his crime on the ground that he has met a Vestal before sentence is carried out.[82] Opimia listens briefly to the facts. It turns out to be a trivial amount of kindling stolen from the head tenant of an apartment block, where the man resides with his wife and four children in one room on the first floor. When she pardons him the wife rushes forward to

---

82. A man condemned to death for some crime was automatically pardoned if he subsequently met a Vestal.

clasp Opimia round the feet in gratitude. Gently she pushes the grubby hands away and orders the driver to proceed.

A male slave conducts her down the passage from the front door of the house into a spacious reception room lined with couches furnished at each end with heavy bolsters. He bows, revealing a tight chain around his neck coupled by a plate on which the name of his owner appears. Having indicated that Opimia should take a seat he retires to inform his master of her arrival. She has only just settled herself on a couch before a young girl dressed in a sleeveless chiton enters, bearing a jug of barley water, a silver cup and a bowl of walnuts coated thinly in honey. Silently she places these next to Opimia who nods and utters a word of thanks. Like the male slave, the girl bows before walking backwards to leave the room. Opimia wonders whether she is a mute or perhaps has no understanding of Latin.

Looking round, she can see into part of the peristyle where stone fish rise from a pool and disgorge thin jets of water, or would do if the fountain were playing. The room in which she sits has a timber roof supported by slim columns painted deep red on the lower half and ochre above. On each wall are depicted scenes from the story of Rome. Horatius defends the bridge over the Tiber against the invading hordes of Lars Porsena. Another wall bears the image of the sacred geese on the Capitol raising the alarm as the Gauls attempt to scale the defences. Opposite, she recognises the figure of Aeneas carrying his father and leading his son from the ruins of Troy, at the start of a journey that will eventually lead him to Italy and the foundation of a city from which Rome will spring. She sits on the edge of the couch, taking frequent sips of the barley water. She picks up a walnut and then puts it down, not wishing to be eating when he comes. A large brazier occupies the centre of the room. She moves to stand by it, warming her hands and savouring the scent of the smouldering pine.

Chapter Ten

The sound of voices precedes Lentulus's arrival. He wears a blue woollen tunic and soft leather sandals. His chestnut curls are damp. Evidently he has just come from the bath. His appearance is leaner than Opimia remembers. She remarks on it and he laughs.

'Campaign food, you know, and days spent on horseback.' He stoops to kiss her on the forehead, then gently leads her by the arm to one of the couches. 'I'm sorry to have kept you waiting. When I did not hear from you, I thought that perhaps you were not going to come. I'm so pleased that you did.'

'I heard that Fabius is to return to the legions tomorrow and thought it impolite not to come and say goodbye. I presume that you will accompany him.' The words do not emerge as Opimia would like, more a gesture of good manners than the leave-taking from a loved one. She looks up and smiles to show what she had meant.

'Yes, I fear we leave at dawn tomorrow.' He is silent for a moment, as if lost in thought, gazing down at the floor. 'Perhaps I should not say this to you, but it is such a great pleasure to be with you again. I have missed you so much.' He half turns and takes her hand in his. For a few moments she allows it to stay there, before gently withdrawing it. She cannot look at him. It would shatter her resolve.

She forces herself to speak words she does not want to say. 'It is a pleasure, too, for me to see you again, safe and well. But we both know that nothing can come of our friendship. It can never be more than that. My presence alone here in your aunt's house compromises my vows as a Vestal.' She looks steadily in front of her, unwilling to witness the effect of her words. Her lips tremble. With a great effort of will she restrains the tears which she feels welling up inside.

Lentulus nods slowly. 'I understand, but you will not always be a Vestal. I can wait.'

The Daughters of Cannae

'What, another eighteen years? I'll be fat and ugly by then.' She laughs bitterly. 'There, I shouldn't even have said that.'

'Perhaps, but you mean everything to me.'

Like the string of a bow drawn just too far, something inside Opimia snaps. She collapses in a confusion of sobs and tears. Lentulus puts his arm round her shoulders and she buries her face in his neck, crying uncontrollably. The pain and tension, the loneliness and isolation of the past months release themselves in his muscular comfort. Lentulus waits patiently, saying nothing. At last she draws back and tries to compose herself, straightening her braids and ribbons, which have become disarranged. Lentulus senses that his arm should no longer be around her shoulder.

'That was very weak of me. I won't be like that again.' A wan smile plays about her lips. To Lentulus she has never seemed so beautiful. He stands to pull her gently upright, placing his arms round her waist before kissing her on both eyes. His lips brush hers and then she reaches up to him, searching with closed eyes for his mouth. It is brief, but it is enough to know that she is loved. A certain serenity of spirit pervades her. She is still and calm.

Lentulus sends a slave to summon her driver. They walk through the house, talking of trivial things to distance their minds from the imminent parting. When it comes, both want it to be quick. He promises to write and stoops again to kiss her. He feels the softness of her hand brush against his cheek and then she is in the carriage. From the door he watches the wheels rattle away over the rutted earth. She turns once to wave and he raises his arm in reply.

Winter melts away into spring. The six-month appointments of Fabius and Minucius have expired, leaving the legions in the field to be commanded by the consuls of the previous year, Servilius and Atilius. In the bitterly fought elections for the new year the Senate have won support for their man, Lucius Aemilius Paullus, an experienced general who has

Chapter Ten

conducted successful campaigns in Illyria.[83] The plebeians, however, have insisted on their own candidate, Gaius Terentius Varro, as his colleague. Varro has no military experience, but is a fiery orator who has whipped up the support of the people with rash speeches in the Comitium, promising immediate action to rid the country of the African invaders. He and Paullus set about recruiting fresh legions to supplement the army tracking Hannibal.

Far away from Rome, in the region of southern Apulia, a river called the Aufidus meanders its way north-eastwards from the Apennines to the soft waters of the Adriatic. On its way it crosses broad flatlands filled with swaying ears of corn. Here the crops mature earlier than further north in Picenum or Etruria. Beside the river, barely ten miles from the sea, lies the little citadel of Cannae, a settlement built around granaries and warehouses in which the produce of the surrounding fields is stored. The sun shines down from a cloudless heaven on the smallholders who are beginning to harvest their crops, though it is still early summer. Men and women bend to their work while carts drawn by white oxen and laden with sheaves of corn lurch along the rutted tracks towards the town. Occasionally a skylark, disturbed by the harvesting, rises from the corn stalks with a shrill burst of song, sailing upwards to dance high in the blazing light before settling again.

In the distance a cloud of fast-moving dust swirls up from the plain. Soon dark shapes appear, travelling at speed in the direction of the town. Black men on horseback, brandishing spears from which red pennons trail in the wind and screaming their paean of battle, cut a swathe through the peaceful fields. Harvesters are impaled where they stand, oxen panic and carts lie overturned in ditches. The Numidians thunder past, heading for the citadel.

---

83. An area of the Balkan peninsula bordering the north-eastern coast of the Adriatic.

Within the hour the Roman garrison is no more than food for flies. Hannibal has seized the stores of grain with which to feed his army and put himself in possession of the fields the shadowing Romans had hoped to reap.

Disconcerted, Servilius and Atilius send to Rome for orders. What are they to do? Should they retreat, or should they attack Hannibal and rely on more distant sources of supply? Aemilius and Varro despatch instructions. On no account is a battle to be risked until they arrive with the fresh levies. 'Then,' says Varro confidently, 'we'll put an end to this impudent invader once and for all.'

Lentulus stirs in his tent. The night has been hot and he has barely slept. He tries to settle again but sleep eludes him. When he peers outside the stars are fading in the sky. Somewhere nearby a horn sounds the end of the last watch of the night. He straps on his boots and drapes his cloak across his shoulders. In the cool air of the dawn he walks down through the lines towards the compound where the cavalry horses are tethered. The horses' bridles clink as their hooves shuffle restlessly on the beaten earth and the air vaporises in jets from their nostrils, blanketing the compound in a cloud of steam. His little mare, already on her feet, whinnies at the sight of him. He canters down to the praetorian gate and out beyond the rampart towards the river which lies a few hundred paces away. There he dismounts to allow the mare to slither down the bank and drink her fill. The beams of the new sun, lapping an opalescent sea, kindle in the palest bronze the summits of the crags far across the plain to the west. The dotted heads of sentries protrude above the rampart of the smaller Roman camp on the far side of the river. Somewhere downstream lies Hannibal's camp, hidden by a small rise in the ground. The armies are no more than 5,000 paces apart. Including her allies, Rome has put some 80,000 infantry and 6,000 cavalry into the field, the

Chapter Ten

largest force she has ever assembled. Today it is the turn of Varro to command.[84]

The tranquillity of the early-morning light, in which droplets of dew from spiders' webs strung between blades of grass create a transient jewelled carpet, and the lazy drift of the river hold Lentulus in their intangible grasp. The image of Opimia and their all-too-brief embrace in his aunt's house becalm his mind. Will he see her again or have the fates decreed that it was their last meeting? He is not afraid of the coming battle, whether it is to be that day or another. Perhaps it is better that he should die in the defence of the Republic, rather than put her life at risk. He has an uncanny sensation that she is aware of his presence by the river, that she knows he is thinking of her. Her smile lingers in his mind's eye. Involuntarily he reaches out to touch her. His reverie is interrupted by the blast of a bugle. Reprimanding himself for neglecting his duty, he mounts his horse and rides swiftly back to camp.

On the main thoroughfare men hurry this way and that. Centurions are barking orders at legionaries helping each other to buckle on their armour while squadrons of cavalry canter past, churning up the dust in their wake. Varro is standing outside the praetorium,[85] his face flushed with excitement. Beside him, hoisted on a pole, hangs the purple tunic signalling the order to prepare for battle. Close by, his lictors wait, curiously incongruous in their togas. Varro is talking in a high voice to Atilius and Servilius who, Lentulus gathers, are to command the Roman infantry in the centre. He notices that Aemilius Paullus is also present, but a little detached from the main group round his fellow consul. In contrast to Varro, his demeanour is composed as he talks quietly to a few cavalry captains. Lentulus cannot make out

---

84. At this time, when both consuls were in the field together, they took command on alternate days.
85. The general's headquarters.

The Daughters of Cannae

what is being said, but from the expression on the face of Paullus he guesses that he does not share the enthusiasm of Varro to offer battle.

Within the hour the legions are filing out through the main gate, led by the standard bearers and to the accompaniment of the military horns blaring out the signal to deploy for action. They wade across the river, shrunken by the summer drought, and scramble up the bank to join forces with the men from the other camp. The cavalry follow, splashing through the shallow water and out onto the plain.

Lentulus leads his squadrons forward to find Paullus, who has appeared beside him, astride a black stallion at least three hands larger than his own mare. On his chest the consul wears a breastplate of worked bronze, seized from the corpse of a Thracian mercenary during the campaigns in Illyria. It displays Theseus slaying the minotaur. His helmet is of polished brass from which burst dark blue plumes, so that his troopers may recognise him in the melee of a cavalry engagement. The cheekplates on his face do not hide a scar running down from one eye to his chin.

The Roman cavalry are ordered to guard the right flank alongside the river, while the allied horse have been deployed on the left wing. Between these formations the infantry are disposed in a solid mass, designed by sheer weight of numbers and force to punch a hole in the enemy's centre. The skirmishers fan out in front of them, ready to launch their darts and light catapults. Lentulus can see in the distance the Carthaginians pouring out of their own camp and fording the river, having observed that the Romans are at last prepared to try the issue in a pitched battle. Paullus surveys the enemy's dispositions, which mirror those of the Romans, with cavalry on each wing and the infantry in the centre. Something in the expression on the consul's face and his detached appearance outside the praetorium embolden Lentulus to speak.

Chapter Ten

'How do you see the battle unfolding, sir? Can we give this African a licking today?'

Paullus turns in his saddle to eye up the young tribune next to him. 'Publius Lentulus, isn't it? I think I served with your father many years ago in Gaul, against the Insubres, if I remember correctly.' His horse is pulling on his bridle and Paullus jerks him roughly back. He looks round, checking perhaps that nobody else is near enough to hear him. 'Well, young man, I'll tell you this for nothing. I would not fight today, not on this terrain. Ideal cavalry country this is, flat as the palm of your hand, just what the Numidians and Spaniards like. I don't say we can't match 'em, but they outnumber our horse by nearly two to one. We shall struggle to hold them. As for our legions, I fear greatly for how they are deployed.'

'Why is that, sir? We have eight legions in the field and nearly as many allied infantry. Surely they will swamp the Carthaginians?'

'One of the first principles of battle, young man, is to deploy your men so that the maximum number can engage the enemy at any one time. Look at the way Varro has crammed our infantry together, in one solid phalanx. His front is too narrow and the ranks are too deep. Only a fraction of the legionaries can come to grips with the enemy. The rest are behind the front line, surrounded by their fellows and unable even to wield their swords, let alone strike at the enemy.' Paullus shakes his head. 'Terentius Varro is the son of a butcher, you know. I wonder if he or Hannibal will be the butcher today.' He leans forward to stroke the ear of his restless horse on whose neck a white sweat has broken out. 'Good luck to you, my lad. Your father was a brave man. I'm sure he would be proud of you today, if he had lived. When the time comes, lead your squadrons flat out. There is no other way.' With that the consul digs his boots into the stallion's flanks and rides away to tour the other squadrons, offering words of encouragement to the captains. Lentulus watches the plumes of his helmet nodding above the throng of horses and troopers.

The formations of the enemy cavalry are gathering opposite them further downstream. After listening to Paullus he screws up his eyes, searching for signs of the red pennons of the Numidians. Of them there is no trace, but he can make out the white tunics edged with purple worn by the Spaniards, among whom bare-chested Gauls gallop wildly, apparently without thought of conserving the energy of their mounts for the coming struggle. The skirmishers on each side have engaged, filling the sky with clouds of darts and slingshot. Behind them the infantry are advancing steadily towards each other, clashing their swords or spears against their shields. The noise is deafening, causing some of the horses around Lentulus to rear up in fright. As the heavy armour closes with the enemy the skirmishers turn tail and run back through their own lines. A trumpet sounds the order for the cavalry to charge. Lentulus draws his sword and shouts at the squadrons around him. The earth shudders beneath the hooves of 3,000 horses picking up speed. Many of the troopers are screaming with pent-up fear. Others choke and splutter in the clouds of dust stirred up by the headlong gallop.

'Isn't this glorious?' Somebody is shouting at him. Lentulus swivels round to see Gaius galloping alongside him, his face lit up and exultant. 'I've been waiting ever since Trasimene to stick this up the arse of some fleeing Gaul.' He waves his sword in the air before bringing the flat of it down on the flank of his horse. 'Tonight, my friend, we'll drink hard and celebrate.'

Moments later they career into the enemy. Gaius is lost to view in the swirling chaos of men and horses. Many of the riders on each side dismount and fight hand to hand on the ground. Abandoned horses gallop off or make for

Chapter Ten

the river, splashing across it to safety. Lentulus shouts to the men nearest to him to stay in the saddle. He has spotted a detachment of Spaniards crossing the river from the far side to join the melee. They will have to clamber up the bank where he can catch them at a disadvantage. At that moment his eye is caught by a Gaul running towards him, his face and chest streaked with blue daub. He wields a long knife with which to hamstring the enemy's horses. His mare senses the danger. She waits until the Gaul is virtually upon her before swinging round and kicking out with both hind legs, knocking the man senseless to the ground. Lentulus reaches down to thrust his sword into his guts.

Urging the troopers around him to follow, Lentulus gallops forward to the river in time to attack the Spaniards as they reach the top of the bank. His men cut down several of them, while others, seeing the fate of their comrades, swing their mounts round in the water and try to regain the opposite bank. The Roman horses slither down into the river to give chase. In no time the water is stained red with Spanish blood spurting from the thrusts and slashes of Lentulus and his men. They make short work of those who, unhorsed by their panicking mounts, attempt to wade to safety. Some of the Spaniards escape to the far side of the river closely pursued by the Roman troopers. The Spanish horses, however, can outpace their counterparts and they disappear over the crest of a low ridge, heading back over marshy ground beyond which lies the Carthaginian camp. Fearing the possibility of an ambush Lentulus brings his little company to a halt. The horses are nearly spent and they canter slowly back towards the river. In the distance the infantry battle seethes beneath a cloud of dust. A dull roar rolls across the plain like continuous thunder under which a grey mass writhes as if some gigantic beast had been skewered to the ground.

Lentulus leads his troopers round a long bend in the river and up to the brow of a shallow hill, which he had not noticed

The Daughters of Cannae

in the pursuit of the Spaniards. He is anxious to rejoin the cavalry battle, but the view is not what he expected. Before him is spread out a still life, carved out of death. Men, whose actions and reactions have been shaped by fear, lie paralysed in tortured lumps. Nothing moves. A kind of peace prevails over the scene, despite the unnatural postures of the bodies brought on by the agony of their passing. Above all a miasma hangs, a stench of blood. His mare picks her way down through the corpses, most of which he realises are Roman. Here and there the shaft of a spear sticks up from a body. The low moans of men pleading for water, or a final swordthrust to end their suffering, accompany him. He comes across a cavalryman, wounded in the leg and unable to move, but still coherent. He tells Lentulus that the Roman cavalry has been put to flight and driven back along the river. Looking upstream in the direction of their camp Lentulus detects the movement of horses galloping away across the plain. They are too far off to distinguish friend from foe, but the injured man thinks they are squadrons of enemy horse wheeling round to take the legions in the rear.

There is no time to lose. Lentulus orders his men forward, wondering what fate awaits them. They have barely moved off when he hears his name being called. He reins in his mare close to a small outcrop of rock on which a man is heaving himself up from a prone position and waving. There is something familiar about him. Instructing his men to wait, he rides over to find that the stricken man is none other than Aemilius Paullus. The consul appears a little dazed and has lost his helmet. His breastplate carries a large dent where it has been struck by a slingshot in the initial charge.

'I think I must have lost consciousness and fallen from my horse.' Paullus tries to stand, but is so unsteady that Lentulus has to grab hold of him to prevent him from collapsing.

'We must get you back to the camp, sir.'

Chapter Ten

'No, no, young man. I shall be all right in a moment.' He looks round, trying to collect his thoughts and remember what happened. 'Where are our cavalry?'

'It appears, sir, that they have been driven back along the river. I was on my way to rejoin them. We have been chasing some Spanish horse further downstream.'

Lentulus unhitches a leather flask strapped to his belt and offers it to the consul, who takes a few slugs and then throws some of the water onto his face.

'Thank you, that feels a little better. My head is beginning to clear. Give me a hand up, would you?' On his feet, Paullus turns to look over towards the infantry battle. For some time he stares, trying to comprehend the scene and steadying himself with a hand on Lentulus's shoulder. 'I can see Carthaginians, Spaniards and Gauls, but I can see no legionaries. Do you realise what that means, Lentulus?' He does not wait for a reply. 'It means that our forces are surrounded.' The anger in his voice is reinforced by his spitting violently on the ground. Lentulus notices that the spittle is stained red. 'I should not have allowed it. I could have done more to dissuade that idiot Varro. All our strategy undone in one day of madness.' His head droops and he falls silent.

Coming towards them out of the dusty haze Lentulus spots a solitary horseman, riding slowly through the cornfields. His left arm hangs limply by his side and he holds the reins with only his right hand. From time to time he slumps forward over the neck of his horse, so that Lentulus thinks he must fall. Then with an effort he straightens up, looking about as if he is trying to find something or somebody. Lentulus points him out to Paullus who is sunk in a reverie of despair. The consul rouses himself to observe the rider who has now drawn close enough to be recognised.

'That's Marcus Scribonius, one of Atilius's aides, unless I'm much mistaken. He looks in bad shape. Better send

The Daughters of Cannae

one of your troopers to fetch him over, Lentulus. Let's see what he has to say.'

They help Scribonius to dismount. His tunic is covered in blood from a deep wound near the shoulder which Lentulus binds with a makeshift bandage torn from the tunic of a nearby corpse. The man cannot stand and they lay him on the rock recently occupied by Paullus, who holds to his lips the leather bottle from which he has just drunk. The water seems to revive Scribonius a little, but his face is grey and it is clear that he has lost a lot of blood. His lips move in the effort to form words which come only faintly and hesitantly. Paullus kneels down at his side to catch what is said.

'I was sent by Atilius, sir, to try to find you and report.' Scribonius lies silent, summoning the strength to speak again. 'Our legions are surrounded and are being hacked to pieces.' His head lolls sideways on the stone. Lentulus leans forward to support his neck in the crook of his elbow. 'We did well at first, punching a hole in the centre of the Carthaginian line. They fell back in front of us.' Scribonius falls silent once more and his eyes close. Lentulus fears that he has gone but then he comes to, though his voice is barely above a whisper. 'We didn't know that Hannibal had posted his heavy infantry on either wing. As we advanced they turned inwards, so that we were being attacked on both flanks at once.'

'That will be his Libyans. He re-armed them with Roman swords after Trasimene,' mutters Paullus. 'He's suckered Varro with the oldest trick in the world, a standard encirclement manoeuvre.'

'The legionaries cannot fight, sir. The maniples are so tightly packed that they cannot wield their weapons or reach the enemy. Their cavalry have chased ours from the field and are now attacking us from behind. It's a massacre.'

These words drain the last energy from Scribonius. His face twitches and Lentulus feels a gentle tremor run through

Chapter Ten

his body, which stiffens momentarily and then falls back against the rock. Paullus straightens up. He has witnessed death in the field too often to be much affected by it. His head has cleared. The situation is too serious for sentiment.

'Lentulus, you must ride to Rome at once. The Senate needs to be informed of this disaster immediately.'

'Sir, I should prefer to remain here and fight, whatever the outcome.'

'Your attitude, young fellow, would doubtless have pleased your father, but there will be other occasions when you can satisfy the family honour. At this moment nothing is more important than informing the Senate of the great danger which threatens the city. By nightfall it is possible that not a single legionary will be left between here and the walls of Rome.'[86]

'Sir, would it not be possible to send two troopers? They are capable men with good horses.'

'Who would probably get lost!' The glitter has returned to Paullus's eye. 'I am ordering you, Lentulus, as your consul and your general, to report forthwith to Rome. Go to the house of Quintus Fabius. He has the respect of the citizens. They will work for him to strengthen the defences of the city.'

'I will, of course, carry out your order, sir.' Lentulus looks steadily at the ground. 'What orders shall I give to these troopers?'

'None. I shall lead them back into the battle. I will not have it said that Aemilius Paullus ran away at Cannae. Now, give me a leg up onto Scribonius's horse.'

'Will you at least take my helmet, sir? I shall have no need of it.'

'Where I am going, Lentulus, they wear no helmets.' He shouts to the troopers to gather round him. 'And tell my

---

86. In fact, according to Polybius, about 3,000 Roman and allied infantry escaped, 10,000 were captured and 70,000 died at Cannae.

217

friend Fabius that I tried to follow his tactics against Hannibal, but others thought they knew better. Good day to you and may the gods speed your journey to Rome. The future of the city may depend on it.' With that the consul sets his horse for the centre of the roiling sea of flesh and iron, where the giant pincers of Carthage are slowly but inexorably crushing the citizens of Rome to a hideous pulp.

There is no time and no place to bury the body of Scribonius. Lentulus seizes the cloak of a dead Spaniard nearby, unhitches the buckle of horn and silver by which it is secured and wraps Scribonius in it, before dragging the body under a rock out of the reach of pecking birds. He will have to tell Scribonius's mother who, he remembers now, is called Servilia and lives on the slope of the Aventine Hill looking out towards the Great Circus.

Instinct suggests that he should travel downstream towards the sea and then swing away westwards across the plain to the mountains, from which he can try to reach the Roman colony of Beneventum. There he can risk joining the Appian Way, perhaps finding posting stations and making best speed to Rome. The Aufidus wanders through the flat landscape almost unwillingly in the direction of the sea, which dominates the horizon like a vast lake of indigo. For a couple of miles he follows its winding course until he notices specks in the distance moving inland from the coast. Their speed soon indicates that they are men on horseback. Lentulus reasons that they are unlikely to be Roman cavalry, but may well be part of an enemy squadron returning from a chase. If he turns away across the plain he will inevitably be seen and captured. Jumping down from the saddle and patting his mare on the neck as if to say, 'Don't wander too far,' he darts into some reeds at the water's edge and wades into the thickest. The horsemen, about ten of them, are approaching rapidly. The water is shallow and slimy, but he squats down and then lies flat with his hands and feet resting in the mud. He reaches down to

Chapter Ten

daub his face with some of the black slime and then peers through the reeds. He is right. The men are Gallic cavalry who, he guesses, are probably returning from the pursuit of Romans who rode right through the initial clash. They canter steadily, apparently in no hurry to return to the fray. None of them wears a helmet and long streaks of hair flop against their naked torsos. One or two have saddles but the remainder use only a rough cloth. Their spears bear the evidence of recent use. One has a head impaled upon it.

At first Lentulus thinks that they are going to ride straight past his mare who has put her head down to graze, unmoved by the Gauls' approach. Two of the riders, however, stop and circle round her. It is clear that she is a cavalry horse who has lost her rider and strayed from the scene of battle. Lentulus can hear the men's voices. He dare not look up, fearing that any movement might catch their eye. By the sound of it one of them is approaching the river and a moment later his horse is splashing about in the water, but he does not enter the reeds, perhaps because of the cloying mud. The Gaul shouts something to the other man and Lentulus fears that he has been spotted. He feels for his sword under the water. The Gaul is within a dozen paces of him. The splashing of the horse recedes and Lentulus realises that the man has rejoined his mate on the bank. After more discussion one of them gallops off in pursuit of his fellows and the other reluctantly follows.

The warm air soon dries his sodden tunic and short cloak, but the smell of the mud lingers disconcertingly. Lentulus points his mare in the direction of the mountains which are now silhouetted by the late afternoon sun. It would be good to find a hamlet or a farmstead where he can get forage for the mare and rest for a short time. She trots over bare, uncultivated land, so arid that it can support only brittle scrub. Towards evening a solitary hillock rises from the plain to the north. Round its base Lentulus can see what appears to be a tiny settlement.

When he reaches it, he finds only the remains of blackened huts and rough stone buildings which have recently been fired. The air is rotten with putrefaction. Neither man nor beast disturbs the heavy silence of the place. The Carthaginians have passed this way.

Wearily he steers his mare once more for the hills. She proceeds at walking pace, accompanied by their shadows lengthening in their wake. The landscape is featureless, offering neither shelter nor any prospect of sustenance. The events of the day begin to take their toll and Lentulus braces himself to stay awake. He has not yet put much distance between himself and the enemy. Rome cannot afford him to be caught. Once or twice his eyes close, only to snap open when some unseen obstacle disturbs the gentle rhythm of the horse. Dusk is almost upon them when the black solidity of a building looms a few hundred paces ahead. This gradually reveals itself to be a small farmstead consisting of three separate sheds of rough-hewn stone. The mare picks up her pace a little and Lentulus guesses that she can smell water. The buildings enclose a yard of beaten earth in the centre of which stands a well with a stone trough beside it. The trough contains a little water which the mare consumes, while Lentulus lowers a wooden bucket which was standing on the lip of the well as if it were expecting him. He takes care to fill his leather bottle before pouring the rest into the trough.

The buildings seem unscathed. The door of one is ajar. He pushes it fully open and immediately becomes aware of a pungent smell from inside. He reels back and then peers again into the gloomy interior. He can just make out a wooden press for grapes and olives, next to which stand two vats. The reason for the overpowering smell is also visible, for slumped across one of the vats is a body covered in flies. A low building of stone close by houses three pigsties, but of the animals there is no trace. A store for animal feed is attached to it, where in a corner he finds a sack containing

Chapter Ten

a small quantity of corn. This he feeds to the mare, wondering whether he will find anything for himself. The third building must be where the smallholder lived. It has a dilapidated appearance, but the possibility of discovering something to eat encourages Lentulus to look inside. The only room discloses the ashes of a fire in the hearth, beside which a pair of crudely carved statuettes, the household gods, have been knocked over. On a table two long trails of ants lead to what look like bits of bread, green with mould, and an earthenware plate holding the remains of a meal. A rough wooden bench and a cot in one corner complete the furnishing. On the floor Lentulus notices the stopper of an amphora. It leans against the wall, cracked and empty. He steps over to an opening in the wall which serves as a window. Outside the last of the light reveals a few gnarled olive trees. The fruit is bitter and barely ripe enough to eat. He chews on a handful. They make a miserable supper.

Here is as good a place as any to rest for a few hours. He contemplates the cot, but inspection shows the woollen blanket to be infested and the woodwork to be in an advanced state of decay. He tethers the mare to an olive tree and makes himself as comfortable as possible on the dead grass beneath its neighbour. Even the smell of his dirty cloak cannot postpone the onset of sleep.

Long before first light Lentulus is slapping water onto his face and feeding the last of the corn to his mare. Until he can put more distance between himself and the Carthaginians there is always the possibility of capture. He must not fail to reach Rome. Even if he cannot fight, at least he can be an efficient messenger. The flat expanse of the plain makes a lone horseman visible from far off. There is nowhere to hide from foraging cavalry. He urges the mare into a steady trot, trying to forget the cramps in his stomach brought on by the handful of olives for breakfast. The comfort of the hills beckons like a mirage that never comes closer. The sun has almost reached its zenith when at last the ground begins to rise. He enters a shallow valley through which a white track leads up towards high pastures. If he keeps heading in a westerly direction he should eventually come across the extension of the Appian Way leading down from Beneventum to Venusia in the south.

The sun warms his crusty cloak and tunic, causing him to remove the former and drape it over the mare's neck. She climbs gamely enough, picking her way through the stones brought down onto the path by winter torrents. Lentulus takes frequent gulps from his flask to try to stave off bouts of giddiness which alternate with stomach pains. At length they breast the pass between two steeply sloping crags to reveal a grassy upland on which sheep are scattered. Higher outcrops serrate the skyline. The going becomes easier as the track flattens out and a gentle breeze helps to subdue the fierceness of the midday heat. Black kites circle in the blue above, seeking thermals on which to soar and contemplate the world below. At a rivulet Lentulus slithers stiffly from his mare to let her drink. He lies back on the grass to rest his dizzy head on a convenient tussock.

He awakes with a start to find a man bending over him. His hand goes instinctively to his dagger before he realises that there is no threat. The newcomer presents a curious appearance. His face is almost black through years of exposure to the Apulian sun. Long grey hair, thinning at the top, hangs in ragged ringlets below his shoulders, which are clothed in sheepskins stitched roughly together to form a sort of sleeveless coat. His legs are similarly covered. In his left hand he carries a shepherd's crook.

Conversation proves difficult as neither can understand the other. Lentulus gestures with his hand that he is in need of food, in response to which the shepherd points with his crook towards a cleft in the hills, indicating that Lentulus should follow him. They set off, cutting across the slope, one foot above the other. The shepherd makes nothing of it, striding over the hillside like a sure-footed goat and

Chapter Ten

turning occasionally to beckon Lentulus with waves of his crook. They round an escarpment beneath which, in a tiny valley dotted with isolated trees, stands a farmstead not dissimilar to the one Lentulus left that morning. Near to the house he can see a patch of cultivated ground for growing vegetables, with a walled enclosure next to it, which he guesses is used to hold sheep.

As they descend the slope the shepherd shouts something in the direction of the house, from which a woman presently emerges. Her face is nearly the same colour as the shepherd's. She wears a woollen smock on which she wipes her hands, and slippers of sheepskin reaching to her calves. It is impossible to guess her age. Having presumably received the message from her husband, if that is who he is, she disappears back inside. Lentulus is ushered through a low stone doorway, down a short passage lined from floor to ceiling with firewood and thence into the single room. The woman is standing at the hearth by a large blackened pot suspended over a brazier of charcoal. She surveys him nervously before turning to the pot and giving its contents a stir. It occurs to Lentulus that she probably thinks he is a Carthaginian. His filthy clothes and stubbly face are hardly indicative of a Roman military tribune. The shepherd is drawing up a stool to a stout table which occupies the middle of the room. One end is piled high with sheepskins.

Looking at him with what he hopes is a reassuring smile, Lentulus repeats several times, 'I am a Roman soldier.' The man appears to understand for he suddenly nods vigorously, then says something rapidly to the woman who looks up from her pot and gives Lentulus an uncertain smile. Having motioned to Lentulus to seat himself on the stool, the shepherd disappears outside while the woman resumes her stirring of the pot, frequently dipping her finger in and then sucking noisily on it. Finally she is satisfied and selects one of a number of bowls stacked by the hearth, into which she ladles a generous helping of the stew. Silently she places it in front of Lentulus and stands back, watching him anxiously. Floating in the thick broth are lumps of mutton and rabbit, much of it still on the bone, together with lentils, beans and slices of turnip. There is the scent of a herb which Lentulus cannot identify. The whole tastes wonderful to his empty stomach. He beams his thanks to the woman who returns them with a smile, showing a neat row of dark brown teeth. He eats greedily, picking out the solid pieces with his fingers before finally raising the bowl to his lips and draining the last of the contents. She fetches some bread to wipe the bowl clean, nodding with satisfaction and more confident now.

The shepherd returns to beckon Lentulus outside, where he finds that his mare has her head down in a bucket of corn. He tries his best to thank the man and to explain that he has nothing with which to pay him. Again the shepherd is quick to understand, spreading out his hands to indicate that no payment is expected. There is one more thing with which the shepherd may be able to help. From the saddle of his mare Lentulus points towards the west and repeats the word, 'Beneventum?' This only produces a frown on the shepherd's face. He seems at a loss until Lentulus remembers that many years previously the Romans had changed the name of the colony from Maleventum because the original name was thought to bring bad luck. The old name is recognised immediately by the shepherd who nods his head and points in the same direction as Lentulus's arm. He is on the point of leaving when the woman comes bustling out of the house carrying a cloth in which she has wrapped bread and slices of turnip. He reaches down to accept the bundle, patting the woman on the shoulder in a gesture of gratitude. At the top of the slope he turns to wave. The pair are standing together where he left them, staring upwards. In unison they raise their arms to him and Lentulus wishes that he had something to give them. How often, he wonders, do they see another human being in this remote spot?

Chapter Ten

Reaching the higher ground he makes good progress, by turns cantering and walking the mare over the gently undulating grassland. At nightfall he pauses by a ravine where a few ash trees have grown up between the rocks. He tethers the mare to one of these and makes himself as comfortable as he can in the lee of a boulder. The moon rises to provide enough light to get on the move again. He follows a narrow path, not much more than a sheep run, in the hope that this will bring him to the road to Beneventum. Around and above, the wind moans in the dark masses of the hills which surge into a paler sky sewn with myriads of sparkling jewels. An intense silence envelops everything in its cloak and for the first time since the battle Lentulus feels confident that the Carthaginians will not catch him. The mare picks her way slowly, but surefootedly, towards a ridge which retreats endlessly before them. With every step another summit comes into view.

His thoughts turn back to the battle. So many of his friends must be dead. Gaius is probably among them. For the first time the full enormity of what has happened is borne in on him. Rome lies prostrate, helpless, though she does not know it yet. He is the man charged with the task of bringing the news of the city's impending destruction: the death of its citizens and the firing of its temples. Even at this moment, somewhere on the tracks behind him, the army of Hannibal, fresh from overwhelming victory, is probably preparing for the march to Rome. And he, Lentulus, who so wanted to fight bravely, and if necessary to die, for the Republic, is once again fleeing from the field. His friends have died honourably in the face of the enemy. He remains, the man who always escapes. He should have ignored the consul's orders, he tells himself, and ridden headlong into the scything Libyans. Better to die fighting than be the wretched messenger of a catastrophe. Rationally he knows he is not fair to himself. Nevertheless the maggot has entered his brain and is feeding there. And

The Daughters of Cannae

Opimia. He must tell her that her brother, the young tribune who rode so exultantly to war, is probably dead, while he, miraculously, has survived again. He longs to see her, to touch and feel her body pressed to his. And yet he dreads it too. How will she greet a man who does his duty by running away? He tries to dismiss these reflections. The consul has ordered him to report to Rome. The matter of his own self-respect is irrelevant.

At last the ground rises less steeply. A soft breeze warns him that the summit of the pass is close. His mare scrambles up onto a small plateau and there beneath them, in a shallow basin surrounded by hills, lies a vast expanse of open land veined by two threads of silver filigree, the rivers at the confluence of which stands the colony of Beneventum. Somewhere to the south the great road must run. As yet he can see no sign of it. In the pale light of the sinking moon shooting stars streak like burning arrows, the skirmishers of some celestial army.[87] Lentulus wonders if the gods too have joined the enemies of Rome. Behind him the darkness is fading into the watery milk of a new dawn as they trot down out of the hills.

Much of the land is brown or scorched where Hannibal's troops overran it the previous year. Lentulus fords a river once traversed by a stout wooden bridge which has been destroyed. Not long afterwards the mare's hooves crunch the gravel of the Appian Way, stretching over the landscape in an endless undeviating ribbon. After the rock-strewn paths the smooth road encourages the mare into a gentle canter, so that by the sixth hour they reach the River Sabatus guarding the southern approaches to Beneventum. A timber bridge supported by three stone pillars leads over the sluggish water to a gatehouse from which sleepy soldiers emerge, roused by the clatter of hooves on the

---

87. Almost certainly the Perseid meteor showers which occur at this time of year.

Chapter Ten

wooden deck. Lentulus orders one of them to conduct him to the town's chief magistrate. In the colonnaded Forum a court is sitting in the open air. The heads of the spectators turn at the sight of the scruffy cavalryman, who seems nevertheless to have an air of authority about him. They stand back to let him pass and approach the tribunal. Not wishing to provoke a panic among the citizens Lentulus requests that the magistrate adjourn the proceedings so that he may speak privately to him. The latter, one of two men elected annually to administer the colony's affairs, orders the people to disperse. He is one Lucius Philo, a second-generation colonist who served under Metellus in Sicily during the previous war.

Within the hour Lentulus is on the road again, bearing a message to the Senate that Beneventum will remain loyal to Rome. He has been furnished with food, a change of tunic and a fresh horse. It grieves him to part with his brave mare, but the urgency of his mission leaves no choice. His new mount is a powerful grey stallion, able to maintain a steady canter for long periods. Philo has parted with him willingly, having expressed the hope that Lentulus may one day be able to return him.

The road climbs out over the hills and into the fertile plains of Campania. By sunset on the following day they are entering the coastal town of Tarracina where Lentulus puts up at the inn for a few hours, instructing the innkeeper to wake him at first light. A thin mist hangs in the dawn air as they clip along past the cultivated fields of Latium, skirting the hills and making good time. When the hamlet of Bovillae comes into view, Lentulus knows that he is only a few miles south of the city. At a roadside inn he pauses to let the horse drink from the trough and persuades the landlord to part with a mug of thin wine and a hunk of bread for himself. The end of the eighth hour is nearly upon them when he remounts for the last stage of the journey. The gravel surface of the road gives way to grey volcanic slabs of basalt, so tightly jointed that the edges are barely discernible.

Lentulus's eyes are fixed on the familiar cluster of low hills above which black sheets of cloud have gathered. To the west the sky is streaked with the blood of a veiled sunset. The gods are telling the city of the grim fate which awaits it. Rain begins to patter down onto the road. Soon it is a cloudburst so violent that the drops bounce up from the smooth surface like a thousands tiny fountains. Jagged bursts of lightning slash the clouds and the bolts of Jupiter reverberate around the hills. A stream of golden fire lights up in sickly white the temples of the Capitol, followed by a crash of thunder so earsplitting that Lentulus fears that the buildings have collapsed. At the Capena Gate the brands lit by the guards in the premature darkness have been extinguished by the downpour. Lentulus is waved through the archway by men who retreat rapidly to their shed beside the wall. He canters on towards the centre of the city. Virtually nobody is abroad in this foul storm and his arrival goes unnoticed, unannounced. The slope of the Palatine rears up on his right. On the far side the Vestals are at prayer, murmuring their supplications for the safety of the city. The solitary horseman passes the Great Circus and veers round to the back of the Capitoline Hill where he dismounts. At the top of a steep flight of steps he pauses, looking for a narrow alleyway which he knows leads to the house of Quintus Fabius. In the semi-darkness he trips over a dog, which growls and lunges at him. Lentulus aims a kick, which misses, and hurries on. The first hour of night has begun when he hammers on the door of the house to which the consul ordered him to report.

Chapter Eleven

216 BC

The news Lentulus brings of the terrible events at Cannae throws the citizens of Rome into the deepest fear and depression, partly engendered by the fact that nobody knows exactly what has happened. Rumours spread that the entire army has been wiped out, that Hannibal is already on the march and will be at the gates of Rome in a few days. Everybody expects an attack at any moment. The women, for there are few men about, take to the streets, wailing and bemoaning the expected slaughter of themselves, following the annihilation of their menfolk. Everybody is in complete despair and several flee the city, hoping to hide in the Sabine Hills or elsewhere, until the crisis is over.

Into this atmosphere Fabius steps with his calming influence. First, he addresses the lack of information, advising the praetors to send reliable and resourceful men out into the country to look for stragglers and survivors of the battle, in the hope of obtaining some news. Next, he proposes that people should remain in their homes to await proper information and quell the spread of unfounded rumours. Instructions are given that mourning should be limited to thirty days to prevent the paralysis of the city and the cancellation of religious festivals. As soon as more news of the battle is available attention can be turned to the

The Daughters of Cannae

defence of the city, including the recruitment of slaves to serve in the legions if necessary.

In the taverns of the city the atmosphere is febrile. A mood of licentiousness prevails, as men and women contemplate the possibility that their last few days may be upon them. It's almost as if the feast of Saturnalia were being celebrated every day, when people do as they like and no questions asked. In one such tavern close to the cattle market sits Vibius, a freedman of no great intellect, but who can read and write passably enough to work as a scribe in the Regia. His job is to trancribe documents and run errands for the Chief Priest and his secretary, a certain Lucius Cantilius. Vibius is not married and lives alone in a one-room apartment near the tavern. He is a regular at the establishment, which is run by Marcus Tubero, sometime centurion in the first legion of the late and disgraced Flaminius when he was fighting the Gauls at the time of his first consulship. Tubero has used his discharge gratuity sensibly to purchase the inn by the market, where he makes a reasonable living from the dockers, small shopkeepers, masons' assistants and animal handlers who inhabit the area. He is an intelligent, straightforward man who keeps himself fit by regular exercise on the Field of Mars.

One of the serving women employed by Tubero is a girl called Pella, upon whom Vibius has had his eye for some time. He fancies her and tonight he thinks he will have his chance, for, unusually, there is money in his purse, a lot of it. Normally he sits by himself, thereby avoiding the expense of buying wine for others. He can nurse one pot of rough stuff for most of an evening. He watches the games of dice being played at two tables in the low-roofed room. Crude tallow candles cast a smoky orange glow above the heads of the participants, bent over earthenware mugs of wine and the small piles of bronze coins in front of each of them. In another corner two old men are engaged in their

Chapter Eleven

habitual game of draughts, using a grid scratched out on the table.

Vibius has been in the tavern since the first hour of the night, watching Pella who circulates among the customers, carrying an amphora in her strong bare arms. Occasionally she pauses to refill a mug, placing the payment in a leather pouch attached to her belt. She responds to his beckoning finger with a friendly smile which serves only to increase his growing ardour, promoted by having drunk more than usual.

'You seem thirsty tonight,' she says. 'Not like you to have more than one mug of an evening.'

'You can fill it up again, love.' Vibius pats her on the bottom as she bends to fill the pot by his side. 'And here's a little something for yourself. No need to pass it on to Tubero.' He takes out a silver denarius and presses it into her palm, together with a quarter – as in payment for the wine. Pella looks round, anxious that nobody should have seen the denarius, then drops it down the front of her tunic. The rent is overdue on the draughty wooden room she occupies with her mother at the top of a tenement block near the river.

Vibius leers up at her from his seat against the wall. 'There'll be another one of those if you see me right when Tubero closes up.' His words are somewhat slurred. Pella makes no reply but smiles, confident that the fresh mug of wine will save her from his attentions later. Vibius, however, is encouraged by her look, which produces in him an eager contemplation.

On one of the tables the dice continue to rattle. Three men seem to be losing, judging by the diminishing pile of coins in front of each of them. The fourth man, however, a large, heavily built fellow whom Vibius has seen occasionally before, is having all the luck. The pile of coins in front of him grows steadily. He becomes more raucous and confident as the night wears on, calling repeatedly for more

The Daughters of Cannae

wine and food. A boy appears carrying a platter of pasties fresh from the brick oven in the back room of the tavern. The man with the winnings waves his hand, indicating to his friends to help themselves before taking two for himself, cramming one into his mouth and placing the other beside him. With his mouth full of pasty he pushes the jugs of his fellow players across the table for Pella to fill. His own jug he slides away from her, so that she is obliged to stretch over him to reach it. Still munching, he pulls her down, forcing her to sit on his lap while she pours the wine. He takes advantage to plant a messy kiss on her cheek, at the same time fondling her breasts with a greasy hand.

Vibius, who is well gone in his drink by now and imbued with a confidence which he would not ordinarily display, shouts across the room angrily, 'Leave her alone. She's mine tonight, not yours, you great oaf.'

The hum of conversation ceases abruptly as the customers pause in their various pursuits. Pella rises hastily from the man's lap, wipes her face on the back of her hand and disappears into the kitchen. The docker, for that is his occupation, is not used to being called an oaf. He sets down the second pasty, which he was about to consume, and lurches to his feet, knocking his chair over in the process. He stumbles across the room to seize hold of Vibius who stands up to receive him. Inevitably they lose their balance and fall to the floor where they roll around in the dirt and spilt wine, each struggling to get a grip on the other's neck and at the same time flailing with their legs in their attempts to kick the other in the guts.

Tubero emerges rapidly from behind the counter where he has been engaged in opening another amphora since business is brisker than usual. The occasional outbreak of violence is nothing new. Indeed it goes with the nature of his clientele, who are more accustomed to settling their differences over women, or anything else for that matter,

Chapter Eleven

by the use of their fists rather than their tongues. The point of a dagger applied to the throat of each combatant is sufficient to quieten things. Vibius grabs at the bench on which he had been sitting, to haul himself to his feet. His belt catches on the edge of it and somehow pulls open the drawstring of his purse from which coins spill out in profusion on the floor. Most of them are silver denarii, like the one he has just put into Pella's hand. The other customers look on aghast. None of them could ever hope to have such an amount of money about their person. Vibius almost falls over again in his haste to gather up the coins. Fortunately for him, the presence of Tubero saves him from several of the other drinkers who might otherwise have helped themselves and made off with what they could. Once all the money has been retrieved, the landlord helps Vibius to his feet amid much muttering at how he could possibly come to be in possession of such a sum.

'No wonder you've had a few drinks tonight. Where did you get money like that, Vibius?' Tubero is well aware of the work that Vibius does and that it does not enable him to carry about fistfuls of denarii.

'Never you mind.' Vibius looks round aggressively. 'Just give me another drink and tell that bloke to keep his hands off Pella.' He steadies himself against the bench, before sitting down heavily on it. The other customers resume their gambling. They know better than to interfere once Tubero has taken charge.

'You aren't having another drink until you tell me how you came by that money. Have you stolen it?'

'Give me another jug and I'll tell you.' Vibius assumes a conspiratorial look.

'No. You tell me where that money came from. Then you can have another drink.'

Vibius pulls Tubero down next to him. 'If I tell you, promise not to tell anybody else,' he giggles.

'I can't do that until you tell me where it came from.'

'Not possible. I got the money for promising to keep my mouth shut.' Vibius starts to giggle again.

Marcus Tubero is an upright man, and not without intelligence. He knows that the Regia is an important part of the city's religious life from where the Chief Priest carries out many of his official duties. If something irregular has occurred there it may be a matter for investigation, particularly if it is anything that might cause offence to the gods. He recalls recent speeches to the people in which Fabius and other conservatives in the Senate have insisted upon the diligent performance of religious ceremonies. The failure to observe these rites correctly has resulted in the calamities which have befallen the city. Having pondered the matter overnight, Tubero decides in the morning to call upon his patron, Publius Valerius Flaccus, consul eleven years ago. Flaccus agrees that Vibius's sudden possession of so much money is a little strange and promises to refer the matter to Caudinus.

The Chief Priest has survived to a great age and is rapidly losing such faculties as he possessed. He hears only with difficulty and his sight is failing, so that in his house and at the Regia a slave can often be heard shouting the words of some document to him. Indeed Vibius frequently performs this task. When Flaccus calls to see him to discuss the incident in the tavern by the cattle market, it is all he can do to make the old man understand. Eventually Caudinus grasps the point but says he really cannot undertake any investigation himself. It is too much for him. He will pass the matter on to the Priest of Mars, Publius Umbrenus, to make some inquiries.

The interview in the Regia between Umbrenus and Vibius does not last long. Under threat of a little physical persuasion Vibius readily reveals the source of the money in his purse. Umbrenus takes care to relieve him of the coins.

* * *

Chapter Eleven

In the house on the Esquiline, Naevia and Opimia await the arrival of Lentulus who has sent word that he is back in the city. The meeting is painful for Naevia whose worst fears are substantially confirmed by Lentulus when he arrives. Gaius has not been seen or heard of since the cavalry charge at the beginning of the battle. Lentulus cannot be certain, but it is most unlikely that Gaius survived.

'I should be deceiving you if I said otherwise. I am certain that he died gallantly in the thick of the fighting, as I would like to have done.' Naevia and Opimia receive the news stoically, seated on a couch while Lentulus remains standing awkwardly before them. Their sorrow is matched only by his feeling of utter shame, that once again he has left a battle and returned home unscathed, leaving so many of his comrades and friends to die fighting for the Republic.

Naevia thanks him for coming to relay such news as he has. Her head is bowed, but she does not weep. Many matrons of the city have lost more than she, husbands and sons as well. On Opimia's arm she walks from the room, dignified and simple in her grief.

Lentulus waits for Opimia to return. His shame is such that he considers leaving without saying goodbye. That would be an unkindness, which she does not deserve. He sits down on the couch where she finds him, taking his hand and seeming to understand his feelings. They remain silent, neither knowing what to say, until her lips brush his cheek and her hand gently squeezes his.

'I'm so glad that at least you survived.' The tears are streaming down her face. 'I don't know that I could have stood it, if both you and Gaius had been killed.'

'I always survive, don't I?' he mutters, almost to himself. 'I can't help this sense of being a coward. I'm ashamed to be sitting here. If it were not for you, I believe I might take a dagger to my throat.'

'Promise me you will not do that!' She flings her arms round him, burying her face against his chest. He lifts it in his hands. The sadness in her eyes is overwhelmingly beautiful, so that he cannot resist smothering her with kisses. The passion of the moment is frighteningly intense for both of them. He draws back, conscious of the status of the woman he has been embracing so tightly. Opimia, too, gasps at the realisation of her own behaviour.

'You must go now.' The words are whispered, as if she does not want him to hear them. Lentulus nods, but makes no move. Opimia stands up, close to him, pushing her hands back and forth through the curls of his hair. He looks into her eyes, smiles and rests his head in the folds of her gown. It lasts only a few moments. Suddenly she turns away and runs from the room. He knows she will not come back. A great lassitude descends upon him.

In the Vestals' house Postumia and the other priestesses wait, apart from Floronia who is missing. It is apparent that Postumia knows where Floronia is, for she makes no inquiry about her absence. She stares fixedly in front of her, unwilling to engage in conversation, as if she were about to undergo some ordeal for which she is steeling herself. Opimia realises that something must be very wrong. It's written in the faces of the others who are equally withdrawn and tense.

A messenger arrives with instructions that they are to present themselves before the Chief Priest. The memory of the previous occasion when they were summoned to the Regia haunts Opimia on the short walk across the Sacred Way. She strives to control the wave of apprehension which increases with every step. As they enter the building she is shaking like a person suffering from a fever. Caudinus indicates a row of stools set to one side of the dais which Opimia remembers. The Chief Priest sits in the same chair

Chapter Eleven

as before, flanked on one side by the Priest of Jupiter and on the other by Umbrenus, who has the Priest of Quirinus to his left. Behind them the twelve lesser priests, whose cults complete the pantheon of gods, are arranged in an arc on rather smaller chairs. All are robed and capped.

'These proceedings,' squeaks Caudinus, 'will be conducted by the Priest of Mars. Unfortunately my hearing these days is not such as to permit me to conduct them myself.' He taps his iron knife against the side of his chair to signal the commencement of the hearing.

From behind the dais, where she has hitherto remained hidden, Floronia is led forward and told to stand before the priests. She does not wear her Vestal headdress and likewise her gown is missing, replaced by a long plain tunic. Her shuffling gait indicates that she is hobbled by some invisible cord or chain concealed beneath the tunic. There is no trace of colour in her face apart from her eyes, which appear pink and swollen. She seems almost oblivious to her surroundings, staring down at the mosaic patterns of the pavement. Opimia can hardly bear to look. Two seats away, Postumia's face is set in chiselled lines. Next to her, poor Livia has clasped her hands together so fiercely that the knuckles show white through the tautened skin.

'You are aware of the accusation against you?' Umbrenus, who is privately relishing the situation and his role in it, speaks in a curiously stilted accent intended to disguise the rougher tones of his birth and plebeian class. His money has certainly advanced him in society.

Floronia does not look up, but nods wearily.

'And do you continue to deny it?'

'I deny all of it, all of it. I am innocent as I have already told you!' She suddenly becomes animated and shouts the words out across the chamber.

'Very well.' Umbrenus turns to an acolyte. 'Let Vibius be brought in.'

The Daughters of Cannae

Vibius steps forward to stand no more than a couple of paces from Floronia. He appears a little shame-faced and does not look at her.

'You are Marcus Vibius and you work here at the Regia as a clerk?'

Upon Vibius's assent Umbrenus leans forward in his chair. The eyes, deeply set in the jowly face, fix Vibius who moves uncertainly from one foot to the other. 'Now tell us what it was you saw four days ago and how you came to see it.' The words emerge from the mouth of Umbrenus as a mixture of curiosity and threat.

'I work here in the Regia, sir, running errands and writing documents for the Chief Priest and Lucius Cantilius. He sent me with a message.'

'Who sent you with a message?'

'Cantilius, sir. He sent me to the Senate with a message for Cethegus, who is standing for a priesthood.'

'Yes, we know that. Go on.'

'Sir, I got half way to the Senate House and then realised I had forgotten my stylus to take down any reply. So I went back to the Regia and that's when I saw them.'

'Saw who?'

'Cantilius and the Vestal Floronia, sir.' Floronia turns her head sharply to stare at Vibius.

'And where were Cantilius and the Vestal Floronia when you saw them?'

'They were just inside the shrine to the goddess Ops Consiva, sir.' There is a stirring among the other priests, horrified that a clerk could have entered the shrine forbidden to all but the Vestals and the Chief Priest.

'You are saying that Cantilius was within the precincts of the shrine. Are you sure of that?'

'Yes, sir. I saw them both there.' Many of the priests shake their heads in disbelief.

'And what were they doing?'

Chapter Eleven

The colour rises in Vibius's cheeks. He stands speechless, seemingly lost for words. The eyes of every person in the chamber are fixed upon him.

'Well, man, what were they doing?'

'They were having intercourse, sir.' Vibius blurts out the words, which provoke an outburst from the seats behind Umbrenus, who holds up his hand for silence.

'Are you saying that they were indulging in full sexual intercourse?' Umbrenus puts heavy emphasis on the last phrase.

'Yes, sir.'

'I deny it!' Floronia screams, pointing a quivering arm at Vibius. 'This man is a filthy liar! How can you possibly taint a Vestal in this way?' Her whole body shakes and she turns her face upwards as if appealing to the gods to be her witnesses.

'Be quiet! You'll have your say in due time.' Livia catches her breath at the insolent way in which Umbrenus addresses Floronia. 'How do you know they were having intercourse?'

'I could see them, sir.'

'Yes, yes. Be more precise.'

'Well, sir, not to put too fine a point on it, she had lifted her gown and was holding it around her waist. Cantilius's tunic was up too, so that I could see he was thrusting himself into her. There was no mistaking it.' Once again a loud murmur rises from the row of priests, some of whom protest that the clerk's testimony is outrageous.

Floronia shrieks at Umbrenus. 'I tell you, Vibius is lying! I have never been near Cantilius. I find him repugnant!' She buries her face in her hands, sobbing uncontrollably.

Umbrenus ignores her. 'And what happened then?'

'Cantilius had his back to me, but Floronia caught sight of me. She gave a little cry and they separated. Cantilius came out of the shrine. Floronia stayed inside. She didn't come out while I was there.' With her hands still pressed to her face Floronia shakes her head, rocking back and forth on her heels.

The Daughters of Cannae

'Did Cantilius say anything to you?'

'Not then, sir. He just walked straight past me. He gave me a bit of a look.'

'I should think he did.' Umbrenus cannot disguise the snigger in his voice. 'You say he did not speak to you then. Did he say anything later?'

'Yes, sir.'

'And what was that?'

'He came to me later that day and told me to forget what I had seen.'

'Anything else?'

'Yes, sir. He gave me fifty silver denarii and said there would be some more, so long as I kept my mouth shut.'

'But you didn't keep silent, did you?'

'No, sir. You persuaded me that it was my duty to reveal what I had seen.'

One or two glances are exchanged among the junior priests, who are well aware of Umbrenus's persuasive powers.

'Very well. You may stand aside for the moment.' Umbrenus confers briefly with Caudinus who cups his ear to listen. He has caught the drift of Vibius's evidence, but not the details. As Umbrenus talks into his ear he watches Floronia, occasionally nodding vigorously. Then, addressing nobody in particular and speaking rather loudly in the manner of deaf people sometimes, he starts to relate the incident many years ago when he had occasion to whip Floronia for letting the Vestal flame go out. She looks round the chamber, seeking some vestige of support, but nobody meets her eye.

Cantilius is brought in, rattling in the chains binding his ankles together. His hands are also bound and he bears the drawn features of one who has been deprived of sleep. Two burly men push him to stand next to Floronia. Each ignores the presence of the other.

Umbrenus begins his examination. His accusations are met with denials on all points. The whole affair is a web of

Chapter Eleven

lies concocted by Vibius to explain away his possession of the money, which has been stolen from the treasury in the Regia. An inspection of the coffers will confirm that a similar amount is missing. Umbrenus concedes that a slightly greater sum than that found on Vibius is indeed missing, but points out that this could just as easily have been taken by Cantilius himself, who had readier access to the treasury, and then given to Vibius in return for his silence.

Nevertheless, Cantilius stoutly maintains his innocence, claiming that nothing improper has ever taken place between himself and Floronia. At these words she turns to look at him for the first time. 'What Cantilius says is true. You must believe us!'

Cantilius warms to his task, sensing that many of the priests are beginning to doubt the evidence of Vibius. He pleads with the Chief Priest to accept the word of a Vestal Virgin and himself, rather than the story of a clerk attempting to disguise a theft in which he has been detected. Beside him Floronia weeps, mouthing the words, 'I am undefiled.'

Tuditanus, Priest of Jupiter, has his doubts. On the far side from Umbrenus, he speaks into the other ear of Caudinus on whose decision the fate of the accused depends. He is for dismissal of the case. There's no corroboration of the evidence of Vibius and Caudinus agrees that he has never previously found Cantilius to be untrustworthy or dishonest. Umbrenus, however, is in the other ear again. He is not convinced. He wants further time to investigate the matter. What harm can there be in a short adjournment? Surely, the important thing is to establish the truth. Eventually Caudinus is persuaded. The following day is one on which no business may be conducted. The resumed hearing is fixed for the day after.

Umbrenus again takes charge of the reconvened proceedings. All are present, as before, to observe Floronia brought shuffling in to stand before the dais. There is an

The Daughters of Cannae

aura of defiance about her, as when she stripped off her bodice to reveal her back before the beating. Opimia tries to catch the eye of her old friend to communicate her support, but Floronia only looks stonily ahead at the tribunal. Opimia prays to Vesta for her safety. A murmur goes round the chamber when Cantilius appears. The chains around his ankles cannot disguise a limp and one arm hangs inertly by his side. His gait is like that of a man walking in his sleep, staring sightlessly in front of him. When he has reached his position beside Floronia the murmuring stops. Everybody waits.

At length Umbrenus looks up and contemplates the pair, before speaking in a sharp voice. 'I understand, Cantilius, that you may have something more to say to us.'

Cantilius inclines his head a little. It appears to cause him some discomfort.

'Very well. What is it?'

'I want to say that what I first said was not true.' He swallows and his body sways a little.

'Go on.'

'I have had intercourse with the Vestal Floronia many times. What Vibius said is true.' The words emerge like those learnt by a child declaiming to his master. Floronia shrieks, collapsing to her knees on the pavement.

'You liar, you liar, you liar!' she screams. 'Can't you see he has been forced to say this? Look at him, he can barely stand!' She continues to shout at Umbrenus who orders two acolytes to restrain her by means of a gag across her mouth.

'Why have you changed your evidence, Cantilius?' He makes no reply, apparently not having heard the question, which Umbrenus repeats.

'I realised,' his voice trails away and he pauses, then with an effort starts again. 'I realised that it was my duty to tell the truth.' On the pavement next to him Floronia falls sideways in a crumpled heap.

Chapter Eleven

Once more Umbrenus confers with Caudinus. After some discussion and much nodding by Caudinus, the latter pronounces judgment in his high-pitched tones.

The citizens have crowded into the Forum where they occupy any vantage point which affords a view of the wooden frame set up on a platform near the great sundial. Several senators are grouped on the Rostra, while lesser folk throng the ambassadors' platform, the steps round the Comitium or even perch on chairs brought out from the shops. The news of the debauching of a Vestal has spread like fire through the city. Now is the opportunity to offer expiation to the gods and to put an end to the woes that have recently afflicted the Republic. All eyes are fixed on the entrance to the Tullianum, the dungeon carved out of the rocky slope of the Capitoline Hill above the Forum. The people give a great shout when the figure of Cantilius appears. He is chained on each side to the arm of a soldier. Slowly they begin their descent into the square. The soldiers half drag and half carry Cantilius down the steps. His feet trail on the ground and his head lolls on one shoulder. The crowd chant, 'Adulterer! Adulterer!' Some spit or throw bits of food, while others merely wave their fists. With leather thongs the soldiers secure Cantilius to the frame, before ripping the tunic from his body to the cheers of the spectators. The white flesh is already stained dark purple and yellow. Caudinus hobbles forward on his stick which he exchanges for a whip composed of thin strips of leather. He holds this aloft, drawing roars of approval from the crowd, before handing it over to one of the soldiers. Like the heads of so many vipers the thongs hiss through the air to strike at their victim. Several in the crowd have gambled on the number of blows it will take to kill Cantilius. They count each one out loud as the executioner slashes into the matted flesh. When all signs of life have disappeared the soldier thrusts a spear into the ribs of the mangled torso to make sure of death.

In the house of the Vestals a cheerless dawn beckons Opimia from her bed. She has not slept, her head churning with confusion and uncertainty. What was sharply etched in her mind so recently has become pale and blurred. Until now it had not occurred to her that the woman she saw in the glade on the Palatine might not be Floronia. Perhaps it was not her. She did not actually see her face, nor that of the man. She does not recognise Cantilius. She could be wrong. The more she tries to concentrate on the scene, the more doubt infiltrates her brain. Her instinct tells her it was Floronia, and yet suppose that it were somebody else. Then, surely, her sacrifice will not propitiate the gods. It may even anger them. A trial has been manipulated to achieve a conviction. That must be an insult to Vesta, which she and her fellow gods will certainly punish by visiting even worse calamities upon the city.

She hears footsteps in the atrium and emerges to find the other priestesses gathered there. Livia is trying to comfort the child Licinia who is weeping openly. Postumia and Tuccia stand pale and silent, apparently wrapped in their own thoughts. Each wears on her head the white cloth appropriate for sacrifice. Opimia realises that she has forgotten hers and retreats back to her room to fetch it. At the sound of a bugle ringing out across the Forum Postumia motions to the others to follow her.

On the far side of the Sacred Way the gates of the Regia are drawn open to reveal in the entrance a strange, forlorn figure, dressed as before in a plain full-length woollen tunic. Beneath close-cropped blonde hair Floronia's face is rigid, as if transformed into white marble. Dark rings surround unseeing eyes. From somewhere inside the courtyard a man appears holding a coil of rope with which

Chapter Eleven

he ties her hands together. From behind, another acolyte produces a cloth which he secures across her mouth, then knots at the nape of her neck. Livia clutches the arm of Opimia to steady herself. The man who tied the cloth pushes Floronia forward and she steps uncertainly through the gates. At the sight of her a collective murmur rises from the crowd who line the street. Somebody shouts, 'Traitor!' and the cry is taken up by others. Four litter bearers set down a chair in front of her. From the steps of the Regia, where the stooped figure of Caudinus stands propped on his stick in company with the other priests, an order is given. The men bind Floronia's feet with cord and lift her into the litter, closing the curtains around her. With the disappearance of the Vestal from view the crowd falls silent, except for a matron who drops to the ground in a faint. The apples in the basket she was carrying roll across the pavement, but nobody moves to gather them up. Once more the notes of a bugle sound sorrowfully over the city.

The litter bearers bend to take up their burden and begin the tortuous journey through the streets. Before them walks the skirted executioner, carrying an axe over his shoulder. A few mourners, dressed in dark funerary clothes sprinkled with ashes, fall in behind the litter. No family members wearing the face masks of distinguished ancestors, no mimics or flute players accompany them. Postumia leads the other Vestals back into the House, but Opimia remains, her eyes fixed on the litter swaying on the shoulders of the bearers, until finally they are lost to view as they climb past the temple of Juno Moneta. The thought that Floronia might after all be innocent tortures her. She feels Livia's arm around her shoulders. The older woman guides her gently into the Grove of Vesta where the thrushes are striking up to welcome a new day. They find a seat close to the path leading to the pool. Opimia calms herself enough to speak.

The Daughters of Cannae

'Will she suffer for long?'

'They say not. I believe it is a relatively painless death. I hope so. The goddess will welcome her back to the earth.'

'I don't believe she should ever have been a Vestal. After all, she did not have the choice.'

'None of us had that choice, dear, though I am happy with my lot.'

Opimia ignores the unspoken question. 'It's so unjust that she should die for the fault of others.'

'Is her death any more unjust than those of the men who fell at Cannae through the incompetence of their generals?'

Opimia is silent, twisting her fingers together and then pulling them apart, until Livia gently restrains her. 'That trial was a mockery. Cantilius was tortured to change his evidence. That was obvious.' Opimia pumps her fists on her lap in frustration.

'You may well be right, dear.' Livia puts her hand on Opimia's. 'But the Senate needed an offering to appease the gods. Perhaps the sacrifice of an innocent woman is more acceptable than the sacrifice of one who is guilty.'

'Do you believe that Floronia was guilty?'

'I cannot say. There are influential men in Rome, senators and priests, who insist that our relationship with the gods must be preserved at all costs. Guilt or innocence is of no consequence to them. When things go wrong, they seek an explanation, something which has caused the gods to punish us. It is the sacrifice that matters, not the truth. Who knows what pressure was brought to bear on Cantilius?'

'But Hannibal is still out there. At any moment he may march upon the city and destroy us.'

'We shall not gain anything by such speculation, my dear.' Livia rises from the seat with a sigh and leads the way back to the house.

Old men, matrons and the children of the city emerge from their shops, tenements and little houses to line the

Chapter Eleven

streets and alleyways. With the approach of the litter their chatter ceases and at the moment of its passing each citizen turns his back, so that the dismal cortège seems to plough a furrow through the throng. Along the Subura and on between the Esquiline and Viminal Hills the procession makes its solemn way, the eyes of every man and woman momentarily averted to avoid the sight of it. The ascent towards the city wall is short and steep, causing the bearers to blow out their cheeks. Now they are on level ground again, following the wall to the Field of the Wicked outside the Colline Gate. Here a low grassy ridge runs out at right angles from the wall, beneath which more citizens are assembled to witness the final act. On the ridge itself the Chief Priest waits by a ladder protruding from a hole hollowed out of the bank. Beside him stand two acolytes bearing a bowl of water, some oil, bread and the milk of a donkey. At Caudinus's signal they descend the ladder to deposit the food and water and to light the lamp next to the covered couch within, before re-emerging.

The bearers, having reached their destination, set down the litter close by the ridge. The curtains hiding Floronia from view are untied. The bearers reach inside to release the cloth over her mouth and the cords that held her. Once again, utter silence descends upon the scene. The crowd watches and waits tensely. At last there is movement from inside the litter and Floronia climbs out unsteadily, for the journey has cramped her limbs. She stands alone, blinking in the sudden light. Caudinus, hunched over his stick, begins to intone a prayer, mumbling inaudibly into his straggly beard. He cuts a sorry figure beside Floronia, tall and slim in her long white tunic, framed by the dark wall of the city behind her. In a final gesture of supplication he raises his arms to the heavens, at which the bearers move forward. Floronia defiantly waves them away and walks firmly to the ladder. For the last time the citizens turn their backs upon her. Slowly, deliberately and silently she descends the ladder, pausing on each rung, until finally her head disappears into the blackness. Caudinus calls on the gods to witness her departure from the upper world. Many of the citizens raise their arms in a prayer to Vesta that her priestess may have a safe and speedy journey, accompanied by the goddess in the flame of the oil lamp. Her passing will be in the hands of the goddess, not the citizens of Rome. They have provided milk, bread and water, thus absolving themselves of the responsibility for the death of a priestess. The executioner carries away his unused axe and the bearers pull up the ladder, before covering the entrance to the cavity with a heavy sheet of bronze over which they pile earth and stones. The immolation of Floronia is complete.

That same day, at about the tenth hour, the two-wheeled carriage of a Vestal passes through the Capena Gate and out onto the Appian Way. Inside it Opimia tries to dismiss from her mind the fate of her former friend, but the vision of her lying on the couch, shivering and in total darkness once the oil in the lamp runs out, lays siege to her. She cannot escape it. Her mules maintain a steady clip until they reach a point near the first milestone. Here Opimia alights, telling the driver to wait. In the gathering dusk she climbs the grassy bank to the family mausoleum close beside the road. The granite façade of the tomb is surmounted by a pediment bearing a frieze carved with the figures of famous ancestors. Urns of black marble draped in laurel decorate each end of the pediment, in the centre of which the goddess of victory reclines on a couch, holding a wreath of oak leaves above the kneeling goddess of Roma. Taking a key, Opimia unlocks the heavy bolts securing the bronze door, which with considerable effort she pulls open. Inside, the clammy air wraps itself around her like a damp cloak. She waits for her eyes to become accustomed to the dark and then reaches up to find what she is looking for. Her fingers walk along the shelf of the niche until they clasp the casket in which the ashes of her

Chapter Eleven

father are contained. Gently she lowers it and holds it closely, wrapped in the folds of her gown. In that gloomy chamber she conjures up the image of Lucius, who appears before her as she likes to remember him, when she was young and he was not disfigured, long before the troubles that have since assailed her and Rome. She remembers the early mornings when she would run to his room and lean against his knees while he put on his sandals, then pass him the goblet of water he drank every day before leaving the house. The bond between them has never been broken, even when she was formally cut off from the family on becoming a Vestal. She always understood that he was not rejecting her. In the dark silence, isolated from the upper world, his image hardens into corporeality. He is sitting with her in the peristyle, his smiling face inclined towards her, and waiting patiently. He knows the question she will put to him, the question to which she knows his answer. She bows her head in acquiescence and he nods gently with approval. It is enough. The image fades and disappears.

Outside, the warm air of the departing day is a relief after the chill inside the tomb. The bronze door groans under the pressure of her hands and she slides home the bolts. She pauses for a moment to pray to the god Pluto that her father may have drunk from the river Lethe to forget the sufferings of his past life and start anew in the underworld.[88]

As she approaches the city the last rays of the sun are gilding the finials on the temple of Capitoline Jupiter, so that they resemble torches held aloft above the gentle undulations of the city's hills, lying like the recumbent bodies of young women. Past the Capena Gate the carriage makes a detour to a small house on the Aventine Hill, where Opimia dismounts and pays a short visit to the

---

88. Pluto was the god of the underworld where the river Lethe ran, from which the souls of the departed drank to forget their previous sufferings.

occupant. It is almost dark by the time she returns to the house of the Vestals, heavy with the terror of the day. The slaves, speechless and frightened, move silently to light the lamps. Postumia and Livia are nowhere to be seen. Opimia goes straight to the temple to relieve Tuccia for the first watch of the night. It is many months since she has been so clear and calm in her mind.

In the morning a rumour reaches Rome that a delegation of ten men, representing about 7,000 legionaries captured in their camp by Hannibal after the battle, is approaching the outskirts of the city. The Carthaginians have released them upon an oath to return after their mission, which is to plead for the soldiers' ransom from captivity. Hannibal has set a price of five hundred denarii for every cavalryman, three hundred for an infantryman and one hundred for a slave. Marcus Junius, the dictator appointed by the Senate to deal with the latest crisis, despatches a lictor to inform the Carthaginian nobleman accompanying the delegation, one Carthalo, that he must leave Roman territory by nightfall. He has agreed, however, to receive the ten men and to permit their leader to address the Senate.

An anxious throng awaits their arrival in the Forum. Some have pushed forward into the vestibule of the Senate House where they are already pleading with the members to find the ransom money and return the prisoners to their families. Lentulus has climbed onto the Rostra to observe the scene. He remains deeply troubled by the manner of his departure from the battle. He is debating whether to return with the delegation and surrender himself into captivity, whatever the decision of the Senate.

At length the shouts of the crowd, many of whom are hostile to these men who have surrendered without a fight, herald the arrival of the delegation on the Sacred Way. They bear no resemblance to legionaries, having been stripped of their arms and armour. Their appearance is more that of a ragged band of slaves, unshaven and

Chapter Eleven

unkempt, shameful travesties of Roman soldiers. With heads bowed they shuffle forward through the Comitium to the steps of the Senate House. The lictors clear the vestibule to enable this forlorn group to enter. Inside, the senators view them gravely from their benches. Marcus Junius calls for silence and the captives' leader begins his plea for the ransom money.

Meanwhile Lentulus lingers on the Rostra, waiting to see what happens. He is by himself and in no great mood to be sociable. Beneath him on the pavement a group of women are talking. They have gathered round one of their number who seems to have interesting news to impart. Lentulus recognises her as the daughter of Publius Umbrenus, Priest of Mars. Mildly curious he bends down to listen, unnoticed by the women below.

'Father says that another great scandal is about to break. You know about Floronia, of course. Well, a second Vestal has gone missing!' The others come closer, eager not to miss a word. One asks who it is.

'I don't suppose I should tell you really, but I overheard the messenger from the Regia say it was Opimia. Apparently she disappeared last night, dressed in ordinary clothes! They're looking for her now.'

Lentulus makes no sudden movement, fearing that it might betray his eavesdropping, but edges away through the crowd on the Rostra. Once out of the Forum he discards his cumbersome toga, which he presses into the hands of a surprised youth, telling him to keep it. Being fit, as any good cavalryman should be, he maintains a steady trot up the Esquiline Hill to Naevia's house. While he waits for her in the atrium Orrius passes on his way to tend his vegetable patch. The old slave greets the familiar figure of Lentulus with his slow smile and a bow. He is followed moments later by Naevia who extends a welcoming hand and wonders to herself at her visitor's lack of formal dress. She seems to Lentulus less tall than he remembers and her

The Daughters of Cannae

hair, drawn back almost severely from her forehead, has lost most of its colour. The lines on her face betray the strain of the later years caring for her husband and the almost certain loss of her son. Nevertheless, she smiles gallantly and ushers Lentulus to sit with her.

In a few words he relates what he has overheard in the Forum. Naevia confirms what he already half suspects, that Opimia has not been to the house. She wonders whether there may not be some innocent explanation for her absence. Lentulus has not mentioned the matter of Opimia's clothing and tries to keep the anxiety from his voice.

'Do you know of anywhere she might go if she did not come here to see you?'

'That's a strange question.' Naevia looks at him steadily. 'Do you think she is in trouble? That business of Floronia must have shocked her terribly. They were close at one time, you know. And the death of Gaius has upset us all.' Her voice falters and she bites her lip in an effort to control herself. Her head sinks onto her breast. Lentulus senses the battle this brave and once vivacious lady is fighting against her emotions. In a few moments she recovers her composure. 'I'm sorry. Sometimes it is very hard. What was it that you were asking?'

Lentulus does not respond immediately, but places his hand on the old lady's arm, trying to convey the sympathy that he feels. She gives him a weak smile, then quietly repeats her question.

'Opimia once told me that you have a villa in the hills at Tibur.'

'Yes, we used to go there every summer. Opimia loved it there.'

'Is it possible that she might have gone to it?'

'I suppose it's possible, but I can't think why. It must be many years since we last went.'

'I will check that she has not returned to the Vestals' house. If she hasn't, I might take a ride out to your villa. I

Chapter Eleven

have a good horse and he could do with the exercise. Perhaps you could give me some directions.'

'Oh, that's very simple.' Naevia describes the route, then holds out her hand for Lentulus to raise her from the couch. He stoops to kiss her on the forehead, takes both her frail hands in his and gently lifts her to her feet. She peers searchingly at him, then nods imperceptibly as if satisfied with what she sees. 'I'm sure you'll find her somewhere.'

Lentulus is on the point of leaving when a slave enters to say that a messenger from the house of Vestals is outside.

'Perhaps it might be safer if this man were not aware of my presence here.'

Naevia indicates a screen behind which he conceals himself, before the messenger is brought in. He has been sent by Postumia, who wishes to know whether Naevia has any knowledge of her daughter's whereabouts.

'It is a most irregular inquiry. The Chief Vestal is no doubt aware that I am not accountable for my daughter's movements. However, you may tell her that my daughter is not here and to my knowledge has not been here. Perhaps I may be permitted to ask what this is about?'

The messenger knows only that Opimia was seen to leave the Vestals' house shortly before dawn, dressed in ordinary clothing. It is disturbing news, but Naevia remains composed.

'I'm afraid I can be of no further help. No doubt there is some perfectly innocent explanation.' With an inclination of her head she indicates that the interview is over. The messenger departs, followed shortly by Lentulus who promises to return as soon as he has any news.

In her distraction Naevia walks out into the peristyle. She hears Orrius scratching with his hoe and goes to a seat under the almond tree. He does not notice her at first and continues his methodical progress round a patch of lettuces. There is comfort in observing this old family servant, freed under the terms of Lucius's will. He has a calm, unruffled air which communicates itself to Naevia as she sits watching him. He finishes the hoeing and, as usual when he has a visitor to his garden, he cuts the best blooms on the rose pergola and offers them to Naevia with a toothless smile. He is a link with a past and happier period of her life. She asks him to sit down beside her. It is good to have his company.

From the house on the Quirinal Lentulus circles round the city wall to avoid delays on the crowded streets. Soon the grey stallion lent to him by Philo is cantering along the Tiburtine Way towards the hills. A shower of rain has cleared the dusty air and the sun, close to its zenith, shines down benignly from a fluffy sky. There are few carters on the road. Those bringing produce into the city have long since passed and will not return this way till dusk. No day could be more pleasant for a ride, if one were disposed to enjoy it. Lentulus's mind, however, is preoccupied by the events of the morning. It seems possible that Opimia has got wind of an accusation of adultery against her as well, and fled. That can only mean that their friendship has been noticed and reported. The atmosphere in the city is such that people will seize on anything, regardless of whether there is any truth in it. What a fool he has been to invite her unescorted to his house. Sooner or later somebody was bound to suggest that it was suspicious. And before that, the visits to Gaius's house where they first met. But surely nobody could infer anything from those. The letter! It must be the letter he wrote to her on campaign. It must have been discovered and fallen into the wrong hands. It is his fault that Opimia is in trouble now. Lentulus digs his heels into the stallion's flanks, urging him to go faster.

The sun is shining straight into the valley tucked between the woody hills. The valley culminates in a rocky outcrop at the far end, which Lentulus recognises from Naevia's description. The track leads him past a rickety cottage near which a farmer is goading his ox forward to plough a narrow strip of earth where he will plant turnips.

Chapter Eleven

He pauses to stare at the lone horseman, then resumes his toil. From here the track begins to rise steeply. Looking up, Lentulus can see the simple villa sitting on the hillside at the head of the valley. There is no sign of life and when he tries the door he finds it immovable. Walking round the house he can detect no sound from within and stout wooden shutters protect the windows. It appears that the villa is deserted. Lentulus sits down on a bench set against the front wall, wondering where next to search. He must get back to Rome and try to find Opimia there. He takes a last look round, unwilling to leave. Instinct tells him that all is not quite right and he turns back to the door. No bolts or chains secure it on the outside. It must therefore be fastened from inside. This is very strange.

A sudden urgency seizes him. He lunges repeatedly with his shoulder, but the door is of thick planks which do not give way. The shutter of the window next to the door rattles with the impact of each shoulder charge. In desperation he prises open with his dagger the crack where the two leaves meet, then yanks them fully open and climbs inside. The room is simply furnished. Dust gives it the appearance of having been unused for a long time. He walks through an arch to find himself in a short passage leading back to the door through which chinks of light are shining in the gaps between the heavy timbers. An iron bolt is stretched across it. Beside him another door leads off the passage. It yields to his touch. In the darkness he can make nothing out until he walks over to the shutters.

Daylight reveals a small bed in the corner. On it lies the huddled figure of Opimia, fully clothed. Lentulus kneels down beside the bed. She is lying on her side with her face towards the wall. Gently he cups his hands around her head and turns it to his own. Strands of hair have fallen across her face. He brushes them aside. The eyes are closed and tiny drops of a brown liquid have dribbled down her chin. With the fold of his tunic he wipes them away and kisses the white lips. When he rests his head against her breast the soft body gives off the last trace of living warmth. His hands search urgently for some sign of life. If only he had been quicker, he might have saved her. A small roll of parchment drops from the bed onto the floor. As he bends to pick it up, his hand disturbs an empty cup lying next to it. He goes over to the window to unfold the scroll. It is the letter he wrote while he was with the legions tracking Hannibal. Lentulus releases one edge of the scroll, which folds itself into his other hand. He cannot bring himself to turn back to Opimia. Instead he stands stock still, gazing from the window out at the valley below. The silvery leaves of the nearby olive grove shine tremulously in the warm breeze. He watches the farmer's slow progress with the plough under the westering sun which illuminates the whole scene in the mellow glow of late afternoon. He imagines Opimia skipping down the hill with her pail to fetch milk, as she once described it to him. Everything is as she would have remembered it.

In the distance, perhaps two miles away, he notices blurred figures in a trail of dust moving along the track towards the valley. Lentulus's trained eye is not slow to guess their purpose. Realising that he must act quickly, he tucks the letter into his belt and, having kicked the cup out of sight under the bed, hoists Opimia onto his shoulder. The stallion climbs easily up the hill into the woods where Opimia and her mother used to walk. By a young oak tree Lentulus sets her down among cyclamen growing at its foot. Keeping well back in the trees he observes a posse of horsemen circle round the villa and dismount. One of them enters by the same window as he used and comes out moments later. Evidently they have found nothing and canter back down the hill. One of them rides over to the farmer and appears to question him. The farmer has seen nobody, so he tells the man sent by Umbrenus. Lentulus watches the horseman turn away to rejoin the others. They ride off in the direction of Rome.

Chapter Eleven

The practicalities of moving Opimia to ensure that her body is not discovered have briefly smothered his anguish which now returns to Lentulus as he looks down at her. This is the consequence of his selfish pursuit of his own feelings at the expense of her safety. He kneels beside her and, taking one of her hands, pleads for forgiveness. The tears flow freely. He makes no attempt to stifle them, until finally he collapses in a convulsion of horror across her body, beating his forehead on the ground. He clutches her face in both hands, kissing it repeatedly and asking her to come back to him. His fingers grip the hilt of his dagger and he contemplates his own suicide as being the only escape from his guilt. But Opimia must be buried and Naevia must be told what has happened. There will be time enough to attend to his own punishment. The daylight is fading and will soon give way to dusk.

He rides down through the woods to find the farmer who is herding his pigs into their enclosure for the night. He asks no questions but he understands. He knows who came to the villa that morning, for she stopped to speak to him and he saw the empty carriage drive away.

With the farmer's spade Lentulus tests the ground to find a suitable spot. He comes across a dry ravine running down through the trees, near which the soil is more yielding than elsewhere. The failing light and a few drops of rain oblige him to work quickly. The root of a tree delays him, but at last he is satisfied. He lays Opimia in a shallow trench, placing in her hand his letter to her. He stands up to contemplate her for the last time. The physical effort has settled his emotions once more and the serenity of her face transfers a little of itself to him. He cannot bear the thought of shovelling earth onto that face and he cuts a piece off his tunic to lay over it. On top of the soil he lays some rocks to prevent animals from disturbing the grave, which is close to the spot where Opimia and her mother used to plait their garlands of ivy and wild flowers. It is raining steadily by the time his work is complete. Lentulus is oblivious of it. He stands still, trying to find the words of a prayer to the goddess, asking her to receive the soul of her brave and innocent priestess. He tries to speak the traditional words to the departed, but can only get as far as 'Farewell' before his voice breaks. He turns on his heel and, without looking back, mounts his horse. It is almost dark. Somewhere on a rocky outcrop high above, a lone animal watches him, then lopes down into the trees and disappears.

In the house on the Esquiline Naevia knows instinctively what has happened. She suspected it before Lentulus left to search for Opimia. They cling to each other, overwhelmed with grief both in themselves and for the other. Her body is frail and yet Naevia retains an inner strength. She steps back, still holding on to Lentulus's hands.

'Only you and I know how she came to die. It must remain that way. There is a rumour going round the city that she had been unchaste and would suffer the same fate as Floronia. Do you believe that she was afraid?'

Lentulus releases the old lady and leads her to the couch. He pauses for some time before speaking. 'The citizens of Rome may think what they like.' He stops again. 'Perhaps she was afraid. Who would not be? But I do not believe that is why she killed herself. Her sacrifice was to save Rome. She saw it as her duty.'

'That's what her father would have wanted. She loved him and she loved you. Perhaps she loved Rome even more. We shall keep her secret and let others think what they will.'

208 BC

Near the town of Venusia in Apulia there lies a hill covered with thick woodland. On one side of this hill Hannibal has established his camp and on the other the consuls, Marcellus and Crispinus, are with their legions. It is

Chapter Eleven

Hannibal's view that the hill might serve as a trap for the unwary, but nothing is to be gained by seizing it. Marcellus, however, thinking to deny Hannibal any initiative, decides to reconnoitre the hill and, if expedient, to occupy it. In company with his fellow consul and a small force of cavalry the veteran commander, over sixty years of age and with many victories to his credit against the Carthaginians, sets out. The majority of his men, about one hundred and eighty of them, are Etruscan allies. Lentulus commands the other forty who are from Fregellae, south-east of Rome.

What Marcellus does not know is that Hannibal, under cover of darkness the previous night, has posted a squadron of Numidian cavalry on the hill, with orders to remain concealed during the hours of daylight. A Carthaginian scout observes the Roman advance towards the hill and signals to his comrades to manoeuvre round behind the Roman column, while the Numidians wait in the woods above. When the Romans reach the the hill, the Numidians attack from the front while the Carthaginians charge them in the rear. The consuls can neither advance nor retreat. In the ensuing skirmish Marcellus is run through by a lance and falls from his horse, fatally wounded. Crispinus is struck by two javelins and the Etruscans flee for safety. The men of Fregellae, however, under the leadership of Lentulus, fight on, until at last they too lose their nerve. Lentulus tries in vain to rally them, but they veer away, taking with them the injured Crispinus. Lentulus alone remains to confront the enemy. He gallops at full speed into the Numidians, cutting down two of them before perishing in a hail of javelins.

Epilogue

In the history of Rome, Opimia, Floronia and Lentulus are shadowy figures. Livy, in his account of the Hannibalic war, tells us that two Vestal Virgins, called Floronia and Opimia, were convicted of unchaste behaviour and that one of them was buried alive. The other, Livy says, destroyed herself. Lucius Cantilius, the debaucher of Floronia, was beaten to death in the Comitium. Livy relates that these events took place immediately following the battle of Cannae. There is no further mention of these Vestals.

Livy also records the meeting of Aemilius Paullus with a military tribune, referred to only as Lentulus, on the field of Cannae, and the consul's instruction to Lentulus to report to Rome. No more is known for certain of this Lentulus.

The suicide of Opimia, if indeed she was the Vestal who killed herself, was not in vain. Despite the exhortations of his generals to do so, Hannibal declined to attack Rome after Cannae, possibly because he lacked the equipment and resources to sustain a siege. Five years later he did march on Rome, but only as a feint to try to draw off the Romans who were besieging the city of Capua, then occupied by the Carthaginians. Hannibal withdrew from the environs of the city without attacking it.

Four Vestals are recorded as having been immolated in the centuries before Cannae. It was to be more than another hundred years before the immolation of another Vestal, Marcia, in 113 BC.